In honor of the

MILLENNIUM
CHRISTMAS

2000

BOOK DESIGNED & PRINTED BY:
C. JOHN COOMBES

EBOOK ISBN 9780982221358   0982221355
PRINT ISBN 9780982221396   0982221398

CLAUS

A CHRISTMAS INCARNATION

A novel by
C. J. COOMBES

Escape to a time
When life was an adventure.

Our nation was young,
And so were her people.
A time of struggle and setback,
Of pain and perseverance.

A time also of freedom, joy,
And the birth of new traditions.
The future was fearful and uncertain,
But no more so than for the children.

For them, let us say,
Fate brought forth a man.
He was wealthy and influential,
He was good-hearted and generous.
A man of conjecture and mystery.
He was there for them, a savior,
A second chance, a hope.

Only one person may have known him.
A person who struggled to understand him
Through the eyes of a child,
Through the heart of a woman.

A disciple named Elizabeth.

ILLUSTRATIONS BY:
C. JOHN COOMBES

THE M HART EDITION
THIS EDITION REPRESENTS THE FIRST EDIT
OF VOLUME THREE UNDERTAKEN SPECIFICALLY FOR A
6X9 PAPERBACK PRINTING

**It would be preposterous
To assert that
Fact is born of myth.**

*Conversely…
It has been proven
Myth is a child of truth.*

BOOK THREE

The disciple

PART TWO

THE M HART EDITION

Eden

Springtime means meadow greens
and sprays of paintbrush red

when ice unhooks long frozen brooks
now waiting to be fed

by winter snow that melts to flow
before a warming sun

that washes sparkling icicles
with drops that fall and run

To rivers headed for a sea
that beats its shoreline bare

with countless untamed trickles
that started way up where

granite crests scrape clouds at rest—
til tortured bruised and black—

til tempers flash—til teardrops splash
below a thunderous crack

That resonates, reverberates,
ricochets tween walls

that tower too high to meet the eye
of those who fear to fall

from that place where birds embrace
nests that touch the sky

where chicklings fledge from their ledge
in leaps to live or die

Much as do the youngest who
are grounded to the earth

leaping up are fawns and pups
playing promptly after birth

beneath the trees now sprouting leaves
to beautify a land

born of barren cliffs that rose
and returned to earth as sand

When in my mind I'm pressed to find
a place I might call Eden

I stroll a mountain trail in spring
and nothing more be need'n

C. JOHN COOMBES

FIFTY-SIX

We pressed on in haste for the next two weeks, all the while being nipped from behind by rain and ever colder winds coming down out of the northwest. Taa knew every inch of the trail as he claimed. It was well traveled, used much by the stage, and led us to Sibley, then past Napoleon, across the Big and Little Hebert Rivers, and onward toward Lexington.

"You wait here. Keep quiet. Keep out of sight. We go to Lexington for business and get supplies, get blankets. After Lexington, we ride seven days to Marion."

We did as we were told, and Taa returned in short time as promised with supplies that one could not obtain with a bow and arrow, such as soap, coffee, and a pot. He brought back a couple of extra blankets, oil clothes, and socks. Taa understood the need to keep warm and dry on the trail.

We left Lexington and then traveled wide open spaces until reaching a river of notable size.

"Riviere a La Mine. It flows to Missouri near Booneville and Franklin. We follow. Tonight we cross."

It went as Taa predicted, and after crossing the river, we set up camp. We arose early the next morning to the aroma of hot coffee—a pleasure missed dearly during the last ten years. It had been another night of rain, but we remained dry and so coffee was sufficient to warm us from the inside. After a light breakfast of rabbit, we were returned to the trail and pressed to make time.

Two days later we came upon the town of Marion, and as before, Taa had us remain hidden just off the trail way. It was late afternoon, and he and the others rode into town and returned with a few fresh supplies, including flour for making biscuits to sop up meat gravy from our kill. The dinner was heavenly.

From Marion we reached Jefferson City late in the day, having traveled just under twenty miles. This time we did not stay clear of the town. Jefferson City was the state capital and it was large and busy enough for us to enter as Indians and not be bothered or draw attention.

For this reason, Taa left us to our own devices at a trading post on the edge of town while he attended to business. He took our horses with him. We had nothing but time, so I encouraged Luke and Gracie to wander about inside while I remained in the doorway keeping an eye on the street. I wasn't specifically looking for trouble, preferring to think I was keeping an eye out for Taa, but it never hurt to keep up one's guard, especially after recent events, or when addressed from behind.

"Sometin' yer lookin' fer, ma'am?"

I turned around to see this stout and well-worn woman of about forty years, I supposed, looking up at me from behind two or three aprons of different shapes, colors, and sizes. She covered the rest of her frame with a heavy knit sweater.

"Oh, no thank you. The two blondes inside belong to me. They had hoped to look about a bit before heading back out on the trail."

"I see'd ya lookin' up n' down the road. Figer'd ya be in need o' directions n' the like."

"Oh, no thank you. I am waiting for a friend to return for us."

"I ken tell ya ain't from these parts. Where ya come from then, if'n ya don' min' me a-askin'?"

"No, I don't mind. Stony Mountains, some call 'em the Rockies."

"Oh, yeh. Heerd o' 'em. Never chanced to see um, but heerd of 'um by folks thet did, folks passin' through. Say, ya come all thet way wit just them leathers an' a blanket? Ain't ya findin' it a bit cold?" Winner's 'bout here, ya know. I got some real warm longcoats inside ya might like. Why don' ya step in here an' let me fit ya to one. Ya'll like it, I promise."

"Oh, that's very kind of you, but I am afraid I have no funds."

"No fun's? How ken ya be a travelin' wit' no fun's. How ya manage t' eat—. Ha!"

A smile interrupted our conversation as it broke wide across the woman's face, revealing what little remained of her teeth. She laughed aloud and I sensed she was directing her laughter elsewhere. I was just turning to have a look when she called out in a husky voice.

"Taa! Ya devil! How are ya?"

I spun around to see him ride up and dismount. He had three fresh horses in tow. I noticed at once they were saddled western style. I looked back at the woman.

"You know Taa?"

"Oh yeah, we do bizness ever' now n' then. Have done fer some time. Come t' spend some money 'ave ya?" she yelled at him.

"Yah. I need warm clothes for Elizabet and the two." He pointed inside at Luke and Gracie.

"There ya go, I jus' got done' a-sayin' I have some nice fittin' longcoats jus' waitin' fer her t' walk in. Com'on now, Elizabet, jus' like I say'd before—fallah me fer a fittin'."

I followed the woman inside, and in turn, Taa followed me. He saw to it that all three of us were fitted in longcoats and boots if we preferred. All three of us passed on the boots. We found them too confining and uncomfortable, but we did buy new leggings and high moccasins. In the meantime, I found the woman friendly enough and unbothered by my questions.

"Oh, I reckin' gots t' be fifteen hun'erd folks living here now-a-days. I'm guessin' a good four or five hun'erd slaves as well. Started out a landin' fer steamboats. Called it Lohman's Landing in those days. Persons fixin' to head west wou'land here and stock up. Ya heerd a Lewis n' Clark? They landed here an' set foot fer western reaches on behalf o' the president.

"Nex' thing, there's a place t' eat, an' a hotel. A warehouse. Then we'z state cap'tal fer a few years before it got moved t' Union. But we still got a cap'tol buildin'. Built the peneten-chury n' thirty six an' thet really started business goin'. Made us a city in thirty-nine. That same year, Mr. Crump built himself a three-story, stone place on the river by the landin' that's become a tavern, hotel, telee-graph office, groc'y store, an' a warehouse. Good place t' settle down if'n yer of a mind."

FIFTY-SEVEN

We concluded our business, with Taa paying "Winni'ferd" her due, and me insisting that Taa remember, I was to pay him in kind for his assistance. Now, secure within our warm longcoats and leggings, we stepped back onto the street. We looked a lot less like plains Indians, and a lot more like half-breeds, or well-seasoned trappers, or settlers who had been too long out of touch.

Taa brought Luke and Gracie over to the fresh horses and handed them the reins. They were a couple of nice-looking Kentucky Saddlers. I knew the breed from years back. They were a very common horse known for their comfortable gait. Taa helped both of them climb up into the western saddles, something to which neither of them were accustomed. It was comical watching them trying to adjust. They were both most impressed with the saddle bags and spaces made for ferrying needs.

Coupled with a parfleche, one could travel comfortably even accounting for distance or weather.

"This for you, Elizabet—an American Saddlebred."

Taa was clearly proud of this horse. Unfortunately, I looked at him with an expression that confirmed my ignorance. When living with the Claussens, I had saddled nothing but the best in my younger years, mostly Thoroughbreds and fine Narragansett Pacers. I didn't understand the significance of this horse that was Taa's gift to me.

"This horse new, new breed, very much wanted. Expensive. My gift to you."

"No Taa—."

"Yes. You did much for me, for Snow on Ground and Little Deer. I not forget."

"Taa! You saved my life! You saved the life of my son and Gracie. Surely, you of all people owe me nothing in the way of gratitude. I owe you my life, Taa. Do you understand—*my life.*"

"Please, take gift."

"Taa, I can—."

"Please, take gift."

Taa didn't have to be a man of many words. He had eyes that told the whole story in detail.

"Oh, Taa. What am I to say?"

I gave Taa a heartfelt embrace.

"When I leave St. Louis, you must take the horse back."

"No—."

"Yes, you shall. I insist. It won't feed well back east."

"Ahhhh."

That he understood. He would accept the gift back for the sake of the horse. We didn't stay in Jefferson, but passed through in the last light of day. Taa had no desire to sleep in the city. For Luke and Gracie, this was another course of wonderment and surprise. This was not just a little one-street collection of shops, but the state capital, an established community of note. There were still pigs running about in the street even as we passed all variety of industry, including grist mills, flour mills, tanneries, and distilleries, not to mention a myriad of lesser businesses.

There was a notable presence of Germans in this community, but there were all manner of immigrants due to the fact that Jefferson's Landing on the Missouri was frequented by many boats, and because the stageyards were crowded with coaches making regular daily rounds to and from St. Louis.

According to Taa, Missourians wanted the capital moved from St. Louis, which was on the eastern border of the state, to Jefferson, which was more centrally located. This move was approved, but the legislature had no desire to suffer a loss of connections or business activity with the port of St. Louis, and so enacted a plan to improve the established farmers' lane and Indian trails from the end of Market Street in St. Louis to the Jefferson City courthouse.

The legislature felt it necessary to supplement the Missouri River access with direct access to the Mississippi, and also construct a reliable mail delivery route. We were now traveling the first "state road" that some called the Manchester Road, some the Jefferson Road, and others Market Street.

All free males between sixteen and forty-five years of age living in the counties along its length were required to maintain it. We now benefited from that enactment and especially the maintenance, as our journey was safer, easier, and faster.

Our visit to Jefferson City gave us sufficient fodder for conversation that lasted the next four hours. The talk kept us engaged and entertained until we approached the western outskirt of Osage, a town situated at the head of a river by the same name. It was well into dark when we arrived, and so we elected not to invest time building a fire, but instead eat pemmican while spreading out our blankets and oil cloths. We were all fully spent and preferred sleep rather than the chore of building a fire.

We slept hard, woke later than usual to a heavy fog, and entered Osage later than we expected. Osage was different. It was a small settlement heavily influenced by the presence of Indians. We were not so much in the minority at Osage, and there was much less wariness on our part. We stopped to breakfast, and did so in view of the residents without concern. Needless to say, our time there, the one place we truly felt comfortable, was brief.

After departing Osage and crossing the Osage River, we rode a day and a half before arriving at the Gasconade River, which we also traversed. Another day and a half's ride brought us directly into New Port, a town situated on the waters of the Missouri much the same size as Marion.

"Three days."

It was hard for us to believe we were now but three days out of St. Louis. Luke and Gracie watched the sun as it moved all too slowly across the sky. They were wishing their lives away gladly in order to make St. Louis as soon as humanly possible.

And maybe they succeeded in speeding up time because traffic suddenly increased dramatically along the road. We had made the town of Manchester, where another road intersected us from the south; it being the road from Springfield. And lastly, we passed through the St. Louis outskirt settlement of Rock Hill.

"Ten miles."

Stagecoaches bent on killing us flew past regularly. They traveled to and from St. Louis and Jefferson or Kansas City, all points between and beyond—every coach to be scrutinized by Luke.

Now, we fell in line with a growing procession of horses and hikers, farmers driving wagons chocked full of produce, chickens, and rabbits, all heading for the public market at St. Louis's levee on the Mississippi.

Impatiently overtaking the wagons were scores of businessmen riding in from points west, Kansas City, Jefferson City, Springfield, or one of the other upper Missouri settlements. All variety of travelers served to build our ranks, heading east along Manchester Road in force, and intent on entering the largest city in the western half of the continent.

FIFTY-EIGHT

Manchester Road eventually left the farms and countryside to enter the periphery of city dwellings, all seemingly new and surging outward in a western flow of expansion. We rode past Chouteau's Pond, a landmark on our right that survived change. I recognized it from my memories of past days in St. Louis.

I noticed that the spoken street name was replaced by the written street name. It appeared fastened atop posts at each corner that sorted out the equally spaced crossroads. Manchester Street was now officially named Market Street.

Many of the minor cross streets were paved, clearly a testament to the financial worth of the city. Each crossroad counted down our progress as we descended toward the levee. Each crossroad marked an increase in congestion of merchants, shops, shoppers, and the day's new immigrants. Market was one of the most important and active streets in St. Louis in the early days. And if that was still true, it led directly to the public market and the Illinois Ferry Landing.

A banner sign on our right, between the streets of Rundlet and Mayne, asked for donations toward developing a large plot of land called Washington Square into a city park. Just beyond the proposed park, yet to our west, between Tenth and Ninth, Chouteau's Pond returned again to touch the roadway. Here the pond formed a large body of water, and looking across this water, in the distance I could see the expansive grounds of a new Episcopal college called Kemper, and also Kemper's Medical College.

Looking down Fifth, I saw a long stretch of two- and three-story buildings bordering both sides of the street. There were numerous boarding houses and storefronts with awnings that covered wares and goods spilled out and stacked high at street's edge. The street was admirably wide and spacious. There were open lots to be seen between some of the buildings that showed a residual of dried-out stalks and stumps, signs of productive summer gardens.

Between Fifth and Fourth Streets, on the other side of the road, the courthouse occupied an entire block. The original building designed in Federal-style architecture with its flat plane surfaces, towering columns, and large radial steps was preserved, but a major addition to the structure appeared to triple its size. The addition was designed in what I remembered to be termed Greek Revival architecture with the foundation of an impressive dome clearly in the making. The display of renovation on such a large scale added greatly to the sensation that St. Louis was exploding in growth.

Another structure, every bit as massive as the courthouse, rose up some five or six stories on the next block north of the courthouse. I only glimpsed the building while we were stopped momentarily for Taa and his companions to talk. I thought it might be the largest building in St. Louis I had yet observed. My attention was eventually drawn away from the edifice by Taa's conversation.

It was at this intersection that, following some discussion, Taa's comrades left our company. They headed south down along Fourth Street in the direction of Carondelet. I understood from the discussions, that Taa was overdue to meet with a party of settlers who had hired him as a scout through the outfitter's station. He should have departed with the others, but elected to continue with us to the river.

Back on our side, at the corner of Third was the National Hotel, one of the few buildings I remembered from my last stay in St. Louis. In those days, it was a newly constructed hotel with the best accommodations. Today, it was more of a landmark, but stripped of its glory and so paled in light of the surrounding growth. I assumed it remained in the limelight due to a new omnibus service that ran from the hotel to a ferry landing farther north along the levee.

I noted that whereas Market Street was one of the principal business streets when I last saw St. Louis, this was changing. Having observed Fourth Street, where Taa's comrades rode, and now looking down Third, I could see that the business community was changing direction.

Market Street was the road traveled east and west, back and forth between farmers' fields and the market on the river, and so was crowded with shops. Now, Third and Fourth Streets, which ran north and south at a right angle to Market, and paralleled the river and levee, outpaced the older Market Street.

Third and Fourth were older and narrower streets, but they ran the full length of the river from one end of the city to the other. They became the focus of new shops that attempted to stay as close as possible to the unending line of docked riverboats and their cargos.

At Main and Market I spied "Jones' Museum of Art, Sciences, and Curiosities"—admission twenty-five cents, children half price. I noted an old flyer from April past announcing the arrival of General Tom Thumb, who was two feet and one inch tall. Someone had written across the flyer, "seven years old, fifteen pounds." Another flyer touted the accomplishments of "The Great Tragedian, Macready, on second tour from England at the St. Louis Theatre at Olive and Third."

Stores crowded both sides of Market Street, especially near its end at the levee, or Water Street as is was also called in this area. In past years, the Water Street levee appeared to have been paved right down to the water's edge, which virtually disappeared beneath that row of riverboat hulls packed in tighter than livestock at a feed trough.

While Luke's and Gracie's eyes scoured every square inch of the boarding houses and storefronts passed, my eyes sought out once familiar wharves edging the Mississippi's shore. I was hoping to see something of the levee that would help me regain a fragment of my former bearings from that location.

Unfortunately, it seemed all had changed except for one enormous open air structure of wood called Market House that backed up against the levee, and effectively blocked any view of the river beyond. It occupied much of the final city block to our right, the one to touch water's edge. The building's backside opened as storage facilities for riverboats unloading their decks of wares, transferring cargo onto land in row upon row of towering crates to be housed. The front side of the structure, with its stores and merchant stalls, faced The Publique, or Public Place, which was both the city market and recreation area.

A portion of all those unloaded goods and wares found their way to this market. All the latest, all the best, all the freshest, newly arrived stores from the Ohio valley and parts east, or New Orleans to the south, could be found in the open air square. So bountiful were the quantities that prices for groceries, wines, and spirits were exceptional. So too, the prices of perishables, meat, fish, and poultry, all very fresh and appealing. The markets offered staples and delicacies for every palette.

A train of Murphy wagons sloped upward from the levee. The train grew longer with each landing of the ferry from the Illinois shore. The new wagon owners were flowing in and out of the stores, buying up their own stockpile of goods, and cramming all of it, along with children into the sturdy beds.

I was in every way overwhelmed. I had nothing on Luke and Gracie, who were equally stunned.

"You were correct, Taa. My St. Louis is only a wisp of memory. I hardly recognize this city. It seems more orderly to me, but more driven, the growth is incomprehensible. I would measure it in hours, not years."

"Yah. Last year, six hundred new buildings. Year before, I think four hundred."

"A thousand buildings in two years. It boggles the mind."

When last here during the early thirties, by my best recollection, there were five or six thousand folks who took up residence in the general area. In those days, sitting on a horse was sufficient enough to be a resident.

"Taa, how many people live here now?"

"I think forty thousand. But they come in last few years."

"I find this flood of immigrants unsettling. I find that genteel air, that social grace and charm I so much loved, is missing. It seems to me that the character of the city is much diminished."

"Yah. This is true. Ask the French. French not happy. French not in St. Louis now. French live in Carondelet."

As in Jefferson City, St. Louis appeared to be awash in Germans and Americans. Here, there was also a notable count of Irish. They were a rude, crude, loud, and pushy lot without the excuse of drink, or because of it.

The faces of St. Louis were no longer those of trappers, furriers, and adventurers, but rather neighbors and merchants drawn by the profitable business climate. St. Louis was less the city of footloose and fancy free land roamers. It was more a place teeming with citizens who stayed put and lived over stores they owned and operated. Stores that bordered every street and were dedicated to outfitting the new generation of wayfarers that were making one last stop before entering those wilds that so intrigued the city's forefathers.

The streets that were once lined with taverns full of hard-drinking, brawling trappers and such, men chasing soiled doves in and out of its doors dawn to dusk, dusk to dawn, were gone. The adventurers, the furriers, the trappers and taverns were a part of an earlier time that was fast fading from memory.

In their place were the gunsmiths, blacksmiths, coopers and bricklayers, bakers and comb makers, carpenters and painters, glaziers and sign makers. Down side streets could be seen well-established saw mills, flour mills, potteries and tanneries, soap and candle factories, brickyards and stonecutters, manufacturers and wagon makers.

FIFTY-NINE

At last the tease of water came to an end. We dismounted and took fair time to stand abreast on the levee at Water Street so Luke and Gracie could savor their first sight of the Mississippi. All of the talk, all of their imaginings, now took shape in the world of the real. For two young people, who knew only of desert and plains, seeing firsthand the massive river that I spent years describing in their youth was an inspirational experience.

Taa and I enjoyed their awe as much as did they. We fully appreciated that this was the first of many experiences to come that would acquaint them with the world Taa and I already understood.

"What does it say? What does it say?" I repeated as I pointed out across the water at a boat starting its downriver leg.

Luke studied the nameplate on the bow.

"Princess May." He looked to me for confirmation.

"Yes! Yes! See, I told you learning letters would pay. All those years of lessons—whoooo-ooo!" I yelped.

"I've been reading all the signs," said Luke with a hint of indignation.

"So have I; flowers, tannery, wares, Jones, cooper," injected Gracie.

"Good for both of you. Now you will put to good use all those hours of study. You will see that my badgering was to your benefit."

Needless to say, it was the sight of Water Street, the unfathomable variety of goods piled door-high as far as one could see, the PRINCESS MAY and the endless row of boats exactly like her billowing steam across the levee and black smoke into the winds overhead, and finally that broad expanse of water called the Mississippi that most affected us.

For me it was every bit as unbelievable, but it was unbelievable change, change I would have never dreamed possible had I not seen it with my own eyes. It was a crushing wave of western technology headed straight for the land of the Tsistsistas. It would be a flood of culture that would never recede.

For Luke and Gracie, it was life-altering, it was an awakening— a new birth. They came from a world where the farthest thing to exist beyond nature might have been some iron-forged wares on a peddler's cart. In fact, wares from Dusty's peddler wagon that I drove into camp many, many, years ago.

For them, to suddenly stumble upon waves of clamorous vessels vying for position, approaching, departing, loading and unloading goods of every nature up and down the riverfront, all being nursed by stevedores and haulers, horse teams harnessed to carts, wagons, and hoists of every description, was incomprehensible. I could see the struggle on their young faces. Their eyes were wide open, as were their minds, but they were drowning in disbelief.

A single riverboat possessed more life than most of the characters loitering about the river bank and street corners. There were simultaneously plenty of, and yet not enough, words to describe the nature of these boats by all who encountered them for the first time.

These steamboats were far bigger, and louder, and far more ornate than anything I had boarded or seen when last stationed here. The old horn-honk or gunshot had gone the way of the keel boat, to be replaced with musical whistles specific to a captain or his vessel. The boats were captivating, if not on occasion enchanting. I almost saw them as rough and surly cousins to the painted up sailing sloops that I recalled on the Potomac.

A quick glance out across the river's currents would capture scores of boats; most all steam-driven, which fulfilled a prophecy from my childhood, and most all heavily laden with goods soon to be transported westward. If the rivers were arteries, then the boats were the blood of life-supplying energy and sustenance to St. Louis, now undeniably the heart of the new west. Like blood, the city pumped commerce in and out, in and out.

Suffice it to say, but for the enormity of the river at their feet to the hot ash and clouds of black riverboat smoke high over their heads; but for the streets seemingly unlimited in number and length, crammed corner to corner with all things imaginable, including scenes of every aspect of city life; Luke and Gracie were left helplessly slack-jawed and silent, too steeped in amazement to utter a single word lest they miss something in their attempt to absorb a great city in all its truly spectacular glory.

Who wouldn't be mesmerized by the intensity of activity and the power of technology spread out before us? I could only imagine what images poured through their eyes, what silent thoughts streamed through their minds. I would have thought them dizzy by the way their heads spun in circles. Their stupor forced me to acknowledge what my heart knew to be true. I was witness to the inevitable end of a way of life that lay to the west. The knowledge brought with it deepening sadness. I wished to turn my mind away from thoughts about Ho'neheveho, Talk-a-Lot, and the future of the Tsistsistas. I wished to rid myself of the guilt.

SIXTY

"Wot happens now?"

Gracie snapped me out of my thoughts. I suspected that her head was so overloaded with stimuli, so weighted down with wondrous sights and sounds, she needed to focus. She had locked

34

her eyes onto mine, searching for a sense of sanity, for simplicity in a city of unbound complexity. But it was Taa who spoke first.

"Elizabet, I must go."

Gracie's eyes unlocked at once and shifted to Taa. Luke and I also turned to face him. The announcement had to come and there was no good time to hear it. We had been a happy lot enjoying life without worry for the last couple of weeks. Not I, not Luke nor Gracie wished to see Shadow Hunter go his way.

"I must go, Elizabet. I am late. I lose much work if I stay. I must go. I know you, Elizabet. You strong. You find your way. Remember, Rachel and Caleb, live on Sixth or Seventh, north, beyond Biddle Street. Be careful to stay clear of Kerry Patch, stay clear of Battle Row, stay east of Eighth and Ninth. Kerry Patch bad, dangerous. Say hello to Rachel, Caleb for me. Tell them, I come by soon."

"Yes, I will tell them. Now, I am holding you to your promise. You promised to take back the horses, Taa. What should I do with them? I won't take them as gifts. They are too expensive. Where would I leave them?"

"Yah, yah, I promise." Taa shook his head in resignation. "Leave horses at Pillar Stout's Livery on Sixth, between Chestnut and Pine, near jail. It near Rachel and Caleb. I speak to Mr. Stout. I tell him you come. He keep horses for me. Look for large Episcopal church on hill at Fifth and Chestnut. Has big square tower. You will see it."

"Very well, Pillar Stout's Livery."

"Yes. Elizabet, you take money. You need it for now. Rooms very expensive here. Very expensive. Not like before when you here."

"Thank you, Taa. I will leave funds at Rachel's to pay you back."

35

"I must go. I have—."

I laid my fingers gently across his lips.

"I know. You have to leave."

I then placed my hands on his shoulders, and pulled myself up to kiss him on the cheek, and then looked him in the eye.

"I will never be able to thank you enough for saving Luke and Gracie, for saving me. You will always be my hero, Taa. Now, go, go, I understand. Go."

I stepped away.

Taa mounted up. It was obvious from his expression and demeanor that he would leave with a heavy heart. I wasn't surprised because Taa had always been a good, caring man. I knew he had pressing engagements, a business obligation in Carondelet, a westward party of pioneers awaiting his return. I managed to get a smile from him as we waved good bye. Like Taa, my smile belied my sadness. It was hard to see him go.

"Until next time!"

"Thank you for everything, Taa. I will see you again, I am certain."

"Good bye, Elizabet. I tell Snow on the Ground; I tell Little Deer, I see you. They be very happy. They thank Great Spirit, make feast. Good bye, Elizabet."

With that, Taa turned his horse around and trotted back up Market to disappear into the bustling crowd. It reminded me of the last time I watched him ride out of St. Louis ten years back. I felt just as disheartened. Luke and Gracie sensed my sadness and made no effort to interrupt my thoughts until I turned to look at them. My face lit up.

"Well, we're back on our own, but we *are* in St. Louis."

"Whooooooo-ooooo!"

Gracie let out a war cry, which carried little weight amidst the noise and confusion swirling about us. Nothing in St. Louis would diminish the look of glee upon her face. Her eyes sparkled with excitement. If she had needed a moment to settle down and collect herself, one would have never guessed as much now.

It was Luke who remained sedate. He spoke hardly a word since we entered the city. Either he had been *reading* a lot, or he had been knocked off balance by the staggering difference between this world and that of the Tsistsistas. What he had hoped to see may have overpowered him, unsettled him, shaken his foundations. I would make sure he didn't come to feel this world made useless all he knew about his other world, about survival and life.

"Wot are we going to do now?" asked Gracie.

I took a moment to study our surrounding and gain my bearings. I pointed to the east.

"First, we go that way to return the horses to the livery. We will have little need for them in the city, and it would be too costly to feed and care for them."

"Then wot?"

"Then we find a room to let for the night, after which we will eat and hopefully get a good night's sleep. Tomorrow, I will seek out Rachel and that should put us on our feet. She will help us get situated."

"Do you know a lot of people here, Momma?"

"No. Years back, I knew a few. Why? Did you think I made up all those stories about St. Louis?"

"No."

"You will learn very quickly that in the white man's world, you must have money to survive. Without the help of Taa and Rachel, right now things would be very difficult for us."

"Do we have a lot of money?" asked Gracie.

"For now, only what I borrowed from Shadow Hunter."

"May I see some?"

"Oh, I want to see money too," said Luke.

I reached into my pocket and pulled out a leather pouch of coins. I was well aware of the weight in my pocket. At first, I was surprised that Taa hadn't handed me banknotes. Notes would have been lighter to carry on his journeys, but then I recalled the many times I was held up because one bank refused to honor the notes of another. I would have thought those matters improved by now, but maybe not. Coins were always good no matter how far west one traveled. Coins were good right through Mexico. Actually, I recalled the Mexican dollars as being the most valuable.

I untied the strings to the pouch and poured a few pieces into my opened hand. I spread the coins across my palm. Luke and Gracie stood before me staring down at the small treasure.

"Look at that."

Gracie placed her finger on one, pushing it into my palm.

"Those are all silver dollars, made out of silver. What does it say?"

"It says one dollar."

"Very good. I used to have coins that were made out of gold."

I handed Gracie one of the pieces to inspect.

"See the date, eighteen forty-three—tells you when it was made. That coin is only a year old, nice and shiny. Here's one that says eighteen forty-one. I've never seen these before. When

I last had coins in my hand, they looked different. In fact, I can't remember any dollar coins dated later than 1804. Apparently, while I was out west the government must have started minting dollar coins again. I have never seen this seated figure—used to be a woman's head."

I was as amused by the coins as were Luke and Gracie. I handed Luke one to inspect. The two of them studied the engravings with interest. Luke began tossing his coin up into the air so as to judge its weight.

"These are nice. I would like to have a headdress made with these," said Luke.

"Silver dollars? You and everybody else," I quipped. "Now give me those back. I can't afford to have them stolen by a pickpocket."

"What's a pickpocket?"

"A person who will bump into you and clean out your pockets without you having the slightest idea you have been robbed. They are very good at their craft, and you will be most unhappy should one bump into you. You are safer on your horse."

I could see that bit of information took hold in their heads.

"Speaking of horses, how will we get around without them? This is a big place," said Gracie.

"Well...look around. In a city, most people walk. Everything you need is close by, so the need for a horse is not so great. There are always plenty of cabbies looking to make a living."

"Wot's a cabbie?"

"Oh, lord. You really do have a lot to learn. A cabbie is someone who takes you around town in his cab, or coach, or wagon."

The wind suddenly changed direction, coming at us from the south, and carrying with it a stench of blood and freshly slaughtered animals that emanated from a row of butcher shops in the Market House.

"Oh! Oh! What a stink."

I turned from the affront, holding my hand across my nose. Luke and Gracie both wore expressions of shock.

"Oh! C'mon, mount up. Let's remove ourselves from this stench and find Pillar Stout's livery so we can give Taa back his horses."

We rode slowly back up Market Street, I allowed Luke and Gracie whatever time they wished to take in the sights. When we arrived back at the National Hotel on Third, I turned north. I was curious to see the theatre mentioned in the flyers down by the levee. At the next corner, it being Third and Chestnut, we came upon a Baptist church. Ours needed to be Episcopal

SIXTY-ONE

Pillar Stout had been expecting us just as Taa predicted. We turned our horses over to the stable as instructed, and collected a sobering amount of money in return.

"My word, Mr. Stout. You have favored me. Four hundred is a handsome price for the horses."

"I wish I might be so noble, ma'am, but the truth o' the matter is that the Saddlebred fetches a good dollar. I've only offered ya fair price on the other two. I 'magine it more 'bout losing track o' costs. Taa mentioned ya bin' in the desert a good long time."

"That I have."

"If I may be so bold as t' suggest ya watch yer funds with care. It's not just on the street ya can get robbed. Presently, ya seem to have a good sum, but a dollar'll not get ya near as far as ya might expect. I've lived here in St. Louis a fair time, an' find that goods as of late cost less due t' the amount o' river traffic an' quantity o' goods arrivin' 'round the clock, day in, day out.

"However, when it comes to a bed an' roof, now that's a different story—good luck with that. St. Louis is barren o' places to lay yer head. The price o' rooms t' let is b'yond reason, outrageous, lunacy best describes the rates bein' asked an' paid. If ya don't find your friend, Mrs. Rachel, an' be given a place to bed down, you'll be needin' every dollar in hand to stay outta the weather."

In the conversation that ensued, Mr. Stout provided good advice about goings on in town, and also detailed directions and distance to Rachel's orphanage. Lastly, he suggested a couple of descent boardinghouses, and repeated Taa's warning to steer clear of Kerry Patch.

"They're a sad lot. Stories are runnin' amok 'bout a terr'ble famine that's said t' be takin' hold in Ireland. I bin' told the Irish are leavin' in droves just t' survive. They're said to be starvin' an' penniless, comin' across with nothin' more'n the clothes on their back t' join friends an' relatives here'n St. Louis. The whole lot's bin' strugglin' to make ends meet, an' so are findin' comfort an' support in numbers. They settle an' stay put, all t'be counted in Kerry.

"Sorry t' say, they ain't findin' an easy go of it there. It's easier to be a negro here an' get a day's pay than be an Irishman. Their situation has made 'em a murd'rous, thievin' bunch jus' t' get by an' the truth is, word get's out, they're shunned. People stay clear. You be sure to stay clear yourselves, or you'll fast come to regret not payin' me mind. Ya hear?"

"We do hear, and we are grateful for your advice and concern."

41

We thanked Mr. Stout, said our good byes, and departed the livery better informed. We certainly departed with a newfound respect for the Irish neighborhoods. Kerry Patch aside, we found ourselves strolling along other streets quite relaxed and carefree. There was a certain bounce to my step, for I understood that once I reached Rachel and Caleb, I would have easier access to the bank and my own funds. At that point, I would be able to repay Taa and support the three of us in comfort.

We continued our stroll unrushed, lost in private thoughts. This part of town was quieter, certainly calmer than those places nearest the river. We looked into the boardinghouses suggested by Mr. Stout, but as he feared, there were no vacancies. As Luke and Gracie studied their surroundings, I studied them. There was no limit to my love for them, but on one issue they plagued me. I harbored a secret, a secret kept from the two of them since their first day in my life. Any person asked would have said it sensible for the three of us to head directly for Rachel's place. There we would be safe; there we would be cared after, but that was not about to happen.

I preferred not to know how many countless seasons, how many years, I had spent envisioning my return to the orphanage, to Boston, to my past. I had replayed my entrance back into that world, my meeting with Rachel and Caleb, my greeting Dorrie, Mary, and all the others, a thousand times over, a thousand times different…a thousand times difficult.

All this rehearsal left me with one unwavering truth. Returning from the dead was not easy. Many would have suffered miserably to think me lost. After all these years without as much as a word, how could I be viewed as anything but cruel and heartless? I needed to return to life with care. I needed to ease myself into Rachel's world without the added stress that Luke and Gracie would pour into the affair. Even if they stood silent, stock still, mouths sewed shut; I would yet feel pressured and out of control.

No, for the briefest moment, I would leave them. I would resurrect alone. I would bow my head and ask forgiveness on bended knees if that would convey a fraction of my deep felt regret.

And so, with Taa's money in hand, and Luke and Gracie in tow, I avoided Rachel's and instead began to reacquaint myself with the city and take note of what other rooms were for let.

"Welcome to my world, Gracie. Not that I recognize it."

I addressed Gracie only because she was older and had spent her childhood sitting around the campfire listening to stories of city life as told by her father. For Gracie, this was all about dreams come true.

"I...I...I hardly believe any of this even though it is everything you said it would be."

"It's everything your father said it would be."

"Truthfully, I remember very little about wot my father said. Wot I remember of his stories are now only feelings at best...dreams. They serve to add a sense of comfort beneath all that you have told me over the years. And all that you have conveyed has not prepared me for this. It's almost too much, Elizabeth. Everywhere I look there is some maggoty *thing*. I don't understand wot all these things are, but they're everywhere. Look at all of that. Wot is all that? Wot's that?" She pointed.

"That's a plow."

"Wot's that?"

"That's a washboard. Every white woman alive knows what that is."

"I fear I will spend the rest of my life asking wot are all these things. I know you told me before, but wot is the name of that lodge...store?"

"Hardware store. That's a hardware store and it's chocked full. Now listen...don't let all this get the best of you, Gracie. You're going to find more things around here than you can fit into your pretty blonde head. But I promise you, everything has a use, and in time you'll get to know it all. Trust me."

The outskirts of St. Louis stretched miles farther than in days past. But there were also communities in the middle of St. Louis much the same as Kerry Patch that seemed as far removed as the outskirts. Even in these catch-all communities, we looked peculiar in our Indian braids and moccasins. However, Mr. Stout's voice was still in my ear persuading me not to spend our money on anything frivolous first thing, including new wardrobes, but instead holding on to our money for room and board. In that frame of mind, I continued to keep an eye open for any boardinghouse that appeared safe and reasonably priced.

Finding a hot meal looked to be easy; there were a good many eating houses. Finding two rooms for the three of us proved anything but. The warnings of Taa and Mr. Stout played over in my head. The issue wasn't even one of price. Price could be debated, but first there had to be a vacancy over which to dicker. Again and again, we were told no rooms were available. To make matters worse, the innkeepers kept directing us closer to Kerry Patch, the only place Taa and Mr. Stout told me to avoid whatever the bargain. I suspected only because sane people dared not venture into that neighborhood, it was there on Ninth Street that I spied a couple of inns hopefully with rooms to let.

Based on appearances, I selected the best of the worst-looking boardinghouses yet to be seen. I hoped the cover belied the contents. I feared not one of these places would be deemed fit for a decent woman, but I was starting to have more than my share of problems walking around with Gracie. We were attracting too much attention. I wished only to get off the street, and hide us in a room for the night.

This was no place for an average woman, let alone a young, emerald-eyed, blonde-headed beauty. All variety of man was attracted to Gracie, but it was the worst sorts that flocked unabashedly toward her like bad rats to good grain. They were unrelenting in their disrespect. The fearless look of defiance in her eyes only served to make the challenge of getting near her all the more sporting.

I knew that Gracie could take care of herself in most any situation. She could fight like a cat and was deadly with a knife, but she was outnumbered twenty to one in this place. It would have been prudent to proceed with caution, but the lengthening shadows of late day were leaving us with fewer options by the minute. We quickly grew focused on finding the safety of a room where we could escape the howls of wolves and their wanton eyes.

I was attracted by the amount of light about one establishment in particular. I deemed that inn to be safest by appearances, and so decided to apply. Unfortunately, as soon as we neared the place, I knew I had erred in my judgment. But at that point, come what may, I was not of a mind to turn back in a show of weakness. I knew things would only get worse, for the day was near ended, the houses filled, our choices fewer, and the men bolder.

Much of the light that bathed the street was at the farthest corner of the building, opposite to where we approached the entrance. That light, which attracted me from a distance, was filling with a number of men. There were now, six or seven, milling around a basin of water set out for barbering and wash. Needless to say, the moment we came into the light, the men were interested in everything but shaving.

"Hey, there! Ha-warra-ya, me sweet! Yay sharr look grand faur-ahn Indyan girl."

"Heh, heh. We haaven't any-ov-us-had a toe headed colleen befaur."

"Yaah, but then we ahrn't the layst bit fussy eyether."

"Iam ov-a-mind to throw a leg over one-ov-em Indyans just now faur the fun-of-et, so I am, I am."

The men were beginning to move in our direction.

"Pay them no mind, Gracie. Don't answer, don't you even look their way, you just keep on walking."

"The mahtter is what, Momma? Ahr yay worried faur yaur colleen, ahr yay now? Yaur a grand lookin' one yaurself."

Another spoke up.

"Apple fell close to the tree, it did."

"Aye! And would I like to fell that tree, I would."

"Would you?"

"Would I."

The gang roared with laughter.

"Hey! What reason faur, ahr yay wearing that Indyan leather? After a show or something, it's dressed up," said yet another.

I hustled Gracie and Luke through the door of the inn and made directly for the innkeeper.

"Aye, ya ahrr a lucky one this night. Six lads up 'n left, wasn't but ten minutes ago. To be sure, I have three. Twice, you'll not be so fortunate. A dollar and two quarters per room, it'll be."

"We'll take them."

"Yes, ma'am. Deck hands, they were. So the vessel might leave ladened by first light, just now, they were called upon to stow goods."

I could hardly be bothered by what means these three rooms came to be free. I promptly paid four dollars and two quarters

46

for the rooms, and would have gladly paid six or eight for the peace of mind. We were at last off the street, but hardly free of the harassment.

I turned from the innkeeper, and barely managed ten steps toward our rooms, when a large framed man put his arms across the hallway and blocked my progress. I took it in stride, but Gracie whipped out that knife of hers so fast I hadn't the time to warn against it. She lay it up hard against the man's throat with such speed that he hardly understood what had taken place. It was a near hopeless situation for me. I turned to her.

"Gracie, put the knife away. Come on, Gracie. Put away the knife. We can't do that here."

"I don't like him, Elizabeth."

Gracie was seething. Her eyes went ice cold. The muscles in her jaw stood out prominently.

"Yes, yes. I don't either, honey, but we can't be doing this right now. Please. Please, listen to me and put the knife away as I say before the innkeeper puts us out on the street."

Gracie withdrew the blade from his throat and stepped back, but she refused to sheath it. Instead, she remained on edge, watching his every move. The man was a brute. He had the sense not to move unexpectedly, but to my dismay, he barely flinched. He was not as unnerved as he was uncertain. I turned to speak to him.

"Sir, you would be well advised to know the girl is all heathen as far as you're concerned. Please believe me, slitting your throat is not an unthinkable way for her to resolve her problem with you."

"Heh, heh, heh. Feisty colleen is she. I like that in a girl. Heh, heh, heh. It's a crack in the hay, I say; it'll take ya to the task, it will."

The stranger was still plenty cocky in front of his friends, but made no attempt to further block our passage. I could see that introducing Gracie and Luke to a new culture might be harder on the new culture than on either of them. If this was a sign of what I was in for, then I was going to have my hands full.

If there was hardly a room to be had anywhere in St. Louis, let alone three rooms, there was also no such thing as a room with two beds. The city was crowded and compacted. The buildings butted up one against the next, leaving little if any room to breathe. The rooms inside these structures were just as small and suffocating. They offered nothing but a bed, no chair, no desk, no amenity or comfort of any manner. It was highway robbery to all, but especially to those of us who chose the gouging over the perils of the street. Not to be daunted, we dragged a bed out of one room and pried it into another.

"There. Two beds in one room."

"These beds are filthy. Oh, lord, Elizabeth, there's a bug, there's another! Look! They are crawling across the straps! I would rather sleep on the floor than on that filth. Luke, you can have the beds," Gracie protested.

I studied the bed frames. Indeed, there were bugs running along the straps.

"I don't blame you, but I doubt you will find fewer bugs on the floor. Sleep where you wish, sweetheart. Just be thankful, you are off the street. I trust you have gained a sense of the brutes about this place. I also hope I needn't explain the importance of keeping the door to this room locked at all times and to remain inside. At no time do I want you to wander about this inn. Under no circumstance are you to let anybody inside, no matter how hard they knock or what they say. If someone yells fire, you best first smell smoke before unlocking that door. If you visit the outhouse, you go together, and you take the knives. Do you understand?"

48

"Yes." Both answered in unison.

"Do I have your word that you will stay put?"

"Yes."

If only for the pleasurable peace of mind, the semblance of sanity, or a prayer's worth of law and order; once we entered our rooms to lie down and rest, we had no ambition to leave. We were all three hungry, but it wasn't worth the likely trouble should we set foot outside the room, especially now that it was dark, and the drunkards were in rare form.

For these reasons, Luke removed what remained of food in our parfleche. We joined the bugs upon the beds, and spread out our small pickings, but soon forgot about our hunger; it giving way to our enthusiastic accounts of all the marvelous things we had observed. We retired early, not by choice, but by surprise as we found ourselves dozing in and out of conversation and awareness.

When next I awoke, Gracie and Luke were both sound asleep in each other's arms. I satisfied myself that they were safe for the night and then awoke Gracie.

"Gracie…Gracie."

"Wot."

"Wake up, sweetheart, you need to lock the door behind me."

"Wot?"

"I am going to my room. You need to lock the door behind me."

Gracie had all she could do to find her feet, but only after I heard her secure the latch did I feel free to find my own bed. I slept a hard, dreamless sleep the whole of the night.

SIXTY-TWO

I had no recollection of lying down to sleep, only of awakening. I awoke to pitch black. My room was coffin-like, it being small and without window. It was not light, but noise that prompted me to awake. At first, the barrage of sounds beyond my door set me to believe the drunks were yet hard at it. Only after contemplating the rudeness of their lot, did I realize that the commotion spoke of morning activities and ascertained the hour was late. At least, late for me, for I was an early riser. I concluded every boarder in the house was in full motion except for me and the two next door. Despite a careful listen, I perceived nothing in the way of movement or conversation opposite the wall that separated us. It seemed, of we three, I had awakened first. I was not surprised.

At my age, I required less sleep, especially when it was as sound as the past night. Or maybe, I was simply worried enough about what next lie in wait for Luke and Gracie that I was shorted on rest, but too anxious to realize it. I knew that I was impatient to get out of bed. I was impatient to find Rachel or else gain my own footing. Whatever the reasons, it appeared I was first to rise and dress. I imagined myself covered in lice, mites, and creatures too small to name. I wanted to wash in the worst of ways, but that was't about to happen. And so, I stepped cautiously out into the hall, half expecting trouble after considering the past night's disorder.

I walked the few steps to the door of Luke and Gracie's room and confirmed my suspicions. They were yet in a deep sleep. After a good deal of trouble trying to wake Gracie, my nearly beating down their door, I finally got her attention. I spoke to her through the door.

"Gracie, listen to me. I want the two of you to stay put. Do you understand me? I know this place is an unending source of fascination, but don't make any mistake about it, you'll find plenty

50

of trouble here without looking for it. If you don't find it in the hallway, you'll find it in the street, I promise. Just stay in the room, rest up, and I will return shortly with something to eat. Afterward, we can walk the city. Do you hear me?"

"Yes."

"Gracie, are you awake. Do you understand me?"

"Yes, Elizabeth. I hear you. I understand, don't leave the room. Don't worry, I am not ready to get up."

"Alright then, I'll soon be back. Now keep this door locked, alright?"

"Alright, I will keep the door locked. I promise."

Gracie was only half awake, and their room was every bit as dark on the inside as was mine. That was a good sign. I turned away from the door believing they would sleep and remain safe for at least a couple of hours before burning curiosity tempted them to do something stupid. I walked down the hall toward the boardinghouse entrance. Now that errant rays of light seeped into the building, it appeared perfectly squalid to me. I needed to leave, the sooner the better.

A full complement of shabby-looking scoundrels swarmed the place, the interior, the front porch, and the street. Murmuring, milling about, coming and going, keeping company with their own kind; they were rude by nature, loud and unkempt. One might have thought me dancing by the way I sidestepped their every approach, intentional or otherwise, as I shunned contact.

Only by concerted effort did I avoid brushing up against them. I felt as though each of them left a little of their residue upon the walls, in the rooms, on the beds…on me. I felt certain that a thick coat of invisible scum covered everything about the place. I kept my hands to myself, preferring to touch nothing as I stepped out into the street.

It was mid-morning by the look of it. I took in a full lung of air untainted by the gaseous eruptions of boarders. Once past their heated stench, the air nipped at me. The sky overhead hung low just above the roof edges, and appeared thickly overcast and gray. Smoke hovered just high enough off the ground to mix with the overcast, and the smell of parlor stoves filled with burning wood and coal permeated the streets. At least the chilly air was invigorating, and it served to remove most of my depressing thoughts about life at the boardinghouse. I knew for certain, I had grown too accustomed to another life, one of clean fresh water that reflected clear blue skies crowning the uninhabited plains.

The cool air seemed to enhance the mouth-watering aroma of breakfast and dinner preparations wafting through the streets and alleyways. Indeed, it proved how healthy was my appetite, and I knew soon enough Luke and Gracie would awake famished. I walked north along the street and came upon a row of market stalls. I was minding my own business picking out some tarts for breakfast when a girl attending the stall addressed me in a bold fashion.

"Why ya dressed for 'n that manner, ma'am? Yer not Indian are ya?"

"What manner?"

I was somewhat annoyed.

"Such as ya are...in them injun skins."

She pointed at the leathers beneath my longcoat.

"Oh, the leathers. Not that it is any of your concern, but I've just returned from the desert, and as of yet haven't had a chance to buy a new wardrobe."

"D'ja see many Indians?"

"Yes, I did. ...A considerable number."

"Really! D'ja have t' kill any?"

Her eyes grew wide with anticipation.

"No, why would I have to do that?"

"They're all heathens, un-Christian, murder'rs n' rapers by most accounts."

"How interesting. I hadn't heard. They were very nice to me. When they had food, such as you, they never sold it. They gave it away freely to anyone who was hungry and wished to eat. I found them to be very kind."

The girl frowned.

"That's strange. Don't believe I ever heard such a thing."

"I suspect not. You probably never will again either."

"Were ya out west a long time then?"

I nodded my head. "Yes, a very long time."

The girl had got me to thinking, and I realized that I had absolutely no idea of the date, of when it was. I looked all around me, up and down the street for signs. I knew it was pointless, but it did seem unusually quiet, like the Lord's Day, but I didn't hear Sunday bells. I simply had no idea at all, for I only knew time by seasons.

"What is today's date?"

The girl looked at me with some suspicion.

"Twenty-eight November."

"Is today Sunday?"

"You jest."

She looked at me as if I was a tease.

"No, I really have no idea. What day is it?

"Fine. It'd a be the last Thursday o' November. In these here part's that makes it Thanksgivin' Day. Truly, ya din't know?"

"Truly, I didn't know. No idea at all. Fancy that. Thanksgiving Day. That is interesting; I would have never known, not in the least."

"It's somethun' ov a heartbreak in these here parts."

"How's that?"

"Well...last year, our late, Governor Reynolds, made a law. Said...in these here parts, the fourth Thursday will be celebrated as Thanksgiving Day. Four months later, he did himself in. He was a man o' conscience an' stood fer upholdin' slavery as a white man's God given right. He earned the respect o' many a good citizen. It was a great loss in this here time o' quarrel. Ya'll be hard pressed t' hear a soul give thanks fer that stroke o' devil's work."

"The devil works in mysterious ways."

"Say again?'

"Merely saying these things defy explanation. I must be on my way."

I paid the girl for the tart and a piece of chocolate, and removed myself from her apparent grief. I was of a mind to head back toward the boardinghouse, but instead of making my return, I found myself walking farther up the road in the supposed direction of Rachel's place. My curiosity was getting the best of me, and I rationalized it better to be poking around unknown streets alone instead of in the company of Luke and Gracie—especially Gracie.

I reasoned I shouldn't be too far from the orphanage, but I also knew I couldn't go running off too long a spell in search of it. Gracie and Luke wouldn't stand to be cooped up in a small room while all of St. Louis was beyond their door to be seen. However, at this moment they were most apt to be yet asleep, and with what little time it would take for me to walk a couple of extra blocks certainly wouldn't be the death of them.

I started off briskly in that direction, but any thought to hurry was soon forgotten as I slowed to absorb the flavor of the neighborhood. It was removed from the hectic pace of the riverfront. The slower pace seemed to reveal the conscience of the city. I confessed myself to be every bit as stunned by St. Louis as were Luke and Gracie. For them it was about seeing an actual city for the first time.

For me, it was about seeing the city for a second time, but feeling it was my first, feeling like I was lost, forgotten, feeling like the city had betrayed me. Like both of them, I too found my head ratcheting back and forth, side to side, taking in everything that was new, but it meant letting go of another St. Louis. It meant parting from heartfelt memories of a distant time and atmosphere that yet tugged at my heart.

There was little to be found of the place I remembered. I did not recognize anything of the streets I walked. My St. Louis seemed as buried and distant from this reality as was my past. I found little more than remnants of the places I once frequented, all seemingly shoved behind a crush of newer reddish-brown, sharp-edged, and windowed masonry walls that looked down upon the streets. The signage on these structures had a more permanent feel; a testimony to the doubtless conviction of the boisterous and colorful merchants, all believing St. Louis was here to stay in a big way. It pleased me to note that at least the crowds retained all of their forefathers' vigor. That much hadn't changed.

It occurred to me, I had never doubled back over ground traveled. Never before had I *returned* to a place, not to mention doing so a decade later. In the centuries old stability of Europe, I supposed after ten years the very same coat of paint might be seen on the very same wall, of the very same storefront, still doing business on the very same street. Nothing of that way of life could be found about this place.

I was bewildered by the magnitude of change that had taken place on this riverbank. I had left a place of wooden structures and returned to a place of brick. Brick, brick—*everywhere* I looked it was brick. Street after street sided with multi-storied brick that only began to instill a sense of stability and permanence found in Europe. It was if all structures wooden had been ripped from their foundations, ripped from their nails, never to be seen again.

I looked eastward across ten years of growth and found myself lost for words. That in itself was amazing, considering I could stand before Luke and Gracie, and prattle on for days describing dresses and dry goods, buildings taller than trees, carriages and coaches and brick-paved roads. I could tell them about everything except the discomfort of change. Whereas I planned on being their guide, I found myself every bit as lost.

I had come upon Biddle and turned east, walking three blocks to Sixth. On Sixth, I began to take in another neighborhood; it wasn't a street that I knew or recalled. The street was a collection of two-story boarding houses, a mix of wood and brick, a street like any other in this area. Some houses had yards and gardens, others were butted up to one another so tightly that light barely entered the crevice between.

I recalled the orphanage originally being closer to the docks and warehouses in the tannery district. I recalled the putrid smell of the area. Obviously, Rachel had acquired new quarters for the children, a place undoubtedly better for their health. I wasn't surprised by this change of address. Judging by the growth of the city, any address close to the water, stink or no stink, would now be very expensive. It made sense that business interests would have gobbled up those properties nearest the river, forcing living quarters farther west, most notably beyond Fourth. Hopefully, Rachel sold out and profited handsomely.

I was both joyful and afraid, overjoyed at the prospects of finding the shelter, and mortified I might discover ill fortune had come to Rachel and Caleb or their enterprise. I pressed on walking along Sixth determined to find the orphanage either here or close by. I saw a young boy of seven or eight coming my way and decided to intercept him, thinking him best to know the where-abouts of a place filled with children.

"Excuse me, son. May I ask you a question?"

The boy didn't answer. He did stop and look at me as if to listen.

"I am told there is an orphanage on this street or close by. Would you happen to know of such a place?"

"Whatsa orfinge?"

"A home with a bunch of children living in it. Maybe ten or fifteen."

The boy turned to look back down the street from whence he came. He pointed.

"Yeah, kids live in the house on the corner. ...On this side o' the street, at the end of the block. It's the big house with the big yard. Are they niggers? My poppa says they're all niggers in that place."

I winced. I felt like someone hit me in the chest, for I knew at once Rachel and Caleb were still running, still fighting for respect.

"Thank you. Would you like to have a tart? I have an extra."

"Yeah."

I handed it to him. He smiled and set off at a run. Now, my thoughts were troubled with the distressing recollections of slavery and inequality. I thought about Rachel, her life of hardship, and wondered how she fared in St. Louis during my absence.

I wondered where the citizens of St. Louis as a whole stood on the issue of slavery. From my conversations with the tart maiden and the boy, it sounded to yet be a way of life. My head was filling with questions of a kind I hadn't known in years. At this moment, I had no idea where the country stood on slavery, and I wished I didn't have to know.

I was amazed at how a couple of young folk could suddenly squander my high morning spirits, leaving me gloomy and down, and fearing what else I might soon wish not to discover. I had returned to civilization, and felt the next of my burdens being weighted back upon my shoulders.

I reached the corner house at the end of the block. Unlike the neighboring houses, this structure had been built back away from the road on a sizeable lot. This was not an affluent neighborhood and many of the dwellings were built of wood, but this structure was built of brick and had an accommodating porch. I stood before the building to study it and the yard, and also the four coaches that were parked around the corner off the street in a side yard.

I was mildly annoyed to find my hands sweating. Clearly, I had just fulfilled my apprehensions and predictions about seeing those from my past. I felt as if a glass wall had been erected between me and the orphanage. As I stood on the street sizing up my courage and what next to do, I noticed that a man crossing the street from the next block was particularly focused on me and drawing near. I grew attentive, and slowly started my way up the walk toward the porch. I chose not to look at him so as to invite conversation, but to no avail.

"Excuse me, ma'am."

I turned to look at the man.

"Do you know where ya are?"

"I believe so."

"I'm fearful, ya might not. That place belongs to a lot of negroes an' Irish, an' no self-respecting white lady would be calling if she knew the truth of it."

"I appreciate your concern, and I thank you. However, there is no need for worry. This is an orphanage, and I support the care of children regardless of heritage. I am here by choice. Thank you again, and good day, sir."

The man squinted at me with an air of disapproval. He nodded his head and walked past. I was irritated, but noticed I had inadvertently scaled the porch steps. To the man's credit, his concerns drew my attention sufficiently enough to temporarily subdue my deep reservations about calling on Rachel.

There was no point in my stepping off the porch to leave. I would be forever embarrassed at my cowardice should I turn back, and so I faced the door. I was adamant to go through with this… for about as long as it took to let out a sigh. After which, I stood there like a statue, yet focused on the knocker, but powerless to strike it. Instead, for relief…a distraction, I looked aside to glance about the porch, noting the commendable attention paid to repairs and upkeep.

I exhaled in a blow of exasperation.

"My god, Elizabeth! Ten dead men to your credit and you can't say good morning to a black lady. Are you serious? You have completely lost your mind," I chided myself.

I forced my eyes back to the door knocker. That door was intimidating. …Again, the wall…dense and impassable—granite.

The door blurred as I sank hopelessly into my thoughts. Like one thousand times before, I questioned my motives, wondering what benefits could possibly come of raking up old mud, stirring up heartache and betrayal. I feared the embarrassment of rejection, the uncertain reception awaiting me on the other side. It would be at first polite, open arms, but afterward the resentment would most certainly take hold.

They had reason a plenty to be angry. Where was the wisdom in rekindling these old relationships? Would there ever be a right time? Sometimes stones were best left unturned. Maybe I should have tried to establish myself in the city and then make myself known and available at a later date. I would then be in a much better position. All these thoughts passed as I gazed at a door knocker awaiting my grasp.

Startled, I caught movement out of the corner of my eye. I turned at once. It was a young black man of about seventeen or eighteen rounding the corner of the house. He was very well dressed. I assumed he must have walked up the drive from the rear yard. He stopped short at the sight of me, but at once broke into a broad and friendly smile. He appeared anxious to assist me.

"Madam? May I help you?"

I felt uncomfortable, awkward.

"Oh, oh. Excuse me, I was just walking by and I uh...I."

I looked away momentarily. I retreated. I was embarrassed at being caught off guard, embarrassed to be stammering. The thought of ten dead men plowed through my head, and with it passed the point of indecision. I surfaced from my emotional quagmire, and looked directly at the young man.

"What's your name, son?"

"Isaac."

"Is that a fact? You're a fine-looking lad."

"Why, thank you ma'am. You are too kind."

"Tell me, are you Rachel's boy?"

"Why, yes, I am. Do you know my mother?"

"Yes, but it's been a long time since we've spoken. Actually, I had hoped to see her this morning, but it seemed a bother. She appears to have a house full of guests. Hence, my standing hesitant on the porch, quibbling with myself as if a dolt."

He laughed easily, and stepped up onto the porch.

"You needn't worry yourself. Folks arrive unannounced all hours of the day."

He went for the door and opened it, so I might pass.

"Why don't you go inside and I'll bring her to you."

"You're certain I won't be a bother?"

"Of course not. Please, step inside and have a seat. I'll call her at once."

"Thank you, Isaac."

I was thrilled to see that Isaac not only had been found, but also raised as a fine well-mannered and engaging young man. I might have thought almost too refined for his years. Or possibly, I desired not to see the distance between his refinement and that of Luke and Gracie. He closed the door behind us, and then walked me though the foyer and into the parlor.

"Please, have a seat. I'll be only a moment fetching Mother."

"Thank you again."

SIXTY-THREE

Isaac walked down the hall to a room on the left and opened a door, which set free the chorus of conversation and laughter taking place inside. The sounds made me feel uncomfortable. I heard him call out above the din.

"Mamma!"

"Yes, honey?" The sound of Rachel's voice passed through me as a wave of warmth that flooded my heart. I felt as if I had been forgiven before my sins were revealed.

"There's someone here to see you."

"Someone hwo, Isaac?"

I heard him hesitate, and then burst into a laugh.

"My word, Mamma, I never got her name. I'll go and ask now."

I observed him turn in the doorway about to walk back in my direction.

"Isaac! Isaac, honey!"

"Yes, Mamma."

"Just have her come in. She must be someone I asked to stop by and join us for dinner. Hwoever she is, just show her in, honey. No doubt, we are expecting her."

"Ahhhhhh...."

I saw him lean back into the hall and look at me. I knew it had to do with the filth of me.

"I think you probably should come to the parlor, Mother."

"Oh Isaac, not now. Please, sweetheart, I don't have time. Show her in. Hwe are all friends here."

"Alright, Mamma."

He reappeared in the hallway.

"But…I don't think so." He whispered under his breath.

He returned to me and offered his arm.

"Would you care to come with me, ma'am?"

I studied the boy.

"I'm not really dressed for this am I. Not to mention washed or perfumed, or any of the little niceties one does before approaching people seated and about to dine. Do you like the smell of sweat, horses, and boardinghouses, Isaac? Are you certain you want me on your arm?" He looked at me and chuckled ever louder.

"My mother says a good sense of humor trumps all miseries. Besides, the Good Lord did give us the wind. Don't you agree?"

"Indeed. Windows as well, I trust you will open them."

Isaac stopped just short of the doorway and looked at me.

"I think this will be interesting, but I think it will be great fun. Shall we?"

"How can I refuse such a handsome escort? Let us go upwind then."

Clearly, Isaac had the great sense of humor. Yet, no matter how I may have joked, the fact remained I was embarrassed. Not only for me, but also for Rachel, because I knew what I was about to do to her dinner party.

I took a breath, turned, and walked into the room on Isaac's arm. I was uncomfortable to say the least. A very large table had been set. I would never escape my childhood training, and noted at once that the crystal and silverware were in proper position. The dishes on the side tables were overflowing and steaming hot. There were a dozen people presently seated at the table, a few more yet standing in conversation, all dressed in their finest attire. I had forgotten how polished and refined people could be at a social function in St. Louis.

It was those seated at the opposite side of the table who first went silent. They had the benefit of an unobstructed view. I passed through the doorway, and the sight of me put an end to their part in whatever conversations were taking place. Those with their backs toward me turned around out of curiosity, and the table talk went silent. Immediately thereafter, the remaining guests yet standing and scattered about the room hushed as well.

Rachel was standing in the far corner, finely done up in a royal blue dress with light blue lace and appointments, but wearing an apron. I was reminded of her lessons and expertise at the stove. Rachel frowned as she struggled to place me. I could see she was wondering if she had made an awkward mistake. Her mind must have been racing through the crowds of street people she encountered daily.

Suddenly the door behind her swung open and Caleb came bursting into the room walking backward followed by a large tray he was gripping firmly, upon which were placed two very large birds. He swung about revealing a broad smile and he blurted out.

"It is time to eat!"

He stopped short at the sight of me, and noted at once the silence now prevalent within the room. Rachel took a few steps forward, her eyes narrowed, her mouth opened slightly as if working to form an unspoken word. She was studying me intently. By the expression on her face I knew she was about to greet me with kindness.

"I am so sorry, but I am afraid I don't—."

"My god! It's Elizabeth...."

My eyes darted to the end of the table. It was Dorrie! Her back had been toward me as I entered the room. She was now twisted around in her chair and facing me. Her hands gripped the chair back tightly. Her eyes were locked onto mine. She stood up slowly from her seat and raised her palms to her face. Rachel was now fixed on Dorrie, trying to make sense, trying to make the connection.

Dorrie stepped forward cautiously, somewhat uncertain, and then lowered her hands so she might hold them outstretched to embrace me. Unashamed, she walked in my direction shaking her head in disbelief. I saw the tears well up in her eyes and spill as she approached. She threw her arms around me. Her embrace was firm and heartfelt, the moisture of her tears damp against my neck.

"Elizabeth?"

I heard Rachel question in a whisper, and then she realized.

"Oh, my word. Oh, my word! It's Elizabeth! Good Lord, Caleb, it's Elizabeth!" As Rachel came running around the table from the far side of the room to greet me, Dorrie leaned back, her face awash in tears. She gurgled in stunned surprise.

"You are not dead? Our prayers have been answered."

She straightened up and then looked me in the eyes.

"Have you any idea how we prayed for you, prayed for your safe return? Tell me you are not a ghost. Tell me it is really you. Look at you. Look at the way...why are you dressed like this? Where have you been? For the sake of angels, Elizabeth, where did you go all these years?"

She didn't wait for the answers. Instead, she hugged me again, only this time with the added embrace of Rachel.

"Ladies! Ladies! Allow our guest some air. Ladies, please. Let her sit. Offer her a chair."

Caleb reached for a chair and pulled it back from the table as Dorrie and Rachel released me from their grip and led me to the seat. I was too nervous to sit.

"We were just about to eat. You must sit and join us." Dorrie insisted.

"No! Oh! Bless you, Dorrie, but I couldn't. I couldn't bear the embarrassment. Such a thing would be entirely uncivil. No lady in her right mind would…. I am not dressed for such an occasion. I'm as ripe as a pig, a bad egg. I would foul the aroma of your best dish, of all your fare for that matter. I would be embarrassed to even think such a thing. The time is not good."

I felt my face glowing hot red with discomfiture. I started to pull back. I now fully regretted taking such liberty, being so rude an imposition solely to satisfy my selfish curiosity. Now I only wanted out, the faster, the better.

"I must be on my way. I promise to return…soon…when I am present—."

"Nonsense! I won't hear of it. We won't hear of it." Dorrie looked offended. "The time could not be more perfect, it's Thanksgiving."

"I should say so!" Rachel asserted. "You must have dinner with us. To leave now hwould cast a sad and severe demeanor upon us all…an unfitting end for a day dedicated to blessings and gratitude, to be sure."

She turned to her guests who were numb with astonishment. Clearly, all were clinging to every spoken word, searching for any clue or indication of who I might be to have such a profound sway on Rachel, Caleb, and Dorrie. I watched Rachel prepare to address her guests.

"Everyone! Please, may I have your attention? Forgive me for this interruption and my obvious state of bewilderment. Please

66

bear with me as I am at this moment overhwelmed with joy, and troubled…to find the words that express the honor given me…to introduce all of you to the finest, kindest, hwoman I have ever had the pleasure to know. It is her doing that has brought all of us together here today. The orphanage….” Rachel bit her lip in order to dampen her emotion. “…The return of my son…my friendship hwith Dorrie, my reunion hwith my husband and…my own life for that matter.

“I owe Elizabeth all these things and much more. I am sure some of you may have heard me speak of her, how she saved me from a certain death, and along hwith my dear friend Dorrie, nursed me back to health. She brought Caleb and I here to St. Louis in the face of many perils. For so many years hwe thought her dead and…and….” Rachel looked at me with a smile. “…she is back.”

Rachel took a moment to catch her composure and study the crowd. With her eyes, she asked for their patience and understanding.

“Please, I beg you might understand that I could never sit at this table today in peace hwithout Elizabeth’s company at my side. I could never live hwith myself if I offered her anything less that all of my heart and home.”

“Please, please join us!”

“She must stay.”

“Who could turn away such an honorable person?”

“I agree.”

“She must stay and dine with us.”

“We must hear more.”

“I dare say, indeed we must.”

“She must stay.”

67

The men folk put forth their argument as one voice. They were very persuasive, but I could not overlook my condition. My stench was more than even I could bear let alone expect others to suffer.

"You are all very kind, so very kind, but I am afraid I could never accept such gracious hospitality at this time. I must confess as of yet, I am unsettled and presently possess nothing more than the clothes upon my back. I have been traveling and only just yesterday arrived. Given a day or two I should better be settled, and in a condition better suited to meet all of you in a manner respectable to you stations. I thank you all the same. I thank you very much. I am sorry for imposing, sorry for disrupting this fine dinner aff—."

"No! Elizabeth. That hwill not do..." Rachel shook her head in disagreement. "...that hwill not do. I insist. It's God's hwill that you are here hwith us today. He is reminding us...He is reminding me this very minute of hwat most hwe should be thankful. It was I hwo had nothing but the clothes on my back hwen you found me. I was every bit as dirty, every bit as filthy, I hwas at heaven's gate, and you carried me back from the grave. You carried me. I could never forgive myself if I allowed you to refuse my hand. You must accept this small gesture in return for all you have done for me." Rachel's eyes moistened. "Look at my boy, Elizabeth. Is he not the most beautiful son for hwich a mother could ask? He hwas lost to me forever, Elizabeth, and he is here hwith me now. Please take my hand and allow me the pleasure of showing my gratitude. It is many, many years overdue." She wiped her eyes with her apron. "Please, Elizabeth."

"Rachel, I am not fit.... I stink, I—."

"Please, Elizabeth."

"We insist, Elizabeth," said Dorrie.

"You are all too kind, too kind, but—."

"We insist—."

"You must stay," chimed in the men again.

I held up my hand to silence all. I then spoke in a determined voice.

"I know your hearts. But, it is not just the stench of me, not just my unfit appearance. I must tell you that I am in the company of two others who are equally unfit to present themselves. I must return to them and see to their well-being. As I've said, we have only just arrived. I couldn't possibly sit to such a meal knowing that they—."

"Madam, Elizabeth."

A stately gentleman stepped away from the table and moved in my direction.

"Madam Elizabeth, Mr. Harold Wilkinson at your service. Forgive me for interrupting, but Isaac has informed me that you did not come by coach. I assume if you walked then your companions must be nearby. May I ask where you board?"

"Over on Ninth by—."

"In Kerry!" Rachel blurted out. "That hwill never do! My hword, Miss Elizabeth, you hwon't live to see the morrow. I hwon't hear of such a thing."

A murmur of concern swept through the crowd. I wouldn't have foreseen the anguish such news would spawn.

"Madam, Rachel is correct in this matter," said Mr. Wilkinson. "Kerry is a most dangerous place, especially for a woman to be walking. My wife and I would be honored if you would allow my driver to bring you to your friends in safety, and return with them to join us. I am certain you will find that we would be most pleased to await such return if it meant you would sit at our table. I sense your presence will enliven the dinner immeasurably. It would do us much good to discuss something other than the usual afflictions of the city, which I might add, never seem to be cured. I can speak for all when I say, we would welcome a fresh voice that seems certain to fill us with wonder and visions."

"Hear, hear!" The room cried out in unison.

"Then it's settled! You and your friends will eat with us," exclaimed Dorrie.

I was outnumbered. I sat momentarily in thought. This situation would end as they saw fit. It seemed best that I concede defeat and accept their wishes.

"As you wish. To refuse further would be equally rude of me. I thank you, Mr. Wilkinson, for offering me the use of your coach. You are a gentleman indeed. Thank-you Rachel, Dorrie; I thank you all for your generosity. This may end up leaving the day slightly tarnished, but you won't be able to say I didn't forewarn you."

The room broke into laughter, and I felt more at ease.

"Elizabeth, would you prefer one of us to accompany you?"

"Oh thank you, Dorrie, but I think it would be wiser if I prepare my friends for this occasion." I turned to the others. "I must beg of you all, your tolerance and understanding for these two of whom I speak, have never been seated at a table in their lives. They have nothing of the refinements of which you are accustomed, but they are fine persons indeed, honest persons of character...people I am most proud of."

"We are eager to make their acquaintance."

"Hear, hear." The men conveyed their sincerity.

"Isaac, would you show Madam Elizabeth to my coach?"

"It would be my pleasure, Mr. Wilkinson."

"I hwill prepare hot hwater and towels for your return."

"Yes! Yes!"

Dorrie clapped her hands nervously. She was giddy with delight.

Isaac escorted me to the coach and made certain I was seated comfortably. He was about to close the door when he looked up at me with laughter in his eyes.

"Miss Elizabeth, You were far more interesting than I might have imagined. I can hardly await your return."

"Wait until you meet the other two."

"Ha, ha."

Isaac nodded with anticipation. He was grinning ear to ear.

"I can hardly await your return," he repeated.

I laughed as he closed the door.

The coach sped away. I gazed out the windows that separated me from the people on foot, the houses, the shacks, the stores, and the dealer stalls that often crowded the road. I was falling back into the folds of my former life, a life that knew a great deal about the wants of others, but suffered none of their afflictions. I had returned to that life for good the moment I set foot into the orphanage.

Neither Gracie nor Luke would need to endure hardships of any kind from this point forward. The line separating the haves from the have-nots was as wide as the ocean for most, yet I crossed from one shore to the other effortlessly. For me the water lay flat and the current held still. There was no lightning, no storm, and no thunderous revelation that signaled my crossing.

As the coach approached the boardinghouse I could see a gathering of men about the entrance to the building. I knew without further thought that trouble was brewing. I feared Gracie and Luke would be at the center of it, and I knew it could prove disastrous for anybody involved.

Having no wish to wait for the driver, I stepped out of the vehicle before it had come to a halt. I pushed my way into a crowd of onlookers that were visibly surprised at the arrival of a coach.

"Excuse me, excuse me, please. Excuse me."

I forced my way into the building and down the crowded hall toward our rooms. It appeared I had arrived not a second too soon. The door to their room was open and the man who had blocked my path the day before now stood in place of the door, bridging the opening.

He was leaning back against the frame with a foot pressed up against the opposite side effectively gating off any attempt to pass. I walked up to his knee and pushed on it.

"I beg your pardon, sir. May I pass?"

"Well now, come after the babes has it?"

"Aye, aye." The rest of his lot confirmed my presence.

As with the night before, the brute's bravery was fed by his friends. He stood up straight and let me pass into the room. He then returned to his former stance, a barrier to the three of us.

I looked at Luke. He was nervous, but not scared. He was Indian in everything but blood. Gracie looked down right surly. I glanced down at her hand and saw the knife gripped in a throwing hold. I turned back toward the man. He made no attempt to move his leg. I stopped to stand at his side.

"What is it with you men? I swear, I'll never understand. For some reason because it is a woman who stands before you with a knife, you find it to be great sport. I cautioned you yesterday to stay clear. Are you so stupid, you can't manage to even consider she could kill you?"

I reached above his shoulder, the back of my wrist brushing against his beard. I patted the doorjamb that his head leaned against. I spoke to Gracie.

"Show him what would happen to his head if it were right here, sweetheart."

I pulled my hand back as the last of my words formed to leave my mouth. The brute hadn't the time to process my request. He still sported that smug 'I couldn't be bothered' grin, one corner of which nearly touched the jamb, the same door jamb that yet supported a head salivating over the view of Gracie. He might or might not have seen that quick dance of light race toward him. Either way, he possessed nothing of the speed or luck needed to sidestep the blur of Gracie's blade.

The knife slammed into the wall with such force that the dry wood split all of an arm's length. The blade point had passed cleanly through the plank, drawing in its handle far enough to nearly disappear. The sudden jar must have been most unpleasant on the man's temple. I suspected his ear was ringing.

"Bloody hell!"

The bully leapt out of the doorway—long after his would be death. He plowed backward into his collection of mates. His trampling over them only added to the rush of pandemonium underway, but for a number of onlookers who were standing behind the wall and startled by the harsh thud of the blade's strike. The sight of steel blasting through the wall was enough to send them also trampling over each other in an attempt, first to get out of harm's way, and later ask questions.

Without a second's thought, I stepped over to the jamb, and starting working the blade loose. Gracie was again ready to throw.

"For your sake, it's a good thing I got here when I did. Gracie skewers rabbits on the run with those knives. And I dare say by now, you have stared at her long enough to see we eat well. Splitting your ribs, or your skull for that matter, is but child's play for her. That little lady will shave you clean at ten feet, blindfolded."

I finally managed to work the blade free. I tossed it onto the bed where Gracie immediately took hold of it. I looked back at the brute, now standing in the hall, his swagger undermined by a red-faced glow. I was growing more irritated by the moment.

"Is this sinking in? Are you getting my point? Right now, your life is hardly in your hands. She is wicked with those knives. If you are supposing that she would find restraint before killing you, then might I suggest you to have a second look? You see her nature, her upbringing? You know an Indian's temperament. She has no fear of you. That's the reason you all kill Indians, isn't it?

"Now, last night, I asked politely. This time, I am telling you to leave us be and go about your business before someone here gets buried. We wish no quarrel with you. Go!"

The man shifted his frame and inched his way down the hall, all the while, all the way, he continued blowing bluster and belligerence. He had cowered before the knife and my tongue-lashing. He was in the awkward position of trying to save both face and hide.

The standoff only fully dissipated when the driver of our coach was heard demanding room to pass along the hallway. The whisperings of a private coach waiting in the street for the three of us seemed to unnerve our adversary far more than the knife. Men were now covering their faces and scurrying out of view, disappearing into the woodwork. The coach connected us to another kind of fear. It was one that the stranger could not assess, but might have known—the strike of the well-heeled. I knew it well.

I promptly instructed Gracie and Luke to go to the coach. They filed out of the room, and I followed then down the hallway past the gawks and stares of the curious. Not a face looked away; all

74

were focused on us, all duly impressed to see a coach awaiting our company. The driver opened the door, and at that point they believed we stepped into the protection and security of the rich and powerful. The door closed and we were suddenly untouchable, invisible to those left standing in the street. It was exactly the kind of escape that infuriated the impoverished.

Once in the safe confines of the coach, Gracie wasted no time scolding me.

"I thought you were coming right back."

"My word, Gracie, I wasn't gone that long. What happened back there?"

"Wot happened? We were sleeping and the door burst open, that's wot happened. I jumped back and pulled out my knife. The brute just started laughing at me. He kept taunting me, going on about how he'd like to stick me with something that I wouldn't soon forget and put me in my place. He said he would drive the Indian ways right out of me. I was just about ready to shut him up for good when you showed up."

"I am sorry, Gracie. I know I shouldn't have gone off. I can only imagine what you must be thinking after waking up to that mess. Plain and simple, this is a rough place, and I shouldn't have wandered off. However, I also have to say that even though you did nothing wrong, you must be careful with those knives. Listen to what I say. It could get you...it could get all of us into a lot of trouble. Do you understand?"

I looked at Gracie and she just looked back, defiantly to be precise.

"Do you understand, Gracie? You can't just go about wielding those blades."

"I understand."

"Good. That is all that I ask. Just take a moment to think things through then go ahead and kill if you must." I looked at her. "I am just kidding; you realize that…yes?"

I looked over at Luke. He was captivated by the inside of the coach. He was captivated by the passing scenery. He was captivated by life.

"How about you? Are you alright, Luke?"

Luke was in his own world, his face pressed up against the glazing and taking in every detail of the street.

"Luke!"

"Yes, Mother. I am fine."

Having broken his trance, Luke turned to look at me with bright-eyed wonder. I was certain he was about to give me an account of something he had just seen. In fact, he did.

"You should have seen the way Gracie stood up to that man! She looked him straight in the eyes and said she was going to slit his belly open from side to side, and pull his insides out, and tie him up with his own guts! She said she would tear his heart out with her own teeth and swallow his soul. She said she was going to peel him like a snake. She really scared him. You should have seen the look on his face."

"That's enough, Luke. I would really rather not hear anymore about it."

"She was brave! She stood right up to him. I wish you would have killed him. It would have been great coup. You would have been praised."

"Luke! I said that's enough of that, for heaven's sake. You don't know what you're saying, and I don't care for that kind of talk. Can we just not talk about this anymore? We have plenty of other things to deal with right now."

I shook my head, allowing it to topple in my hand. I closed my eyes and wondered. How *was* I supposed to take a knife-wielding, blonde-headed girl with a killer's instinct, and her like-minded sidekick, my son, and prepare them to be seated at a Thanksgiving dinner with some of St. Louis's best in the space of a coach ride? It seemed all my years of teaching were for not, maybe it would be impossible. On the other hand, it was I, who cried to be a mother.

"Alright, you two. Now, listen up...."

SIXTY-FOUR

When we returned to the orphanage, I noticed at once there were several more carriages and coaches in the street. The driver pulled over to the curb and stepped down from his bench to open the cabin door. I stepped out first and stood to the side as the driver assisted Gracie and Luke down to the street. There were a good many unknown faces smiling excitedly from the front porch, a few of which darted back inside.

Seconds later, the front door flew open, and Rachel and Dorrie came running out, past the guests and descended the steps to greet us.

"Come, come. Welcome all. Please, come inside."

Tugging on our arms, they escorted us back up and inside.

"Hwe are preparing everything for you. I haven't had sufficient time to muster up clothes. I didn't know hwo needed hwat. But the tub hwater is good and hwarm and ready as hwe speak. Fresh towels have been set out for all."

The folks waiting in the foyer eased their way into the parlor, and were followed by the gentlemen smoking on the porch. Most of the ladies spilled out of the dining room. There appeared to be upwards of thirty guests, and the air was filled with excitement. This was three or four times the earlier number of guests. I saw the front door open and yet two more entered. Rachel called out in a clear voice.

"May I please have your attention? Please! May I have your attention?"

The guests grew silent, and you might have heard a pin drop had it not been for the voices of children that could be heard horsing around in back of the house.

"I hwould like to introduce you all to a dear friend of mine, Elizabeth Claussen. I am afraid I haven't had the pleasure of being formerly introduced to her companions, but, Elizabeth, if you hwould do us the honor...."

"Certainly." I stepped forward. "It is my pleasure to meet you all. I am deeply embarrassed for the disruption I have caused, and I also must apologize for our dress and foul odor. We have just arrived in St. Louis after ten years in the wilds, and I wasn't expecting such persuasive welcoming party.

"That being said, allow me to introduce this perfectly gorgeous woman at my side, Gracie Castleman. As a child of only ten years, she saved my life, and has lived with me ever since. I have no idea how I would have been able to survive many of my ordeals without the joy and comfort of her spirit and encouragement.

"And this young man, here...well...this is my son, Luke."

There was an audible gasp from both Dorrie and Rachel. I looked in their direction and witnessed unreserved wide-eyed astonishment. My eyes locked onto theirs as I continued to speak.

"He is my pride and joy. He is all that I live for now. He has fulfilled my life. I will have my hands full teaching him the ways of St. Louis and the places I call home. He has blood in him that is as wild as the western desert, and I pray that he doesn't lose it all in order to master the social graces that will be expected of him in this new world."

There was a round of applause and cheer, and much good will offered us.

Rachel had always been a head servant, and knew precisely how to handle situations like this. She took charge.

"Now, I beg your patience. Hwe must allow this dear and special guest hwo honors us to have a brief rest to freshen, and then return to awe us with stories of hwonder and places afar. Please enjoy our hospitality until that time. Thank you."

She approached me.

"Elizabeth, I have laid out a selection of clothes I hope you and Gracie might find to your liking. One of our guests, Mrs. Becker, had gone back to fetch a change of clothes, which her son has outgrown. She believes they will fit handsomely on Luke. Isaac, I am afraid, is too tall and thin."

She turned to her guests.

"If I may have your attention, once again please! In light of the number of friends that have joined us, I have decided to ask if you might support my decision to make this a less formal affair. Mr. Hwilkinson had been gracious enough to send for his chef and table maidens. I assure you they promise to tend to our every need, and hwill be compensated generously for having given up their holiday in our behalf.

"Hwe must also thank, Mr. Barron, hwo has sent for a couple of cases of hwine for those of you not hwolly disciplined in the principles of temperance. Hwe have set up additional tables, and I hwould ask that you feel free to step up to the table and select hwat you hwish. In short time, an assortment of dishes hwill appear regularly to curb your appetite, hopefully to your liking. The table maids hwill dress your plates, and assist you to your tables. I believe hwe will be much freer to move about and mingle hwith the fresh faces and especially our guests of honor, Miss Claussen, Miss Castleman, and Mr.…."

I looked at Rachel fully understanding her sudden uncertainty.

"Dennison. Luke Dennison." I offered.

"…Mr. Dennison." Rachel continued. "Please feel free to imbibe and make acquaintance hwile I hwisk our guests off for a hot invigorating bath. Thank you for your patience—and good appetite."

Rachel in all her cleverness had freed me from the concern and discomfort of having Gracie and Luke sit at a formal table. They would have looked like animals. Not that I didn't spend years explaining table manners and protocol, but it still remained to be known if either had ever so much as seen a fork or a table knife, let alone handled one. There was so much for them to learn. I knew they would do well. It would take time, yet I knew they would excel for they had character far beyond their years and young faces.

This being Rachel's house and undertaking, it was Dorrie who stepped up to escort us to our baths so that Rachel might be free to attend to her guests. Dorrie had hoped to smother me with her affections and attentions, but I begged her to honor me by going to Gracie. I whispered my plea.

"Dorrie, I can only laugh as I try and imagine what Gracie must be wondering. She must be eyeing the soaps and fragrances, and the corset, the dress and slips. I showed her a dress awhile back and she was utterly dismissive of anything that held no place for her knives.

"You must assist her, Dorrie, for me, you must. And whatever you do, don't laugh at her. What-e-ver. you-do, don't laugh at her."

I started laughing, trying hard to contain myself. "She is all spit and grit behind those green eyes and if she glares at you just one time, I promise you will know your position."

Dorrie pouted in jest, but understood my predicament. She set off at once to attend to Gracie.

"Ohhhhh."

I moaned with disbelief as I inhaled the fragrance of the soaps put out for my use. I reached for one of the towels and pressed it up against my face. It was made of cotton, thick and soft. Rachel had not left me to myself. I was tended to by a servant who remained silent, yet smiled easily and seemed eager to scrub my back.

The pampering drained me of all my anxiety. I found myself dazed, dozing, staring into the soapsuds that floated across the warm comforting bath water. I blew on them and watched as they drifted away. My mind drifted to dry sand and weed blowing across the hot flat desert, and I recalled the fears I endured believing I might never drink again. I thought of my parched lips and my insane obsession of saving urine in a jar. I remembered the prayers. I thought of the freedom I was given each time I discovered a spring-fed pond, a source of life, life to last a few more days.

I thought of that dear singing rambler, Luke, and how we had danced together in the rain and how incredibly wonderful the wetness felt on our skin. I thought of Gracie and how she drew me into that freezing mountain stream...so many joys associated with water, so many memories that haunted me. I knew my life was rich with experience, but I didn't know why. I suppose like all others, I wondered if I would ever know the reason for my being. Maybe, it was all about my Luke. *The chosen one....* What silliness.

The maid brought my clothes and helped dress me. Dorrie came in just as I was finished with my powdering. She took my arm and escorted me from the dressing room to the staircase. We stopped momentarily to look down upon the guests at which point she leaned in close to confide.

"I must warn you, it appears as though your son possesses an attraction that brings out the cat in our ladies. Is he made of catmint?"

From our height, I looked over the crowd and tried to stifle my laughter.

"My word, have they no shame? Will you look at the way they are fussing with his braids? You know, he is suffering to be on his best behavior," I replied, barely able to contain my amusement.

"The poor thing doesn't dare do anything but stand there and answer their questions. I think you need to rescue him."

"I told him in the coach, should he embarrass me, I would show him the full extent of my historic temper. It's fortunate he is yet young enough to fear a mother's wrath."

We descended the staircase and Dorrie passed me off to Rachel, who was waiting to escort me toward her guests. I glanced over at Luke, who was surrounded by women and so shot me a glance of desperation. I simply nodded and smiled, knowing it would be hard for him to get in trouble as long as he was encircled by so many lady admirers. They were captivated by the wildness that was clearly visible in his eyes and demeanor. They were captivated, he was caged, and I was free to roam, more or less. I chuckled lightly under my breath, for I fully expected to spend my night having to watch his every move as long as he remained in such structured confines.

I was distracted by a murmur that passed through the crowd, and turned to follow the eyes of others. I found myself gazing up at Gracie as she descended the staircase on Dorrie's arm. I was completely taken aback. I was simultaneously jealous—remembering when I was the picture of youth—and prideful, an adoring mother, mesmerized, stricken speechless by the sight of her. I swallowed hard, strangled by emotion that was apparent to all in view of my eyes.

This formerly rough and tough purple-faced orphan was now looking to me for approval or explanation. I wasn't sure which, but she was nothing if not an angel of perfection floating down to highlight the skill of God's handiwork. Bound up within the constraints of a dress that was gorgeous, a dress that enhanced her natural beauty beyond stunning; she held the room in spellbound silence.

A polite applause acknowledged her entrance. It was a very moving moment for me. I opened my arms to accept her.

"Gracie…. You look…heavenly. Look at you. You are dazzling. Do you like the dress?"

"Wot are you crying for?"

"I'm not crying. I'm just happy. Someday you will understand."

"I don't believe you used to wear these."

"There was more to my life than sweaty leathers."

"How do you move in such a thing?"

"You will get used to it. I trust you haven't forgotten how you used to dream of such dresses when your dadduh spoke of them. I promise, he and your mother are at this moment beaming proud in heaven."

Dorrie stepped forward.

"She cleans up nice, no?"

"Who would have known?"

"You should have seen the look on her face when we held the dress up for her to put on. I asked her if she liked it. It took five full minutes for the fear to leave her face." Dorrie laughed.

"Pray tell, and she said…?"

"How do you know front from back?"

We both began laughing at which point I looked at Gracie and elbowed Dorrie.

"She's glaring. What did I tell you about that frosty stare?"

We each took one of Gracie's arms and led her into the crowd.

Gracie was blushing like a little girl. She knew nothing of restraint, but at this moment, so out of her element, her innocence was pure and intoxicating.

The dress not only lit up Gracie's eyes, but also the eyes of every man present, especially those of the younger men. She was very mindful of this particular kind of attention and her clumsy pursuit of it would have made any mother die of embarrassment.

I made a point of explaining some of the cultural differences that dictated her actions and unabashed mannerisms. Gracie and Luke were assertive in everything they did. Under normal circumstances, in my opinion, they would have been flawlessly rude, obnoxious beyond comprehension. But the guests were tolerant and most forgiving of the unpolished nature these two possessed.

If anything, the guests were fascinated by these glimpses into a distant world they often attempted to imagine. The women of Christian upbringing went silent when Luke took a piece of meat with his fingers and then offered it to the four directions. It was innocent enough, but the impact it made amongst them was evident in their expressions.

The children would certainly have been branded as pagan heathens, but for the fact I was Luke's mother and Gracie's guardian. Blonde braids and pretty dresses couldn't cover up the nature of the beasts, yet the beasts couldn't overshadow my standing with those guests of Rachel, Caleb, and Dorrie.

The guests understood I was somehow mysteriously connected to Christopher Claussen. Throughout the evening, they pried. Their curiosity was most evident, but kept at bay behind good manners. They skirted direct questions by recalling accounts of Claussen, his influence and accomplishments. They spoke of his land holdings and shipyards back east. They spoke of his legendary vision, his western railroad ambitions and undertakings, his investments that were now returning profits to satisfy a god. I concurred, adding that Mr. Claussen was the invisible force to be reckoned by all who did business of any consequence. I added nothing else.

The night was a draw, tit for tat, everything in balance. Whatever Luke and Gracie may have lacked, may have failed to bring to the table, my presence compensated by stories and mysterious connections. And so, the evening was enjoyable start to finish, and after the guests grew weary from the hours of eating, drinking, and merriment, Rachel called it a night.

SIXTY-FIVE

The next morning, I awoke to the sound of children playing. They were outside somewhere off in the distance squealing and laughing excitedly. In my mind, yet behind eyes working to open, I imagined them romping about and playing with abandon. Listening to them forced a smile even in my half awake state. Their exuberance shaped my morning mood. I greeted the early light; jumped from my bed, threw on a robe, pushed and pulled a little on the hair, and headed for the kitchen. As I passed along the hall, I salivated for the mouth-watering aromas of bacon and coffee, cinnamon, vanilla, and spices, scents of breakfast that hung heavy in the air.

The clinking of silverware and china perforated fragments of conversation that filtered out of the kitchen and floated down the hall to enter my ears. I felt light-hearted and cheery upon entering the room, and was made even more so upon seeing Dorrie and Rachel, both seated at the table. Their eyes rose to greet me as did their great welcoming smiles.

The smell of breakfast permeated the room. Apparently, the orphans had been fed, though none were to be seen with the exception of three girls washing dishes and cleaning up.

"Come in, come in and have some coffee," Rachel insisted. "Don't mind the mess."

"This takes me back. It reminds me of breakfasts on the schoolboat."

"Yes, it does." They laughed knowingly. "And at times, just as chaotic."

"Did you sleep well?" asked Dorrie.

"Yes, very well, thank you. I was dead tired. It was an outstanding evening. The two of you certainly know how to host an event. I hope I didn't make a fool of myself. I haven't had a glass of wine…well…glasses of wine, in a decade. Hoooh."

The room went quiet. Rachel and Dorrie were staring at me.

"What?" I smiled. "Was I that bad?"

They laughed.

"No, you were an absolute delight. Those stories—I think half of St. Louis fell in love with you last night. My word, Elizabeth, I can't help but to look at you. Rachel and I were just saying what a shock it was to see you walk through that door. I still can't get over it. It gave me goose bumps. It still does. Look!"

Dorrie began rubbing her arms briskly. She stood up from her chair and pointed.

"I know; I don't believe it myself. I woke up this morning, and I saw a ceiling and four walls. I was in an honest to goodness bed, and alone, no bugs trying to cozy up. It was odd, indeed."

"Come, come. Sit down, Elizabeth. What can I get you, coffee or tea?"

"Coffee sounds wonderful."

I pulled out a chair across from Rachel. She looked at me as if mesmerized. Finally, she frowned and rolled her big brown eyes.

"I hwas soooo embarrassed."

"She must have told me that a hundred times last night," said Dorrie

"It's true! I hwas. I am. I swear I didn't recognize you. I am looking at you, and I know it hwasn't because you have changed that much. I mean of course you have changed, hwe all have, but at this moment you seem no different to me than the day I last saw you. I didn't accept knowing you because you hwould be the last person on earth I hwould have imagined to see hwalk through that door.

"We gave up hearing from you, gave up seeing you years ago. I thought you hwere long, long, since dead. I just remember staring at you and sensing a distant familiarity, something of a past dream. I very nearly died of shock hwen the truth of it sank in."

"Rachel, if it makes you feel better, I *should* have been long since dead."

"Honestly, we did. We all thought you had come to a sad end," confirmed Dorrie. "I mean, land sakes alive, how many years has it been? You yourself said you have a son...you said what? He is ten?"

"Yes. That makes it at least ten years since last we were together, more like twelve. I left St. Louis in thirty-two. ...Lord, thirty-two, I can't believe it myself."

"Now, Elizabeth, you can't expect to hwaltz back into our lives hwithout facing the questions begged to be asked. First, you must tell us about Luke's father. Hwo is this lucky man? Hwere are you hiding him? Honestly, I can't imagine he'd allow the likes of you to hwalk Kerry unescorted."

"Oh, no. No, no, no. This isn't a good time to delve into that, maybe later. I am afraid Luke's father is no longer with me, and the memories are painful. I have to be in the right frame of mind to revisit that part of my life."

"Oh. I am sorry. Ohhhh...forgive me, Elizabeth. I didn't mean to pry. How rude of me." Rachel frowned.

"Not really rude, Rachel. The same question I would have asked—."

"Well, what about that Mis-ter Claus-sen? Yesss?" Dorrie jumped in. Her eyes lit up as she drew out his name. "I still recall, when back in Tonawanda, how you would go on and on about him—praising all his virtues. You had a *thing* for that man—."

"I most certainly did not."

"Oh, ho, ho, I think you did," Rachel teased. "I think you just forgot. I remember all those things you used to say about how kind he was, and how he supported you the whole of your life.

How he could do no wrong. He was a god in your eyes. I remember, yessss?"

"Nooooooo. I'm saddened to see the state of your memory, how it fades." I teased. "You exaggerate. You embarrass me with such nonsense. Yes, I did think very highly of Mr. Claussen. I still do, but I never thought him a god."

"Well, pardon me, if I beg to differ. I have an excellent memory and I well remember the sparkle in your eyes whenever you mentioned his name."

"Oh, please." We all laughed.

"Anyway..." Dorrie continued. "Last night you mentioned having found him, but I never got to hear more. Now, I am dying to know. I can only imagine how thrilling that must have been. So, tell us. We want to hear all of it, every little detail—no secrets. Was he happy to see you? I'll bet he just about *died* when you showed up knocking a thousand miles from home."

Dorrie was thrilled and she laughed excitedly.

"Yes, I think he might have," I responded.

"And? And?"

They were both leaning forwards waiting for the words to fall out of my mouth.

"And, and...well—," I stammered.

"And that is all wot you will ever know."

I spun around to see Gracie standing in the doorway also dressed in a robe. Rachel and Dorrie looked up at her in surprise, but now awaited her explanation.

"It's all very dark and mysterious—."

"That's enough, Gracie," I interrupted.

89

"Christopher Claussen is the only man's name I have ever heard cross her lips. She will say he is the most mysterious, most kind and gentle man to walk the earth. She will tell you he spends his life helping others in need, especially children, countless thousands of orphans, but that is all. I can't tell if he is a man or a god. Is he a dream? Can someone that perfect be real? Elizabeth will never reveal more. I remember when she was pregnant. She was talking to him in her sleep and scared the living daylights out of me. These are secrets of her heart that—."

"Alright, this conversation is finished. I apologize for Gracie. Apparently, she has a great deal more to learn about manners, and exaggeration as well."

In fact, I was shaken. Those were the most direct words I ever heard come out of Gracie's mouth in regard to my most private affairs. I wondered if she had waited years to find someone who knew me as well as did she, someone with whom she could compare notes. Her comments greatly added to my discomfort regarding this conversation. It impressed upon me my guilt, my denial of my deepest conviction. In my life, Claus *was* a god. Now, I suffered to reject the notion, and so returned from my thoughts to find Gracie still on a roll.

"...no exaggeration. And what I lack in manners, I make up in honesty. I love you with all my heart, Elizabeth, but you are every bit as secretive as is your Christopher."

"Ha! Now there's a gal hwo knows Elizabeth. Isn't she though? I agree," added Rachel.

"Enough, Gracie. That is enough. Now, if we may change the subject, I must say that I was overjoyed to find you here, Dorrie. What a surprise. How did that come to be?"

Dorrie looked at me with concern. It was written all over her face. Gracie stole away my control of the situation, and I wasn't happy about it, but Dorrie was sensitive enough to give it back.

"Well, my boys are out on their own now. Things slow down in New York this time of year in the sense that we offer many classes, but not while traveling, because the canal is closed down. I am sure you remember."

"I do; I do."

"Rachel and I have kept our friendship alive by letter over the years, and finally three years ago when the last of the orphans were moved out of this building, she asked me to 'come on down for a spell' and spend Christmas and the holy days. And I did. I am no longer connected to the boats, but spend most of my days in the office. I am free from the seasonal restrictions of the canal, and so vacation when it suits me. I came down with my youngest boy, Jack, that year, and he came with me again last year, but this year I'm on my own. It gets cold down here to be sure, but Buffalo is perpetually buried beneath a mountain of snow. I guess I'm getting old, too old, and I get sick of it. So, here I am."

"I have to ask. What became of the Schueller's and...."

"The Gunnicks?"

"Yes. The Gunnicks. How are they?"

"All passed. Opal was the last to go. She died two years ago. It's as if they wished to remain together in the afterlife. And I am certain they managed it. They supported the schoolboats ambitiously, and by the time Opal passed, we had twelve boats. The boatyards now allow us the use of their boats during the winter months for school. Oftentimes, we float their newly built boats down the canal in spring to show them off and advertise their sale while we use them for classes. They even build them to accommodate us until they are sold, you know, put companionways in the bulkheads adjoining the holds. You would be very happy to see what your hand has accomplished." Dorrie nodded approvingly.

"Well, let's not forget it was never my hand. Mr. Claussen funded every dollar. Whenever it's about children, his pockets are deep. I am confident his heart hasn't changed. He believed in you, in helping you get back on your feet, and he believed in your knowledge and expertise. He would be very pleased to hear of your success."

"I can assure you Mr. Claussen's heart has been ever more generous. I am told he insists that his freight move only on board or alongside schoolboats under my management. It was because of the increase in his freight that more schoolboats had to be put in service in order to comply. We have profited handsomely by his hand. But...Elizabeth, you are killing me. Did you, or did you not, find him?"

"Yes. I did find him."

"Ohhh.... You appear to have misgivings. Please don't say he was put off by your visit."

"No, Dorrie, he was a gentleman. He is always a gentleman. He will always be a gentleman."

Rachel and Dorrie sat hanging on my every word, waiting in silence that I found uncomfortable.

"Forgive me, but I really don't want to talk about this."

"Oh, of course. And we shouldn't mettle, Dorrie," said Rachel.

"I suppose.... I apologize, Elizabeth. It's just that we spent years thinking of you, wondering how you were getting along, wondering if you found Mr. Claussen, or whatever it was that your heart longed to find. In time.... In time, if you wish to tell...."

"Maybe, in time. So, are there no orphans here at all?" I asked.

"Not anymore," said Rachel. "Hwe had to make it an office. The number of orphans in St. Louis is staggering. In the last few years it has become an embarrassment for the city, actually that doesn't describe it. It is all of a nightmare.

"So many immigrant families have been torn apart by disease and death, hweakened by their travels, that the streets are filled hwith their orphaned offspring stealing and vandalizing in order to feed themselves. In fact, the first hwave of orphans came in thirty-two hwen you hwere leaving. Cholera broke out here, and I don't remember how many died, but the city had hundreds of orphans.

"There has been so much growth here that the city is drowning in bad hwater, sewage, garbage, and filth. A lot of immigrants die under these conditions and leave children behind that cannot even speak English. It is often impossible to support a hwife or consider marriage and so there are bastard children beyond count. There is no extended family out here to take in these children so they roam the streets half starved.

"Those churches that hwere given assistance from the city made an effort to address the problem by providing food and shelter. But hwe have been through a terrible recession for the last few years and money to support the needy is scarce.

"And then one must understand that negro children are not allowed or accepted into the public housing for hwite orphans. Because Caleb and I already had an orphanage with predominantly negro children, the public institutions hwere more than happy to assist us in expanding our service."

"Come, sit, Gracie. Have some tea and join us. Sit, sit." said Dorrie

"Hwe oversee six homes hwith just over one hundred children mostly negro and Irish. There are a lot of Irish immigrants just hwest of us, starting about Ninth Street as I assume you discovered. They call that area the 'patch.' The area is even hworse off than

93

it appears, and suffers all the ills of impoverishment. They say life expectancy in the patch is fourteen years.

"Caleb and I live in this house. Hwe stay here to manage the homes. Hwe usually have a few orphans living hwith us hwo are in transit, getting ready to step out. But, for the most part, this address is used for meetings and business matters, including entertaining and fund raising as you saw last night. Mostly, hwe beg before the city's affluent to help place and provide for the children. The children you see hworking about and cleaning up come from the homes to help us hwith dinners and said activities. They are usually older and looking to leave. It's a tough step to take."

Rachel took a well-deserved breath.

"Rachel…does Mr. Claussen assist you as well?"

I was most curious to know if Claus had continued his donations to those places connected specifically with me.

"Oh, yes, most certainly. Like clockwork, there is a deposit made into our account every three months for eighteen hundred dollars. Hwe see nobody, hwe hear from nobody, but every time hwe expand, so too does the deposit…usually about three hundred dollars per home. Mr. Claussen's charity remains the core of our funds. I trust his support far more than that of the city. He not only provides us financial relief, but probably more important, peace of mind. All in all, I hwould say that the orphanage is reasonably secure. It has grown considerably, more than you might have ever imagined.

"As for Caleb and me, our lives…they have become routine. That is, if hwe overlook the brewing issues of slavery and freed blacks. If hwe overlook that then our diversions are simple, our plans inconsequential. There is little more to us, hwereas it is you hwo is filled with hwonder and interest. I know I asked last night, but there hwere so many interruptions that I must ask again, hwat are your plans now? After all that you have been through, hwat's next?"

"Yes! Do tell! What great adventure next lies in store? I can only imagine," said Dorrie.

I reached for my coffee and sipped the hot savory liquid. I watched as Rachel set a cup of the orange spiced tea on the table for Gracie, and then motioned for her to have a pastry. Gracie promptly began sniffing the tea like a dog. Rachel turned back to me for an answer. I returned my cup to the table.

"At this point, I am unsure. I must first say that my return to St. Louis was sudden and entirely unexpected. We were abducted—."

"Abducted!" yelped Rachel.

Dorrie and Rachel were shocked at hearing the revelation, but it was especially horrifying to Rachel, who knew the terror of abduction firsthand.

"My god, hwhat happened?"

"That is a long, long, story, Rachel, best left for an afternoon tea. Now, I simply wish to say that I never had a moment's time to consider what would be my plans once in St. Louis. I was so preoccupied with surviving the journey, keeping Gracie and Luke safe, that I never gave much thought to anything past finding you and the orphanage. I suppose now that I am back, I am mostly of a mind to make amends. I would like to right my wrongs here in St. Louis, and then go home, back to Boston.

"So, a big part of my being here is to assure myself that when I leave you will believe when I say that I know it was cruel of me to put you both through the torment that I did, and that I am filled with remorse when I think of it. I will never be able to apologize sufficiently, and I hope you will find it in your hearts to forgive me. You had every right to believe I abandoned you at the worst of times. I vanished and it cannot be denied. I cannot explain the desert. I can only ask you to understand that at the time there was no other way for me. If things had been different...well, if things had been different, I wouldn't have been gone for twelve years.

"When I leave you, I will go on to face Mary. I know in my heart that she will forgive me for what I have done. That is her way. But...there will be fences to mend. You said that at one time you had correspondence with her. I do wish you could know her by more than just her letters. I wish you knew her face and her eyes. She has the heart of an angel. She once cared for me as a child when I was deathly ill. I will never forget. I love her dearly.

"I want you to understand that I have done things, not just here in St. Louis or Boston, but also during my time in the wilderness that I regret. These things haunt me and I must right my wrongs in my own way at my own speed. You might know I now speak of the reasons I am so secretive—*thank you very much*."

I shot a sharp glance at Gracie. I turned back to Rachel.

"Actually, as long we are on the subject, I would be indebted to you both if you made as little mention of my return as possible. I have very good reason for the news not to be made public."

"Secrets, secrets, secrets," exclaimed Gracie. "I told you, Elizabeth is all about secrets."

At once, I thought of the greatest secret of all which was that of a ten-year-old boy fathered by a man who knew nothing of his existence, and when introduced to my dearest Mary, would be recognized at once as the flesh and blood of Mr. Christopher Claussen. Gracie's ignorance grated me, and I must have appeared annoyed or even angered, because at once I saw a look of regret sweep across her face.

"Very well, Gracie. Then, this is a secret. And it would mean a great deal to me if this secret is kept close to breast, for I may have brought you here with only the shirt on my back, but I carry baggage of another kind. It is invisible to you, yet it weighs heavily on me to this day. I make many of my decisions based on these connections to my past, some good, some not so good, but not *one* of which you know."

The room went silent. The pressure passed from me to Gracie. She buckled.

"Forgive me. I was being smart, but I didn't intend to be disrespectful. If it felt that way, I apologize. I apologize, I'm sorry."

I softened my expression.

"I don't need your apology, sweetheart. I need you to understand that we are now in a different place, a different time. I face a different set of fears and concerns; maybe not bears, or abductors, maybe not scoundrels, but for me, fears nonetheless. I have issues to address that are difficult, complicated. Wrongs to right, and that is never easy no matter how deep one's remorse. Forgiveness and understanding won't be up to me."

"Have no fear, Elizabeth," said Rachel. "You needn't seek forgiveness in this home, for hwe know your heart. Hwatever drove you to your deeds, hwe know they hwere done for the best. As for your secret, it is safe hwith us, but I can't speak for all my guests. You all made quite an impression on them. In fact, I hope you hwill consider staying here and spending time hwith Dorrie and I through the holidays. Our friends will be greatly disappointed if you leave on short notice."

Dorrie's eyes lit up.

"I can help you teach Gracie and Luke the many things you want them to know. I would love to. Oh, Elizabeth, it would be wonderful to have your company over Christmas. I can't think of any way to make the season merrier. Please say you will."

"Besides," said Rachel, "it's time you pitched in and started answering Christmas letters. Those original fifty slips you used to talk about, hwell, I'm here to tell you, hwe now get hundreds of cards and letters at Christmas. It's gotten completely out of hand. Everybody is either sending or dropping off letters of good hwill and news. It isn't just the orphans anymore. It's everybody!" Rachel complained.

"What do you think, Gracie? Have you ever celebrated Christmas? Would you like to stay with us for the holidays? You want to learn how to read?" asked Dorrie.

"I can read. Elizabeth taught Luke and me both how to read. I'll show you."

Gracie reached for a page from the *St. Louis Republican*.

"No, Gracie, no—."

Rachel stood up from the table, but Gracie was possessed by her assertive Indian nature.

"No, please, I can do this listen."

She charged into the article, reading slowly, methodically, but with good form.

"On Friday last, the…coroner held an…inquest at the house of Judge…Dunica, a few miles south of the city, over the body of a negro girl, about 8 years of age, belonging to Mr. Cordell. The body…exhibited…evidence of the most cruel whipping and beating we have ever heard of. The flesh on the back and limbs was beaten to a jelly…."

Gracie stopped reading. She started to read further, but to herself. She then paused to look up at us visibly shaken.

"Wot is this?"

"I am so sorry, Gracie, I didn't—."

"No!"

I stood up from the table.

"No, Rachel. Let her read it. Let her know about your life. Let her learn a little something about the wonderful institution of slavery. One thing I noticed in my twelve years' absence: nothing appears to have improved.

"You read it, Gracie. You have spent weeks learning all the wonderful things of the white man's world; the fine things, the clothes, the books, the streets, the shops, the wonders of technology. I think maybe now it's time for you to learn some of the shameful accomplishments for balance. Read the rest of the article."

"Oh, no, please, Elizabeth. This isn't necessary—," Rachel pleaded.

"Rachel, I have raised Gracie from her youngest years and there is no need for me to stop teaching her now. Read it, Gracie, and learn."

I sat back down at the table. Rachel and Dorrie remained silent. Rachel sat back down; she was upset, maybe embarrassed. Gracie continued on.

"...The flesh on the back and limbs was beaten to a jelly -- one...shoulder-bone was laid bare -- there were several cuts, apparently from a club, on the head -- and around the neck was the...inden...tation of a cord, by which it is supposed she had been...confined to a tree. She had been hired by a man by the name of Tanner, residing in the...neigh...bor...hood, and was sent home in this con...dition. After coming home, her constant request, until her death, was for bread, by which it would seem that she had been starved as well as un...mer...ci...fully whipped. The jury returned a verdict that she came to her death by the blows in...flicted by some persons unknown whilst she was in the employ of Mr. Tanner. Mrs. Tanner has been tried and...ac...quit...ted."

The room was silent. Gracie fingered a second clipping folded within the newspaper. After studying it for moment, she again began to read.

"I yesterday visited the cell of Cornelia, the slave charged with being the a...ccom...plice of Mrs. Ann Tanner (recently ac...quitted) in the murder of a little negro girl, by whipping and starvation. She admits her par...ti...ci...pancy, but says she was com...pelled to take the part she did in the affair. On one occasion she says the child was tied to a tree from Monday morning till Friday night, ex...posed by day to the scorching rays of the sun, and by night to the stinging of my...riads of mos...quitoes; and that during all this time the child had nothing to eat, but was whipped daily. The child told the same story to Dr. McDowell."

Gracie looked up at us.

"October? This just happened?"

Rachel nodded.

"Here?"

Again, Rachel nodded.

Gracie, looking somewhat pale, stared at Rachel. Rachel smiled weakly and commented.

"You read very good, Gracie. Elizabeth taught you hwell."

After reading the article, Gracie continued to ponder the meaning. She read the article over repeatedly to herself. She was determined to dissect every detail, to understand, and so spoke up every few minutes to demand that we help her with unfamiliar words, their pronunciation, and explain their meanings. The lesson only served to emphasize the horror of the event.

"You always live in fear of these things?" asked Gracie.

Rachel studied Gracie for a moment before speaking. I believe that Rachel wished I not hear the embarrassment of her reality. These horrors highlighted the difference between her and the rest of us in the kitchen. These horrors inferred that she alone was an animal. The simple shading of her skin barred her from being a part of our world, the world where lived those dear to her.

"Yes, Gracie. Caleb and I have to be very careful. Hwe hworry always for Isaac. Hwe hworry he should make a small mistake and be taken away from us again. If I were to pick up that paper and read it in public as you have just done, there are those hwo hwould have me whipped at once or hworse. I cannot venture out after dark hwithout a pass or I could easily be jailed and taken away. There are many who believe all free slaves that arrive in Missouri married, as did Caleb and I, should be immediately separated, reduced back to slave status, sold, and removed."

Rachel came to direct her comments to me.

"The problem in Missouri is that there are equal numbers of people hwo support and condemn slavery. This makes for fevered battles between the parties, and so emotions run very high— emotions that bring out the hworst in people."

"Is it worse than when I left in thirty-two?"

"Absolutely. No question. There is now upward of five thousand slaves between the city and county, and countless more passing through the auctions. Slavery has become a very big business here, and business is brisk at the courthouse every hweekend.

"The slaves are confined in Leyman's Slave Pen on the south side of Locust, east off Fourth. There is a pen at fifty-two Second Street, another not too far from here on Chestnut Street between Sixth and Seventh. Thomas has a pen next to the jail. There is a pen just south of Market on Fifth that deals only in children five to sixteen years of age.

101

"Caleb and I are speaking more and more of taking Isaac north to Canada hwere hwe believe he will be safer. And it isn't just us. Friends that are abolitionists are hwarning us more frequently to leave St. Louis. They believe hwe have become too visible due to the growth of the orphanage. The pro-slavery faction believes those children should be returned to the business."

Gracie kept her eyes locked on Rachel, and I could see her blonde head working its way through a thousand questions she wished could be asked. Rachel stood up under the pressure of Gracie's stare and walked over to the sink. It was Dorrie who broke the silence.

"Well, that was very good, Gracie. I guess you can read, just as you said. I vote you open all the letters we'll soon be getting, and read them to us."

Dorrie was desperate to dispel the pall suddenly fallen on the room.

"You like cakes and cookies, Gracie? Rachel, can bake up a storm. I'll bet you never went out to sing Christmas carols. I know—." Dorrie's eyes suddenly lit up. "Rachel said she heard that Ludlow and Smith may allow the Farrens, a couple of local actors, to make use of the theatre for a Christmas play. That, you would enjoy."

"Last night was the first time I had cake. I like cake. Christmas sounds like fun."

Gracie was yet distant. She passed right over the Christmas play. She had no idea what theatre was about, but the comment caught my attention, and having felt the lesson was learned, I moved to acknowledge Dorrie.

"You know, I passed by the theatre on our return from the public market."

"Did you?"

"Yes. I saw a flyer for one Mr. Macready, an Englishman, performing at a theatre on Third and Olive, so I passed down Third just to see it. I must say, in size it seemed quite an impressive theatre, but outwardly—."

"Oh, Elizabeth. It is spectacular," said Dorrie.

"I am afraid like most things, it wasn't here before." I pined.

"No, I'm trying to think…you left in spring of thirty-two. The theatre opened in the summer of thirty-seven. July of thirty-seven," said Rachel.

Dorrie looked over to Rachel. "Wasn't Mr. Mcready the spring act this year?"

"He hwas. He is a very accomplished actor, but I understand turnout hwas poor and the theatre hardly profited. In fact, I am not sure if Ludlow and Smith can keep it open for business much longer. Between the recession, a flood that nearly hwiped out half the state, and the lack of culture and taste in our community… hwell, times could be a lot better for the theatre. They never finished the façade. To this day the building is incomplete."

"It is a shame because the theatre is beautiful inside," added Dorrie. "There is a parquet in front of the stage fitted with chairs so each gentleman has his own place and so there remains no need for quarrel. You see clearest and hear most distinct from the parquet. Above the parquet are two levels of boxes, and a gallery, which has the cheapest seats at half price. The parquet and box seats are priced the same at one dollar. I believe the theatre holds close to fifteen hundred patrons all told."

"It is quite large," confirmed Rachel who moved to rejoin us. "The ceiling has two skylights. It is covered hwith canvas and painted hwith muses. At the front side of the gallery, above the offices, is a gentleman's saloon. There are also boxes in the gallery now for freed persons of color. It is nice indeed. You hwould love it, Gracie, I promise."

Gracie shrugged.

"There is so much to see. I never gave a thought to wot I would do, once I reached St. Louis. My whole life has been about getting here. Are we going to stay in St. Louis, Elizabeth?"

Gracie looked at me as if she were only half a step ahead of worry about her future. No doubt my indecision and the horror of the newspaper story did little to diminish her insecurities.

"I don't know, Gracie. I need some time to think things over. Everything has happened too quickly for me to make sense of it, and at this point I am still sorting out my wits. I'll soon decide, I promise. But, rest assured, you will be taken care of."

"Oh, for certain!" exclaimed Dorrie.

"I should say!" agreed Rachel.

Both Dorrie and Rachel rushed to quell Gracie's concerns.

SIXTY-SIX

The determination was scribbled across their faces, written in their eyes, spelled out between lips pressed thin. Dorrie and Rachel sat directly before me, or more precisely, boxed me in from across the table, where they stared me down and awaited my answer.

"We're hwaiting."

"Fine. What do you want me to say? At this moment, I am of a mind to depart for Boston as soon as possible. Time has come for my return to Boston, and I wish to show Luke and Gracie the East Coast. I think the experience will be good for them."

"I don't want to hear it," said Dorrie.

"I don't hwant to hear it," repeated Rachel.

"Ha...I beg your pardon?"

The quickness of their reply caught me off guard. My mouth hung open in surprise as if I were about to cough up a laugh.

"The idea you should go traipsing about in the dead of hwinter hwith a child and young lady is lunacy, Elizabeth. I have *six* guest rooms in this house. I beg you to count them. Hwe have plenty of food to go around, and my cooking has done nothing if not improved. I cook more now than ever. How can you not allow Luke and Gracie a rest after the terror they have endured, being abducted and half starved?"

Rachel's eyes grew wide with disbelief.

"Honestly, Elizabeth, you can't expect us to believe after twelve years dead in the wilds, now you suddenly have a schedule to which you must adhere. I think not," said Dorrie.

"Stay with us the hwinter, enjoy the holidays, and then strike out the first of spring."

"I don't know, Rachel. Spring is another three or four months away. I fear if I stop now to rest, I will never find it in me to travel farther. I doubt I would ever leave St. Louis and return myself home."

"How are you planning to return? By hwhat route?"

"I admit, I have barely thought it out. I have the children to think of; need I say, they play a major role in my decisions—."

"Elizabeth, please lend me your ear, listen to what I say," said Dorrie. "To leave now and attempt crossing the Illinois swamps before they freeze is nothing less than lunacy. It would be murderous. Better to wait until late January. The weather is then settled, the National Road is frozen solid and travels much better, and the godforsaken mosquitoes are killed off.

"They completed the National Road as far as Vandalia. That was in thirty-nine, and since then it has been improved westward right up to the Illinois Ferry Landing. You can ride down to the levee, take the ferry across to Illinois and head east on the road for the entire eight hundred miles if you can stand it. You can follow it all the way to the Potomac, and then board a ship making for Boston.

"Otherwise...otherwise...*otherwise*...you can wait until March when the ice floes pass, and leave with me." Dorrie leaned across the table to bore a hole through me with her eyes. "We can book passage on a riverboat headed down the Mississippi to Cairo, and then steam up the Ohio to Louisville or Cincinnati. We change boats there and travel a ways farther upriver between Wheeling and Pittsburgh, where we head north to Erie on the lake by way of the Beaver Erie Canal. From Erie, we can take a stage into Buffalo, or pay extra and board one of the lake ferries at Erie making for Buffalo. They depart daily.

"The boats are very comfortable. They cater to passengers now more than ever. The journey would not only be tolerable, but time spent aboard a riverboat would be wonderfully entertaining for Gracie and Luke. It would spare you much worry for their well-being and safety, and you would arrive at about the same time had you trekked all winter across the swamps. Here look at this."

Dorrie produced a page from the newspaper and handed it to me.

106

ST.LOUIS & CINCINNATI PACKET

Captain George P. Talbert is presently fitting out a handsome new steamboat in Cincinnati named the AMERICAN CHARM.

Intended expressly for river trade and the ferrying of passengers to and from St. Louis, Mo. in comfort. Every detail of the ship appointments are being perfected per his direction including the exhilarating Texas deck. When complete the ship promises to raise the standard for furnishings, comfort, efficiency, and low pressure safety.

Captain Talbert possesses considerable experience and knowledge regarding the peculiarities and vagaries of the Mississippi and Ohio currents. Bookings are now being accepted for passage from St. Louis to Cincinnati departing March 15, 1845 water permitting.

DEVON, MERRICK, PEARL & CO.
AGENTS.

PITTSBURGH, LOUISVILLE, CINCINNATI
and all intermediate landings.

The newly built steamer MARY WREN. Joseph Fairchild, Master, will run as a regular Packet.

The light draught, fast-running, freight and passenger steamer will avail its services for the entire season water permitting.

For freight or passage apply on board. Officers will provide strict and prompt attention to all matters of business.

DEVON, MERRICK, PEARL & CO.
AGENTS.

Having read the postings, I handed the paper back to Dorrie. She continued with her need to persuade me.

"To take the stage along the National Road is by far the cheapest and most direct route, but it will simply beat the three of you to death. A thousand miles of stump, rock, and rut jarring travel. It would serve you well to know that stumps along the road in Illinois need only be cut to fifteen inches. Can you imagine? You might just as well be scaling castle walls. Just catch a wheel on one of those anywhere along the length of the state and I promise you a toothless laugh from that point on. I would think the decision plain as day.

"Once we make Buffalo by boat, I could then accompany you on one of the schooboats down locks to Albany just as we did years ago. And there, at that point, I will say good bye and take my leave. But there, at that point, you can next book passage on the railroad that departs Albany directly for Boston.

"Now, I *am* putting forth a sensible proposition for your consideration. You can't possibly find fault in my intention. You traveled the swamps, and you have floated the canal. I beg you consider the hardships of travel on Luke and Gracie, and if considered, the choice should be obvious."

There was no room to wiggle. Dorrie had positively sorted out her attack beforehand and trounced me. I sat silent. I took a breath.

"Obviously, you have given this a great deal of thought. I see the merit in everything you have proposed, but I need a little time, Dorrie, a couple of days or so if I am to make a decision that in the end I know I will stand by. Would you allow me that?"

"Most certainly. Oh, of course. Elizabeth...Rachel and I will support you in whatever decision you make. We just thought that with you being gone for so many years, and our knowing what all has changed in regard to travel; we might be of help. If I were to escort you back along the route I have taken thrice, then we would both sleep better of a night. We only ask honest and thoughtful consideration of our proposals."

"Bless you both. I know you have only my best interests in mind, and so I promise you every consideration. You have my word."

* * *

After a few days of relaxation, conversation, and deliberation, I was of a mind to accept Rachel and Dorrie's invitation to stay. I decided that they were correct in arguing a prolonged rest would be in the best interest of us all. It would save us the misery of facing winter on the road. It would, for the first time since our abduction, offer me a chance to make sensible plans.

Meanwhile, I believed St. Louis was likely the most suitable city to introduce Luke and Gracie to the white man's world. It was yet rough enough around the edges to allow unconventional behavior room for forgiveness. And then there was my utter lack of ambition to face the swamps of Illinois. There was a memory unfazed by the passing of time. Only in the dead of winter, when the ground was frozen and serpents asleep did one dare venture into that hellish place.

Finally, a fear almost as paralyzing…the thought of facing Mary; I might wait out a winter, a year, an eternity. No amount of time would ease my trepidation, but moving that day out another three months wouldn't worsen the situation or be the end of me.

"Fine, Dorrie. You leave me little space for other considerations. I'll stay. We'll stay. You already seem to have thought out every angle for my benefit; you leave me speechless."

"Yes! Yes. Wonderful."

Rachel and Dorrie cheered in unison. They whooped it up, dancing and prancing about the kitchen with delight.

By cowering before the threats of baked hams and sweet potato pies, I opened up a world of opportunities for Gracie and Luke. I provided them a stay in the perfect environment for making their transition from one life to another.

I could hardly overlook how kindly everybody had taken to them, accepting their background with understanding, and showing such willingness to teach them the subtleties of social grace and protocol. St. Louis was still a place where the course mingled with the refined, where the haves and have-nots lived side by side. It was a city where Luke and Gracie could gain a solid footing in their new life.

During our stay, Gracie was nudged gently into recognizing the expectations of a lady. Given a little encouragement, and spared the fear of ridicule or embarrassment, she eventually warmed to the prospect. I was made to laugh, for she acquired reasonable poise and civility in record time, but could never quite shake that streak of wilderness in her character, or the need to step out back and throw knives.

Luke set out on his own personal quest to discover all he could of man-made artifacts in his new world. He developed a ravenous appetite to understand the workings of gadgets and things mechanical, and Rachel, Dorrie, and I used a number of these items quite effectively as 'carrots' to keep him in line. As long as Luke minded and exhibited an air of civility, I would buy him just about anything to feed his curious mind.

Gracie had a number of years on Luke, but both were old enough to appreciate how knowledge could be gained though reading and also listening to their elders. This proved nothing short of a blessing for me. Reading remained a welcomed challenge for them as might be expected, for they now witnessed the value of being literate and the truth of my predictions. Listening attentively to Rachel, Caleb, and Dorrie in order to learn was the way they were brought up by the Tsistsistas. They had spent their youth sitting at the campfires to hear the oral stories and lessons of their elders. All in all, they progressed admirably, and I couldn't help but be proud, for in the way of the Tsistsistas, their success did me honor.

Something else came of my decision to stay. Gracie proved to me that she had the wherewithal and tenacity to survive on her own. It was a bittersweet realization, a first indication that her life would lead her away from mine. I knew at this time she yet looked to me for direction, for security and support, and that she would have been emotionally crushed had I turned her out to fend for herself.

Not to worry, I could have never imagined such a separation, for she was as much a daughter to me as was I to Lady Rebecca. It would have torn out my heart to see her hurt or leave. Even so, I was becoming all the more aware of the contentment and independence both she and Luke had come to enjoy here in St. Louis. But, St. Louis wasn't our home.

SIXTY-SEVEN

A little over a week after our arrival, December 7th to be exact, the St. Charles steam ferry blew up, down on the levee. One Mr. Bell was killed outright, and a good number of others were injured. It was a massive explosion that rocked the neighborhood, and although tragic, it seemed a fitting introduction to what typified our new life amidst the hustle of St. Louis.

Through Rachel, I had been given the necessary introductions to establish connections that would improve my finances. Obtaining a loan was a simple matter in part due to the many gentlemen at our welcoming party offering to sign in my behalf until my own funds arrived.

I wasn't long in the waiting. I had asked for a full account of my holdings and was amazed to discover how well my investments had performed. I was indeed wealthy in my own right, shockingly so. Twelve years of accrued interest and growth during my absence did wonders for a portfolio filled with Claussen-inspired direction—especially railroad investments.

My financial situation, now much improved, left me free to settle in with Rachel, living and laughing, the three of us eating like pigs, as days turned into weeks. Before I knew it, we were all dressed in attire fit to walk the colorful bustling streets of St. Louis in search of Christmas gifts. I was becoming familiar with many of the grand buildings constructed in the last few years such as the Roman Catholic Cathedral, the Episcopal and Presbyterian churches, the Lucas House Hotel, and the Jesuit Seminary, which was an impressive Greek Revival edifice constructed out of solid limestone blocks. We paraded in and out of stores, and wasted much time taking frequent rests in the numerous coffee and pastry shops.

In particular, we frequented the recently completed Grand Planter House Hotel, the largest and most exclusive hotel in St. Louis or anyplace west of the Mississippi. It had a couple of nice coffee shops and rivaled anything in New Orleans or on the East Coast.

It was completed in forty-one, and like the courthouse next to it, occupied an entire city block. The building stood four stories tall with a partial fifth. It dwarfed the structures that surrounded it. It had an observation deck twenty feet above the roof that covered the front entrance and offered one a grand view of the street and river activity.

The detail and appointments of its interior were spectacular and included a fabulous staircase that spiraled upward through four complete revolutions. There was a ballroom on the second floor that positioned the orchestra on a raised platform seven or eight feet above the dancers. The dining room was immense and boasted a full beamed and paneled ceiling with classical pilasters, delicious food, and impeccable service. There were one hundred and fifty rooms.

Gracie and Luke were beside themselves with disbelief. How could children who knew only of life in a tent possibly accept something so spectacular? Their heads were tilted upward, eyes fixed on the overhead turns of the staircase. All the while, Dorrie was telling them about her stay.

"I stayed for a couple of nights on my first visit, much to Rachel's objections, but I am glad I did. The rooms all had venetian blinds and Berlin grates for burning coal. And on top of that, I was told by the staff that each room had its own private call bell connected to the front desk."

"That stay must have cost a fortune," I quipped.

"Actually, the prices were quite reasonable. I think a week's stay with meals might have been ten dollars."

It was fun just sitting in the lobby of the hotel and watching the businessmen and merchants alike flowing through the place conversing aloud or deep in thought. Luke and Gracie had retained everything of manners and protocol that I had taught them over the years. Once they overcame the initial excitement and wonder, once they settled down, those years of lessons surfaced. Their real hurdle was more along the lines of learning to control emotional outbursts, pigheaded stubbornness, and overbearing assertiveness—traits that might serve them well in the wild, but worked against them in society. At least in my company, they remained calm, behaved, and were quick to adapt to surroundings like the Planters.

In spite of its splendor, there was one notable flaw. It could be seen clearly in the absence of Rachel. The Planters forbid any person of color to enter. Rachel was always in need of tending to business whenever talk of Planters came up. Luke and Gracie were quick to surmise the injustice, and I believe the lesson would go a long way toward forming their characters for the best.

We walked much of the city, but the levee was far and away the most entertaining. It had been grown to extend up and down the river quite a distance since last seen by me. It was now completely paved in cobblestones and below Market Street was a large flatboat landing that catered to the thriving wood market also there at the wharf.

All along the levee on Front Street, old taverns, eateries, and boardinghouses were disappearing or left compressed between the tightly packed construction of two- and three-story stone structures that were commission houses and wholesale grocers.

The levee roiled day and night without pause. It swarmed with life. It was packed with people of every description, frantic clerks buzzing in circles around unloaded goods, idlers hard at work or hard at drinking and scraping, casualties of hard times, drunks, Indian beggars moving crowds like wolves move sheep, hordes of immigrants babbling in Spanish, German, French, Indian tongues, and English.

There were circuses, and entertainers, musicians, magicians, hunters, trappers, farmers and fruit sellers, well-dressed merchants, prostitutes, peddlers and porters, reporters, runners, teachers, skilled craftsmen of every sort. There were the wealthy and well-heeled; there were the ragged and run down. Every expertise, every walk of life, was represented upon this narrow sloped band of stoned pavement that bordered the river. At first the multitudes of people seemed to walk about mindlessly avoiding carts, wagons, teams of horses and oxen, drays, and cabs at they bounced back and forth between the boats and the buildings. On closer scrutiny, one could determine the general movement wasn't so mindless, but flowed westward from the water to flood the city and beyond.

The draymen calling out their commands, the clatter of wheels crossing the cracks between cobblestones, the clopping of horse hooves, the hollers of hawkers and vendors, the bells and whistles, the blasts of steam from riverboats, the captains' calls to board, the cabbies' call to board, the tickets sellers bellowing best prices, deckhands yelling for lines, hotel runners hollering, all of this boisterous bawling cacophony of noise held one's attention to the point of eliminating the need for conversation at the table. Not to say that conversation couldn't add a little something to the mix.

"All of this was under water this spring past," said Dorrie.

"Under water? Oh, you mean from the flood?"

"It poured. The talk in the shipyards hwas to build arcs. Nobody laughed at them. The rains never let up. It hwent on for days, and hwe all knew that the river had been high to start. The city knew it hwasn't going to bode hwell and so started preparing for the hworst. They had no idea," said Rachel.

"Yes, I saw the signs of flooding all along the river. We saw the state of affairs in Independence."

"Independence! Oh, my hword, Independence hwas a total loss. There hwas talk of rebuilding the town, but the river had changed its course to such a degree that the town hwas abandoned. Folks couldn't see it ever being a port again," said Rachel

"I thought as much. Luke and Gracie wished to see a town, so we left the trail in order to view Independence—nothing but rubble. It was unbelievable. And stink. My word, there were a couple of places in the bottoms that we happened upon while riding down near that area where, I'm here to tell you, the stench of rotting trees was disgusting to say the least."

"Oh, yes, I know. You should have smelled it during the heat of summer. I assure you hwatever stench remained to linger in the cool air of November hwould have seemed fragrant by comparison," said Rachel.

"All of Illinoistown…this entire levee was under water." Dorrie cast her hand to the east, and then swept across the whole of the riverfront. "The water flowed up Market Street as far as Second before abating. The first story of these buildings—all the buildings along Front Street, were entirely submerged. Boats coming upriver were mooring alongside the buildings and dropping passengers and goods off at the second-story windows. Most of the traffic was tying up at Cahokia. The water in the streets was twenty feet deep. The river crested thirty-eight feet above low water. Can you imagine, thirty-eight feet?

"Rachel and I walked down and stood at Second one morning and observed in disbelief as trees, haystacks, fences, entire herds of animals, and their barns floated downstream as if in a parade. We watched homes, in fact I don't believe you can think of anything we didn't see float past."

I took in the distance of the levee, the width of the river, the rise of the land as it reached Second and gasped. It was impossible to fathom the amount of water necessary to fill such a tub.

"I can't imagine."

"You never will. I saw it with my own eyes and I'm still unable to imagine. No amount of words will ever describe the havoc," said Dorrie.

"It hwas an ordeal," said Rachel. "So many found their selves homeless and ruined that the poorhouses hwere chocked full. Every bed we had, and the many more brought in hwere full. Our floors hwere covered with bedding for nearly three months hwhile folks tried to regain their footing. We only emptied the house of boarders a few hweeks before you arrived."

Silence overtook us as we plowed through our personal visions of the catastrophe. To see the activity now, one would never know; one would simply stare across the levee while sitting over coffee. There were still plenty of signs on buildings indicating high-water marks, but unless told or specifically looking for such scars, one would never notice. The glory of the morrow's promise healed the heartbreak of yesterday's horror. And so life went on in spite of past tragedy, leaving the levee a wonderful experience for anybody and everybody, especially for Luke and Gracie...or for that matter, me as well.

The season swallowed us whole. Rachel and Dorrie understated the number of Christmas letters and cards that circulated. It seemed to have grown into a national event. I rolled up my sleeves and pitched in by taking quill in hand. I knew none of these people. Rachel filled us in on what senders she remembered. For the majority that remained, we simply wished them the best. The reading and writing was immensely helpful practice for Luke and Gracie.

There was an irony amidst all the hustle and bustle of the season in that I found myself torn between my hopes for the future and my longing for the past. All the merriment promised was provided. Luke and Gracie were having the time of their young lives, and it would seem impossible to be sad. Yet, I so missed Ho'neheveho. I still worried myself sick over Talk-a-Lot's outcome. I missed all the Tsistsistas each and every one. I visited them frequently in my dreams, and cried to be torn away upon awakening.

SIXTY-EIGHT

A half an hour after dinner, Luke and Gracie returned to the kitchen table per my request. By that time, Dorrie and I had finished clearing away dinner and cleaning up. Caleb was off to finish repairs on one of the houses, and Rachel dismissed the help as soon as the dishes were washed, dried, and shelved. Only the whistle of a teapot now disturbed the quietude.

"Alright then…tea is ready. …Time to relax, thank you, Lord. Anybody wish a cup before I sit?"

It was impossible to turn down a cup of Rachel's spiced tea. The aroma was intoxicating. Who wouldn't wish a cup to savor and chase off winter's chill. Having emptied the pot in one pass, Rachel set the kettle aside and took up a chair to join us. I blew across the steamy surface and took a sip. All awaited my announcement, and so I placed my cup back on the table.

"As you know, I have—."

No sooner did I open my mouth, when a minor disturbance was heard at the front of the house. The door was heard to open followed by muffled sounds.

"Who is that?" Gracie whispered in alarm.

I said nothing. We five sat in silence, holding our breath. A draft of cold air swept across the floor and drove a pang of nervousness through us. With some apprehension, we turned to face the doorway and whoever might make an appearance. Hopefully it was not an intruder, but someone familiar enough to enter freely at this late hour.

"Mrs. Cook? Are you there?"

It was the gentle and respectful voice of a male adolescent who apparently had come to pay visit to Rachel.

Rachel rose from her chair at once and moved to leave the kitchen. I saw her eyes open wide with surprise as she recognized someone in the shadow of the foyer. She broke into a broad smile, and greeted the boy with much enthusiasm.

"Hello, Daniel. How are you?"

"Fine, Mrs. Cook, an—."

"Hwo's that? Is that Anna—?"

"Yes, m—."

"And Lena, is that you, honey?"

"Hello, Miss Rachel."

"Is there someone else—?"

"Is Tomias, Miss Rachel."

"Tomias? Hwell, I'll be—. How many more of ya are there? My word, hwat are you all doin'? C'mon in, c'mon. Get yourselves out of the cold. For the love of God, I haven't seen your faces in ages."

One after another, a growing line of boys and girls of differing ages entered into the glow of light that leaked out into the foyer. They poked their heads into the kitchen. Over every shoulder appeared another head, and I assumed all heads were Rachel's wards at one time or another.

I looked at Dorrie. She returned my glance with an expression of bewilderment. Clearly, a reunion of some nature seemed to be underway. The rooms began to fill with orphans, all talking to one another, joking and seemingly oblivious to winter and their hardships.

Most of these adolescents were of color and I knew they only managed to walk about in number because Rachel's house was so close to Kerry Patch. Other than the Irish, who were never confronted by sane persons, few whites with any wits about them would question a gang or group, no matter how few, moving about the patch. And yet, I would have thought that even in this area, such a large congregation of negroes would be reason for the authorities to be concerned; they drew too much attention.

I soon realized that this crowd of adolescents was rekindling old friendships. It was obvious that most knew each other, but after a few moments, I also noted that much of the surprise and greeting appeared to be taking place inside the house. It seemed that the party might not have arrived as a group, but responded individually to invitation.

"Give me a moment; I'll be right back."

My curiosity prompted me to leave Luke and Gracie in the kitchen for a moment so I might peer out the front door. I made my way through the crowd now numbering some twenty or more and stepped out onto the porch. Three youths stepped around me to enter the house. I looked down the street and confirmed my suspicions that these urchins were trickling in by ones, twos, and threes. Was it possible that Rachel would forget one of her scheduled events? I thought not, and returned to the warmth of the kitchen.

"Alright, you might as well go about your business. Obviously, Rachel has something underway. They are yet filing in, and I saw plenty more coming up the street."

Luke jumped up from his chair and plowed into the swirl of commotion. He became an instant celebrity. Unlike whites, the darker skins of negroes were closer in looks to the Indians who were familiar to him. He moved amongst them with ease. Gracie, now older and occasionally less impulsive, remained seated alongside Dorrie.

"I suppose my announcement will have to wait until tomorrow. I don't mind, but I am surprised I heard no mention made of tonight's activities. I think Rachel, plain and simple, forgot."

Dorrie threw her hands up in wonderment.

"I don't believe there were any activities."

"Really? Judging by the number of people streaming in, I may beg to differ. Something was supposed to take place tonight."

"No, even if she forgot, she wouldn't have forgotten on every day leading up to tonight. I would have known about it for sure. Rachel isn't secretive about anything. In fact, she goes out of her way to prepare me for anything taking place during my stay."

The point begging to be made was that none of this was any of my business. Like Dorrie, I was merely a guest in the home of a very socially active woman. As once I was, and as Dorrie became, Rachel's life was now devoted to children. Through the doorway, I could see her floating about these orphans and young adults as if she were an angel guarding over her flock. But the more I watched, the more I grew uncomfortable. On the surface, to all present, these goings on seemed joyous and impromptu, but I sensed something deeper, something unspoken. This sudden and unexpected rush of greeters worked my surprise slowly into anxiety. I heard Rachel's voice carry over the top of a gathering that was now tenfold greater in size and growing.

"Hwat are all of you doing here? I don't understand."

"Mer' n'me jus' stopped by t' pay a hello."

"Yeah, we din't know you had orphans comin' over."

"We heerd ya'll hat white injuns puttin' down fer a night. We hat t' come fer a look n' see."

"So'd we.

"An' us."

Dorrie was second to rise from the table and head for the reception hall. There was now excitement in the air, enough so that Gracie opted to join her. It seemed pointless to sit alone in the kitchen and so I also rose to my feet and followed suit.

As soon as I stepped through the doorway, all eyes flashed my way in unison. Nobody but me would have realized the split second event, and panic stole my breath. It happened so fast that I wished it to be my imagination. Maybe I was overeating. It seemed logical the crowd would uniformly glance at anybody who exited the kitchen and popped into view. Likewise, if the crowd uniformly glanced at Gracie when she passed into the foyer, how would I have known? I collected myself, but the damage was done. My instincts were shaken and I was suspicious. I questioned if this unexpected crowd had anything whatsoever to do with "lookin' n'seein' white Indians."

This event was uncomfortably close to those past unexpected appearances of distantly connected children. It was a pattern I was beginning to recognize with unwelcome accuracy—that sudden stampede of orphans and street urchins walking out from the mists, from the shadows of the wood, from out of nowhere.

I worked to keep a smile in spite of my uneasiness. I began building an invisible wall to protect me, to assist in my retreat. As I backed away mentally, I concentrated on finding some common thread in their conversations, in their questions or comments, but there was nothing. Their voices blended into an undulating drone, a sound that moved through my head in waves. My mind may have struggled to make sense of the unknown; it may have held some small desired reservation for normality, but my soul understood this reunion to be as far removed from an unplanned event as heavenly possible. Here was the harbinger.

The crowd of energetic youth pressed in on Luke and Gracie. They questioned the two about everything, everything imaginable by way of children's curiosity. Rachel, Dorrie, Luke, Gracie, all interacted freely with one another amidst this throng. They had little hope of noticing how the children related to me, wary, stand-offish as a whole, preferring to acknowledge me with a thousand glances.

Unlike Luke, Gracie, and the others, when I was approached, I was rarely asked where I had traveled, or what I had experienced, or anything about my life. Instead, I was asked variations of a question that conveyed the single theme I had suffered to discover. Of what state was my constitution, my health? How did I feel? It seemed as if every question asked was meant to satisfy their concern about my well-being. Why should they care? Was there but one child in the crowd whom I knew?

Voicing my concerns or making any noise based on tenuous instincts regarding these spontaneous gatherings would only have earned me the praise of backslapping lunatics. It would also have likely scared the ever-loving wits out of all those dearest to me. This was and might very well continue to be a dreadful secret forced upon me to be kept to myself.

I was shaken. I excused myself from the facade of festivity and sought the solitude of my room. I readied myself for bed, all the while listening to the commotion downstairs. The hair on my body stood on end like quills upon a rankled porcupine. I felt it to be much more than the chill of winter's air. I climbed into bed and drew my covers up tight. I fell asleep at some point after entering deep contemplation. I wanted to understand why I was convinced that children, for whom I dedicated most of my life, hovered about to haunt me?

SIXTY-NINE

Aside from the residual exuberance of the past night that was shared by all but me, the day moved on in its usual peaceful, if not mundane fashion. We finished dinner, and I asked Luke and

Gracie to remain and help clear the table. Later, when all were again seated amidst the aroma of Rachel's spiced tea, I made a second attempt at my announcement.

"I ask you first...to listen carefully to what I say, and then when I have said my piece, you may ask your questions and we can discuss all that's been said."

I paused to gather my thoughts. I looked directly at Luke and Gracie.

"I have said many times, especially as of late, that we would depart St. Louis for the East Coast. Our departure is now near. Spring is well upon us, and I expect we shall leave for Boston as soon as the water permits. The ice is much diminished upon the river, and the boats will soon be returning in number. Passage is already being booked as we speak. Dorrie is yet committed to staying in our company, and for that I am very happy...more than happy...grateful, for she is well versed in the required bookings.

"Rachel and Dorrie have watched over the two you with care, feeding you well and seeing to your every need. I know aside from the list of worries I suffer as a mother, aside from knowing you are happy and feel secure here in St. Louis, you are both well-rested and strong enough to travel. For that reason, time has come to prepare for our departure.

"St. Louis has been a grand place to learn much of the white man's ways. It is a forgiving place for those yet rough around the edges, but as I have also said on many occasions, St. Louis is not our home. I live in Boston and that is where I believe we shall settle. When we arrive there, I should hope to open my apartment providing I still possess one. If I do not, or if it proves too inconvenient to meet our needs, then I will find suitable accommodations for the three of us elsewhere.

"I must impress upon you that the journey is not a matter of days but one of weeks. Our patience will be tried, but in comparison to what we have been through it will seem a holiday cruise. Nonetheless, in order to keep the trials and tribulations to a minimum, Dorrie has argued successfully that we book passage on boats whenever possible. It will make for a longer but gentler trip. I am certain that you will find your time aboard the riverboats to be sensational, the scenery spectacular. It will be one experience of the white man's world that you will find most rewarding. Now, having stated my mind, I would like to know if you have any concerns about these plans or our future?"

They looked at each other and then back at me. Luke was first to speak. It wasn't a question so much as a confirmation.

"We're going to Boston."

"Yes."

"How long will it take?"

"I would think a month given good fortunes."

He said nothing more.

"Gracie? Have you no questions? Nothing you wish to say."

"Do we have to go to Boston?"

The question left me slightly puzzled.

"Ahh. Yes. Boston is my home. That is the place I know. That is the place that best provides us with the opportunities for a successful future. Does that trouble you? Is there a problem? Would you not care to see it?"

Gracie's crystal eyes were locked onto mine. She was deciphering my every move, my every breath, my most minute expressions.

"Well…I…I like…St. Louis…. I like St. Louis. I don't…."

My heart stumbled. It suffered the bittersweet sting of her words. It was the first time Gracie had ever pulled away from me.

125

It was so faint a move, so short a distance, but I felt it as if an axe had been swung to split us worlds apart. My chest pressed in upon me. At last, the reason for the *children*. I knew. *I knew.* The realization sent my tears to the brink of flooding forth.

It would be wrong of me to push the issue, to test her love, her loyalty, but it was as if I needed to increase the mounting pain of losing those bright eyes that brought so much to my life. I would rather have my heart shredded at this very moment than wait for what I now knew would soon arrive regardless.

"Are you saying that you would you rather stay? I would understand. I would be brokenhearted, Gracie, but I would understand. St. Louis has always been the city of your dreams since you were just a wee thing. It was the place your father wished you to be. I would understand if you prefer to stay."

Gracie took a deep, nervous breath. She looked around the table, studying each of our faces, wondering as do so many of the young—what were her abilities to fend for herself? When was she supposed to take that first step away from the arms that cradled her for as long as she could remember?

The outcome of this discussion would impact Rachel in no small way should Gracie decide to stay. Both Dorrie and Rachel remained silent, preferring not to sway Gracie in her decision or contribute in any manner to my anticipated heartbreak should it come.

Gracie finally spoke and did so with great heart. My tears were ever so ready to give me away.

"Elizabeth, I can't remember ever a time in my life when I wasn't traveling. I traveled with my mother and father; I traveled with you and the Tsistsistas. We traveled the full breadth of the desert, north and south, east and west. And until now, I have never known what it meant to have roots, to think of a place as being home, even if only for the shortest of time gives one a sense of security.

"I can't say that St. Louis is the place I would always call home, but I can say that I am anguished to consider leaving yet again for parts unknown. I believe Boston is *your* home, Elizabeth— but, *it isn't mine*. I fear, as much as you enjoy seeing me in a dress and powdered, I will never find comfort in that refined culture of which you so often speak. I throw knives, Elizabeth. I throw knives. I will always throw knives."

I nodded, my head held high, but the tears began slipping down my cheeks. I bit my quivering lip to keep from appearing weak. I did my best to be strong, considering I had not enjoyed the benefit of notice. I said nothing. I nodded. I nodded.

Gracie rose from the table and came around to my place. She wrapped her arms around me in the nick of time. Her hair draped across my face and veiled me in privacy so I might close my eyes and let the flood run free. I felt Gracie shudder with sorrow. I felt the heat and moisture of her face next to mine, which only served to deepen my grief. I struggled to regain my composure. It was difficult.

"I am alright, Gracie. I am alright."

I pushed her back away so I could look into her face. She was unable to face me; she looked down to the side.

"Look at me, Gracie…. Look at me, honey. I love you so very much. Never question it."

Her gaze met mine. Her green eyes glistened, shimmered behind a patina of emotion. I wondered how those tears could remain so colorless after having graced those incredible eyes. I spoke to soothe her.

"I will have to learn to live without you by my side. That will be painful for my heart. But small girls grow up and become women. And you are nothing if not a woman. You are strong, you are confident, and you make me proud, Gracie. In time, Luke will also grow up and take his leave. I reckon you are helping me to prepare. I l-love you."

I closed my eyes and sobbed quietly as I pulled her back into my embrace. Rachel, after motioning Dorrie and Luke away, took leave of the kitchen. Gracie and I remained together at the table for many hours accepting our imminent separation, recalling the many stories of our time together and speaking of our hopes for the future.

SEVENTY

And so passed the Ides of March. As soon as the treacherous ice floes and floods of spring subsided, our packet, the AMERICAN CHARM appeared at the levee as promised. The day following its arrival, a Saturday, the twenty-second of March, Dorrie, Luke, and I stood at the gang plank packed and prepared to depart St. Louis, bound for Cincinnati.

We took our leave amidst a smothering of embraces, good bye kisses, and tears. When time came to give my final farewell to Gracie, my spirit was utterly crushed. There was no point in believing I might keep my head high, or rise above being a blubbering fool. She was in every way a daughter to me and more. We shared experiences beyond those of any mother and child. I knew all too well the ease with which a person could lose the bonds of love so close to the heart. I held her before me, kissed her, and took one last look to form the image of the face and eyes I would keep with me forever.

I knew well to study her face. It was the same study I undertook a decade back when I last looked into the face of Mary, forging her speckled amber eyes into my memory. In fact, soon after I set Gracie free, it was that very image of Mary I feared to face.

"Promise me, Rachel, you will watch over her. She has yet much to learn. Please, *I beg*, don't let her kill anybody."

"*Elizabeth*, I'm not going to kill anybody. My word! I promise!"

"Be wary of men, Gracie. You are too beautiful and they will track you like wounded prey."

"I'll be careful. I can take care of myself around men."

"I know." I looked at Rachel. "Please don't let her kill anybody."

"That's enough, Elizabeth. I said, I'm not killing anybody."

We all laughed. It was badly needed laughter, for just behind my smile was a throat choked off with emotion, the words becoming ever more difficult to pass.

"Alllllllllll abooooooooard—Americaaaaaan Chaaaaaarmmmaaaaaaah!"

The ship whistle echoed off the buildings up and down the levee.

"Alllllllllll abooooooooard—Americaaaaaan Chaaaaaarmmmaaaaaaah!"

The captain made his last call, it also being echoed by deckhands, associates, and agents up and down the levee. The furnaces were stoked, the boilers brought to pressure, and black smoke was hurled high above the towering twin stacks. The escapements blew explosive blasts of white steam.

"Ladies, I beg you board at once. Please. We must keep to the schedule."

The captain himself moved to terminate our good byes. We were being hustled, herded up the plank, the last to board. The plank was hauled high off the levee, and would have tumbled us onto the deck had we dawdled but one second more.

The lines were tossed, and the boat shuddered from stern to bow. The enormous side-wheels began to rotate, slapping the water, flinging it forward, as it reversed the massive vessel out from its cramped quarters. The levee drifted away from us and so too did Rachel and Gracie.

I cried. I couldn't help myself. I had lost my daughter and dearest companion. As they grew distant, I sensed the cover closing forever on the richest volume of my life story, a decade of devotion and love, a decade of laughing, crying, playing, feasting, starving, a decade of living hand-in-hand, side-by-side facing all that came our way. A decade to be tucked away to memory. My heart was shattered.

I excused myself from Dorrie's company. I went to my stateroom. I found it accommodating. I tried to distract myself by focusing on my cabin amenities. I guessed the cabin to be about nine or so feet deep and maybe ten feet wide, slightly wider than deep. My door opened up against the left wall. Before me was a table up against the same wall and upon which there were a towel, a wash bowl, and an urn filled with water. Up against the opposite wall at my right was the bed. Against the back wall, between the bed and table was a chair to be used as either a seat or a toilet. My bags had been placed neatly upon the floor. I stepped over them and dropped onto the bed. I grabbed the pillow and buried my face as I exploded into sobs. Even my love for Luke could not soften the loneliness I suffered. My pain was acute.

It took hours for me to release all the hurt. I had settled myself by way of exhaustion. Feeling perfectly numb, I arose from my tear-soaked pillow, and moved to make myself reasonably presentable. I removed myself from the cabin. Outside, not too far from my door, stood Dorrie at the railing. I knew she had been standing vigil. She said nothing, but placed her hand upon mine.

I trembled, but there was nothing left in me to cry. She picked up my hand and held it to her lips. She kissed it.

"Be strong, Elizabeth. The depth of your pain reveals the extent of her care. Gracie will never forget you. Not for the briefest second. Rest assured, you may not have been her mother, but you may have been more."

I could only nod my head to express my thanks. The remainder of my day was a perfect blend of depression, anxiety, and stress. I went from suffering the loss of one dear to me, to suffering the gain of one lost and dear to me. I had departed St. Louis without forwarding Mary any prior notice of my impending arrival in Boston. Truthfully, I was too worried to let her know. I was afraid if she had time to think on all the pain I had inflicted upon her, she would be so angry with me that by the time I arrived, there would be no hope of restoring our relationship.

The AMERICAN CHARM steamed down the Mississippi without event. Luke had long since disappeared to investigate the workings of a steamer. There was nothing whatsoever to distract me from my depressed state. I was left to my thoughts as I watched the wilds beyond the riverbanks slowly pass.

I was the worse for company and conversation. Dorrie was patient and stood quietly at the deck rail. She said nothing, but remained at my side for support. Her friendship and understanding needed no words; it was both soothing and welcomed. How ironic this fateful twist from our situation years ago in New York. It was true that Dorrie's son had been killed, but that tragedy came with finality. I felt as though my child had been kidnapped by fate, and I would go to my grave worrying, wondering what would become of her life.

We made no intermediate landings between St. Louis and Cairo, and for that reason, and the fact we were aided by the current, we arrived at Cairo and the confluence of the Ohio the following day at noon. I was most surprised to discover how substantial was the flow of the Ohio. It led me at once to question why anything below Cairo should be called Mississippi instead of Ohio. The Ohio was indeed grand, surpassing my assumptions in every way.

From the Mississippi River, Cairo seemed hidden from view, but once rounding the bend and starting upriver against the Ohio current, the city unfolded to our port side. It displayed a well-planned levee, certainly insignificant in size when compared to that of St. Louis, but no less crowded with activity, it being the last Ohio landing before navigating the upper Mississippi toward St. Louis, or the lower Mississippi toward New Orleans.

The town appeared somewhat peculiar upon closer scrutiny. At first look, it appeared to enjoy its levee, an active dry dock, and a shipyard. From the boat we could make out a number of sawmills, a large two-story wood-framed hotel, a warehouse, and what appeared to be an iron works industry. There were even a good number of residential cottages. We spotted a general store operating out of a riverboat.

What was lacking was the expected hustle-bustle of merchants, businessmen, and townsfolk. It seemed as if all but those about the docks had abandoned the place. The peculiarity was confirmed when Dorrie was told that some twenty or thirty families were all that remained in this nicely situated port. By what I saw, I might have assumed a hundred folks were bent on earning whatever wages possible by doing business with the docking riverboats. The number of empty well-constructed buildings suggested the majority of townsfolk had died or packed up and left in a hurry, most likely the result of an epidemic.

We were to remain in port until dawn of the following day. The afternoon was devoted to the transfer of goods and passengers, and the captain determined it preferable to spend a night in port rather than risk an unnecessary night on the water. We would depart at first light.

I had no desire to go ashore, and for good reason. It was a chilly March night, not only due to the still early spring temperatures, but also because of those March winds that were blowing across the water from the southwest. It was the dampness carried in that wind that kept one from venturing forth. Dorrie and I stood on the promenade and watched the dots of lamplight spread across the town until the shadows of nightfall obscured every detail and feathered darkness around each golden flame. The mists were growing thick and impenetrable by the time we retreated to the cabin.

The AMERICAN CHARM had been furnished every bit as luxuriously as promoted. The accommodations and appointments were first class in every respect. The main cabin was all of two hundred feet in length, at least twenty-five in width, and sixteen or more in height. The ceiling was paneled in bird's-eye maple with cross beams and pillars built of contrasting mahogany. In the light of day both woods were unsurpassed in their luminance, a mirage of shimmering gold. Running the full length of the ceiling on both sides were gorgeous windows of stained glass. The windows were framed in black walnut. The space that ran between each window was also covered with bird's-eye maple, but fully detailed with exquisite patterns of floral marquetry.

A spectacular table was centered in the cabin and also ran full length with the exception of breaks every twelve chairs for the benefit of servers to cross from side to side. Along the walls, between each portal to the promenade, were individual tables that seated four. The wood-planked floor beneath the tables was worked to a high polish. At each end of the cabin, there was also a highly polished stove that was used to assist in food service and to provide warmth during the nights and early mornings.

Aft of the main cabin was the ladie's cabin. It was closed off by a large double door. It contained every detail and appointment of the main cabin but tenfold more spectacular. With the ornate carvings and gold leaf adornments, it was clearly designed to keep the women pampered and stayed put, whilst their men were gallivanting on deck.

The most notable difference was the number of fulllength mirrors that made this smaller cabin appear to be broader than the main cabin. In fact, it was broader. The main cabin was forced narrower by the promenade decks that flanked it on each side. The ladies cabin was not so flanked. Instead, each deck ended at the outer entrance doors to our cabin. We were therefore two decks wider by inside measurement.

The stained glass windows were much larger in height and provided superior lighting and cheerfulness during the day. Four small parlor stoves served to spread gentle warmth evenly to be enjoyed by all. Whereas the chairs of the main were hardwood with cushions provided upon request, ours were padded and upholstered in the finest material.

"May I bring you ladies hot tea?"

"Please do," replied Dorrie.

There was plenty of conversation to go around. A goodly number of ladies shared the cabin with us and it was here that I learned Cairo had more than a thousand residents barely two years prior. Many had emigrated from Scotland, but the company handling the immigration had failed, and with it went the town. I listened with interest. I was comfortable. I turned to Dorrie and spoke.

"Oh, it feels wonderful to sit. These chairs do a superb job of pampering us. If ever I was rewarded by paying attention to good advice, it is now. I must confess that sitting here next to the warmth of a stove in such comfort frightens me to think I had considered booking a stage. You saved me, Dorrie. I am duly indebted."

"This is a very nice steamer is it not? You know, the nicest of the lot are east of Louisville. They run between Louisville and Pittsburgh, but are too large to pass through the Portland Canal at Louisville so are forced to remain upriver. I was told the canal is about fifty feet wide. Of course the boats need to be narrower, but there is also at times a stiff current that makes navigating the canal perilous even for the smaller boats. You must appreciate how my limited funds have saved me from the tribulations of boarding large luxurious steamships that are unable to squeeze through the canal.

"In fact, it was my limited funds that prompted me to attempt the overland route on my first trip out to see Rachel. I endured and swore never again. I was sandwiched between two of the largest, most disagreeable and uncivilized males I ever set eyes upon. I rode with those barbarians for some four hundred miles between Columbus and St. Louis. I ate the worst food imaginable, and was played upon in a most embarrassing manner. I was allowed twenty pounds of luggage and ended up carrying more dust and dirt than luggage. I repeat, never again. I spent most of my life on the water, and after that horror, I intend to spend the remainder of my life on water."

"I say, one cannot complain about this pampering. I am impressed."

"Biscuits, ladies?"

"Thank you."

"Do understand, Elizabeth, the packets I book don't pamper one to this degree. Not even close. I haven't stooped as low as deck passage, but aboard more than one of those boats, first class was closer to bringing your own food and soap than not. In fact, when one observed the utter filth of the cabin and staterooms, it was only natural to prefer eating your own food. Only God might know what manner of slop was in theirs.

"I recall my return trip three years back when we landed at Cincinnati only to wake up the following morning with four inches of late spring snow covering the roof and decks. That was topped by a steady cold rain that never seemed to find its way off the boat. Instead, the snow soaked up the water and passed it straight through the roof as freely as if we had been standing in a field. Fortunately for the captain, it then passed straight through the floor to be soaked up by our beds beneath. And for that bit of bad luck, the boat failed to sink."

I laughed at her stories. I loved them, but the sound of her voice was far too close, too gentle, too soothing. It was making me drowsy, and behind heavy eyes, I was purring inside like a spoiled kitten. I tried to break out of my contentment.

"I suppose I must suffer the chill outside and find my son."

"I suggest you sit back and relax. You've had a day, and Luke can't travel too far on a boat. He'll be fine."

"Ohhhhh—."

"He's fine, Elizabeth. Lay back and relax. Take a nap. Your heart needs a rest in more ways than one."

"You know, Dorrie…I remember once being told that ladies cabins were only constructed out of a need to keep women out of sight. In spite of the costs to furnish a cabin in such splendor…. It was considered money well spent…because it put a near end… to the number of gentlemen dying in duels…over women's honor. That is why…no man…is…allowed tooooooo en…ter…this…."

I was quite embarrassed to open my eyes and see Dorrie and Luke staring at me.

"It's time to retire to our cabins," said Dorrie.

"What time is it?"

"Late."

"I feel like I have been hit by a horse. How long have I been asleep?"

"All of three hours," stated Dorrie.

"Oh, my word. You can't be serious. What have I been doing, sawing logs amidst all the respectable company?"

"Mmm-hmmm. A little of that…you were tired, Elizabeth. You still are. Luke is here now, so let us go below and bed down for the night."

SEVENTY-ONE

It was with a fearful start that I awoke to the most frightening pounding, shaking and shuddering. My eyes snapped open and awaited my head to gain its wits. I looked at the porthole and noted nothing more than the faintest hint of dawn's light filtering in.

As I freed myself from the grip of sleep, I understood us to be getting underway. The captain was determined to mind his schedule when departing St. Louis, and hadn't found a change of heart since that time. I assumed that Luke would also be awake and bounding from his berth so as not to miss a thing. For that reason, I decided with utmost reluctance to trade the warmth of my bed for the disagreeable cold of morning. In spite of the dim light, I could see the plume of my breath as a spasm shuddered through me.

Once up on the promenade, I glanced through the cabin doors and was eased by the sight of Luke sitting down to breakfast. I was then calm enough to go to the ladies cabin and cozy up to a stove while awaiting Dorrie. She wasn't long to arrive, and as we conversed over a well-prepared breakfast, the sun rose to illuminate stained glass windows that flooded the entire cabin with the most glorious hues. How better to start one's day?

The Ohio River proved to be the most genteel course I ever chanced to know. I longed for the giant paddles to still themselves and rid us of the incessant trembling underfoot. I wished them quiet only long enough to experience the full tranquility of these waters. There was not as much as a ripple of disturbance to ruin the perfectly placid surface before us.

It was the very opposite of stumps and stones, and cut-a-ways to be crossed by the stagecoach. But that being said, the mists, the damp and chill of early spring were intolerable enough to keep us inside and nearby the stoves. At no time were we able to long stand on the promenade before mid-morning, and even then, it was often uncomfortable before near approach of noon. However, from noon 'til time to sup, we sat bundled up on deck and watched with great interest the passing of the country.

We steamed past Paducah, Kentucky, which populated the mouth of the Tennessee River. It did a brisk business with the steamboats and was noted for being the farthest landing upriver that did not freeze over in winter.

A number of colorful stories were relayed to us by passengers about the pirates of Cave-in-Rock. It seemed the pirates or outlaws had, besides a habit of stealing boats floating past, a penchant for pushing couples off of the cliffs above their cave. There was no mistaking the cave when we came upon it. It appeared to be fifty or sixty feet in diameter, a highly visible opening in the whitish-gray limestone face of the cliff at river's edge.

Right up there with the passing of country was the passing of boats. Last night it had been said four or five hundred steamboats worked the rivers, and that number failed to take into account all other flatboats, rafts, barges, and manned vessels.

Unlike the rivers of the far west, the Ohio had a great number of notable islands the length of her course. What I found remarkable about these islands was the way in which they were densely covered with timber and luscious vegetation. They were thick with wildlife. In no way did they mimic the flat and barren sandbars or tow heads of those rivers of my past.

We watched the countless small collections of cottages and farms that sprouted up wherever the swamps and bottomlands would allow. Many of these places drew income from the felling of trees in the bottoms that were then chopped and stacked for steamboat fuel. They were structures small enough to hide behind those stacks of wood and the dwellers earned just enough income to fuel their existence.

Their thread of existence was a far cry from Louisville and especially Cincinnati with its two miles of river frontage. We arrived late afternoon on April sixth and stayed over the night but remained aboard. From our vantage atop the Texas Deck we were able to spy the concentration of stores, shops, and bars that catered to the profusion of riverboats. Some fifty to sixty vessels a day were docking at this port. As in St. Louis, Cincinnati hosted a notable German community, but also a more recent influx of Irish.

Cincinnati called itself the 'Queen City', and it probably was if one took into consideration all of its industry. GAYLORD, MORRELL & CO., iron and nail manufacturers; BICKNELL BLACKSMITH AND REPAIR SHOP; QUEEN CITY SHEET IRON & COPPER SHOP; and the MAHOGANY SAWMILL were but one quick glance of the businesses that flanked the upstream side of CASSILLY'S ROW, that being a long stretch of four-story buildings connected and following the river bank for a quarter of a mile. There were a number of holding pens and slaughter houses that produced pork. This was substantiated by our dinner selection.

A number of church steeples stabbed the sky in the distance of a cityscape almost without end when seen from our place at the river. One of the passengers informed us that a particularly prominent building rising up from the upper ridge of Mount Adams, which effectively pressed the city against the river's edge, was an observatory newly constructed a year or so before.

The building struck a note within because it was dedicated by John Quincy Adams, who was president just prior to my years spent in the wilderness. He was known for his support of education and science. He was a most intelligent and resourceful man who stood apart from most by his outspoken support for the abolition of slavery. In spite of every attempt by politicians to silence him, he feverishly attacked the horrors and immorality of slavery and all those who condoned its preservation. He was a man who fueled both the wrath of politicians and promoters of slavery, and my wholehearted admiration.

Thursday morning, April tenth, we docked before sun-up in Wheeling, West Virginia. There we spent the breakfast hours awaiting movement of freight to and from the holds. We were underway shortly after breakfast, the river being calm and yet covered in heavy mists.

Our next stop was to be the last upon the mighty Ohio— Pittsburgh. And so we relaxed. We enjoyed our lunch and teatime, until distracted.

"Dorrie, have you noticed anything odd about the men on board."

"Funny you should say as much. I was just about to ask you the same. They seem to be scurrying about in alarm. Should we be concerned?"

"I wonder where Luke is off to?"

"I wish I could hear something of their conversations. It's obvious that something is amiss."

"Oh! Look there."

A woman at the starboard cabin door was pointing eastward. The majority of women seated in the ladies cabin rose to their feet and moved to step out onto the promenade. There was a chorus of gasps to be heard. Dorrie and I followed suit and were last to exit. Looking out across the river in a southeasterly direction we took notice of a massive dark region of sky. At first it appeared to be a storm, but as time went on, it appeared more to be smoke.

"It's a forest fire," said one.

"Of course. You are exactly correct," said another.

We were all perplexed, but the woman's suggestion seemed most plausible. It certainly eased my mind from thoughts of the boat sinking. I only turned from the eerie sight when I caught glimpse of Luke coming my way.

"Mother, did you say we were making way for Pittsburgh?"

"Yes."

"Have you heard? The men are saying Pittsburgh appears to be on fire."

"Do they?"

"Pittsburgh!" gasped a woman, now staring at us in horror.

The revelation reverberated through the group of ladies.

"Yes, ma'am, that's what's being said."

I placed my hand upon Luke's shoulder.

"Well, I guess we'll soon find out. Now stay out of trouble. Do you hear?"

"Yes."

I turned him about and sent him on his way. Luke retraced his steps back along the promenade. I looked at Dorrie.

"I can't imagine that being the case. How could that be possible? Judging by the smoke, if he speaks the truth, it must be a dandy of a fire."

"Indeed, it must."

Our gaze returned to the smoke-filled sky, but there was little more to be said, and so conversations picked up where they left off, many of the ladies returning to the comfort of their chairs in the cabin. In spite of numerous engaging conversations, a cloud hung over us…literally. Late into the day, the riverboat completed its leg along a miles-long bend in the river, and was now headed on a southeastern course. This put the plume of smoke over our bow and far closer to the eye.

Now came the first boats headed down trip from Pittsburgh. The men were hollering back and forth in passing.

"What goes Pittsburgh way?"

"Fire! Fire! Half the city's burnin'. God's wrath to be sure."

"Folks are runnin' fer their lives."

"Ya won't be dockin' there tonight lessin' ya wanna trim yer planks t' the waterline."

"Docks are gone!"

We all shifted from starboard to port rail to hear the latest of news coming our way. During our approach to the city, the wind changed to a southeasterly breeze and carried smoke and ash to our decks. It made filth of everything and forced us inside for the sake of our clothes. We were in the ladies cabin when the captain made an appearance. We quieted ourselves and gave him our ear.

"Ladies, a moment's interruption if I may…. I imagine you have looked across our bows, and I gather but what conversation I have heard, it is unnecessary for me to point out the disastrous event that has befallen Pittsburgh. I have not come to alarm you,

142

but to assure you that we are in no danger. However, I must point out that our landing, along with most others along the Monongahela course, has burned to the waterline.

"We are presented with an inconvenience to be sure, but a minor one. More important, no peril awaits our arrival. Our associates have sent word directing us instead to take the Alleghany course. It appears Allegheny City has been spared the conflagration. However, at this time, there are countless vessels ferrying fire fighters and fleeing persons back and forth across that leg of the river, and it would be unwise, unsafe, and certainly inconsiderate of us to contribute additional mayhem in those waters.

"For that reason, our pilot has determined to suspend any further travel upstream until conditions are more favorable. I am told the fire is intense, but moving slow now that the wind had eased. Word has it that the worst might be over. And so, begging your patience, I trust your wait will not be overly burdensome. I have nothing else to add at this time and so will take my leave. Rest assured I will keep you updated as the situation progresses. Thank you for your time."

The captain turned to take his leave.

We followed the captain out of the ladies cabin in time to see a large tangle of charred and flaming wooden pilings, beams, and lumber float past.

"Look at that."

Dorrie pointed across the water.

"Must be one of those landings."

"Most likely ours." Dorrie quipped.

We were but one of many riverboats stranded downstream. Rather than burn up all of our fuel to hold position in the current, the pilot cast lines to shore, tied off to the trees, and shut down the boilers. Most all the passengers and deck hands stood along the rails and lost themselves in their thoughts as they watched the shimmer of flames in the distance. By late evening, the traffic had diminished measurably, and the pilot ordered the boilers to be fired up. We cast off, taking our place in a long line of vessels given preference at what docks remained along the Allegheny. The sky was growing dark everywhere but above the glowing remains of a once thriving port.

"It's unbelievable. Frightening. Heartbreaking."

Conversations on board were muted as if to be respectful. One group of women stood in the eerie light, bowed in prayer, bibles in hand. Neither Dorrie, nor I spoke a word as we steamed slowly past the embers of what once was half of Pittsburgh. Most of the city was now a cloud of illuminated smoke drifting off past the horizon. The AMERICAN CHARM slipped into an ash-covered dock on the north bank of the Allegheny. This city may not have burned but it surely looked bruised beneath the smudge of soot and ash.

"I was just thinking about how many times I mentioned the unsurpassed tranquility of the Ohio. Who would have guessed such a turn of character? It won't be something I shall soon forget."

"Nor I," said Dorrie. "I was worried about getting to our packet, but we have put in closer to the A&H docks than planned."

"Judging by the confusion, I suspect that will prove to be a blessing. I suggest we wade into the crowds at our own speed and search out a cabby. Luke, you stay right close to my side. The crowds are unsettled and frightful. You lose sight of me and we may never meet again. Do you understand?"

"Yes, Mother."

"Good. Now, take a firm grip."

144

I clasped Luke's hand as we went ashore. We were fortunate to have nearly collided with a cabby just returned to the docks. And so, without waste of time, we were ferried to the A&H PACKETT 4, a steamboat that serviced the Franklin-Pittsburgh traffic along the Allegheny River. The majority of those bystanders in our wake were staring across the river at the memories of their lives. My heart went out to them. I was certain after all that we witnessed in Pittsburgh, nothing following would amount to anything more than humdrum.

"Were ye on the river a fair spell, ya know, waitin' to land?" asked the cabbie.

"Four hours to be sure, maybe five," I responded.

"Yer lucky, I'll give ya that. The captains won't leave the docks, an' the traffic is backed up to Cincinnati and Louisville."

"For what reason?" asked Dorrie.

"Any cap'n lucky 'nough t' be tied up at Allegheny is booked full. All them folks fleein' Pittsburgh got no place t' sleep. Them steamers are lettin' out all their cabins an' deck space fer lodgin'. They ain' gotta buy a stick o' wood t' fuel the boilers. They just gotta stay put an' make a killin'. You best hope ya get outta Allegheny right quick or ya might not be makin' passage yerselves."

We took the cabby's advice to heart and made sure our packet for Franklin was indeed embarking. With our informed perspective, it was obvious how true was the cabby's claims, for many of the steamers we passed appeared to be overcrowded from the road.

Luckily, we did embark as planned and so steamed up the Allegheny River. Signs of the disaster could be seen all along the river but for the number of steamers and vessels tied up to shore or to one another forming large rafts. The pilot had much difficulty and delay in landing at Kittanning. The docks were in a state of confusion.

A good many hours were lost at Kittanning, but afterward, the journey upriver proved eventless and the docks at Franklin were as of yet minimally affected by the distress downstream. From our landing in Franklin, the following day we booked passage on a stage for Erie.

I understood Dorrie to have said we would travel twenty-five miles to Meadville, thirteen miles to Waterford, and finally fifteen miles to Erie. I believed she was badly mistaken. Judging by my back, I would have ascertained three times that distance. I stepped out of the coach, numb from head to toe.

The last leg of our journey before arriving at Dorrie's home would be on a lakes packet from Erie to Buffalo, New York. Tonawanda was but a short distance farther than Buffalo. Once we arrived in Tonawanda, we took a few days to rest in the privacy and comfort of Dorrie's home that sat on a ridge and commanded a respectable view of the canal. I was saddened not to have again seen her boys, Jack and Kenneth. They would be all grown up, as was evident by news from a neighbor that the boys had recently departed for the falls at Niagara. Dorrie was disappointed. She conceded with disheartenment that it was their favorite place to visit.

Dorrie now spent very little time on the boats. However, due to her offer to care for Luke until I was settled in Boston, plans were made for the three of us to remain together canalling eastward to Albany. In Albany, we would part company. Luke would return to Tonawanda with Dorrie and I would continue on to Boston. And so we traveled the canal. We did so in one of three newly built boats that were of a very unusual design and only lightly laden with goods.

"My word, this is a strange boat if ever I saw one," I commented. "Why would anybody pave the bottom of a boat with stone?"

146

"Hey! You are still a canaller deep down in there somewhere. You are right. Even I have never seen one built quite like it. Usually, a wagon unloads its goods into the boat at one end of the canal and the reverse takes place at the other. I am told this hull is designed to hold a fully loaded wagon and team—no loading or unloading. The team is driven on and off across bow or stern. The stone is to keep the boat riding low in the water so it better clears the bridges. Apparently, the cargo will be light or tall, or both.

"And as strange as this boat may be, what is far stranger is that no one knows for whom the boats were built. There are three, but it was mandated that I, and only I, oversee their delivery to Albany. I have no idea who made such a demand or why. I would have thought it to be Mr. Claussen, as instructions of that nature are usually his doing. But in this case, despite my inquiries, it was never said to be."

Our float along the canal was most rewarding for me as it brought back innumerable memories from my first days on the canal and the events both heartbreaking and heartwarming. One thing was for certain, the canal of old and the canal of present were nothing alike. Where I remembered fields and farmers throwing vegetables at us, now there were only buildings, warehouses, and merchant stores. The canal was hemmed in by commerce that lined its banks often as far as one could see. What would never change was finding Albany at canal's end, and so we did. I looked at Luke.

"Well, Luke. I must leave you. I expect you to be on your best behavior. Promise me you will act like a gentleman while in Dorrie's care. Promise me."

"I promise."

"I must get our apartment and personal matters in order. As soon as I have done so, I will send for you. It won't be long."

"I understand. I will be fine."

I looked at Dorrie.

"Need I say, this is much harder on me than on Luke?"

"He'll be fine. There is plenty here at the canal to keep him entertained for a lifetime. Now, promise me that after you send for him you won't disappear for another ten years, leaving me to wonder and worry."

"I promise."

"I'm not convinced."

"I promise! I promise! I will write. I will keep in touch."

"I will hold you to your word…that much I promise."

"You must come visit me in Boston for a holiday."

"That would be nice."

"I will send for Luke within the month."

"Don't pressure yourself. I will enjoy having him, and the boys will show him about. Send for him only after you are good and settled."

"I will."

I nearly crushed Luke with my embrace, an embrace he barely tolerated. I took Dorrie into my arms, and our embrace was long and meaningful. I felt my emotions rising and so released her.

"You are a fine friend, Dorrie."

"You as well, Elizabeth. Go with God."

I boarded the Western Railroad Ferry at Albany, and crossed over the Hudson River. On the east shore, I was taken directly to the Western Railroad yard. There a train would take me across the State of Massachusetts to Boston by way of Pittsfield, Springfield, and Worchester. This was my first time ever setting foot in a railroad car. It was a larger, more accommodating version of a stage coach fitted with wheels that were fixed to ride the rails.

I was joined by many travelers on the leg between Worchester and Boston. The coaches were packed full. That section of track was so well traveled that aside from freight, tickets for passengers were now being routinely sold for sixty dollars a head.

Even before purchasing tickets, my thoughts were of Christopher. How could I find myself involved with a train and not think of him? Railroads were his life when last I saw him. I wondered if he had ever returned east to see how many passengers, and how much freight rolled along the rails to fulfill his prophecy.

I felt my heart grow heavy with sadness at the thought of him. Oddly, I felt nothing of humiliation. Even now, knowing I was about to see Mary, and how she would soon recognize Luke as Christopher's son, I felt no embarrassment. The realization was inexplicable, but I would not be one to complain.

SEVENTY-TWO

Over a span of two months, I had departed St. Louis, Missouri, aboard a riverboat; coursed by Cairo, Illinois; Louisville, Kentucky; Cincinnati, Ohio; Wheeling, Virginia; the fires of Pittsburgh, Pennsylvania; rode stagecoach to Erie; sailed packet to Buffalo; rested in Tonawanda; canalled to Albany, New York; ferried across the Hudson; and rode a train across the State of Massachusetts until reaching rail's end in Boston—*my home.*

In one respect, my return to Boston was no different than my return to St. Louis. Both times, I had traveled eastward, passing through one neighborhood after another, not recognizing the place. Just like St. Louis, Boston could only expand westward away from the waterfront. For that reason, most of what I observed upon entering from the west was new and therefore unsettling.

For me, this newness of Boston's outskirts was not only mind boggling; it was thoroughly disheartening. It was a sensation, as I said, unsettling, not at all pleasant, and by far worse than my experience passing back through that western gate of St. Louis. I absolutely did not want to be surprised, or amazed, or dazzled. Boston wasn't a place I once visited or passed through in one direction or the other. Boston was my home, my roots, my security. I wanted it to be unchanged. I felt as though it had abandoned me during my absence.

I could only imagine one thing worse than not recognizing my home upon return, and that was not being welcomed back. I would imagine open arms and smiling faces, friends tugging on my clothes, eager to pull me into their embrace. I practiced for conversations I hoped to have with long-lost acquaintances around tables of coffee at old haunts.

But reality had a way of bruising one's hopes and dreams. I stepped off the train at a station I had never seen, to be ignored by crowds of people who never knew I existed, and who never cared I had been so long away. I studied each and every face, searching for that one sign of recognition, that one set of eyes that would look twice, and with opened arms say welcome home, Elizabeth.

"We have missed you."

The words slipped quietly passed my lips. I looked about me. The doors that opened and closed no longer graced the houses and stores of my memories. They had become portals in a picture of time present. The doors that opened to my past had long since closed. I had shut myself out to wander the earth for so long that I had become a stranger in the one place I thought I might never be forgotten. That city of my youth, so intimate in my life, was to be irrelevant. I had thought of Boston Harbor as my safe haven. Instead, I came home to find it had cut me loose, set my soul adrift without remorse. Strangers passed me by all the while engaged, talking, and laughing.

I left my baggage in a boarding room near the train station so I might walk the streets unencumbered. I hoped to find those places that would allow me to piece whatever fragments of familiarity I might discover back together for my comfort. I wanted so badly to rebuild the bridge back to my past. Maybe it was my soul's yearning to find my Mary.

I returned to the station for my baggage and hired a driver. I asked him to take his time so I might reacquaint myself with the city. We trotted past a small park, and I was uplifted by a planting of spring flowers that showed exactly as I had remembered them when a child many years before my departure for the west.

At last, I reached the road that scaled the ocean bluffs and would eventually wind its way past the stone front of Mary and Allen's cottage. It was here where I asked the driver to stop. I paid him for his time, tipping him handsomely for indulging me. I watched him spur the horse back toward town.

I turned to face the direction of my fears. I started up the grade, and my steps became progressively shorter and more labored. It wasn't due to the effort of climbing, or the weight of my bags, but to the burden of remorse, the weight of conscience and cowardice.

To my joy, this neighborhood was old, firmly established, and less changing. It was still much the way I remembered it, the feel of the road being familiar, the look of the homes and lawns being basically true to memory. I practically knew every brick in this road, and I counted the number of bends unfolding before me by memory.

Eventually my count came down to one, and I found myself rounding the final curve, watching as the road straightened to parallel the ocean cliffs. Now, but ten minutes' walk at most, ahead to my left was Mary's home.

The sun pressed down gently on the grasses and spring growth yet unaccustomed to its light and warmth. You could almost hear it growing, sprouting to gorge on that wondrous energy. There was no wind, but the air about me seemed to jump as if tickled by trees whose leaves it brushed, and so twirled about me in puffs. Except for the crows carrying on in a stand of trees up above, the world was silent and seemingly sensitive to my footsteps on the pavement. I felt loud and exposed. I felt I was an intruder soon to be unwanted.

My eyes were locked dead onto Mary's place, fearing that she would suddenly come walking out the front door or around the corner from the side yard with a rake in her gloved hand. I took note of the trees that shaded a large lot across the street from her cottage. I grew up playing in that lot and knew every tree like the back of my hand. I was soon carried away by feet that fled to the safety of those majestic old oaks. I hid my bags.

Within the security of the massive trunks, I was able to dart from tree to tree and look safely across Mary's yard from a string of vantage points. I was desperate not to be seen, and found myself tip-toeing, baby-stepping my way through the fort of bark. I studied each window of her house hoping to glimpse a passing hint of motion. I studied the front yard and the trees and lawn that graced it. From one tree to the next, I managed my way past the house, watching as the view of Mary's garden spread out before me, and it was then, as I might have expected, I saw movement.

There she was. Mary.

SEVENTY-THREE

I was certain it was Mary, and so promptly strangled my soaring emotions. She was on her knees, bent over the flower bed working the soil. As I ascertained the woman could be no other, she suddenly straightened her back and turned to glance across the road directly toward me. I froze where I stood. Motionless, my breath hung in my lungs. Ever so slowly my body slipped back behind the girth of the old oak.

This person, this friend-sister-mother-mentor who cared for me the whole of my youth, this person whom I trespassed, whom I wronged, this person who suffered me such remorse was now there before me in plain sight. The intensity of my trepidation gripped my stomach like some vile sickness, some poisonous affliction that forced me to double over with cramps. Writhing in discomfort, I rolled back around the tree, safely out of sight, and there I squirmed until the butterflies passed through me.

I worked to relax. I reminded myself that my fears were in my head, self-made, only what I chose them to be. My lack of confidence was my own doing, and I should settle my nerves and face my responsibilities like a woman who conquered the worst of the wilds for a decade and then some.

After all, I believed at some point Mary would accept me; she would understand, maybe not at first, but she would understand. It was her way, and I wasn't about to accept that her heart had changed and become unrecognizable during my absence as did much of Boston and its many cold-hearted landmarks.

It did me good to see Mary in her garden. It was the place where she was relaxed and most at peace. It was the place where we passed years discussing every aspect of our lives. The garden was where I had always approached Mary for advice. It was our place.

Mary stood up. Again, I cowered behind the tree. I looked briefly away from the house, back across the lot of old oaks—but very briefly, for I could barely rip my eyes away from the sight of her. I watched as she grabbed a hoe and began scraping the earth. She chopped away at all that winter had compressed and hardened.

She was stepping back and forth, and her restlessness stalled my approach. I waited for her to settle down, for I wanted her to again face the ocean, to turn her back on me. Maybe, for my benefit only, time brought me an opportunity the moment Mary dropped back to her knees. She bent over and attacked the earth with determination and full attention. She again faced the bay, and it seemed as though at the very second all was in place, I was practically thrown onto the street by some estranged part of my being. I stood on the pavement petrified by the thought of her catching a glimpse of me in the open.

I sprinted away from the oaks, bolted across the road, and next sped across Mary's front yard studying her minutest moves as I approached. I knew, should she turn about at this moment, I would implode, and any vestige of courage I possessed would dissipate like spent breath, leaving my intentions to crumble in disarray.

Thankfully, I traversed the distance of her yard yet unnoticed. I rushed along the side yard leaving myself no time to wonder what I might say, but more important, leaving Mary no time to beat me to whatever words would pass between us should she be forewarned.

I was so close. It was ridiculous to imagine I might now effect an escape unnoticed should I lose my nerve. I suspect for that reason, my anxiety was displaced by a wash of peaceful resignation. Or maybe, I simply understood I was now at the mercy of Mary's reaction for better or worse, and I was now helpless to change my fate.

As I neared her, I slowed my advance to the silence of well-placed steps, one before the other, until the distance between us was brought to a close. Mary was humming a song, and the sound of her voice instantly brought me back to my childhood.

For the briefest moment, I relived a myriad of memories and melodies that once floated upon the warmth of her breath while I lay at her side with eyes closed, held within the security and solace of her embrace. It was so during the perils of our journey on the high seas; it was so during my days of sickness. It was so during lazy spring mornings on a blanket covering the grassy cliffs that overlooked the bay.

I couldn't bring myself to steal away such pleasure from my ears, and so rather than call out to her, I directed my shadow to announce my arrival. I laid it across her busied hands as they hovered about the sprouting flowers that she carefully tended. I stood immobile for two seconds of eternity, two seconds that provided all the time needed to allow an avalanche of anxiety and mixed emotions to rain down hard upon my heart.

Mary turned her head upward. She threw up a hand to shield her eyes from a sun suspended above me. After so much living, so many years, the sight of her face moved me deeply. It moved me to my core, and I was thankful that the brilliant rays of the springtime sunlight prevented her from noting my trembling and tormented expression.

"May I help you?"

I had great difficulty speaking.

"Hello, Mary. I'm...home. I'm home."

I couldn't get the words out without choking. Thereafter, I could only nod my head to signal the truth of it. My days of loneliness and wandering, loving and hating, killing, starving and feasting, my days of pregnancy and childbirth were behind me. Now, I was just a girl who wanted nothing more than the love I had always taken for granted, for unlike the weathered looks of me, my heart could still be young and in need.

I laid my hand across my mouth, and then up across my face, as if yet requiring the protection offered by those giant oaks across the street. The sun hardly stopped the sobs that slipped through my fingers. The sobs that suffered to tell what Mary could not see.

As quickly as I had broken down, so too did I shore up. My tension eased, but I felt awkward, embarrassed. I caught my breath.

"I am sorry, Mary. I didn't wish to blubber. You'd think by now I would have outgrown those...I have so longed for the sight of you.... Mary.... I don't know if you can imagine what I...have gone through...to get back to your garden."

This time I was openly racked with sobs. This time I couldn't hold back, for I was too emotionally exposed to contain my sentiment. Mary rose to her feet and wiped her hands off on her apron. She pulled my hands away from my flushed face so she could replace them with her own. She drew me toward her and kissed me gently on the forehead, then my cheeks. She looked at me with those flecked amber eyes. They were filled with acceptance, understanding. They were filled with heart.

"Oh, God, Mary...how I have missed you," I cried.

Mary held my face in her hands and momentarily absorbed the sight of me. The longer she studied my face, the broader became her smile.

"It's been a long time, Liz. None of that matters now. You made it back. You're home. There's no need to cry. You're home, and aside from a bit of wear for weather, you appear sound in body. Spirit, well...I'm not so sure."

Mary's smile was now broad and inviting. She took hold of my arm.

"Come. Let's get you off your feet. Let's go inside and I'll put on some tea."

Mary led me across the yard toward one door that still remained open to my past.

"Where are your bags?"

"Hiding behind a tree in the lot. They can wait."

Nothing further was said as we walked. I stepped through the back door that entered the kitchen, and was at once overwhelmed by a sense of relief. I had found something of my former life that I knew to be real, something familiar enough to reach far, far into my past. I was bleeding emotion.

It wasn't that I was happy; it wasn't that I was sad. It was as though a dam had formed in my heart to hold back the years of heartbreak and longing, the years of worry, the years of embarrassment for my actions, the years of being strong for others. It was as though the dam was at last allowed to give way, discharging tears of emotional entanglement, every possible feeling let loose to flow, and so I cried. I cried hard.

Mary had accepted me without a word of reprisal. She was the one untainted, unchanged connection to who I had been as a person. She would return my past to me so I might bring balance to my present. Mary would always be Mary. Mary would always love me. It took a while for me settle myself. Mary held me all the while, caressing me, stroking my hair and smothering me in kisses, just as she had done during the youngest years of my life. She prepared our tea, but between the stress of journey and my irrepressible emotions, I was so drained of life that she set the kettle aside and led me upstairs.

Mary opened the door to my room and showed me in. These walls welcomed me like no other. She leaned over my bed and drew back the covers. She then straightened up, but kept her back to me as she spoke her thoughts aloud.

"I remember making you tea at your apartment once long ago, Liz. I remember turning away from the stove to see you fallen across your table crying in the worst of ways. I was moved ever so deeply by your distress, pained by your suffering. I could not fathom what it was you needed—what it was you were compelled to seek. You were always a driven soul. It was simply that facet of your character that forever made you unlike the rest of us. I have thought on those things many times over the years. I never knew why you cried so hard that day, Elizabeth. And I don't know why you cry so hard now."

She turned to look at me. She motioned me toward the bed.

"Take a nap, and you will awake refreshed and settled. I will make us up a hot pot when you come down. If after all these years my believing you dead, you come returned to me, then honestly nothing would seem impossible to overcome. Whatever it is that troubles you, Liz, it will be managed and set straight soon as we sit to tea. It always worked that way, and I suspect it always will. Now…rest yourself."

Mary tucked me in. She kissed me and although I may have grown into a middle-aged woman, the sensation, the effect of her love and affection was intoxicating, exactly as I needed it to be. Mary looked at me for a moment and smiled.

"Allen won't believe his eyes."

With that, she turned to take her leave. She exited my room, pulling the door behind her without further word.

I listened to Mary humming as she descended the staircase. Her song faded away into the silence, and I imagined her to have gone back to the garden. I gazed across my childhood bed; a bed given to me by Rebecca at the Barrington, later moved to the infirmary, and again moved to the cottage. A bed that was flooded with feelings, recollections that poured out of me in tears to soak and soften the hardness in my heart and persuade me to let down my nearly impenetrable guard.

The afternoon sun slipped through the window, smearing its melancholy light about my room, pressing down upon my bed and closing my eyes. I drifted back through memories strung end to end, memories of my going away dinner—memories of my summer stays—memories of my earliest days—memories of Christopher.

SEVENTY-FOUR

I awoke to a different light. It was an old familiar light I knew from years ago. It used to work its way quietly into my room, prying my sleepy eyes open to view highlighted collections and coveted possessions. It would pass through the framed panes of glazing that made up my window to the world. Outside, it would dance lightly across the waters of the bay so I might see beyond the ocean's horizon to where lay dreams of the future and faraway places.

Now, through half open eyes, I sought out those once familiar imperfections, those panes of glazing that distorted the clarity of my world and forced me to center some distant object into the vignette of circular waves. How fitting they should exist in my window to life, representing the deceptions and illusions I had grown to encounter.

In any event, I had learned to recognize those distortions, and I understood the tranquility of this morning was no deception, for there was nothing in Mary's world that I should fear. I might have thought such understanding was reason for my feeling so invigorated. I might have thought the invigoration came from the comfort of my own bed as I stretched across it. I yawned. My eyes opened wider to flush away my sleep and clarity returned with a surprise. I raised my head and looked around.

"Morning...morning? Really?" I said aloud.

I propped myself up onto my elbows and focused on the daylight coming through the window. It was far from the melancholic light of afternoon that I last remembered. No wonder I felt entirely rested and energetic. To my embarrassment, I suddenly realized that not only had I nearly nodded out during Mary's tea, but I went on to sleep soundly through the remainder of the day, and then 'saw logs' the whole of the night to boot. For the briefest moment, I considered conjuring up some excuse that would explain away my rudeness, but that proved futile. Fact was I passed out like a pigeon-eyed drunkard trying to track two moons.

Obviously, the serenity about Mary's cottage and my bedroom in particular quelled every anxiety I had managed to muster. I awoke bright eyed and bushy tailed, and now sported a broad-faced grin. From the invulnerability of my bed, I wanted to wish the whole world a good morning. I inhaled the tantalizing aroma of Mary's breakfast. It filled me with impatience and a wish to leap out from under my covers and embrace life.

Today, I would do good by Mary. She was my soul mate, and on such a fine morning, I felt confident I would work out all of my failings for the best. I went downstairs happy to see her and hopeful for our day.

I entered the kitchen and was mildly disappointed to discover that Mary wasn't sitting in her usual place at the table. In fact, the table was unoccupied and the aromas were only a lingering sample of what fare was enjoyed during my slumber. Apparently, it was later in the morning than I presumed, and so I walked over to the door and looked for Mary in the garden.

"Good morning, sleepy head."

I spun around.

"Oh! Mary, you startled me. I thought you were in the garden."

"So, how are we feeling this morning? I will say you look better, you look plenty refreshed."

"I feel wonderful. No, I feel better than that, I feel fabulous. I swear I haven't slept that good since…well, since the last time I slept in that bed."

Mary said nothing. She smiled but looked away. I sensed her change at once. The sensation shot through me like an arrow. Mary and I would always be emotionally connected. When she sobbed, my tears fell. While I slept, Mary had ample time to wonder whether or not my years of silence was callous disregard for her suffering during the years of prayer I knew she had offered in my behalf. I sensed her retreat. I sensed a fresh distance between us. I stared at her. I deserved everything she thought of me.

"Mary…I can't imagine what you must think of me. Last night, did you ask yourself how I could have been so heartless, so cruel? Did you ask yourself where I got the nerve to push my way back into your life, and why you didn't just throw me back onto the road? Even a saint would have asked such things, and if you didn't, I would have been amazed.

"I don't believe there can be anything I have done in my life that I regret more than leaving you to believe the worst had come my way. That is why I have returned. To see you, yes, of course, that is foremost; but also to repair the damage I have caused. As God is my witness, I swear you deserve an explanation."

"No. No. It isn't necessary, Elizabeth. You aren't a child who answers to me."

"But it is necessary, Mary. Please. Please. I beg you allow me to redeem myself. I have carried this burden of guilt and it will go with me to my grave unless I earn your forgiveness. All the years of my absence, I prayed that I might be blessed with one chance to tell you how much I love you, how much I longed for your smile and kindness. You were always with me during the loneliest hours of my life. In my heart, you have been with me always, and I am here to tell you how grateful I am, how many times you saved my sanity. I am here to make amends. I must make amends."

My voice cracked as my throat tightened. I continued.

"All I ask is another chance at yesterday's tea, another chance to sit with you at the table or in the garden as we did in years past. I want a chance, Mary, just a chance to beg your forgiveness."

"Liz, darling, there is nothing to forgive. You owe me no apology. Your life led you down a distant path. I understand that."

"Oh, Mary.... If it were only that simple. Please...the kettle. Sit with me and talk. This has been my prayer for more years than I dare count. Please, let's have our tea."

If the plea wasn't in my words, if it wasn't in my voice, it was in my eyes; and so Mary obliged me. She poured tea as I asked. Not one, not two, but three kettles' worth in order to sustain us as we wore away the day in conversation. The sun swung its shadows from one side of the room to the other. During its arc, we carried our tea, blankets, and conversation out into the garden to bask in the rays of an early summer sun. Neither cloud nor breeze swept past to steal away the heat, and yet for all its glory, the heavens failed to bring me comfort that compared with the warmth of Mary's affection.

I began by giving Mary a full account of my travels up through the Hudson Valley, and along the Erie Canal, including the tragedies that befell Dorrie and Rachel. I told her about the schoolboats. I told her of my journey through Michigan and the bitterly cold winter in Chicago.

I told her about Taa killing the Indian in Illinois, and my first time in hectic St. Louis. I went on about my riverboat excursion up the Missouri and my brush with death at the rapids. I told her about Dusty and his wagon, about his ghost, and my desolation in the desert, and how I talked to her in my mind for days on end. I went into great detail about my time spent with the Tsistsistas, and I told her about the tragic death of Luke Laredo. To my surprise, and Mary's unease, I even gave account of my killing the three bandits.

I told Mary that I had succeeded in locating Christopher, and that he was healthy and more prosperous than ever. I told her about his railroad and his life in the mountains. I told her all about how I met Gracie, how a little girl saved my life, and how I went on to raise her for the next twelve years. I told her about how Gracie and I lived together amidst the Tsistsistas.

Well into afternoon, with a plate of cookies in hand, I finally brought Mary with me through my fearful abduction, the mob attempt to burn us alive in the store, my reunion with Taa, Rachel and Dorrie, my heartbreak at leaving Gracie behind in St. Louis, and at last my return to her garden.

When I finished, we sat in silence. I believe Mary found it difficult to comprehend the extent of my experiences; the height of my exhilaration, the depth of my suffering. Many, many times during my accounts she shook her head in disbelief and offered me a full pardon. Her mind was spinning in circles as she attempted to organize my life into something to which she could relate—something sensible enough to be put to memory.

"For all these years gone by, my strength came in knowing that you would understand, knowing you would forgive me no matter how grievous my sin. I wouldn't allow myself to doubt it,

Mary. I couldn't allow myself to doubt it. I dreaded the fear of facing you. I have suffered the fear of this reunion since the day I first disappeared."

"Elizabeth…. If I have said it once, I have now said it a dozen times. I cannot fathom how you survived your ordeals. I keep reminding myself that the Lord has truly blessed me with your return. In my head, I keep saying that He has given me something back that by all accounts should have been forever lost. It's not our choice to dictate the ways of fate. And fate may have taken you from me for reasons I will never understand. Fate may have hardened your heart in ways necessary to protect you, but I know your heart. No matter what sins you may have committed, I can't imagine anything the devil might do that would change you. God chose your path. I believe you did suffer to face me. I believe you are sincere in what you say. I believe to see you again before me, to hear your voice again here in my garden may be the last great joy of my life."

Mary let out a long breath.

"I also believe that you are keeping something from me," she said. "I don't know if you are protecting me from something, something painful…something disconcerting…. But, I can see it in your face, Liz. You wear an older face, but one rarely changes one's wrinkles. I have read those wrinkles too many years to know different. Every time you pause and step back into your thoughts, you bite your lip, Elizabeth—just as you did when a child. So, why are you biting, what are you hiding, Liz? What haven't you told me?"

Why those eyes? Why must I face those all-knowing eyes? Just as I had feared, all these hours Mary was reading my soul. She was this very moment reading my most intimate secrets while we sat facing one another with eyes locked. She was hardly older than me, but a mother figure nonetheless. I was guilty as charged and so dropped my eyes downward to collect my thoughts.

"You're married."

"What?"

"You're married! Is that it?"

I just looked at her. I was lost for words.

"Come now, Liz, what is so difficult to tell me? It must be noteworthy indeed, being you would choose not to mention it over tea."

Mary's voice faded out of my awareness as I delved deep into my soul where lie that promise that I would never be ashamed of my son being born a bastard. He would be spared that insult, and would only know of my pride. To my astonishment, even before gentle Mary, I felt something inside of me bristle. I took a measured breath and then turned to look Mary square on.

"I have a son, Mary."

It was obvious that the revelation stunned her more than all my hours of stories combined.

"A son," she stated flatly.

"Yes."

This time it was Mary who was lost for words. I sat there nodding my head with assent and waited. She raised her eyebrows high and offered me a look of sheer wonder.

"Well, if I were to say I hadn't nearly fell out of my chair, I would be lying. So, allow me to begin anew...." Mary cleared her throat. *"A son?"* This time she said it with surprise and a good measure of elation, making up for her previous response of outright shock.

"Congratulations, Elizabeth. I am very happy for you. I promise, I am. I'm not sure why that came as such a shock. I think maybe the way you presented it. It came out of nowhere."

"Thank you."

"Allen is going to collapse. You do realize."

I laughed. "Yes, I suppose he very well might."

"Now then, tell me, please, how old is your boy? What is his name? What does he look like? Does he take after his mother or his father?"

"His name is Luke. He just turned eleven this spring. He is the most beautiful child, Mary. Of course, I know, what else would I say; I am his mother."

Mary remained dumbstruck. She was boring straight into my soul with those flecked amber eyes. She squinted as if searching for some logic to my admission. Then relenting, she blinked.

"I...I...I am lost for words, Elizabeth. Honestly, I don't know what I am supposed to say. Am I to ask if you are married or widowed? Am I to ask why are you traveling alone with no man? I mean, we have conversed all day, and you make no mention of your son until this late hour? I don't understand. Is there a dark side to this, something you are preparing to tell me? Is he here with you, or are you about to leave again? Does this mean you are soon returning to St. Louis? I don't understand why you wouldn't make mention of your son?"

"No, no, no, Mary. It's nothing of the sort. I have no plans to return to St. Louis, Boston is my home. I'm so sorry, you must find me deceitful in every way, but that is not my intention. You must believe that I carried nothing but regret for years, nothing but remorse for leaving you and Allen to worry your selves sick.

"I so want you to know the truth of it. I was determined that nothing might overshadow my explanation, my apology for what I have done. It would have been crass of me to go on about my son and the joy he has brought me as if to skip over the grief I

166

caused you and Allen. I wanted nothing, not even the news of my son, to diminish my apology.

"All that I have said is honest and truthful. Only, much of what I said took no account of Luke's coming into my life. Clearly, he is the center of my world and many of my stories are about Luke's life as well. I would love to tell you more if you wish to hear as much. But I must warn you that when it comes to Luke, I might never shut up."

Mary stood up. She folded her blanket as she stared down at me. I hoped the chill I felt was only the sun losing its warmth and the sea breezes now coming inland off the sea and nothing more.

"Let us go inside, Liz. It's getting too chilly for me, and it won't be long before Allen returns home. I really must get his dinner going, but trust me when I say, if ever I was all ears, it would be here and now. So follow me inside and don't stop talking on my account. Are you married?"

"No."

I gathered up my blanket and followed Mary back to the house.

"Is the boy here in Boston? I assume he must be."

"No."

"No? Is he with his father—?"

"No."

"Does he have a fa—? Dear, God, I didn't mean to ask that. It just came out. Incredibly rude of me."

"My word, Mary, you don't know how to be rude. But, for your peace of mind, yes, the boy does have a father. Unfortunately, that remains to be the only story I prefer not to share at this time. It has been a difficult relationship; one I am certain you will know part and parcel soon enough. I have never long held a secret from you, Mary. I just have scant desire to dwell on that matter now. In time…in time, you will know everything. Soon, I promise. Most likely, sooner than I prefer."

"I understand. Tell me only what you wish. Is Luke now in St. Louis? Is the father someone I know?"

"Okay, too many questions for now. I have said all that I intend, except that Luke is not in St. Louis. He is staying with Dorrie in Tonawanda, and could be here within days of my summons. I plan to send for him as soon as I open up my apartment. Which reminds me, I never thought to ask, do I still have an apartment?"

"Yes, as a matter of fact, you do. Allen and I go over regularly and air it out. But, I must say there is a rather peculiar story attached to it."

"Is that so? Well, it's about time someone offers me a tale, especially a peculiar one. Please, *do tell*."

"Well, to be truthful, Liz, after a great many tears, I did finally give you up for dead. We had been receiving your letters periodically. I remember the Potomac, the Erie, your letter from Chicago and all the ice upon the lake. I remember reading many of the things you recounted today in those letters. As you know, after you decided to boat your way up the Missouri, we lost all track of your whereabouts. Allen and I knew you were in the farthest points west, and after years of no word we finally assumed the worst. I mean it was so unlike you not to keep in touch.

"I recall that day too vividly for comfort. It was the morning I sat down and wrote Mr. Claussen to say I thought it was time to close your place up. You see, after you disappeared, and everyone feared the worst, Mr. Claussen saw to it your rent was paid up and all expenses covered from that point on. It was that way for five years before I was of a mind to write him regarding my fearful conclusion that you had come to a tragic end.

"I never received a letter in return, but some months later a messenger appeared at the door and handed me an invitation from Mr. Claussen asking if I might join him for dinner the following day. I agreed and a coach was sent for me as promised. We had a fine private dinner at his residence in the Barrington, and afterward he asked if I might accompany him to your apartment.

"I went inside with him and he spent near an hour in silence going through all your belongings. I saw him standing at the back of the kitchen chair almost as if you were sitting there before him. He was upset. I could see it in his face. He was very upset, Elizabeth.

"Anyway, he suddenly spoke up and said no, he had no desire to close the place up. He stated most assuredly that you would be back. Now you might imagine, I had only recently given you up for dead, and to hear such a statement was most heartbreaking. I broke into tears and begged him to share any news he might possess regarding your circumstance in order to spare me suffering over your disappearance.

"Mr. Claussen, seeing the error of his ways, apologized profusely for upsetting me by such blunder. He went on to say that he was not aware of any factual news that might make account of your well-being. He claimed there were stories, legends of a blonde ghost in the desert, and although such rumors could have meant anything, it gave him reason for hope. He told me to have faith and that he believed I would see you home. With that he returned me to my house, and asked if I might see to it that he was posted should anything be required. Naturally, I agreed, and the rent has been taken care of ever since."

My feelings for Christopher were suddenly stirring after so many years dormant. They were feelings from long ago, feelings I was never able to manage. Feelings I had no desire to dwell upon. I took Mary's hand into mine and I kissed it, and then held it up to my cheek.

"I have done many good things, Mary. I have also done many irrevocable things that bring me no honor. I have tried to right my wrongs. Please believe that. I want your forgiveness, Mary. I want you to love me as you did. I want back the relationship we shared. Please."

Mary gazed upon me with her gentle amber eyes.

"I cried for years believing I had lost you, Liz. When I looked up, and saw you standing there, I forgot about all the heartbreak. My remaining fear was hearing you say...you were only passing through."

SEVENTY-FIVE

Allen arrived home. He was retired from his profession in words, but not in action. When he walked into the room, the brutality of passing time became evident. Allen was at least ten years Mary's senior and nearly fifteen years older than I. His age was clearly branded into his face and although I made no sign to show different, the change in his appearance leveled me. To my joy, his mind was sharp and his personality robust. His arms reached out to take me in his heartfelt embrace.

"Elizabeth, Elizabeth, Elizabeth, I am drowning in joy at the sight of you. I have been impatient all day to return home. However, before another word is passed, you must tell me one thing."

"What?"

"Did you bring back all those books you borrowed from the library?"

I struck him on his chest.

"I didn't *borrow* any books. I owned those books and I trust you aren't about to start all that again."

"I couldn't help myself. Last night, Mary told me that you had arrived, and that you were so tired you fell fast asleep. I replied that if I were still hauling that trunk of books around the country, I too would be tired."

The three of us laughed heartily.

"My word, Elizabeth. You have been missed. I am pleased to see you go on in good health. You look fit. We worried a great deal for your well-being. Actually, we worried a great deal for your life—."

Mary interrupted.

"I assure you, Allen, she understands well the truth of it and has come to me with much remorse. Let us not now dwell on sorrowful things, and instead be seated. Dinner is ready."

We enjoyed a fulfilling dinner together. Now it was my turn to listen, and I insisted they tell me as much about the boys as they could manage. I had forgotten how wonderful was the feeling of family and the confirmation of love through freely expressed affection. I was drowsy with contentment. I was home.

The following day, Allen and Mary brought me to my apartment in the city. As expected, the neighborhood was both the same and entirely different. Allen was quick to point out the many new buildings and improved streets, those under construction and those that no longer existed, always sacrificed for the sake of progress.

The vibrant atmosphere Allen painted was a far cry from the disillusion and frustration I recalled during the years of my departure. I was pleased by this change. It lifted my spirits because I understood Luke would enjoy the sense of vitality that abounded. I dreaded to think I might have lost Luke, as I did

Gracie, to the explosive growth and indescribable hustle bustle of St. Louis.

It took twelve years' time to find me standing again at my doorstep, standing again on my front porch. I raised my key and fit it to the lock. It spun, clicked, and stopped. I felt a twinge of anxiety as I gasped the door handle firmly and pressed my thumb upon the latch. It released. I swung the door open wide and stared.

A massive breath of silence flowed past me, across the porch, and down the steps to the street. It was as if my apartment had deeply inhaled all the energy of my existence in those days. It held that breath inside its walls, making it the unchanged atmosphere of the rooms until my return. Now, it was as if a giant exhalation of musty breath and memories blew past. It swirled about me, brushing me with broad strokes of recollections I had locked inside for safe keeping.

Now it was my turn to inhale deeply. I stepped across the threshold with Mary and Allen close behind. Allen immediately went to the windows and drew back the curtains. Light flooded in and set the treasures of my past crying for attention from beneath blankets of dust. I picked up my favorite porcelain cat, blew off the years gone by, and pressed it to my lips. I closed my eyes and let the past rejoin the present.

"The few things in my life that haven't changed."

Mary walked over to assist Allen in opening a certain window that had settled into a permanently closed position.

"This place offers me a chance to regain a footing in my past before I lose it all to a son who will fill this place with his own collections."

We spent the afternoon airing out the place. We uncovered the furniture, dusted, dusted, and dusted. Allen managed to open most of the windows and a warm summer breeze carried off all the smoky particles we stirred. We made the place livable, and although my plans were to move in at once, Mary was having no part of it.

"Elizabeth, you asked me for my forgiveness and I offered it freely in spite of my desire to knock you silly for all the hurt. But now that I have, I will accept nothing less than your company day and night at least until Luke joins you. I won't stand for anything other. I've said my piece and I will not have a change of mind."

Allen looked at me and rolled his eyes. I wasn't about to utter a single word to the contrary and so we closed the windows, and I again locked the door to take my leave. Mary took my hand and holding it firmly, she led me to their coach. She sat down inside, not saying a word. We three spent most of the ride back to the cottage in the privacy of our thoughts. Mary stared out her window as she patted me on the leg. I thought she might have been crying.

SEVENTY-SIX

On the first day of June, I sent for Luke. I could hardly wait.

Mary and Allen politely insisted on my having space, a moment alone on the platform to greet Luke when he stepped off the train. They preferred to remain nearby in the background until I had a chance to suffocate Luke with hugs and kisses.

Inside, I was giddy at seeing the train as it approached the station. I tried my best to stand still with some composure as the passenger cars slowly came to a halt. I searched nervously up and down the length of the train, hoping to spot that golden mop.

"Do you see him?" asked Mary.

"Noooooooo. Nooooooooooo."

My head was bobbing back and forth, up and down as I worked to bend my gaze around passengers that stood in my way. Then he appeared.

"There! Luke! Luke!"

I waved my hand furiously. Luke nodded in my direction.

"Liz…Allen and I will be waiting inside the station by the door."

"We'll be right over there." Allen pointed to the platform entrance.

"I'll be back at once."

I ran along the platform to greet Luke. He was walking toward me with a broad grin on his face. My heart leapt from my chest. It slammed against my breast as if speeding me forward toward him.

"Hello, honey."

"Hello, Mamma."

I took him into my embrace and might have crushed him had he not been such a barn of a kid.

"Oh, I have missed you." I stepped back to look at him. "Did you have a good trip?"

"Yes, Mamma. I never rode a train before. It's a fine way to see the country. It seems odd not to see desert anywhere. You can't see very far, but I enjoyed it."

I hugged him again.

"How was your stay with Dorrie?"

"Wonderful. I had a great deal of fun. I met a lot of students. Do you think I can have a tutor? I think it would be a good idea."

"I am sure we can do something, but right now, I have someone you must meet. Do you remember me speaking of my good friend, Mary?"

"Yes."

"She is here with her husband, Mr. Sawyer. They brought me to the station to meet you. Come now, let me introduce you."

I was immediately aware of changes taking place. Luke was not wearing his hair braided on the sides, but instead it was pulled back into a pony tail. Dorrie had bought him a new outfit. To my utmost surprise, Luke was wearing boots instead of moccasins. This was not a small development. In fact, as I studied his feet, I was mostly stunned.

"Boots? Do they hurt?"

"Not so much now. They did at first, but I liked the look of them so I kept wearing them until they broke in. They are well made."

"I see that. Did Dorrie help you pick them out?"

"Yes."

Luke was attacking the white man's world without restraint. I knew there would be more surprises to come with each passing day.

Mary and Allen stepped out from the station and met us on the platform. We stopped and I presented Luke.

"Luke, this is Mr. Sawyer and his wife, my closest friend, Mary."

"How are you, sir. Ma'am."

Luke held out his hand and Allen grasped it. They shook. I was amazed. I had taught Luke and Gracie proper decorum, but it seemed as though Dorrie must have been preparing him for his arrival in Boston. If nothing else, I was proud. And in that frame of mind, I found myself focused intently on Mary's expression as Luke offered his hand to take hers.

To say that Mary was taken aback was nothing if not a colossal understatement. Stunned barely described the stricken expression upon her face. Her stare was unshakable, fixed securely as if nailed to Luke's forehead. I believe her complexion went white as she turned to me with a look of utter incredulity. Behind those wide open amber eyes were volumes of words unwritten, hours of speeches unspoken, a million questions Mary was too polite to ask, and I too rude to answer, but there was now no question about one thing.

She knew my last untold story.

SEVENTY-SEVEN

Luke received his tutor within days of his arrival. It brought back memories of Mr. Gaines to both Mary and me. He had been a very good tutor to both of us, and we were left wondering whatever became of the man. That being said, our curiosity paled in comparison to that of my son.

Luke's curiosity was insatiable. He divided his time between staying inside to study his books, and going out with Allen to study the city. There was no one better to introduce Luke to Boston than Allen. He was born here and being a doctor the whole of his life, he knew every aspect of Boston both good and bad. Luke adapted to his new surroundings far better than I had hoped. It seemed he found Boston appealing, almost gratifying, but for some reasons difficult to explain.

I would have expected him to share Gracie's comfort with St. Louis and wish to return to that wild anything goes arena, especially when knowing Gracie would remain there. In fact, Luke's wish to return to St. Louis had been one of my greatest fears, and I prayed those longings would never come to pass.

Luke once asked me where "things" came from as if everything in the white man's world came out of a singular saddlebag. I came to believe that in some way Luke was searching for the sources to the many wonders he encountered in the western world. Boston had a fair measure of the vitality and invention visible in St. Louis, but possibly something additional, something deeper, something unseen yet magnetic.

Boston possessed a sense of aged foundation, a place of long grounded knowledge. There was a certain wisdom that prevailed here, a wisdom gained from a collective experience. It was a resource to be found in the mature neighborhoods and reflected in the solid granite structures and public systems that supported the city. It was a place of established innovation and manufacturing. It was the source of the many things that caught Luke's attention. And it shared a sense of adventure with St. Louis, for it too was a major port to the outside world. At least for now, Boston worked for Luke.

Luke had also become particularly fond of Mary, and I supposed this had to do with his years of listening to me speak of her. After overcoming her initial shock at the sight of him, Mary allowed Luke to fill the space left vacant when her boys, Josh and Juny, left the nest; not the space of house, but the space of heart. She never once made mention of his looks, his undeniable connection to Christopher.

Luke would carry-on, telling Mary about what kind of behavior I had said Mary would or would not have approved as he grew in years. I could plainly see how it flattered her to hear it. She would laugh with embarrassment and scold me for making such a demon out of her.

"I was never that strict."

"Yes, she was," I whispered.

At eleven years, Luke was a master at playing Mary. She was always running off to make up a fresh batch of cookies, and practically hand-feeding him. The two of them swelled my heart with joy as they whirled about each other.

Clearly, we still were not moved into my apartment. Clearly, we might never be. Mary would become overwhelmed with heartbreak, and would wail at any hint of my taking Luke away from her. The house was big, the rooms numerous, the pampering and accommodations above and beyond. I saw us going nowhere.

Even Allen made it clear he preferred us to stay as long as we wished. He enjoyed the added commotion. The house seemed lost for life since the boys had moved on, especially during the Christmas season. Bowing to his insistence, and a full understanding that Mary was in her glory, I decided to put moving out of mind until after Christmas.

For Luke, as for all children, the Christmas season was something to behold. Decorated Christmas trees were now very much a part of the holiday décor. The orphans' annual letter exchange had become something akin to an enterprise and Christmas cards were criss-crossing paths all across the country. Responding to cards and letters sent by the original fifty orphans was very much a part of Mary's Christmas ritual.

I lent a hand in opening and answering cards as well, but my writing didn't stop at season's end. In the fall of my return, I began writing articles and short stories based on my experiences living with the Cheyenne. I wished to bring a balanced view of the red man to the ignorant, and justice to the innocent. Anything and everything having to do with the Wild West or Indians in particular was in high demand, and so request for my articles kept me busy right through the Christmas season.

What came entirely unexpected was the United States annexation of Texas and the war that appeared imminent. The East Coast clamored for any information relevant to that far away frontier, and my detailed descriptions of high prairies, steppes, and mountains drove the sale of my articles to astronomical levels. They proved profitable even prior to completion. I couldn't write fast enough to meet the demand, and so during my first year home I enjoyed a very profitable income.

Everything I wrote was under the pen name Blonde Ghost. I couldn't help myself from cashing in on the irony of Wilpen's legends. The thought of it provided me with endless laughter over glasses of port while writing. On a more serious note, I used the pen name to ensure my efforts to remain invisible in Boston were not undermined.

I was writing a prolific amount of material, my insights and opinions being requested by numerous papers up and down the Atlantic coast. I found myself growing ever more fearful of having my true identity revealed. I had no desire at this time to have the masses calling on me to again undertake my work in charity and thereby pitch me back into the glare of the limelight.

Even worse, I lived in fear of Christopher discovering Luke. I made this matter very clear to Mary.

"You must promise me, Mary. You won't ever, ever volunteer anything about my being here to the charities or Christopher. You must promise me. Mary…swear to me."

"What am I supposed to do, Liz, lie to him?"

"I didn't say anything about lying. I said, please don't divulge any information that would lead Christopher to believe I am here. I will be frank, Mary. If Christopher discovers I am here, I will leave at once. Luke's going with me, and you know you will miss him dearly. And that is a threat, not a hint."

"How unkind of you. Fine. No need for threats. You have my word, my promise. But if he asks me directly, I will not lie. I will not lie for you, Elizabeth."

"Nor would I want you to. No lies."

Mary never looked away when I mentioned Christopher. It was a subtle challenge on her part to have me admit what was obvious. I knew that she wondered when if ever I would confess a connection between Luke and Christopher, a connection of which she was positive. I doubted I ever would. I believed the price too steep. And so, Mary kept mum about my presence, never breaking her promise until….

* * *

"Good morning."

I stumbled into the kitchen, dragging my feet as if I wore lead slippers.

Mary turned from the window to look at me.

"Good morning. Kettle's still hot. You slept late."

"I know. Odd. I was really tired. I feel half dead. I stayed up too late writing last night. I managed to finish the article, but now I can't wake up. What are you looking at?"

"Some kids playing in the lot. I hope they're not up to some mischief."

"Neighbors?"

"Well, friends of neighbors, at least that is what I thought at first, when there was three or four. Now there's too many. I think they came out from the city."

I poured my tea and walked toward Mary. "What are they doing?" I asked as I stood alongside her to look out the window.

"Just staring at us."

The minute they saw me at the window, a ripple moved through the group, and I knew. I choked on my tea. It was still hot and it traveled down into my lungs. I held my cup up and Mary took it at once as I convulsed.

"Are you alright? Liz? Elizabeth?"

I was choking, unable to speak, unable to express myself. The coughing forced tears into my eyes. I wondered if I would breathe again or not. It took a full moment for me to recover a breath and by that time, I was fully on all four looking down at the floor.

"Good lord! Are you alright?"

Mary placed her hand on my back and leaned down to find my face.

"Don't die on me. C'mon. Can you make your way to the table?"

I was yet unable to speak, and so only nodded that I was able. Mary helped me to my feet and walked me over to a chair. I sat down and dropped my head. I was swallowing hard, trying to loosen my throat. I was waiting for my voice to come back. When it did, it was hoarse.

"Where is Luke?"

I must have looked panicked.

"Is something wrong?"

"Where is Luke, Mary?"

"He's in the garden reading."

I rose to my feet and walked over to the door. I opened it and studied the yard. He was seated there with a book as Mary stated. All seemed in accord.

"Where is Allen?"

"What is it, Liz?"

"Do you know where he is?"

"Allen is in the back yard trying to fit a new handle to my hoe. I broke it yesterday. Why? What is this about?"

I walked back to the window and looked out to the lot across the road. There were now eight or nine children. Many of them watching the house. I stepped back.

"Elizabeth. Will you please tell me what is going on? You look white as a ghost. Are you feeling ill?"

"I'm fine."

"Well, I never would have guessed it by the way you're acting. You're scaring me."

I looked at Mary and I couldn't hide my fear.

"It's the children. It's those children."

"What on earth are you talking about?" Mary looked back out the window. "They're just urchins—street urchins from the city."

"No." I shook my head. "No. Something's wrong, Mary."

I left my tea on the table and removed myself to my room.

I wasn't fine.

* * *

I wasn't fine, and the children knew it. I didn't know how they knew, but they knew. Two days later, I was fully infected with influenza. I had only been in Boston a year, but the change of climate from arid desert to the damp of sea must have been my undoing. I was morbidly sick.

"Sixteen or seventeen. I am not sure what you want me to say, Liz. I asked Allen to see what they were up to. They weren't up to anything. They did ask how you were doing. Allen thought that strange, but he must have mentioned you were sick. Anyway, he just asked them to hold down the noise, to simmer down, so you could get your sleep."

"Luke?"

"Luke is fine. He is downstairs reading as always. He is worried for you. Now let's try and drink some of this broth. Allen says you've got to get something down. C'mon open up or I won't hear the end of it."

My only thread of pleasure was in believing that the children were here on my account and not because of Luke or anybody else. This was about me.

* * *

"...I don't know, Liz. More. Maybe twenty or twenty-five. Maybe thirty or thirty-five, I don't know. A lot. It's all nonsense, Liz. Nonsense, going on about this gibberish."

I barely understood her words. I knew if the numbers continued to increase the situation would worsen. And so, my influenza turned into pneumonia. My state of health deteriorated to the point whereby nothing of me remained save my skin and bones.

Luke was at my side when I signed my will in the presence of Mary and Allen. A day later I succumbed to the savage grip of brain fever and delirium.

SEVENTY-EIGHT

Christopher Claussen scaled a steep rock-strewn trail that led to a favorite bluff. This was his escape, a place that brought him peace. From here he could see far out across a distant crest of snow-covered mountain peaks. He could take in the movements of wildlife scaling and descending the slopes. He could look down and follow a creek far into the remoteness of the valley below. At these heights, the breezes that buffeted his hat never gave up winter.

He stood his ground against the gusts and vagrant flakes of snow as he removed first his gloves, and then a letter from his breast pocket. Holding it carefully, he studied the penmanship before turning it over to read the return address. He broke the seal and opened the envelope. He removed the contents, unfolded the fluttering pages, and pressed them against the saddle. Christopher went on to read.

Honorable, Sir,

I beg you forgive the poor quality of the ink and my inability to express myself in this matter with clarity. I pray my letter finds you in the best of health and spirit, being that I thank the Lord for it at this time.

I am distressed to convey my inability to partake in said high spirit, but for having been pitched into the deepest state of sorrowfulness. Our beloved Elizabeth has been transported to the very threshold of heaven by the ravages of influenza and pneumonia.

She has penned her last will and testament before Allen and myself, and I am now torn by conscience as I take unforgivable liberties to write you regarding this private matter in which I have gone against my word, a pledge of secrecy.

I beg you find compassion in lieu of anger, having read such disclosure, for I am certain this letter comes as an unfavorable revelation. I say this knowing well your own anguish in years past, having failed to discover her whereabouts.

I have never asked, nor have I been given account of what difficulty took place between Elizabeth and yourself, this being in no part my business, but I have gathered it a profound matter, for it remains an affair closely guarded by Elizabeth and unre-vealed even upon her deathbed. Only for my recollection of the pain in your heart, and admitted regrets, do I now take up the pen and pray I have undertaken the less grievous path.

I convey, Elizabeth returned to Boston in the spring of last year, some twelve years after her departure from your care, some six years or thereabouts after our meeting pertinent to the upkeep of her apartment. Only by sheer resolve, did I not faint at first sight of her, being wholly unsure if I observed her flesh or spirit.

I beg you value; she was not the same person who left me years before. She departed a younger sibling; a girl of glad intelligence, articulate, accomplished, determined in every way, but still pure in heart and innocent. She returned to me a woman apart, still younger than I in years, but entirely beyond me in her scope of experience and strength of character. I found myself standing before her in awe. It was with difficulty that I put aside the Elizabeth of my youth, who for so long had been my child of sorts in order to accept this remarkably strange and wondrous new person.

Although she claims different, I cannot imagine how I would soothe her, for I feel awkward cradling this person so versed in self survival, so formed by inner conviction and strength. She is nothing if not an inspiration, and I found myself willing, if not compelled to do as she bid. It is for this reason I have kept my word to her and maintained my silence.

I pray not to make anyone the fool. I swear before Almighty God, may he bless us, that she has made use of your name but in kindness only, yet always with a sense of sadness about her eyes. There is some longing or need she represses deep in her heart.

Should you feel any obligation to reconcile your differences while she possesses a breath of life, you must do so in haste. I believe with sincerity any word from you, brief as it may be, would do more to raise her spirit than the best of doctors in Boston, including my dearest Allen, try as he might. I pray you consider. May 1, 1846

Respectively, your servant, Mary Carol Falgren Sawyer.

PS: Elizabeth remains under my care. You may post her at our residence.

Christopher folded the letter. He raised his head and gazed eastward into a wind that whispered. His thoughts traveled a great distance.

Early on the morrow, with letter in hand, Christopher Claussen boarded his private coach and headed east out of South Pass. The train quickly gained speed as it rolled along the Rocky Mountain Railroad toward a rising sun.

SEVENTY-NINE

Mary turned away from the rising sun and the ocean beneath. The early morning sea breeze breaking over the cliffs this day were too crisp for one to kneel comfortably in the dew covered garden. She tightened her wrap and began rubbing her arms. She gave thought to the rake and hoe in order to keep warm, but instead began wandering; making observations, giving thought to what chore most needed her attention until ending up in the front yard where she was called out.

"Good morning, Lady Sawyer."

Mary looked up to see the children across the road waving at her. Mudlarks...everything but the mud. The memory never escaped her.

"Good morning, Lady Sawyer," they called out.

"Good morning. How are you doing today? Aren't you cold? It's so chilly this morning."

"Yes, ma'am."

Mary looked at the tattered collection which had again grown.

"I thought you told me you were all leaving. It looks to me as if those of you who left have come back thrice the number."

The children looked around the lot. A boy named Gregory whom Mary had come to know approached the road.

"Yeah, there's only 'bout six o' us now."

"I know. I saw the mess your lot left behind. So what now goes? Why are your friends coming back?"

Gregory looked around.

"Don' know. Been said a lot o' kids'r comin' from the docks. They's always been down by the docks; always been fer's long as I can 'member. Don' know why they're comin' us this ways. Not much been said. I know it's warmer in the city. There's more t' eat there."

"Well, if that is true, then why do you stay?"

"Don't know…. Feels safer here. No one tries t' chase us or grab the girls. In the daytime, it's easier t' find food in the city. There's always sump'in t' eat; but durin' the night, at least when the weather warms, it's quieter an' safer t' sleep here 'cause we can all stay together as a group.

"Summer's usually quite nice in the woods at night. But fer the last week, it's been too cold, so we been sleepin' in the city fer warmth. That's why everybody was leavin'…to stay warm. Don't know why all them kids'r back."

Mary walked up to the road and stopped on her side just where Gregory and a few of the others stood opposite.

"Are you hungry?"

The question stirred the children before her like a giant spoon.

"We're always hungry."

188

The rest of the group passionately agreed with quips, nods, and laughter.

"How would you like to make a deal to your advantage?"

"What's 'at?"

"If you clean up the mess you've made, so I don't have to look at it, I'll send out some food and drink."

"Yes, ma'am! We'll do it!"

"Well, then, get to it."

"Yes, ma'am!"

Mary turned to head back toward the house, but she was stopped by a question.

"Lady Sawyer?"

She turned to look back at Gregory.

"Yes?"

"How's Missus Claussen doin'?"

The question unsettled her.

"Missus Claussen? You mean, Miss Dennison?"

"Yeah. She feelin' better now?"

"Did you know she was sick?"

"Yeah. We all know she's sick. We were worried for 'er."

"How would you know such a thing? Are you also a lot of peeping toms?"

"No ma'am. Don' ya 'member? Mr. Sawyer scold us fer makin' too much noise? He said as much then. Said she be needin' 'er sleep."

189

"Oh. I suppose he must have. She is doing much better, thank you. I will let her know you asked about her."

"That is good news, Lady Sawyer. Bye then!"

Mary waved back. There was something odd about what just occurred. She couldn't put her finger on it. She shook it off and again started back toward the house. As she glanced down the street, she was taken by the sight of children walking up the lane for as far as she could see. It was a troubling sight. Why would so many leave the warmth of the city? Where would they go? What if they harbored ill-conceived plans? She stepped upon the porch of the kitchen door, reached for the handle, and stopped in thought.

"Mrs. Claussen?" Mary suddenly spoke aloud. "Mrs. Claussen? I can't imagine ever calling Elizabeth, Mrs. Claussen. Where would they get that?"

It didn't seem possible that Allen would call Elizabeth, Misses Claussen. She immediately thought of Luke. The boy was the key. Bewildered, Mary looked over to the lot. Her momentary question was erased by the sight of the children picking up their litter. That pleased her. She opened the kitchen door and stepped inside.

Mary was no stranger to charity, especially when it came to helping orphans and the like. She had spent too many years prior in the proximity of Elizabeth and her work. Mary paid little mind to the expense of preparing food for the children across the street, because monies were always available to her for these things.

She went ahead and gathered up her bread and sweets and broke out whatever was readily edible from the pantry and started carting food as promised. Each time she crossed the road, she was disturbed to see additional groups of children spaced out, two here, three there, all walking lazily up the lane. After carrying

190

her sixth large tray of food over to the salivating creatures she threw up her hands in resignation.

"What is going on here? Gregory?"

"Ma'am?"

"Tell me, son. Why are all these children coming up the lane? What could they possibly hope to find here? You told me it's warmer in the city, and I'm telling you right now, Gregory, I do not have enough stores in my pantry to fill all those bellies."

Mary looked at him with consternation.

"Don' know, Lady Sawyer. There's been talk—."

"Talk about what?"

"Don't know ma'am. Talk 'bout somebody comin'."

"Somebody *who* coming?"

"Don't know ma'am, that's just what's been said. They're comin' up here from the docks."

Mary turned from Gregory, and glanced back down the road at the arriving children. "Hmmmph." She returned herself to the house. Once inside, she called out to her servant.

"Laura!"

"Yes, ma'am."

"Ah, you're still here. Are you busy this morning after chores? Can I enlist your service a while longer?"

"Yes, ma'am."

"Good. I want you to take the pull-cart down to Mr. Sullivan's bakery and fill it up with whatever he has in store. Return to me as soon as possible so we might then hand it out to those unfortunates across the lane."

"Yes, ma'am."

"I prefer not to put money in your pocket, Laura, knowing it a temptation for sticky fingers that abound in that mob of urchins. Do tell Mr. Sullivan, I will be by soon enough to pay him. If he hesitates, ask him how often one buys out his entire stock for the day. Now be off quick."

"Yes, ma'am."

After about an hour's wait, Mary began to grow mildly impatient. She kept glancing out the window for her servant's return, only to be further unsettled by the sight of this crowd of children growing without restraint. It was getting out of hand, she thought to herself. You couldn't just plop a hundred children in an empty lot. The neighbors must be out of their wits by now.

Instinctively, Mary reached down to open the kitchen window and let in the cooler air. It would delay the discomfort of heat from the afternoon sun and the oven. It was just then that her attention was drawn back to the road as the sounds of clopping horseshoes, multiple horseshoes, echoed up the road and through the space of her opened window.

Mary observed how the children began to collect in and around the road. It was reason for concern. She pressed her head up against the glass, looking to her right, straining for the first glimpse of a carriage or wagon to appear. All of this was upsetting to say the least.

Should the children force an unplanned stop, Mary shuddered to think what fear would be put into a neighbor's heart at sighting this horde of miniature outlaws. Feeling in part responsible for their collecting on her lot, she rushed through the kitchen, out the door, and around to the front yard. She was fully of a mind to scatter these children far and wide, and to offer whatever assistance the driver might require.

To Mary's surprise, four impressive black horses came into view drawing an equally impressive black coach. She threw her hand above her eyes and studied the vehicle. It was not the standard well used and abused cabbie, but substantially larger and newer if not new. The horses were handsome, well-groomed animals. The driver called out for the horses to halt.

Mary was somewhat confused, trying to sort why the coach stopped, and to recall whether the children forced it to do so, or whether it stopped for the benefit of the children collected to receive it. Suddenly her heart skipped a beat.

"Oh, Lord. Oh, Lord, it's Mr. Claussen. Oh, my God, it's Mr. Claussen," she spoke aloud to herself.

She was somewhat frightened to think he might have traveled such distance to call in person—to respond to the letter. She turned to look up at Elizabeth's bedroom window. Mary raised a hand to her mouth as if to hold back words too unsettled to pass her lips.

Mary looked back to study the coach. The window blinds were pulled back, and she confirmed the occupant's identity before the driver had stepped down to open the door. Mary's impulse to rush forward and greet Mr. Claussen was quickly damped by the mob of children. Their entire lot was too undisciplined to make way for the man and give him due respect.

"Shooo! Shoooo! All of you, shooo!" Mary hollered to deaf ears. "Mr. Claussen! Is it really you, sir?"

"Yes, Mary. I am arrived. How are you?"

"I am blessed to be well, thank you, sir. I apologize for these urchins. I have no idea what brings them—."

"Ho, ho! It's of no concern to me, Mary."

Christopher stepped out onto the pavement and stretched. The children swarmed him at once. They made no pretense about begging for handouts.

"What do you rascals want?"

"Anything!"

"Money!"

"Sump'n t' eat!"

"You're all beggars. I should have known. Each and everyone one of you. If I give you something, what do I get in return?"

The swarm went silent. They were mesmerized by this giant of a man. They had never conversed with anybody of his standing, and as soon as they fully realized it, they became unsure of themselves.

"I enjoy children, especially these unruly scrappers who live underfoot. They are forced to be wiry and clever minded to survive. If they go against the law, they hang, if given a chance to support it, they become passionate leaders. They have more grit and stomach at ten than any ten at their age. Mary, do you know any of these brats?"

"Only Gregory. Right there. The older."

Mr. Claussen spied the youth.

"Gregory the Older, is it?"

"Yes, sir."

"Tell your motley bunch, I will dispense one dollar to each person who should promise to remove himself from this place and return to the docks or what other place he happened from. Can you do that?"

"A dollar, sir! Do I understand ya? A full dollar!"

"You do, Gregory. Have them form a line at the back side of my coach."

"Yes, sir! At once!"

Gregory could not contain his excitement.

"And Gregory…."

"Yes, sir."

"Tell them, once given the dollar, if I or any of my party should catch them, I take my dollar back. You have my word on that, and I have never broken my word."

"Yes, sir! I shall tell 'em, indeed!"

"Very good, now be off. If all goes well, I'll see to it you are paid two."

"Yes, sir!"

The crowd began deserting Mr. Claussen for the driver. No longer the focus of attention, he moved toward Mary. She again glanced toward the cottage, concerned about the view from Elizabeth's bedroom window. She looked back to Mr. Claussen.

"Was your trip agreeable, sir?"

"Trips are never agreeable, Mary. It was long, and for that reason alone, I must inquire, is my dearest Elizabeth still with us?"

Mary, didn't answer, but instead broke into an expression of exuberant joy.

"Yes. Yes, she is, sir. It is better than that. She remains bedridden, but she's over the worst of it. Her strength is returning by the day, and I believe her recovery, if not miraculous, will be in the least, complete. I suffer to think you may now believe your trip of no consequence, but I assure you nothing could be farther from the truth. I am convinced you are yet her strongest remedy. I am thankful you have come. At best, I hoped for your letter. I wish I had known; I would have prepared. Would you care to call on her?"

"How would that now be acceptable without her invitation, without a request? If she is indeed better as you say, I could never impose."

"To speak frankly, sir, I dare say the fuss brought on by a forewarning would do more damage than the dismay of not being properly powdered. If you will allow me but a moment to clear the house, and ensure Elizabeth is not in an embarrassing way, you may then have your privacy with her. Afterward, I'll put out something to refresh you."

"I'm most appreciative, Mary. Elizabeth and I have much to discuss, but it needn't be done this day. It can wait if I find she is too weak. I'll await your word. In the meantime, I need to stretch, and would enjoy a stroll in your garden. I'll take in the ocean view from your cliff, if you'll allow me."

"By all means. The breeze is more agreeable now. Most of the flowers are coming into bloom. The roses are wonderful this year and look at those peonies. Aren't they just spectacular? Take your stroll, and I'll pour a quick cup of tea to refresh you. I'll be quick, you have my word."

"Mary?"

"Yes?"

"Did you tell her that you summoned me?"

Mary dropped her eyes.

"No, sir, I did not. I swore an oath to secrecy, but I fear in spite of our closeness, she would be terribly upset with me. I hope you understand."

"May I suggest that we not say anything about the letter or my arrival this day? Let her assume I had business in Boston and it

196

is for that reason, I dropped by to pay my regards to you and Mr. Sawyer. I shall be as surprised as the next to find her here. I think it best for everyone at this time, if she wasn't to know different."

"Oh, thank-you, Lord. I am most grateful, Mr. Claussen."

Christopher Claussen started across the yard, at which point Mary ran back toward the house. Almost at once, two servants exited the kitchen and approached Mr. Claussen with hot tea and biscuits. They then took their leave and proceeded to walk the trail that overlooked the bay.

A moment later, Mary stepped out of the door. She signaled for Christopher to approach.

"She made herself presentable of her own accord this morning. She has returned to her bed for a nap. She saw nothing of your arrival."

Mary pointed to an upper window.

"She is in that room; go up the staircase and turn back. Her door is open. I will join the servants for a short walk. I will return in half an hour if that meets with your approval."

"You are most accommodating, Mary. Bless you. I am in your debt."

Christopher finalized his thoughts as he watched Mary walk down the path. He turned away from the ocean view and moved to invade the quietude of the Sawyer house. Inside, he looked around the kitchen with curiosity. The silence felt uncomfortable, deathlike; it bothered him. He recalled Mary pointing to an upstairs room.

A staircase at the far side of the kitchen caught his attention. He moved toward it. At its base, he looked upward, following the handrail to the landing above. A murky haze of daylight floated in the air overhead. He scaled the first step and clenched his teeth as the plank, straining under his weight, immediately let out its complaint with a long, drawn out creak. All would know a stranger was about.

He continued against the chorus of creaks and groans until reaching the upper landing. At that point, he stopped and peered into the rooms. In one room, he noticed fresh flowers on a window shelf, undoubtedly cut from the garden by Mary. He headed in that direction. His movement toward the door was arrested the moment he saw Elizabeth lying on her bed. He hesitated to approach as a rush of emotions raced through him. In silence, he watched her until his anxiety passed.

It passed quickly once he realized that she was asleep. He was nervous, and so having been provided a moment to simply observe her without fear of rebuke or complication was a blessing of no small measure. For the longest time, he stood there absorbing her essence. He inhaled…lavender. In his life, it was the fragrance of love.

Elizabeth was faced away from him. Her hair flowed across her pillow as thick and full as it was in his memory. It was still rich with blonde color, but now graced with subtle strands of white highlights. He longed to hold her tight against his chest. He wished to crush her in his embrace until their spirits merged into one.

With hat in hand, his massive frame squeezed through the opening. He walked up to her bed and prepared himself. Unlike his heart, she did not yet stir. His anxiety rose, his chest pained him as he cleared his throat.

"Elizabeth…Elizabeth?"

Elizabeth turned her head to face his voice. Christopher noted that unlike him, it was hard to believe she had aged. She was yet incredibly attractive, in fact, seductive was a better word. She appeared untouched by the years that had separated them.

In his eyes, she was every bit the child, every bit the woman he had adored. He was moved with emotion. He cleared his throat and again gently called out her name.

"Elizabeth."

EIGHTY

I was wandering in that place where dreams mix with reality to shape half-truths that leave one unsure of what is or is not. I felt Claus at my side, and his voice filled my head as if he had entered it. I heard him call out to me. The sound of his voice filled my heart with bliss.

"Elizabeth...."

I was returning from my sleep with enough wits to be dismayed. I knew that I had been dreaming, and that such contentment only existed in the murky depths thereof. I felt as though I had been awakened prematurely against my will, and my eyes refused to welcome the light. After four or five blurry glimpses, I assembled an image that stood out of place. It was of a man, an enormous man standing silently beside my bed. A man with a hat in hand.

I looked at the stranger with a dulled sense of indifference. There was something familiar.... I thought it some dream-distorted vision of Allen. I remained focused on the face. It was buried behind the brilliance of a full white beard. The man stood there unmoving, like a ghost looking down at me within the privacy of my room. It was but a snap before I understood myself not to be dreaming, and that this man was not Allen. I was jolted awake by fright, my senses instantly charged.

Who was this oddly dressed...leather...a gun...then there was that fragrance. I inhaled, and memories began to stir, connections, visions, images of a time when.... My eyes went wide. Oh, my Lord!

It was Christopher Claussen!

For the love of God, the man had white hair. There...*went my heart.*

"Claus?" I cleared my throat. "Claus, is that you?"

I raised my head off the pillow, hardly believing I was awake. A smile broke across his face. I simply could not believe my eyes.

"Am I dreaming? Is it truly you standing at the side of my bed? My God, what are you doing here?"

I was amazed, to say the least.

"I've come to see you. And I must say, even having faced death, you look radiant," he answered.

"Aha. I'm not that groggy. A wee exaggeration to be sure," I responded.

"Were you referring to death, or to radiance? Either way, I beg to differ."

"My God, Claus, what are you doing here?"

I barely believed my eyes. More important, why did I care? It was so good to hear his voice. It resonated through the room. It resonated through me. I was yet very much under the seductive haunt of my dream. I yet felt those nocturnal emotions that apparently enhanced my desire to now absorb everything of his presence. It was so much easier to deny my lucidity, to believe the remnants of sleep clouded my good sense and desires. It was too easy, and so I allowed myself more.

I reached out for him, and he obliged by stepping closer to take my hand. He leaned over and kissed it. He then sat carefully upon the edge of my bed. I supposed there was little point in denying my thrill. I might as well have been a stammering fourteen-year-old.

"You look lovely, every bit the beautiful woman I recall from years ago. Tell me, how do you feel, Elizabeth? You must tell me what I can do for you. Anything, anything at all, anything you need, and I will see to it. I have been deeply worried about you... worried beyond my ability to say. Tell me, now, in all honesty, how do you feel?"

"Better. Not great, but better today than yesterday. I pray, tomorrow better than today. I've returned from death's doorstep, but I never realized how, after two months in bed, one must learn to walk again." I took a breath as I studied the man before me. "I must say, it does me good to see you, Claus. I had hoped to hate you forever."

"Hmm. Lucky for us both that such feeling has kept you alive."

We had a good laugh.

"I am nothing if not amazed, Elizabeth. I am yet unable to accept we are again speaking. I honestly thought you dead ages ago. For years...years, I suffered to think you passed over having never heard my plea for forgiveness. I swear I have lived in regret every day since I left your side."

Again, I laughed.

"You find that amusing?"

"I find it near word for word, my confession to Mary. Regret? Oh yes, that's a feeling I know all too well. It certainly eats away at one's soul. Does it not?"

"It does indeed. And it has. As I hear your voice, I thank the Lord for His mercy, for this second chance to say in person how I came to see that my pathetic apology was worse than my crime. I was upset, Elizabeth. I believed with all my heart that I had failed you, that I had taken advantage of you. My actions were admittedly careless and rash, and ultimately proved heartless and insensitive. I've had to live with the truth of my stupidity ever since—for years, a long, long, time."

"Come closer."

I reached for the side of Christopher's face, and I stroked it once lovingly with my hand. I then grabbed two fists full of his beard and yanked him down forcefully to within inches of my face. He cried out with pain. His arms fell to each side of me like bent pillars, saving me from the crush of his falling weight, but leaving him unable to pry away my fingers.

"Ooooowww, ooowww, oouuucchhh!" His eyes watered.

"How many years! How many years to figure out that I loved you?"

"Oooowwwwchhh! Elizabeth, that hurrrrrrts! I was told you had but little strength. I see that is not the case."

"Hurts? Hurts, you say? I shall tell you about hurt, the kind of hurt that doesn't go away, the wound that festers. It's called *humiliation*. Like you, I had to live with it for years, as you have just said, a *long, long* time. You were a bastard, Claus, intentional or not, stupid or not, and I don't mind saying it straight to your face. You earned it, you *bastard*."

Our noses nearly touched as I stared into those limitless blue eyes. I then released my grip. He turned his head with a moan and then squinted at me from the corners of his eyes as if to say "*yours is coming*." Then without warning, his arm slipped beneath me, and I was lifted off the bed. Locked securely within his embrace, he smothered me with kisses, not inappropriately, playfully to be honest, but certainly scandalous under the circumstances, and without invitation.

"Oh! Ahh! Oh! What...are...you...."

I used what strength I had to push him off me at once.

"Oh! You pig!" I sneered.

He wouldn't release me, but my outstretched arms held him at bay.

"I have come from a world away to say I cannot live a single day more without you, Elizabeth."

He grinned at me. He *grinned* at me! What a boar!

"Well! Tell *that* to my son! …Luke! Meet Mr. Claussen."

* * *

Now, there was a blow to be admired.

Christopher reeled from the impact of my words. His head snapped around to face the bedroom doorway. There stood Luke. Immediately, Christopher looked back at me. He was entirely red-faced and searching my eyes for some sign of a prank. He was desperate.

Having seen Luke staring at us from the doorway, I knew Christopher's first move would be to dismiss any thought of indiscretion, for his character was impeccable in that regard. Yet, there he was holding me in his embrace high off the bed; his lips barely inches away from mine. He was caught in a painfully questionable act. Gently, but abruptly, he returned me to my pillow before backing away, and literally shrinking with mortification.

As he moved to put a respectable distance between us, he stumbled clumsily over my bed stool. The misstep landed him again upon me and the bed. He broke his fall, but ended up on his knees, his torso lying across my legs, half on, half off the mattress.

"Do be careful, Claus. Are you alright?"

"Oh, for the love of God, what else might I do?" he mumbled.

Luke and I paid him close mind as he steadied himself. Bent over in that awkward stance, Christopher appeared comically crippled. In a most embarrassing manner, and with much animation, he reached out for the footstool, placed it back onto its feet, eased his large frame erect, and took a deep calming breath. He shook himself, adjusted his coat, and then looked directly down at me.

"Your *son*?"

I flashed my thinnest, most vindictive smile.

Christopher's hair would have turned completely white if it hadn't already looked like snow.

"Damn me to hell, Elizabeth. I had no idea you were married. Please tell the boy this isn't what he thinks."

"It looked to me a *whole lot* like what he thinks."

"Please! Elizabeth!" Claus's stunned expression pleaded for salvation. "In the name of God, have you *no* mercy?"

He was desperate to save himself, to save us both from disgrace.

"And what would you have me say? How *am I* to explain such deplorable behavior to my son? Maybe you should explain your egregious transgression and ambiguous intentions to both of us. I for one can hardly wait to know *what* you were thinking."

Yes, I did exaggerate, did I ever, but it served him right. For my sake, I wished to cherish putting him through a bit of hell. It was pure elation to be in charge for once in my life. Christopher stared at me with burning eyes that might once have seared my soul. He then turned away from my taunts and looked squarely at Luke.

"I meant no disrespect, son. You have my word of honor. I meant no disgrace toward your mother. She is a fine woman and—."

"Luke...." I interrupted.

"Mr. Claussen is indeed a very old and dear friend, now mostly old, but I did in fact grab a handful of his beard and pull him off balance. The unexpected fall onto my bed was in no manner his doing. It was a thoughtless prank on my part; and I assure you, he did not know I was *married*." I stressed the word married. "Please, be a gentleman, introduce yourself and be off. Tell your *father*, we'll be having a guest for dinner."

"Mother?"

Luke was smart enough to appreciate a monumental lie, and so bit his lip. Christopher, on the other hand, now having an opportunity to take in the sight of Luke, appeared as though he had been clubbed senseless—this final blow being considerably worse than any dealt prior. If a person thought Mary had been stunned by the sight of Luke, a person only need look at Christopher. His eyes were riveted to the lad, as my eyes were riveted to him. Christopher scrutinized every hair on my son's blonde head, the blue of the boy's eyes, Luke's every expression and mannerism, the build of his frame...no part of the boy was left unstudied.

Luke moved boldly toward Christopher, and extended his hand in a gesture of friendship. Christopher was visibly overwhelmed; his mind must have tripped all over itself, for he was whispering gibberish. His was in a state of utter confusion, utter astonishment. Of this, I had no doubt, for bewilderment formed every line in his face and dropped his jaw slack.

Claus turned toward me with a look of incredulity. He slowly returned his gaze to Luke and received his outstretched hand.

"Mr. Claussen." My son acknowledged him.

"Mr...."

"Dennison. Luke Dennison."

"Yes, of course. It's a pleasure to meet you, Mis-ter Den-nis-son."

The name rolled off Christopher's tongue in slow thoughtful syllables. To my detriment, it was not only Christopher who now was sizing up the obvious, but also my son. Luke had been far slower to realize the similarity between himself and the man standing before him. I believed it wasn't the physical aspects that drove Luke's rabid assessments, but rather the ridiculous realization he might have a flesh and blood father standing within reach. After a lifetime of curiosity and questions, how could that have seemed anything but impossible?

Unified in their incomprehension, father and son grasped each other's hand. It was a firm grip, a yet unrealized bond. Only I could sense and appreciate the spirit of their shared blood. Their hands remained clasped, but went motionless. Time dragged as I absorbed the sight of them fulfilling fate's desire.

I had unbolted the door to my deepest dread. Christopher was looking at his own reflection. Every inch of Luke, from head to foot, was a duplicate of himself, only forty years his junior. I understood that from this moment forward, Christopher would stop at nothing to take charge of Luke's destiny. I was on the verge of losing everything.

I felt suddenly sick to my stomach. Things now would move very fast as I had always presumed. I suffered the first real terror of losing my son, not to a wife, not to battle or misfortune, but to the god-like seduction of Christopher N. Claussen and his empire— to wealth beyond comprehension. From the day of Luke's birth, my foremost fear was the moment that Christopher would render me defenseless, powerless to protect Luke from the rush of his persuasion. I moved at once to halt that rush, to break his spell.

"Luke darling, say nothing more, and allow us our privacy, please. Mr. Claussen and I have some catching up to do before your father arrives."

They released each other from the grip, but the bond was struck. Luke was every bit as bright as the next and although not prepared to be entirely stunned, he appeared shaken and perplexed. He turned to look at me as if asking were I capable of being that sinister.

"*My father?*"

Luke presented me a play on words—a play on meanings. He understood there were mysteries to be unraveled. I returned a play in kind.

"Yes, honey, your father. Now go, go on, shoo. Tell him, we have company."

Christopher had released Luke from his grip, but not his gape. My son could not yet comprehend to what extent he was the exact representation of the man that stood before him, nor did he understand the effect he was having upon that man. Luke only perceived a threshold had been crossed and so moved to obey my wish. Without further word, he left the room.

As Luke exited, Christopher followed him to the door. From there, he watched Luke cross the landing, descend the stairs, and disappear from view. Christopher was unable to remove his eyes from the boy. He stood motionless, his mind undoubtedly numbed by the revelation. His head then pitched forward, stopped dead by the strike of chin on chest. He was surely scrambling for sensibility, for sanity and explanation. I supposed the vision of Luke filled him with vertigo. I wondered if his conclusions would leave him overjoyed or bitter and resentful. If Christopher himself had given birth, he could not have produced closer twins. How could he not know his own son?

I knew Christopher needed time to digest this unexpected revelation. I suspected inside he felt badly betrayed by me, but if so, he kept his feelings masked. In fact, he went overboard to avoid any mention whatsoever of their evident likeness.

"How utterly barbaric."

"Pardon?"

"I have again disgraced myself. I am not sure how I manage it, but I swear, Elizabeth, Mary made no mention of your marriage or your son. I had no knowledge of such relations. It seems, should my past actions not be sufficiently loathsome, I need only see you again to further my foul nature. Now, I arrive at your bedside while you lie infirm, and cause additional injury with my misguided heart. Am I *entirely* incapable of acting favorably in your presence? Apparently so, and having admitted as much, I will now take my leave of you. If you can find any place in your heart for forgiveness, Elizabeth…."

Christopher walked directly from the room. He was a proud man. I had pulled the rug out from beneath him, leaving him to fall to the lowest esteem. His sudden departure caught me off guard. Would I allow my own pride to prevail, only to feel my insides go dead?

"Claus! Stop! Please, don't leave. I took no offense, I swear."

I heard his boots cross the landing. I heard the staircase creak beneath his weight as he started down the steps. I called out to him.

"I would wish you reconsider. I would wish you stay for a spell. Please, return to me…. It would do my constitution much good…. It would lift my spirits…. Claus, please…."

I listened. The creaking steps went silent. I was grateful.

"Please?"

I waited out the silence. After a moment, he spoke to me from the staircase.

"How can you ask such a thing? How can you mean what you say? Does the joy of a family so easily put my misdeeds behind us? Do they become that insignificant?"

Then after a pause, he continued in a lowered voice.

"I am unsure which is worse."

"I do mean what I say. I mean every word. Please, Claus. Return to me. We have so many interests to discuss. It's been far too long a time."

I waited. Finally, I heard the creaking of the staircase move across the landing. Christopher reappeared in the doorway. This time he carried an air of frustration.

"Come in. Come here." I patted the bedside. "Sit with me."

He entered the room obediently, and sat quietly upon my bed. He was undeniably disconcerted. He was yet lost for words. I could see there was some tragedy in his eyes as if he had witnessed his greatest treasure slip through his fingers, something very dear. I might even say I saw a misting of those blue orbs—that is to say if this man ever had it in him to cry—something I sincerely doubted.

Under that thick skin of his, it had to be emotional helter-skelter like popcorn going insane, thoughts flying about every which way. The notion he might possess a son must have been beyond his wildest conceivable imaginings. Not to mention, a son being raised by another man…. I struggled to enjoy the sensation, but it wasn't the joy I anticipated. I held so much power over him at this moment; I should have been giddy, but found myself far from it.

"It does me wonders to see your face after all these years, I like your beard; it's thick. I like all that white hair. My word, what a crop of white.... It suits you." I smiled. "I can see you're eating well."

He ran his fingers through his hair. He took a deep breath and shook his head. No words came out.

"Have you nothing to say?"

His eyes shifted in my direction.

"You have a fine-looking lad for a son."

"Thank you. He looks a lot like his father."

Christopher's eyes were fixed upon me. They narrowed, but he yet lacked the courage to ask the obvious. The room became uncomfortably quiet.

"A continent away, a decade apart and that's it? You make a poor excuse for company, Claus."

"I think I've already said plenty. I'm such a fool, Elizabeth. How could I have overlooked the possibility of you being married with family? I don't know. I suppose isolation out west has its price; it whittles away at one's intelligence. But I am most astonished that Mary made no mention of it. I fear she must have believed I would never have replied or returned to Boston had I known."

"Would you have?"

"Ahh...I suspect not. What reason would there be; to bring you more grief? I think a great deal of Mary, but she has her husband and family to care for her. She needs nothing from me. And now, the same holds true for you."

"Seeing that you mentioned it, why *are* you in Boston?"

Christopher flinched. He was weighing something in his mind.

"Forgive me, Mary." He uttered an apology to the heavens. "It would be much easier to say that I was here on business, and I chose to stop by and pay a visit to the Sawyers, but that wouldn't be the truth of it. The truth of it is that Mary, bless her soul, was so devastated by your condition, she determined to break her oath of silence and so informed me by letter of your pitiful state. It was her wish that I write you, for she believed my words would bring you comfort. Of course, I now question how likely would that have been the outcome. Let it be known; Mary had no idea I elected to make the trip.

"I find no fault with Mary. You needn't worry. But I am flattered, Claus. I honestly wouldn't imagine anybody taking such an arduous journey in my behalf. What ever would possess you to do such a thing after all these years? Surely, you must have considered to what extent our lives might travel in different directions."

Christopher sat on the bed and studied me. I knew well the look. I remembered how he used to stare at me as if soaking up the sight of me until his soul was fully satiated. It was always his last gesture before leaving me. He began to reflect.

"I was high in the mountains, high above the cabin in the upcountry, when I read Mary's letter. I remember looking across the top of the world, at all that God had created to edge the sky and grace the valley below, and I thought to myself, of all that I can see, nothing compares to the one thing I cannot. And that was you, Elizabeth. Having been given the chance, even if only for a moment before your passing; I knew nothing would stop me from going to your side. So, I departed South Pass the following day without an hour's delay.

"Upon my arrival, I was told that you had regained your vigor. I had expected to hear much worse, and so was overjoyed as you might imagine. But then, I was also apprehensive. It meant that I would have to finally face you. No matter how many years have passed, I would have to unbury my shame. I would have to acknowledge my stupidity, and offer you my apology.

"I came up those stairs not knowing what to expect, to see for myself, and I can only say that I was entirely overcome by the sight of you. I wished only to hold you. I wanted you to know how good you were for my eyes, for my spirit. I wanted you to know how sorry was I.

"It was a long time ago, Elizabeth, but I remember being so preoccupied with righting my wrong that I thought of nothing else. My mistake has weighed heavily upon my soul since that unfortunate day. I never escape it. I would rather have died than not made one final attempt to hear your forgiveness."

Christopher took a deep breath and then changed the subject.

"In any event, I am elated, overjoyed, to see you are doing well…that you are married and most of all that you are happy. The knowing certainly makes my departure all the more agreeable. Tomorrow or the day after, I must go back to where I belong. I departed South Pass with little notice, and I have much pending business that awaits me. You know my life better than most…no rest for the wicked."

Christopher rose to his feet. He looked down at me with a heavy heart. I was lost in my own reflections of desperation, back when my own need for forgiveness, Mary's forgiveness, was paramount. Forgiveness was something I understood, and such understanding softened my heart and opened it to accept his apology.

"I needed to hear you say it hurt, Claus. You have never been anything, but most kind and generous with me. Yet, I wanted you to tell me it wasn't entirely my fault. I wanted to believe you might have suffered over my disappearance. Know it was my only recourse, my only gratification."

"Elizabeth, I freely admit to you, the hurt was unbearable. And I am first to say it was not your fault. God above certainly knows as much. But why, at some point, did you not tell me you were alive? Why did you let me think you were dead for so many years? My God, all this time I thought there was no one left in my life whom I might again adore, and then to discover that you have been alive all along? How many wasted years? I would have made up for my injury to you a thousand times over. A thousand times, Elizabeth, had I been given the opportunity.

"My feelings are so confounded, now that I see you again. I don't know...should I kiss you or spank you? Should I cry or be angry? I stumble to find any coherent thought other than to ask, *why* would you do such a thing?"

"Oh, Claus, Claus, Claus," I sighed with resignation. "I could never begin to convey how humiliated I was over what I had done. In my eyes, I amounted to little more than a whore. When you turned away, I believed I had destroyed everything that was us. If I were anything, but a coward, I would have taken my life. I couldn't bear to face anybody, especially not you. I couldn't return to Boston; I couldn't bring myself to face Mary. The embarrassment was unbearable, insurmountable. All I wished to do from that day on was to die in obscurity and escape my shame. Actually, if you must know, I came damn close to succeeding. Thank the Lord I didn't, for I never realized at the time that I was...."

Pregnant! Oh, my word! I thought to myself. *What am I saying?* I stammered as I rushed to change course.

"I was...ah...was going to discover more about my life, ah... you understand, to live for. Gracie. Gracie came into my life. That's what I am trying to say."

"Gracie?"

"A child under my care. Later I will tell you about her."

"Elizabeth, I never meant to put you through such torment. You were always my joy. I wanted to give you everything. But what you asked of me was overwhelming. Your request left me lost. Your words made sense, your argument was valid, but my heart...."

"It wasn't just you and me that night. When you were in my arms, I kept seeing Rebecca. I tried to put her in the past, but I have never overcome Rebecca's death, Elizabeth. You know that better than anyone. I felt as though she was standing there at the side of the bed.

"After you fell asleep, I struggled to justify my actions to her, to myself, but I could not. My only feeling was one of shame and betrayal both to you and Rebecca.

"Years ago, I had an affair with a girl named Brig Rings. She was as full of life as any woman I ever met. She had the ability to make me laugh, to help me put aside my pain. Yet, I always knew that she captained a ship, and like me, she also had to sail away. That fact allowed me to have her companionship without the threat of a permanent relationship. She wasn't free to displace my memories of Rebecca, and so I was safe."

Christopher stood towering over me with his hands in his pockets. He was as big as a locomotive. He was what my son would become. I thought of Christopher as a railroader traveling back to a distant wreck so he might place one derailed car, one derailed hope, after another back on the track of time. He wanted to leave me believing repairs were complete, believing the damage was no longer visible, believing our lives would roll on smoothly forward. I listened to him and, sadly, I believed him.

"You are now a married woman, and I have nothing to lose by these accounts. You were so very attractive. You deserved better than me, Elizabeth. You deserved a man who would cherish you and your affections above all else, not compare it to a love taken tragically, a love buried too deep in one's scarred heart to be pried out.

"You are so much a part of my past, so much a part of my life, with or without Rebecca. I love you, Elizabeth. I always have, you must believe what I say is true. I longed for you at my side on every occasion, and I would have you with me now if that were again possible.

"But having said as much, I couldn't have lied or pretended that Rebecca wouldn't have been a part of our lives until I went to my grave. I'll never escape her. I have no desire to escape her. That night you asked me in desperation to be patient, to understand. Can you do so now, can you understand? Can you forgive me?"

He had the power to mold me. Even at my age, I could barely make my own decisions in his presence. I had no choice but to forgive him. It was what he needed. It was what he wished, and in one ironic twist of fate, that made it my crusade.

"All I have for you is love, Claus. You are a good man. I owe you everything, and it is true, I do understand better than anyone about Lady Rebecca. Know everything worked out. Time does that, Claus. Would you sit me up please?"

Christopher leaned over the bed and brought me up to a sitting position. I dangled my skinny legs to the side.

"I must look a fright."

I tried to put some order to my hair.

"Never in my eyes, Elizabeth. Never. You are a beautiful woman. You have always been beautiful inside and out—a beautiful child, a beautiful girl, a beautiful woman. I am sorry I cannot show you how you fill me with desire."

Christopher sank to his knees. He took my hand between his. He then kissed it with the deepest of feeling and respect. I kissed him gently on the top of that thick cloud of white hair. He looked up at me.

"Elizabeth." He shook his head. "I am the fool. Why shouldn't you be married? You are such a fine woman. I can't believe my arrogance. I am embarrassed. Forgive me the liberty I took, my insensitivity. I didn't mean to disgrace you before your son. As always, I am stupid to the bone."

"Don't fret, Claus. Son, or no son, I am not married. I could never marry. I lied for a moment's pleasure, simple revenge at your expense. As before, I hope it hurt. If it didn't then lie, it would do my pride well. Truthfully I haven't been kissed since last in your bed. I rather enjoyed your advance."

Christopher went rigid. Only his eyes lifted, and he gave me that snake in the grass look. He turned to look through the bedroom door and into the hallway now empty. I knew Luke was immediately returned to Christopher's mind. What a jolt it must have been to see my son's face. Nonetheless, this was my secret, and I would be hell bent before I revealed anything. He looked back at me, and I was ready and waiting.

"You say then, you're not married?"

"Not in the least, never have, probably never will be."

"You are *not* married," he asserted.

"No. Why should I be?"

"Everything you have said, all this deceit is for nothing more than the benefit of my agony."

"And my pleasure. Let us not overlook that."

"Then you should indeed be pleased. In fact, your pride should soar, for the words cut through me like a knife. The thought of you belonging to another pained me as dreadfully as your disappearance, possibly worse."

He twisted his head in search of an explanation.

"Why?"

"Why not? You're such a hard man to hold, Claus. For once, I felt I had you in my hand. Short lived I grant you, but nevertheless, admit it, for a moment there you were mine."

I made a clenched fist out of my hand and shook it.

"I had you—right here."

Christopher let go of me and sat back on his haunches. I waited.

"It's true. No one has kissed you but me?"

"No one."

"The boy, he is or is not your son?"

"Every blonde hair on his head is mine. He is special, isn't he?"

"That boy. Excuse me, your boy, *your son,* I should say. He is your son by blood then, not adopted?"

"Adopted! I should say not! He is mine, all mine, flesh and blood. Damn good breeding, if I say so myself. Terrible time having him. Big boy, isn't he, much like you. In fact, he reminds me a great deal of you. I suppose it has to do with all that blonde hair. Maybe even the blue eyes. Same shade, I think. I often looked into those eyes and wondered to where did you run. Yes, Claus, I imagine you probably looked a lot like that when you were his age."

Christopher glared at me. I could only wonder what must have been going through his mind—seeing his self like that.

217

"Did the boy's father pass on, if I may ask?" He began to pry a little less delicately.

"Lord no! I'm sure he's around somewhere. One day the man just walked out of my life. Never saw him again. It was up to me to raise Luke on my own, and so I did. That's all that matters, I guess. He's a good boy. You'd be proud of him."

Christopher watched me. The game rolled on.

"Elizabeth...Is there any chance I might know this boy's father?"

"It wouldn't surprise me. Who don't you know? But I don't care to discuss the man. You see, the scoundrel left me when I needed him most."

I looked at Claus with an expression of suspicion. A grin crept across my face.

"Why such interest in my son, Claus? Are you looking to be a father?

"Elizabeth, I beg you stop this ruse. You must tell me. Am I the boy's father? Did you not say that no one has kissed you but me?"

"I beg your pardon? What you *am* is arrogant!"

"Forgive—."

"I am entirely offended by your presumption—."

"Forgive me, Eliz—."

"Did no one tell you...*kissing* is not what makes babies. In fact, I should scream to the heavens 'Yes, Claus, I kissed you. You and only you. Of course, you are Luke's father. Can't you see it? Can't you see the likeness? Everyone else certainly does.

"That is precisely what I should do. What mother wouldn't guarantee her son an empire filled with more wealth than even

God knows how to oversee. But, alas, my dear Claus, that would forever leave you to wonder whether or not...I lied for the money."

With that, I shut my mouth.

Christopher rumbled inside, an explosion boxed in with ribbon and bow.

EIGHTY-ONE

Christopher desperately wanted me to confirm Luke as his son. To hell with that; I would not. From the moment he shook the boy's hand, he knew he was a father. It was instant. I wasn't surprised. As I told him, Mary saw it at once. Allen saw it at once, and so did everybody else. It was impossible not to see it. When Christopher arrived in Boston, it was as if the blue dog came sneaking around the red dog house. One look at the pup, and...well, what more need be said. In spite of how it looked, I wasn't about to serve up my ties with Luke's father and sever my ties to Christopher's son. My secret was my leverage.

Only my eyebrows failed to rise over the fact that more than a month had passed since Christopher's arrival, and he was still coming by the cottage. In spite of Mary's private convictions about Luke, even she was astonished by Mr. Claussen's hovering. Maybe, I shouldn't say astonished, pleased might better describe her feeling. If two people on earth could fully appreciate the wanderlust that permeated Christopher Claussen's soul, it would be Mary and me.

Whereas, Christopher's predicament was brutally awkward, for me it remained quite comical. Oftentimes, an outsider would happen by and strike up conversation in the yard. The outsider would be talking to Christopher, and upon seeing Luke approach, would stop the conversation a moment to compliment Christopher on a fine likeness of a son.

"Good looking, boy, broad shouldered like the old man...."

"Chip off the old block, if ever I saw one...."

"Remarkable resemblance...."

Christopher could only smile and stand silently nodding his head, feeling like a fool spouting guarded responses.

"He's a fine son to be sure."

"He's a hard worker to be sure."

"He's respectful to his mother to be sure."

"What father wouldn't hope for such a lad?"

"What father wouldn't be proud?"

Christopher would say almost anything except *'my son.'* He didn't dare utter words to support such assumptions, for Luke was directly impacted by such talk.

My discussions with Mary concluded that Christopher was unwilling to leave Luke. To date he had been making various excuses about having to address affairs of business down at the docks, matters that were keeping him at the Barrington longer than he anticipated. Most of what he said, I took to be truth. But every available moment free of those matters, those affairs of business, was spent with Luke.

Weeks passed on and it was becoming obvious that some changes were in order.

"Mary, I think the time has come for Luke and me to move into my apartment."

"I know. I told Allen it was coming. I understand. You and Mr. Claussen need your privacy. It seems since his arrival in Boston, I hardly see hair or hide of Luke anyway."

"It's more than just a matter of privacy, Mary. It's a matter of wearing out our welcome. Luke, Claus, and I now outnumber you and Allen in your own home. You know, Luke would never leave, but the situation makes both Claus and I very uncomfortable. We feel it rude of us to continue in this manner."

"It's no bother—."

"I know, I know, Mary. That's the problem. For you and Allen, it would never be a bother. You would let us stay forever. And we cannot. We cannot, Mary. It's time for us to say thank you for all you and Allen have done and move on."

"It's not my place to argue, I know, but I'm going to miss you. I'm going to miss our applesauce pies and teas in the garden."

"Oh, no, no, no, Mary…now, I never said anything about giving up any of that. I said it was time to move. I never said anything about throwing my life to the dogs."

Mary started laughing. We hugged each other and laughed. I couldn't imagine anything changing between us, but it was time to set up house in a place of my own. I wanted a place where Christopher could enjoy Luke in privacy. I was now fully recovered from my illness, and strong enough to make the move into my apartment.

Unfortunately, my apartment had only two bedrooms. Luke was assigned one and I the other. The thought of sleeping with Christopher after such a disastrous affair years ago was out of the question. Not to mention, we weren't living out west, and in Boston the Blue Laws made any sleeping arrangement outside the bonds of marriage overtly scandalous. In Boston there were still too many folks who remembered Lady Rebecca announcing my adoption, too many folks who believed I was Elizabeth Claussen, Christopher's daughter.

Christopher was keenly aware of these beliefs, and so preferred to retire at his suite in the Barrington. His routine had become one of arriving most mornings in his coach with breads and pastries for our breakfast. He then contented himself by spending the following hours at my side in polite conversation, except when making forays into town with Luke or to paying visits to his shipping concerns at the harbor, and even that was usually with Luke in his presence.

He tried to talk me into moving into the Barrington where all the amenities of the wealthiest lifestyle were at my disposal. I declined respectfully, gently reminding him that the Barrington was Lady Rebecca's home, and he made no further mention of it. Instead, one morning while having our coffee, he proposed an alternative.

"Elizabeth?"

"Yes."

"Do you remember Mr. McKenny? He and his family lived next door to Allen and Mary, on the south side."

"Yes."

"I met him this morning when I stopped by Sullivan's for our pastries. While we awaited our turn at the counter, we struck up a conversation, and he informed me of his intention to move his family to New York. Apparently, he has been offered a partnership in an insurance agency, which he believes will prove to be most lucrative.

"I took the liberty of asking what price he intends to place on his home. He gave me his price, and I assured him that I was very interested in purchasing the property. I said I would get back to him presently with my decision. The idea of a quick sale served to please him immensely, as you might imagine.

"Whether or not I purchase will be determined by you, Elizabeth. If you would wish to live with me in that residence, I would surely have it by Christmas. If not, of course, I will decline and eventually return myself to the Rocky Mountains. You have my word, there will be no dishonorable demands made upon your good nature. The house and grounds are spacious both inside and out, and therefore offers Luke and yourself ample room to enjoy your privacy when needed. In the very least, it will not give rise to incestuous speculation. The house is too large for a widowed father alone.

"And of course, it goes without saying; you would be calling distance from Mary, and a stone's throw from her garden. As for myself, I would be overjoyed to have you and Luke nearer to me. It would bring me great pleasure to again care for you in person, and need I say anything about my affection for Luke. So, I ask that think over these matters, Elizabeth, and inform me of your wishes. You must tell me what you would have me do."

"I have nothing to think over, Claus. I think it's a splendid idea. I believe your influence will advance Luke's position in life as it did my own. He will be a very fortunate boy to have such a mentor within his home."

And so it was with mixed feelings that I closed up my apartment for good. It had been the place I called home for some twenty odd years, but tragically a place that remained empty for most, and sadly, one that never offered me the comfort I enjoyed at Mary's.

The move was fast and painless. Christopher had a local firm, JL Richards Livery and Undertakings, pack my furniture and belongings, and transport them to our new place. Much of my personal belongings had been packed months back in order to make room for Luke and his mounting collection of interests.

I had also considered removing my lifelong bed from my room at Mary's to our new place; but in the end, it felt too much like cutting the umbilical cord to my foundations. The bed stayed in my bedroom at Mary's, along with my many childhood possessions.

For every item left behind, I imported twenty. Christopher provided me an unlimited allowance to be used as I pleased, and I spent all of a month buying furniture and accessories to furnish empty rooms. As long as I was pleased with my acquisitions, Christopher remained silent.

Christopher seemed to settle in to our home with little effort or concern. The extent of his comfort in the new residence was brought to light one evening when he and Luke brought home some very special guests for a holiday dinner and drinks. It was Marion McCurry and his wife Virginia. I wouldn't have known him from Adam. He was now getting on in years. I dare say the man was in his seventies.

They led a troupe of chefs from the Barrington Hotel who promptly went about preparing a meal of no small proportion. The evening was a raucous affair with loud and boisterous conversation of shipping, memories, and stories from the past.

Marion was genuinely overjoyed at the sight of me, and claimed that laying his eyes upon my still beautiful face brought back a sea chest of memories long since forgotten. They told more stories about me as a child than I could have ever imagined lived by one soul. Luke sat at our table and got an earful of those stories and times. He was trying to imagine life aboard a ship that coursed the oceans for months or years at a time. He kept looking over at me, and I believe it was the first time that he viewed me as much more than just his mother.

I had forgotten to what extent the world swirled about Christopher wherever he set foot. I don't believe Mary and Allen could recall having such a good time in ages. We were reckless with drink, and rocked in our seats as we tried to recall many of the old songs of the sea. We pined sorely for Darin O'Kurk, God rest his soul, and we toasted him lavishly. On that night, between family and friends, the drink, the food and merriment, our house was christened a home.

I hadn't enjoyed a Christmas season the likes of these days since I was a child at the Barrington under the care of Christopher and Lady Rebecca. My years with Mary and Allen brought wonderful holiday memories as well, but not the level of excitement that I recalled in my younger years in the Claussen household.

I would have written such recollections off to memories made through the eyes of a child, had it not been for my present state of mind. I was so happy, so uplifted, so enamored with life and the season of Christmas. I knew it was because I was in the presence of Christopher. To be around the man was to be free of worry, free of heartache or need. It was to live in God's light.

Not only for me, but for many others. Christopher carted Luke about town in style as they oversaw the delivery of food and toys and trinkets beyond count. Crate load after crate load was hauled up from the docks and ushered through Boston's streets to every orphanage known in the area and beyond.

Unlike Lady Rebecca, who sweet talked the wealthy into donating, making such generosity known and admired in those circles, Christopher's generosity went unseen by all except those in the streets. At the gutter, in the camps of the homeless, in the homes of the impoverished; there were the stories of his glory. In those places, and in the hearts of the urchins that moved like mists through the dark, would be found the name of Christopher Claussen spoken with reverence; not for his success in business or his wealth, but for his benevolence. If Christopher hadn't impressed upon Luke the joy of doing for others, then Luke learned it himself by example. Christopher overlooked no child.

Raising Luke to be moral had been my responsibility and only my responsibility for more than a decade. It was that way by season or by month, by clock or by sun. It was that way in the best of time and the worst. It was also plain as day to see how Christopher longed to be allowed inside our intimate relationship.

In spite of Christopher's efforts to be officially named Luke's father, I remained unresponsive to his plight, not dismissive, but supremely cautious. After all, there were no plans in store for us to wed. In Boston, that would have been impossible, and I would never have entertained any such proposal in any event.

Unfortunately for Christopher, without marriage, without adoption, without my acknowledgment that he had fathered Luke, he couldn't positively say the boy was of his stock. He was unable to either make any demand or take any liberty with the boy. Without my blessing, Christopher would never be able to tell the world that Luke was his flesh and blood, his pride and joy.

Aside from this impasse, substantial as it was, I believe that Luke filled a deep-rooted need for purpose that haunted Christopher as far back as I could remember. Christopher lived to provide for Lady Rebecca. Later, he channeled that need to provide toward me. But now, to have a son, to give heart and soul, to offer the world to his own flesh and blood, this was the quintessence of Christopher's existence.

Luke brought peace to Christopher. I wouldn't say Luke changed the man, I would say he brought out a facet of his personality that had been buried by too many years alone. Christopher appeared more relaxed. He laughed easier. His eyes sparkled with a fresh vigor. I would have alleged that Christopher actually encouraged Luke to distract him from his sphere of commerce, and if true, that was a side of Christopher that possibly only Lady Rebecca and I had ever seen.

The Christmas season came and went as did the cold of winter. The bond between the three of us was strong and close. Luke and I rarely stepped outside the house unless in the company of Christopher. Over the course of trips about town, I came to believe that Christopher commanded more respect from those around him now than in his younger days, if that was even possible. It was true that he was a great hulk of a man, and crowds would part way for him on sight, but I decided it had to be due more to the thick crop of white hair, and the chiseled look of his white beard that when combined gave him a most distinguished look, a look by far more impressive in later years than in the vitality of youth.

Even I now related to Christopher differently. All my years of awe and respect, even my fear of his displeasure, were behind me. He had taken me to his bed and made a woman of me. Whether I admitted it or not, he had fathered my son, and for better or for worse; he would be forever the man of my heart. Christopher always made me feel special. I always felt as though I was the focal point of his attention, and I imagine because of it, he could do little wrong in my eyes. The attention he paid to Luke only served to further strengthen my positive convictions about the man.

Christopher often acted similar to Tandor, the Sawyers' retriever. I would watch him pace back and forth like a tail-wagging dog, waiting impatiently for Luke to finish his lessons so they might be off on a run. Occasionally, they would return home at a late hour, as on the night of Luke's thirteenth birthday, a night when I voiced my express dissatisfaction with Claus.

To be honest, I feared little, because not only was Luke in the best of company, but the boy could take care of himself with or without Claus. I raised my great fuss mostly to corner Christopher into an admission that the boy was mine to celebrate, not his, and he would do well to respect my feelings.

My admonishments exasperated Christopher to be sure, and after observing the look in his eyes, I strongly suggested he not say anything that he might later come to regret. If he had an opinion to express, he instead felt it best kept quiet and close to heart. I was upset and so retired for the night.

EIGHTY-TWO

"Where are you?"

I spun around.

"Oh. Hello, Mary. I never heard you come in."

"That's an understatement. I said hello, and you just stood there staring out the window all somber looking. What's on your mind?"

"Mmmm."

"I baked some cookies, so I thought I'd bring over a batch with spiced tea. I put them in the kitchen. Do you have time for tea?"

"I'll put a kettle on."

"Liz! Where are you? I just said that I brought a pot of spiced already steeped. Come, let's sit. Are you in there?"

"Mmm."

I shrugged. I followed Mary to the kitchen and sat down. A tray of cookies along with the tea pot were sitting upon the table.

"Oh, those smell good—cinnamon."

"Enjoy."

"Thank you."

I picked at a cookie. I had little appetite.

"You're not yourself."

"What?"

"I said, you are not yourself. What's the matter?"

"Why would you say that?"

"You were quiet yesterday. But today, you are practically comatose. Those are freshly baked cookies and you barely tasted one."

"I'm fine."

"Well, something's troubling you. I can see it all over your face, and you're fidgeting. You're worried."

"You know me far too well, Mary."

"I used to think so. That may have been true once, but I'm not so sure anymore. You are a lot more mysterious to me now than when I used to hold you in my arms. You're a different person. Not for the better, not for the worse, just different, more pensive, it seems to me."

I sat there hearing her words. My mind felt numb to some extent. Much like the old expression, 'the gate's closed, but the cow's gone.'

"I want to ask you a question, Mary."

"Fire away. Today, I feel as if I have an answer for everything."

"Do you remember that day long ago, in Lady Rebecca's coach, when that old fortune teller said I was the chosen one, and then ran off like a scared rabbit?"

"If I hadn't, you've reminded me a time or two through the years."

Mary laughed at her recollections. I smiled, but my eyes were downcast. I was considering how some private thoughts might be better left unsaid. I was having a change of heart.

"Well, go on. You were special, and I was jealous. So what of it?"

"Ahh, actually, it was nothing. It was nothing…silly thoughts. So…what's our Allen up to today?"

"Allen? Allen nothing. What were you about to ask? You get me all curious and then say it was nothing but silly thoughts. Spit it out, girl. What's the question?"

"You're going to think I'm a lunatic."

"Think? Are you kidding? You are a lunatic. Now spit it out."

I took a deep breath. I knew before saying another word that Mary would never accept what troubled me. I just wanted desperately to share my insecurities with someone even if the other person was left doubting my state of mind.

"Have you noticed how many children are outside—across the street?"

"Have I noticed? How could I not notice? You must tell Mr. Claussen to stop giving those kids money. If he wasn't constantly catering to them, they wouldn't hang around. He can't keep coming home every night and hand out coins and trinkets. Was there ever a day this summer when you didn't see ten or twelve of them camped out in the lot? My God, they pray to see a sign of him. They'll waste an entire day waiting around to pick up a dollar or two. I've forgotten how nice it is to be so young that you can waste away the hours without remorse."

"Haven't we both. My word, where have the years gone? But, you know Christopher as well as me; and I don't have to tell you the man lives to wander amidst those rascals. He always

230

admired their spunk. He's coddled those strays for as long as I can remember.

"Christopher has spent a good deal of time with his charities. He has always said that as long as he is in Boston, he intends to look into his funded organizations, confirm needs are being met and books are in order. According to him, most of these urchins are accounted for and being cared for in town. And that seems to be the case because the lot has been empty for the most part. It's just that the last few days there has been a change."

"You bet there has," asserted Mary. "The last few days they have been coming in by the droves. There must be forty or fifty over there right now and I saw more coming up the road as I walked over. That was the main reason I stopped by. I'm worried about what the neighbors make of it.

"What takes place between you and Mr. Claussen is none of my concern, but for the sake of the neighbors, I felt compelled to ask if you or Mr. Claussen had something to do with the gathering. Has he got one of his projects underway? It seems they are all coming up here from the docks. I figured he must have put out word or something, and they're looking to make some money. Should we look into having food brought up? Do you know anything about this? Do you have any idea what's going on?"

"I do."

"You do? Oh."

"I think so."

"You think so? Okay...you do or you don't know?"

"I am certain they are not here to make money."

"Alright, I give up. Where is your head, Elizabeth? Am I missing something?"

"Mary…I know this is going to sound ludicrous, like I've lost my mind, but every time children gather in my presence like that," I pointed out the window, "within a day or so, something traumatic happens to me. I don't mean to say something bad happens, just something traumatic. …Usually something that makes me cry—cry really hard."

There was a moment of silence. Mary picked up a cookie and began nibbling on it, but she didn't take her eyes off of me. I had unnerved her, and I knew she was sitting there wondering what exactly I meant by that flurry of unsettling words.

"So you think something is going to happen…something to you? You think that these street brats are harbingers of no good and something is going to happen to you."

"I didn't say anything about no good."

"But harbingers nonetheless."

"Possibly."

"That certainly was not the information I was expecting to hear. I'll give you that."

"Do you remember those weeks I was deathly ill?"

"Are you serious?" Mary's head tilted. "Which of us was taking care of you? Of course I remember."

"But do you remember the collection of children in the lot those days before I fell ill?"

Mary hesitated. There were deep furrows cutting across her forehead.

"At this point, I am trying to remember when there wasn't a gang of kids in that lot. Actually, it seems like ever since you arrived in Boston there have been kids in that lot. Let me see…I remember we had quite a few the day that Mr. Claussen arrived.

They came up from the docks. We put food out that day. Oh, yes. I remember he offered each one of the rascals a dollar if they would leave. Within moments the place cleared out right to the last one. I do remember that. I remember thinking, it was funny the things that money could buy."

"How many were there?"

Mary frowned. The question puzzled her.

"I don't know. I remember they ran out into the street...at that point...I imagine thirty...forty...maybe more. ...Enough to stop a coach. I wouldn't have paid that much attention except I first thought the coach belonged to one of the neighbors. I guess I don't understand why you would find a group of kids in the street or in the lot to be that unusual. They wander. They wander all across the city. They haven't really bothered us. I mean, for the most part they've kept to themselves and stayed out of trouble. They haven't yet stolen anything, at least that I know of."

"The last day I looked out the window before I was fully bedridden, there were seventeen children by my count."

"Oh, wait a minute! I remember now. Of course...you never stopped asking about those orphans while you were sick. But, Liz, you were delirious. You were out of your mind with fever. You said all kinds of meaningless gibberish. Somewhere in that head of yours, you were obsessed with those urchins. You were always talking to them in your dreams, but you were really sick, Elizabeth. Neither Allen nor I ever saw anything that caused reason for concern."

"You just said when Christopher arrived, there were thirty or forty. When I became deathly ill, there were at least fifteen or twenty that just showed up out of nowhere. When I was in St. Louis, they filled Rachel's home just hours before Gracie was to tell me that she was leaving me. When I lived with the Tsistsistas, a group of children collected around me the day Luke was thrown

233

off a horse and lie unconscious for a day and a half. I don't believe I ever cried or prayed so hard in my life. As soon as he started showing signs of improvement they disappeared. There were more, maybe fifty or sixty, I don't know, maybe a hundred that appeared in the clearing below the cabin when Christopher and I separated in the Stony Mountains. That day I only wanted to die.

"When Luke was born. There were children everywhere. They were just playing. They weren't doing anything out of the ordinary. But, they were everywhere, Mary, everywhere. There shouldn't have been anything strange about it at all. But it *was* strange."

"Maybe you are just sensitive to children because now you have Luke. It was like when I had the boys. Not a thing having to do with little boys escaped my awareness. I noticed everything that surrounded little boys, mine or otherwise. I swear, sometimes, I felt as if I was the world's nanny."

"The day I became pregnant the children began collecting in a nearby clearing. I was so upset; I closed my self in a cabin so I wouldn't have to endure their stares. They frightened me. The only problem, Mary…Luke was the very last thing on my mind. I had no idea I was pregnant. He wasn't planned."

Mary's face flushed. Her eyes dropped to her hands. Whereas, Mary retained all of her proper New England manners, I had long since abandoned mine. All too often it showed.

"When I think about it, I can remember times, years back, like the day I found Rebecca's coach. I remember the proprietor of those huge warehouses complaining about the children milling about. You probably don't remember me telling you about it. It was that day in the kitchen when I cried. He said they never left. They would always say they were waiting. They waited for Claus to return. What did that man say? What was it? Oh…oh, yes… Santa Claus of the sea. That's what it was…he said, they waited for Santa Claus of the sea."

I vented all of the confused, insane, preposterous, nonsense that was bottled up inside. Mary just sat there looking at me across the brim of her tea cup. She was visibly nervous.

"Well. I am not sure what you want me to say, Liz."

"I don't expect you to say anything, Mary. I am only asking you to remember this conversation. You shouldn't have a problem; it lacks nothing for being bizarre. Maybe, in a week you will be laughing at my expense, and I will feel like a complete fool. But this time, this one time, I am predicting something will occur. I will soon witness or endure something traumatic. It will most likely upset me to the core. I can feel it. The more the children, the worse the event; I know it, Mary. Promise me you will be there for me. Promise me you will stay by my side. I beg you be my witness. Those children have come to warn me."

I must have looked every bit as crazy as I sounded because Mary never uttered another word. She sat in silent concern, looking down at the table. She placed her cup onto the saucer. She then rose from the table and excused herself. I most likely scared the ever-loving daylights out of her because she left the house without as much as a good bye. I assumed that Mary feared I had completely lost my mind, no doubt, the result of my fever. I didn't call out to her. I didn't try and stop her. I had no desire to apologize or repent for the nonsense I sputtered. I felt anxious, troubled, and I didn't want to be bothered.

I turned back to the window where I continued to observe the homeless misfits. I could feel them watching my every move. I felt myself break out in a sweat. It was due to an attack of panic. A sudden fear that maybe, in fact, I was losing my mind. I thought of the Tsistsistas.

I thought of the spirit world in which they believed. I thought about how much of their lives were governed and directed by their communication with their ancestors, the spirits of the dead, the spirits of the animals, the sky and earth. I recalled how a medicine man passed his burning sage over me, and how he called on the spirits to cleanse my soul of demons. I recalled how much better I felt after his ritual. These experiences swayed me. After living with the Indians for a decade, I didn't go around professing my belief in spirits, but then I also didn't go around denying it.

I remained at the window and contemplated. Was I seeing children or spirits? I slipped into deep trance-like thought. My mind was now completely focused, and I was unaware of any petty distractions. I looked backward into time. I hunted for clues. I sought out answers.

It occurred to me that the warning may have arrived days ago, heralded by the very first of the children to come up from the docks. It may be that I, being so comfortable with my day-to-day life, had failed to notice anything beyond my isolated world of contentment. Had I become thoughtless? Had I become selfish? I raked through my brains to recount every hour of every day.

There were too many children. A sign of this size would be no small matter. They frightened me. My heart would have run away had I not reminded myself that on every occasion they appeared, they always came to warn me. They always came to ask about my well-being. If so many children arrived to watch over me, then this had to be about Luke or Claus, the shrines of my soul.

As a mother, Luke was my first concern and I went over everything about his life during the last few days. It all seemed perfect. He seemed happy. His studies were progressing rapidly. He had voiced no concern or complaint. Over and over, I scoured every memory for any clue to the contrary. I found nothing.

I then directed all my concentration on Christopher. When I considered concern or complaint, I found nothing. When I asked myself about his happiness, my chest suddenly collapsed. The breath was driven out of me. This revelation wasn't something I discovered, this was presented to me. It was here I would find my answer.

I delved deeper, following my feelings. There was something. I brought my memories of him into focus. I pored over his every expression, his actions, his moods—*the look in his eyes.* And so it was, I found my answer. It was a subtle change, an almost imperceptible cooling of Christopher's affections for me.

Now I could see the way in which he avoided my eyes when we spoke. He appeared fine and jovial on the outside, but his eyes began to tell a different story. They drifted. He tended to look away more often when we conversed, as if subconsciously irritated by the sight of me. His eyes were often distant as if he were looking into another world, a place he would rather be. He had become less talkative in my world. I began to recall how, now and then, he would distance himself while in my presence, at times quietly moving away, at times leaving the room, or taking a walk without saying a word about his stepping out. His congeniality, his good humor was less apparent. As of late, I realized he had grown considerably more restless.

Most notably, I could see how Christopher's eyes were focused on Luke. He was made drunk by Luke's presence. Enlisting actions that cried out louder than the words Christopher was not allowed to speak, he made it known at every opportunity; he wanted to be recognized as a father. It had been brought to my attention that Christopher was suffering embarrassment at the hands of others, who were circulating brow-raising rumors about his questionable connection to my son.

Christopher was cornered. I knew he had no desire to cross me. He knew that he couldn't afford to cross me, for he sought to hear my words, my admission that he had a son and heir by blood. He prayed to pass on a dynasty to Luke. He hardly dared dream that his lifetime of work might not dissipate into oblivion, but rather be built upon and reinforced by a son who would share his same ideals. His eyes begged me to be a part of this splendid child who held so much promise in so many ways. It was all in the eyes.

Only I could grant these dreams. Only I held the key that could unshackle his heart. Only I could offer him the freedom to express his pride. I knew he would do anything for me, anything at all, for only a hint of hope that I might someday give him one thing in return.

I resented the pressure, the sense of obligation. I went out of my way to make sure I asked for nothing. I made certain I owed nothing. I was no match for Christopher Claussen, and I feared the quicksand of his power and persuasion. I feared his ability to instantly strip me of everything should he choose.

Christopher had mounted a one-man crusade to disavow the rumors and common misbelief that I was his stepdaughter. Dismantling forty years of accepted myth was no minor feat, and yet, failing to do so would leave him the father of his daughter's child. For a man who lived larger than life, a man who lived in stories told by others, legends of greatness from sea to sea; Christopher was being reduced to chasing down rumors that worked to suffer him the worst form of dishonor. Incest.

The scandal was titillating. And so attempts to defend his honor, might well have been impossible. The harder he tried, the worse it looked. Christopher, being intelligent enough to under- stand as much, held his tongue, but would see a return to his life out west as his only option. He could leave the unfairness of a myth behind in Boston, but could he leave a son? Never. This is what I knew. This is what I feared.

Claus would be determined to sway Luke into accompanying him back to the wilds, a place where Luke was very much at home.

I might refuse to reveal Christopher's relationship to Luke and possibly lose my son to his persuasion. Or I could grant Christopher his one wish, and know for certain I would lose Luke forever to the wonders of his father's world. The future of this country followed the tracks of a railroad. The future of my son and Christopher's dynasty would ride together on those same rails.

As I stood watching the children, it was as if they were filling my head with an insight into these things of which I had paid too little attention, these things heretofore swept underneath my consciousness. Pains placed beyond cups of spiced tea and freshly baked cookies, pains put out of mind beyond horizons at great distance from chairs in the garden.

I had now looked back and realized that a fine crack, which had formed in our relationship, one to which I may have chosen to disregard, was now a crevice about to engulf me. This fracture was called resentment. It was the acid eating through Christopher's heart.

I returned from my contemplation. I wrestled with my position regarding the relationship between Luke and Christopher. I felt no remorse for my actions, for I had not led Christopher on with false hope or pretense. Maybe I was jealous of their relationship, the way Luke turned to Christopher for advice— ground that was once mine alone. Maybe I was afraid to reveal the truth that I feared losing my grip on the only two men I ever loved. Maybe I suffered from that age old mother's fear of losing my baby. Whatever the reason, I understood that I held one card only. I alone could name Luke's father, and as long as I held that card, I controlled everything. Once I laid it down, everything controlled me.

EIGHTY-THREE

I was now distracted from such deep agonizing thoughts by fresh activity across the road. A number of men arrived with a wagon. I watched as two men dragged large bolts of canvas off the bed. Others reached over the sides and lifted out a sizeable quantity of poles.

The bolts were unrolled and as the poles where spaced out, I understood that a large tent was being raised for the children. Mary was moving full speed ahead, caring for the unfortunates as was her way. I was rather amused by the fact that shelter and attention was being given to the very same children that I was convinced were here to foretell my impending misery.

Mary probably needed distance from me. I hadn't talked to her the last couple of days, at least since our conversation in the kitchen. It was for the better because I wasn't in a mood to join her or walk over and be a part of the activities taking place across the road. I was entirely preoccupied with these children, who made me agitated and irritable. I preferred to remain in the security of my house and brace myself for the approaching manifestation.

I siphoned off my anxiety by making cookies and pacing through the house while they baked. Back and forth, passing from one room to the next, I glanced across the road out of each window. Maybe it was, maybe it wasn't in my head; but I would have sworn on a bible that their eyes followed me window to window as I paced.

It went thus, for some time before my last couple of glances observed a marked change in the crowd. The random activity of previous hours now appeared suddenly focused with an increasing number of children looking along the lane toward town. My heart skipped a beat.

Mary suddenly rushed by the window barely an arm's reach away. She was walking hurriedly toward my kitchen. Something was up. I moved toward that room.

"Elizabeth? Elizabeth!"

Instead of walking into my house as would have been her custom, she knocked rapidly. The respect shown was a sign of her lingering discomfort.

"My word, Mary. Why are you knocking on my door? Are we that upset? For the love of God, come in. What is it?"

"I must talk fast. I came as quickly as I was able, but Mr. Claussen is fast on my heels. I cannot stay but a moment."

"Did something happen to Luke?"

"Yes and no. Luke is fine, but Mr. Claussen is very upset."

"About what?"

"Let's go to the window where we can watch for him. I don't want him to see me here. I only came to forewarn you that there was an incident at the Presbyterian community center about an hour ago, and the man is in a foul mood and fit to be tied. You best be prepared."

"Mary, please! What happened?"

"Well, you know this morning I asked Luke to go with me down to the community center. I thought his experiences out west, living with the Tsistsistas and all would prove invaluable being that we were hosting a fundraiser for the benefit of the local homeless Indians."

"Yes, I know, I know."

"Yes, yes. Well, Mr. Claussen stopped by to see how Luke was doing. You know how he is; he never leaves that boy's side. He had finished whatever affairs he had at the docks and so came

241

by the community center. He came over to greet me, and we were off to the side discussing the decorations and looking over some of the exhibits when a bit of a ruckus caught our attention—what are those urchins looking at?"

"What?"

"What are they looking at? They look restless. Is Mr. Claussen coming?"

"No, no, I don't think so." We both stared intently down the road. "I don't see anything. So, go on, tell me what happened."

"I don't know if you know or remember the Fargo boy...."

"Ahh, vaguely...tall, red head, upper crust."

"That's the one. Well...the boy fancies himself to be quite an authority on Indian matters. He certainly knows more than most, and I suspect he never anticipated being anything less than the last word on how the exhibits would be displayed at the center.

"Unfortunately for Mr. Fargo's ego, Luke, who generally keeps to himself unless approached, was happy to offer his advice on the quiet, and so answered every question asked of him with obvious knowledge. In short time, Mr. Claussen and I were as captivated by his answers as was everyone present with the sole exception of Mr. Fargo. As Mr. Claussen and I observed it, much to the consternation of Mr. Fargo, Luke suggested that a freshly erected tipi be rotated so the entrance might face east; the direction of the rising sun, that being accurate by Indian custom.

"It was at that point that Mr. Fargo completely lost his humor, and in fact reduced himself to a mean-spirited and insulting cad. He was aware of Luke being without father and promptly called him an Indian bastard in front of the entire group. He accused Luke of using the venue to construct respect for himself in lieu of his lack of surname and unfortunate breeding.

"Elizabeth, we were all taken aback by the insult to be sure, but in my shock, I turned to face Mr. Claussen, and I must tell you…. I have never seen such a look of rage upon his face in all the years I served. I don't believe I have ever seen such rage on any man's face. I lacked the courage to comment or make any mention of what words had passed. I couldn't bring myself to say a word about the incident, but for the extent of his apparent anger. I left him with Luke and pressed my buggy to reach you."

"Was Luke alright?"

"Truthfully, Luke held the high ground in every way. You would have been proud. He took the insult in stride. Instead of striking out, he brushed it off. I have come to know Luke's spirit and I have no doubt he had it within him to drop the fellow in his tracks. Thankfully, he remained a gentleman and so earned the respect of all present."

"It reminds me of my ordeal as a server at the Barrington—."

"As it did me! It most certainly did. And, I believe what made matters worse, was Mr. Claussen's overhearing Luke offering an apology for his behavior and for acting braggy if that was how he had been perceived.

"I rushed over at once, Elizabeth, for I fear Mr. Claussen shall return home in the foulest—."

I abruptly shifted my gaze through the window; a motion that cut Mary off mid-sentence. I stepped quickly to the farthest window. From there I studied the mood of the children. The children had gathered in force. I could feel fate shifting before my eyes. I next heard the high-stepping hooves of Claus's coach horses clopping up the road. I saw it round the corner and fast approach the house. My heart raced.

"He comes. I must leave. Do take care, Elizabeth."

"That I shall. Go! Go, before he sees you."

Seconds after Mary ran across our back yards, the coach was brought to a halt at the front of her place. I watched as Luke jumped out onto the road. He turned to wave to Christopher. He appeared calm and in a good way, but instead of coming home, I watched him cross the front yard to Mary's door. There would be no reason for Luke to go to Mary's unless trouble was brewing. Was this the first sign? The carriage continued on to our yard. My chest felt tight. My heart was pounding. I didn't know what to expect.

I stood worried at the window. I glanced one last time across the road and felt no joy in seeing the field of children looking back at me. The back door swung open and startled me as it slammed into the side of the house. I heard his boots pounding their way through the house. I knew. I looked away from those forlorn faces beyond to see Christopher coming directly toward me. His eyes were reddened by rage. Their fury staked me in place. I stood unable to move. He was overtaken by something terrible.

"Luke! Luke! The boy looked up at me! And he asked me! 'Mr. Claussen... are...you...my...my.... Are you my...*father?!*'"

He spoke as if his words and feelings were jamming up hard, one behind the other, until all hell broke loose, and the word *father* exploded across the room, shattering the peace, blowing past me with the roar of a thousand lions. I felt it rumble through me like a blast of thunder. I was panicked to my core.

His fist upended the dining table, sending it flying across the room, scattering chairs, crushing a hutch stacked with dishes. They came crashing to the floor seconds ahead of the paintings and planters that had been affixed to the wall. I was petrified. His eyes were livid, swollen, tears pouring out. He was out of his mind, thrashing in blind anger. I backed away, but he came straight at me like a runaway bull. I was pinned between the wall at my back and his boiling temper in my face.

"What do I tell that boy! That boy? No! My son! What do I tell my son! Do I lie to him? Do I say I am not, when I know in the heart of my heart he is my very flesh and blood? Do I tell him that his mother lies by her deceitful ways, not by what she says, but by what she does not? Do I tell him how she keeps her deepest secret from me—*from him*? Tell me, Elizabeth! What would you expect of me when I stand powerless as my son endures the worst of insults!

"This god-damned charade ends now! This dance of deception you insist I do in front of family and friends, and before whomever else it pleases you in order to humiliate me. This ends now!"

He plowed his fist into the wall with such force, I wondered if the house would come down upon us. If I hadn't achieved insanity with thoughts of prophetic children, then surely I reached it now as my temper flashed white hot before this monster of a crazed creature. Call it instinctive, animalistic, a mother's fight for her young, call it insanity, but this was to be a fight to the finish. It was spit and gnashing of teeth, as my screams railed against his.

"And what charade or dance is that, Claus?" I screamed.

He brought his massive fist down upon the side table and drove plates, silverware, and the trays of my baked cookies skyward. He bellowed.

"The charade I endure to appease you, the charade that has made me the laughing stock of the city! You know bloody well, of what charade I speak!"

I recoiled and then struck out.

"You will shut your mouth! You will shut your mouth! I will not be spoken to in that manner! If you have so little respect for me, then you may leave at once, or I shall remove myself to Mary's!"

The arteries on his neck appeared as though they were about to rupture. I could feel the heat rising off of him.

"As you wish. As you wish!" The words passed through his teeth like the hiss of a snake. "I trust you of all people surely must understand what beguiles me so. I am frustrated! I am angry! I am deceived, Elizabeth. I have done everything in my power to please you, to prove I am a worthy father, everything! I have run out of both plans and patience. I am lost for direction. What further must I do? I ask myself, what is the point of remaining in this house, in this unwinnable situation between you and the boy? You haven't given me a son; you have only shown me the son I should have had. I find I love you and I detest you with the same heart. I wish only to hear the words that will bring me the joy of dreams, the words that will put some final purpose to my existence—words that only you can voice. Yet, it is not in your heart to be so kind. You prefer the path of cruelty. You much prefer to see me suffer...."

"Suffer! How *dare* you speak to me of suffering!"

Christopher disappeared behind a sudden flush of my tears.

"Spare me the grief of knowing this has burdened you," I snapped, my voice now climaxing with emotion.

"I never said it was a burden! Not once did I say it was a burden!" he countered.

Christopher began to stomp like a wild bull trapped in its pen. I could feel the weight of his steps shake the floor, but I too was angered. I couldn't stifle my sobs. We were approaching an issue too close to our hearts to be controlled. We were delving into a state of raw emotion. There could be little chance for reason. Christopher would fight for his right to claim Luke, and I would fight to the death to keep my son on my terms, to the death! The temper of my youth had surfaced, the fury that allowed me strike viciously against all odds.

"Spit it out, Claus! Pray tell me what you mean to say. Is it out of your control? Is it too uncomfortable for you to partake in something your hand cannot guide? Is it something like being left on a dock as a young girl with no one to wipe away your tears, while the great ship REBECCA and her captain head out to sea? Is it like waiting day after day, week after week, for something as precious as a letter? Maybe it's like praying on your knees for months that someone you love will show his face at your birthday party or graduation. Or is it more like being left carrying a child, and believing your life is ruined and your decisions have been made for you, and you can do nothing, but wait, and wait, and wait, and cry, and cry alone? It was always in your *absence* that I suffered, and I wouldn't wish that misery on anyone, especially not you, who has always had the means to leave when it suits you, when the heart gets too heavy to bear. Don't let me keep you, Christopher. You may leave! You have always left! Go! You can go! Go, now! Get out! Get out of here! *Get out!!*" I screamed.

I threw a remaining tray of cookies across the kitchen and showered him. He raised his arms in defense. The pan sounded like a gong struck as it ricocheted off his elbow and careened into the wall. My tears gushed forth in torrents, making visible the feelings that I discovered reached far back into my childhood. I was saying terrible things, things that were painful. I wanted the words to slice him to ribbons. I wanted to bleed him from the heart, as had I for far too long.

He had been wounded. I could see it in his face. It went pale for just a second, his breath taken from him. I had knocked him off balance. My win only served to instill a hint of regret. In spite of my anger and my heartless tongue, I could never deny that Christopher had done his best. I knew he was right in many of the things he said, right to be angry, but I was afraid to admit it. I knew I wasn't fighting from a rational point of view, but rather from my instincts as a mother. Christopher had everything to offer Luke, I had only my love.

The expressions of anger and now possibly embarrassment were quick to return, as he regained his momentum. I watched the fury again paint his face red.

"Damn me to hell, woman! What I mean to say…what I mean to say… You know what it is I am saying. Why do you insist on torturing me so? Have I done you so much wrong that you would hang my own blood before my eyes as punishment?

"For the sake of God, if you will not say the boy is mine, at least have enough pity on my wretched soul to say he is not! I beg of you that. At least I might then be able to get on with my life. Can you not find it in your heart to release me from…Ahhggg."

Christopher's face froze into a mask of agony. He slammed his fists against his chest as if to knock himself backwards for some purpose. He staggered into the table, driving it across the floor before crashing down upon the chairs. The force of his fall splintered a chair, severing its leg, as he fell to the floor.

I was stunned, immobilized. My rant lodged in my throat. I didn't understand what was happening until…. The vision of children flashed before my eyes and I knew. I knew immediately. I screamed out in anguish, I rushed to him and dropped to my knees. He lay unconscious, pale and drenched with sweat.

"Claus? Claus. Claus!" I was terrified. "Claus!"

Screaming, I ran blindly out the door and across the yard toward Mary's house. I was barely aware of the children now mobbed in my yard, now in Mary's yard. I ran through their number.

"Mary! Mary! Help! Mary, help me! Oh, God have mercy." I dropped to my knees and bawled.

"Liz! Liz! I'm coming!"

The kitchen door flew open so fast it nearly ripped itself off the hinges. Mary charged outside to assist me.

"My god! What is it, Liz? What has happened? Liz, what has happened?" She threw her arms around me. A profound torrent of drool, snot, and tears mixed and worked to drown the words I struggled to choke out. I managed a breath.

"Oh, God have mercy. Oh, God. It's Claus. It's Claus, Mary. He's collapsed. He's collapsed. I fear he's died. Please, Mary." I buried my face on her shoulder and wailed in anguish.

"Allen! Allen! Allen! Quick! It's Claus! He's in a bad way. Be quick about it!"

"Please, Mary. Please, don't let him die. Please, don't let him..." I begged as I sobbed. My tears washed across Mary's neck.

Allen and Luke rushed to the house.

"I must go to him, Liz. I must see to Allen's needs. Stay put and calm yourself, I will be back as soon as I might."

Mary kissed me and ran off toward the house. I was unable. I was too anxious to sit and so rose to walk the garden in the company of the children. I prayed between my sobs. I swore upon my soul, I would do whatever was asked of me if only the good Lord would allow me the company of the man I loved. If only for just a short while longer, only long enough to tell him.

The children remained close. I returned to the bench, and they began to sit down in the grass all about me. I bawled uncontrollably. Through my tears, I saw these girls about me crying. I didn't know why they were crying. I didn't know who they were. Why were they here? I lowered my head and suffered.

Mary appeared back in the yard after about twenty minutes and sat down alongside me. She lifted my face and gently wiped away my tears with her apron. She placed her arm around my shoulder, pulling me into her embrace. She kissed me over and over.

"He didn't die."

I burst into another convulsion of sobs. Mary tried to console me.

"I have often wondered why God had put so much turmoil into your life, Liz. Sometimes, I think if we don't love and hate and laugh and cry on a daily basis, then we forget what life is all about. In the end I think emotion is all that matters. It isn't the amount of years we live that marks the length of our lives; it's the amount of emotion we have endured. I believe that, Liz. That is why you have lived so much more than I."

"Claus is recovering. I'm sure he'll be fine. He's as strong as a bull. He is a bull, but he'll be confined to bed for a while, and we'll have to keep an eye on him. Probably tie him down, I don't doubt, but he'll be fine, I'm certain."

"Oh...thank you, Mary. Tell me it's true. Say...it's true. Please, keep telling it's true."

"It's true, it's true. He'll be fine, I promise you."

"It was my fault. He was so angry with me over Luke. He wanted me to say he was the father. He wanted me to tell him. The insult at the center drove him insane. He was beside himself."

"Did you tell him, Liz?"

"No.... I didn't.... I am sure I would have, but it all happened so fast."

"I think the time has come, Liz. He is every bit as good a man as he has always been. He is generous with everyone, and he has gone well out of his way to prove himself to you when it comes to matters regarding Luke. I think the time has come to settle the matter. It is time to recognize your family. You may end up killing him if you don't, I'm afraid."

"You are right, of course. I can see that, and I've known it all along, but it's not as easy as you might think. It isn't nearly as easy as I might have wished. I couldn't just wake him up in the middle of the night and say, 'hey, by the way, Claus, that boy you like so much, he's yours.'"

"I think you can do much better than that, Elizabeth."

"I suppose. I guess it's just that I have never really come to terms with giving up any part of my son…even to his father. Luke has always been mine, only mine and nobody else's. It takes some getting used to, Mary. Once I say, Claus, you're the father, he is in command. He is in command, Mary. That is very difficult for me to accept. He is a very powerful man."

"I promise you, Liz, your fears are groundless, you'll see. Anybody can tell Claus is too good a man to allow you to feel anything less than supported in your role as Luke's mother. You worry too much, Liz. Now go in and stay by your man. After all, he crossed a continent to kneel at your bedside as I recall, not Luke's."

It was true, and I cried at the recollection. Mary encouraged me to stand up from the bench, and go to Christopher. As we walked back across the yard the children moved gently with us. I felt as though they were guiding me back. I looked at them and nodded.

"I understand. I understand. Thank you."

* * *

Mary left me at Christopher's side. I remained seated next to him day and night as he regained his strength. I fed him, I washed him; I tended to his every need. This I did willingly, for it was the first time I was ever able to give back something of the care that he had always provided me.

251

Christopher collapsed in April. His recovery took longer than we had hoped, but it gave Christopher and me the time needed during the months that followed to talk intimately as never before.

"I didn't know. I didn't have the faintest idea. I mean, I was certain I would know if I was pregnant. You have to wonder how a body cannot possibly know it's pregnant. I thought I was yet suffering the effects of the snakebite. I thought I was suffering the effects of my sunburn. Pregnancy was the last thing I might have thought. The Indians had to tell me, can you believe it?"

"Did you believe them?"

"Of course not. I thought they were uncivilized dolts. But within minutes of my telling them that they were out of their minds, I had flashes of the women who paid call on Allen at the infirmary and I knew. How many came in the door sick, and walked out the door expectant."

"Were you afraid?"

"I was terrified. Horrified was more like it. I thought my life was at an end. Poor Gracie. I think she worried more for me than I did myself."

"If only I could turn back the hands of time. I am so sorry I wasn't there for you, Elizabeth. Fate has been cruel to me as well."

"Fate, now there's a thought. Fate as snapped me like a whip from one emotion to another, from one world to another, from one life to another. Who can make sense of fate? At this point, whether for better or worse, it's in the past. You know, Claus, I remember the moment he was born. I don't know if I was conscious or not, dreaming or not, but I heard you talking to me. You kept saying he was beautiful. You kept saying, 'Look, he is so beautiful, so beautiful.' I believed you, and I had to see for myself. I finally opened up my eyes and the sun was shining on him and I knew. I knew what that old fortune teller meant so many years ago. I was the chosen one."

"And you named him, Luke, after the man who died to save you."

"No."

"No?"

"No."

I looked deep into Claus's eyes and let loose my last hold.

"I named him Christopher Lucas Claussen. But, you can't enter that in the Tsistsista's birth records. They have no such thing. It would have to wait until my return to Boston. I guess that time has come."

The revelation choked me up, but I gave Claus his son. He was so happy he cried. We both cried. We kissed and it wasn't a kiss filled with remorse or shame. I wasn't taking anything from Rebecca or Claus; I was only traveling down the same road of fate, as were they.

It was July, and Christopher was back on his feet and getting around without assistance, but the ordeal had weakened him considerably. This was obvious to us all. His heart beat with a mere trickle of its former force, and he was slowed down considerably. In contrast to the frailty of his frame, his mental acuity remained as persistently sharp as ever.

The attack was now history, but it scared me beyond all reckoning. It opened everybody's eyes and set us all to thinking seriously about our futures and what things we wanted most out of whatever life remained. The discussions were long and in depth, and in the end, Christopher and I agreed that we were most impassioned by the challenges that lie ahead out west. We decided to sell the house and finish out our lives at Christopher's residence in Northpole, a mere speck of humanity at the foot of the Bighorn Mountain range. It was a place where I could look eastward across the open plains and see the Tsistsistas in my dreams.

EIGHTY-FOUR

"The last time I did this it was only to be for a few months. Do you remember? It took well over ten years to find my way back."

"I would rather not think about it."

"I think I am all cried out. Maybe I am getting old and insensitive."

"That is something you'll never be, Liz"

"Maybe not insensitive, but old…? I can't tell the future Mary, but Claus is over sixty, and I fifty come December. I fear in the worst way I will never be back. I may have recovered from my illness, but not without proof that my best days and health are behind me. I don't know, Mary. I spent so many years longing for your company, to eat applesauce pie and drink tea in your garden; and in the space of a breath I find myself once more leaving. I can't bear to think we might never see each other again. I swear…I swear…I only do this for Luke. I could never work up the courage or find the heart to leave you on my own."

"Oh, Elizabeth, my dear. You must be strong. I don't doubt how you feel. My heart breaks as does yours. I share those same fears. But you were born to be on the frontier. It's in your blood. It's as much a part of you as the hair on your head. It was all over you when you returned. Your spirit was wild with it. It's where you belong, Elizabeth. Besides, I have little doubt that Gracie is out there somewhere longing for you as you did for me. Go to her."

"Will you write me, Mary?"

"Of course."

"Promise me, Mary. You must promise me you will write. Promise you will never forget me."

"I promise you. I will write to see how things go for you. As much as I hate to see you leave, I will say I am happy to see you leave with Mr. Claussen. It does my heart more good than you can know. I would rather it be this way than for you to live out the rest of your years alone in Boston. Luke will run off as all boys do."

"We'll never marry."

"Does it make a difference when you rule the world?"

"No, I suppose not."

"Be happy, Liz. Life is so very short…just be happy. You've waited far too long. You deserve it. Now go. Enjoy what good years remain."

"I love you, Mary."

"Take care, Elizabeth, I'll pray for you every night."

"I love you, Mary."

I held my tears at bay as our coach pulled away. Horse shoes began striking the pavement as if a metronome tapping out time and distance before Mary's cottage would disappear around the bend and old majestic oaks. I leaned out the window desperate for every last glimpse of Mary and Allen as they waved their good byes. My eyes were fixed upon them until the old oaks finally hid Mary from me as they once hid me from her. I was embarrassed to cry so hard in front of Luke, so I continued to stare out the window with closed eyes that left me blind to everything except for my memories. The breeze failed to dry my wetted face.

Christopher passed his arm across my breast from behind and drew me backward into his embrace. I dropped my head into the cradle of his arm and quietly let myself grieve. I had no reason to believe I would never see Mary again. It was a bittersweet suffering to leave one half of your love behind in order to proceed forward with the other half.

Our journey began by backtracking along my previous eastbound passage on the Boston-Albany railroad line, but did so only as far as the New York-Massachusetts border. Whereas my previous eastward journey had brought me from Buffalo to Albany via the Eire Canal aboard Dorrie's boat, Christopher was far too interested in discovering what progress was taking place along eastern railroads.

For that reason, we forfeited the tranquility of calmer canal waters for passage aboard any available railroad car regardless of smoke, ember, ash, discomfort, or inconvenience. Christopher sought to discover any usable advances in technology or profitability along the rails that he might introduce to his enterprise out west.

We crossed the Hudson and so started across New York traveling through the Pine Bush region aboard the newly named Albany and Schenectady Railroad. This line began as a sixteen-mile stretch of track that bypassed a dozen locks on the Erie Canal. What had recently taken Dorrie and me an entire day to navigate on the canal, Claus and I had completed by train in half an hour.

We changed trains a number of times, even crossing to the north side of the Mohawk River aboard the Utica-Schenectady and Syracuse-Utica Railroads. We then closed back in on the canal to enter the city of Rome.

Because the railroad passed close by the canal at Rome, it was there that I previously arranged by letter to meet Dorrie. Christopher encouraged me to take a long lunch in Rome, so I might visit with her a final time. I was delighted to see her boys standing beside her to greet us. They had grown into tall and handsome young men now in their mid-to-late teens.

Dorrie and I were hardly embarrassed to run across the platform and embrace, and wasted little time in doing so. Dorrie was glowing. She moved to embrace my son.

"Hello, Luke. I see you made it to Boston in good health."

"Yes, ma'am."

"I want you to see the boys, Elizabeth. They begged I let them come to the station to see you."

"My word, look at how tall you are. I can't believe it. Come here, now, come on, I need hugs! It's been too many years."

The boys came forward, their faces sporting great smiles.

"Hello, Jack."

"Hello, Miss Claussen."

I turned to look at the expression on Christopher's face, and then back to Jack.

"Well, Jack, actually it's Miss Dennison. Let me see you must be what...sixteen, seventeen years old ?"

"Nineteen."

"Nineteen! Unbelievable."

I looked up.

"Hello, Kenneth."

"Hello, Miss Dennison. It's a pleasure to see you again."

"Do you even remember me?"

"Yes, ma'am, very much so. I remember you saved us from hard times."

"Well, I don't think you remembered that. You were too young in those days."

"No, I do remember. I remember my father dying and you staying by my mother's side. I remember you telling me that I would be taken care of. I do remember."

"Well, I am impressed. How old are you now?"

"Twenty-one."

"And a very good looking twenty-one. You have your father's features. He was a handsome man as I recall."

The boy blushed profusely.

"Okay, boys, you already know Luke. Why don't you take him along for awhile? Stay out of trouble and in the area so I can find you when we head back."

"Yes, mum. Good bye, Miss Dennison."

"Good bye, boys. Don't run off too far, Luke."

The boys headed toward the canal to busy themselves. Now, an older gentleman came forward.

"Elizabeth, may I introduce you to my escort and very good friend, Mr. Benjamin Dorset."

I accepted his hand.

"Mister Dorset."

"The pleasure is mine, Miss Dennison. Dorrie has filled my head with accounts of your travels and, more important, your generosity."

"All exaggerated to be sure. Mister Dorset, my dearest friend, Mister Christopher Claussen."

The two men greeted each other warmly, but it was the meeting of Christopher and Dorrie that would inevitably overshadow the commotion, handshakes, and embraces so far displayed. Through me, each had heard a lifetime of stories about the other, and whereas Christopher looked forward to this introduction with anticipation, Dorrie was filled with apprehension.

Christopher viewed himself to be meeting a woman who undertook his interests to heart, spreading hope and opportunity to the uneducated and impoverished. Christopher was aware of the fact that his funds had been invested in the schoolboat initiative. It was obvious to him that Dorrie had wasted no time in educating herself and taking full control of the helm. He could not admire her more.

Dorrie viewed herself as finally being able to thank the one man who not only saved her and her family from certain ruin, but provided her a chance to envisage and realize her potential. She was humbled by him. She understood that it was through Christopher's generosity that her success had come to fruition.

With a crimson-flushed face, Dorrie objected to my reminding Christopher of how through her colorful background, her education, as well as her close ties with the schoolboat and its rotating staff of instructors, she had earned herself quite an honorable reputation along the canal from one end of New York to the other and beyond. I reminded him that she was called upon frequently to lecture at the local lyceums throughout upper New York.

It was at this point that Dorrie moved to sidestep the limelight and save herself from the embarrassment of our attention and praise. She took hold of Mr. Dorset's arm and suddenly blurted out how last summer during one of these noted lectures, she met her escort, Benjamin.

"He is a well-known banker and widower in the Syracuse area. I am not sure what he sees in me, but I am blessed to have his acquaintance."

"*Close* acquaintance, if I may add. It is my sole focus and heart's desire to court Miss Whipsman. I have vowed to obliterate any obstacle that stands in my way."

"I haven't seen too many obstacles. Who wants an old lady?" Dorrie laughed.

"I should have asked this lovely lady for her hand the first time I saw her cross the street from a city block away. I was smitten even at that distance. I found the courage to introduce myself, but soon discovered Miss Whipsman was so independent and successful in her own right that she has absolutely no need of me. I lost my courage."

Mister Dorset threw his hands up in a show of despair.

"The man is too modest. I rely on him for everything these days. I cannot count the times he has come to my aid. He has a head for business and a heart for comfort. I should be so lucky to have such a man at my side into old age."

"She did say she might consider accepting a proposal providing the right man might happen along and promise to take her to Niagara Falls for the ceremony and a holiday. She sets her sights high and drives a hard bargain."

"Ha! In spite of his silver tongue, the right man is squarely within my sights, but I haven't seen him on his knees as of yet, even though he questions whether or not we would make Syracuse our home. It leaves a woman to wonder whether she must hint or holler."

Mr. Dorset was visibly taken aback. Dorrie's matter-of-fact public disclosures caught him completely off guard. Then to the full measure of our disbelief, the man dropped onto his knees in the middle of the station platform and presented Dorrie an invisible box, which he opened before her.

"Forgive me, my love, for not having the foresight to keep your ring in my pocket at this very moment. Yet, I would say its luster would lack before the glow of my heart if you should fill it with joy by accepting my request to have your hand and heart in marriage. I swear before God, Mr. Claussen, and your dearest of friends, Miss Dennison, that I would place no other before you from this day forward until God calls us away. That I swear if you will have me."

Mr. Dorset had turned the table on Dorrie and clearly knocked her off balance. She immediately broke into tears and began to nod her head in acceptance. Finally, after a struggle to regain her composure, she found the words.

"I will."

Mr. Dorset rose to his feet and took Dorrie into his arms. They kissed. Dorrie then turned to me with outstretched arms and a fresh bout of sobs.

"I'm getting married."

"So it seems. Congratulations."

Christopher immediately stepped forward to congratulate Mr. Dorset. He then insisted we all spend the night in Rome and celebrate this wondrous and unexpected occasion over a dinner to be long remembered. We set off at once in search of the boys and the best hotel and inn Rome had to offer.

The air was filled with excitement as we conversed about every subject with vigor. Christopher was always the curious one, and full of questions about the area and its interests. Mr. Dorset proved to be an energetic and enthusiastic conversationalist and did not disappoint.

"Rome is quite an interesting place, more so than many of the historical sites of the area," said Mr. Dorset.

"Dorrie never told me anything special about Rome. I thought you knew about everything along the canal."

I kidded Dorrie. She was quick to jump into the conversation and defend herself. After all she was the supposed well-known and respected speaker and historian in these parts.

"I do know everything about this place and more, but you were never one of my students and I wasn't about to bore you with a mouthful of details. I could go on telling you about every town from one end of the canal to the other. What would you like to know? Rome? Rome was formerly called Lynchville after Dominick Lynch. Unfortunately, in spite of his great accomplishments in building his city, its citizens didn't much care for him. One day they took a vote and decided to call the town Rome just to spite him."

"And before that it was called the Expense Lot, because of the enormous expense incurred while trying to survey this inhospitable terrain," said Mr. Dorset.

"Yes, you are correct. And for a hundred years before Lynchville, it was called the Oneida Carry. It would have been possible to voyage a thousand miles by water between Lake Ontario and the St. Lawrence River, had it not been for one unwilling three-mile stretch of ground between the Mohawk River and Woods Creek. For three miserable miles, everything coming or going by way of the rivers had to be carried."

"There were only two routes into the interior of the continent, and the Mohawk River Route was one. The carry was very important in those days," injected Mr. Dorset.

"And when were those days?" I asked.

"I imagine since the dawn of time for the Indians," he responded. "But for the Europeans and settlers it was important

262

back to the late sixteen hundreds, and the Carry played a big role in both the French Indian and Revolutionary Wars," he answered.

"There were a lot of forts built on that small piece of ground," said Dorrie. "Fort Oneida, Fort Williams, Fort Bull, Fort Stanwix...I'm missing some."

"Fort Craven, Fort Newport, Fort Wood Creek," offered Mr. Dorset.

For Christopher, Dorrie and Mr. Dorset proved to be a treasure trove of interesting facts about the area. Christopher was taken by Dorrie's character and enjoyed listening to her give accounts of the history along the canal, but in time, he and Mr. Dorset arrived to modern times and their conversations eventually came down to the war with Mexico, railroads, and the financial opportunities on the western frontiers. The men stayed fully occupied with those discussions for the duration of our stay, and so left Dorrie and me to converse freely beyond earshot.

"I recall you saying before that you no longer spent much time aboard the schoolboats, but I thought you loved Tonawanda."

"Oh, I do. But my duties being entirely administrative, even after taking the boat yards into consideration, it still proved increasingly inconvenient to be located so far on the west end. If I am to spend my day in an office then I might as well be positioned centrally. It just makes good business sense.

"The move is long overdue. For some time now, I've been putting off what must be done. To be honest, it was seeing you and the fresh breeze you blew into my world that got me off my buttocks. Seeing you made me feel like a change was needed. It's never been a problem about where to go. As many times as I have been up and down the canal, I knew Syracuse was the only place I would consider.

"As soon as I got Luke off to Boston, I made moving my priority. So now, I still oversee the itineraries, class schedules, and student and teacher applications for the excursions. I still oversee the shipment of cargo up and down the canal, but I do it all looking out a window with a different view.

"We also invested more funds into stationary classrooms and sleeping quarters in Syracuse. Instead of basic education, the schoolboats are being used increasingly for cruises past the historical sites. It works out better this way. Living on the boat in close quarters can be trying. The classrooms are much better for attracting students from afar, and to allow separation of boys and girls."

Dorrie went on to tell me about how her need to establish banking in Syracuse led to her making acquaintance with Mr. Dorset, and how that meeting blossomed into a most splendid relationship.

As for me, I could hardly compete with Dorrie's hectic lifestyle. I gave account of my joy to be reunited with Mary, and the subsequent tears and sorrow of my departure. I gave account of Christopher's heart attack and now weakened condition. I confided without reservation that Christopher was indeed Luke's father. After all, I had but little choice to spell out what was already more than obvious in Dorrie's eyes. Well, I should say except for the blonde hair. Christopher's blonde hair was seen only by me in my memory. It must also be said that Christopher and Luke came to me beforehand to say they would make no mention of their relationship until they heard it first from my own lips.

Dorrie and I found no end to the stories we shared with relish, many to amaze, most matter of fact and often trivial, but one in particular caught my attention.

"Do you remember those strange boats we delivered to Albany—the one with the rock bottom?"

"Yes."

"I actually saw them pass back this way, locks up, headed for Buffalo and the steamers."

"So, to whom were they delivered?"

"No idea. But you know how the canal news travels. It was rumored two of those boats were laden with a number of large crates that were fitted with wheels. Most rumors claimed the crates were filled with hardware and goods headed to the far west, there was some talk about a good many toys as well.

"The reason I mention this isn't so much because of the boats, but because I had heard one of the boats was supposedly carrying a spectacular red coach, the likes of which nobody had ever seen. Not only that but it was also rumored that magnificent team of white horses were also driven on board.

"Now, the reason I am telling you this, and correct me if I am wrong, but I could swear that somewhere way, way, back, ten or twelve years ago, when we first met, you told me a story about an amazing red coach. I am sure of it. Otherwise, why else would that stick in my head?"

How strange that this conversation, a trivial one having little to do with anything, turned out to be the one that shook me to my core. It was little more than a *"by the way"* anecdote from Dorrie's perspective, a conclusion to hours of discussion, but the comment leveled me.

"What's the matter?"

"Nothing. I was trying to remember having such a conversation."

"You look pale, Elizabeth. Did I say something…?"

"No, not at all. It's nothing. To be honest, my stomach is mildly upset. Coffee does that, especially when combined with all the traveling."

I wasn't lying. My stomach was upset. It twisted into a perfect knot. Also, I honestly didn't remember telling Dorrie anything about Lady Rebecca's coach. In all my time as of late, most of which was spent in Christopher's company, Lady Rebecca's coach and what became of it never once entered my mind. It had never been discussed. How incredibly strange that omission seemed to me now.

How strange, too, was the knowing that my last recollection of her coach was when I discovered it under tarps and dust in a warehouse that was also filled with crates of toys. The coincidence was too remarkable—boats that were built special, a mandate that only Dorrie take command of their delivery—there was far more to this than mindless chance alone. I would question Christopher. I was fully confident he would have an interesting explanation.

EIGHTY-FIVE

At the end of our day together, we asserted in unison the pleasures of making these acquaintances, shook hands, embraced, and kissed.

"Please try and make it to St. Louis this winter. I would so love to have you join Rachel and me. As it is, Luke spends all his time with Christopher on business, and I don't see how St. Louis will prove any different."

"To be honest, Rachel was my only plan, but now as I am suddenly engaged, I no longer am sure what the future brings.

At least you will have Gracie. That must be a joy for which you can hardly wait."

"Oh. Gracie...." I shrugged. "I can only hope. I have been unable to reach her. I am sure she is off in the wilds throwing knives to her heart's content."

Christopher spoke up to address Dorrie and Mr. Dorset.

"I wish to repeat our intention to winter over at the Planters while in St. Louis. Should you care to make the trip, know that you are both invited to join us as guests—all expenses paid for the duration of your stay in St. Louis's finest establishment. If that doesn't entice you to come see Elizabeth, then I don't believe anything will."

"Oh, my, Mr. Claussen. That is a most generous offer. I am embarrassed to consider such generosity."

"I agree with Dorrie wholeheartedly. We could never sufficiently thank you," said Mr. Dorset.

"Don't concern yourselves. This is an act of pure selfishness on my part. I am driven to please Elizabeth. If she wishes to see you this winter, I will do whatever I might to see that happen."

Dorrie turned to me.

"My word, Elizabeth, how can you stand to suffer such devotion?"

"Already, I am lacking. So soon? Is it possible?" Mr. Dorset whined.

We all laughed. We laughed for our last time and then turned from each other to go on with our lives.

We split the boys apart, and set off to make our arrangements. As we departed Rome, l looked back one last time and was most heartened to believe Dorrie had at last found happiness beyond the ashes of her past sorrow. It seemed we were both embarking on what would appear to become a memorable year and hopeful future.

We passed by Auburn and spied Syracuse from the station. Previously, I had only known Syracuse from the canal. From either vantage, it seemed a vibrant place for Dorrie and her fiancé to call home. Syracuse then fell away to Rochester. At Rochester we boarded the Tonawanda Railroad, which brought us past Batavia, past Attica, and finally to our destination at the farthest major city in western New York—*Buffalo.*

Whereas, Massachusetts and New York had rapidly expanding rail service, Pennsylvania had none whatsoever. In order to travel west from Buffalo, one could travel the shoreline by stagecoach or sail Lake Erie aboard a packet. Neither route was for the faint of heart. The lake could be most treacherous when sailed westbound, and if one easily suffered the ills of sea-sickness, she could be laid up for days afterward.

Yet, avoiding the rough waters meant confronting roads that rightfully earned the worst reputation for a thousand miles in every direction. Many of the old corduroy log roads had been improved with the newer milled planks. But in traveling circles, that particular stretch of road along the shore of Lake Erie by Cattaraugus Creek and Four Mile Woods had reached the realm of folklore. There could be found the worst mudhole in the world. Oftentimes, passengers were called out from their cabin to push the coach through knee deep mud at the cost of apparel and disposition.

Claus bypassed the area by booking passage on a steamship belonging to one of his interests. He had little doubt about his decision as he went on to explain.

"It was said, one night on that infamously bad stretch of road, the entire lot of men, women, and children passengers were called out of the comfort and warmth of the cabin to assist the driver, already straining to assist the oxen now employed to assist the horses whose bellies were scraping the road due to the depth of the mud.

"As they slogged through the mire, one of the passengers came upon a hat lying atop the slop. Being a nice piece, he went for it. But upon raising it from the mud, he was astounded to discover a man's head beneath. At once, he called out for assistance from the others, believing the man desperate to be freed of his predicament.

"Instead, the stranger politely declined, explaining there was no reason for alarm. He was in fact riding his best steed, at last now standing sure-footed upon solid rock."

EIGHTY-SIX

We were to steam west out of Buffalo toward Eire, again the reverse of my voyage with Dorrie. Our coach stopped at the dock alongside a most remarkable vessel. I observed the name emblazoned in a large sweeping arc along the enclosure of the side wheel.

"THE FALLS."

"Yes, THE FALLS. She is one of a new line called Palace Steamers. She operates in conjunction with the railroad in order to navigate the Great Lakes waterways. She ferries passengers and cargoes between Buffalo, New York; Detroit, Chicago, and various stops en route."

"She certainly lacks nothing for size."

"Indeed she does not. At nearly two hundred and fifty feet bow to stern, and thirty-five across her beam, she currently stands as one of the world's longest steamboats, and most assuredly surpasses anything on these waters."

As with all things, be it coaches, boats, or trains, Christopher beamed. I did, however, note that the entire lower deck of the boat was consumed by the stowage of cargoes and wood for the boilers, whereas the upper deck was reserved and outfitted expressly for the pleasure of passengers. It was obvious the boat was only recently commissioned for service. Not even pesky spiders had managed to foul the pristine look of her decks.

Apparently, Christopher had a notable investment in the line because we were met at the dock by the ship's captain and three of his crew.

"Good afternoon, Mister Claussen. I am pleased to welcome you aboard; and you as well, madam."

"And a good afternoon to you, Captain. Your ship shows grand upon approach—impressive indeed. I must say I have been looking forward to viewing her. I am also impatient to embark, to see her underway, in spite of it being the shorter leg."

"Then I must take it upon myself to ensure that while on board, you and your company enjoy every amenity my crew and I have to offer. I assure you, madam, for however short your time on board, you shall be pampered as never before. Please allow me to show you your cabins."

The crew saw to our belongings as the three of us walked across the plank to the grand cabin. At first foot on board, Christopher turned me slightly. I supposed so I might hear him speak, or he might look at me.

"This is our first time together aboard a vessel since the REBECCA."

"Yes," I reflected. "So it is."

"Enjoy."

We moved across the promenade and passed through the doors to the grand cabin. I was at once awed by the magnificence within. The passengers were being provided every need and distraction imaginable as they mingled in conversation. Everybody was smiling. Everywhere was laughter to be heard.

If the boat was nearly two hundred and fifty feet in length, the grand cabin had to be but scant few feet shorter. Its ceiling was arched end to end, paneled in white, and adorned profusely in gold trimmings giving one the sensation of entering a king's palace—a grand cabin, indeed.

Overhead, skylights beyond count were fitted with stained glazings and butted one another to saturate the inner atmosphere with the full spectrum of light. All those crowed together beneath the flood of beams were painted with patterns of rainbows. As we made our way aft through the cabin and its kaleidoscope of color, I counted some twenty-five staterooms, which doubled would have totaled fifty in all split evenly between port and starboard. With its spectacular parlors and saloons, and the highest quality of furniture and carpets, THE FALLS rivaled the best comfort of the renowned Ohio riverboats, and so we arrived in Erie impressed and no worse for wear.

Erie was the place where Dorrie and I had disembarked the coach that we employed to ferry us north from the Pittsburgh area. Christopher dismissed the line coaches, preferring instead to book a private packet on the canal. It would float us one hundred and thirty-six miles down the Erie-Beaver Canal in company with a number of other very large rafts—to be more precise, *three* other very large rafts. I noted a great deal of attention was paid Christopher by all those in the party of rafts. I was no fool, and surmised that as always, where was business, was Christopher.

Any thoughts of our passing within the vicinity of Pittsburgh without Christopher making a call were absurd. For this reason, we took a coach from Beaver upriver along the north bank to Allegheny. Pittsburgh was under widespread construction following the fire and lodging was easier to obtain in Allegheny. It was there that I spent two days resting while Christopher attended to business with Luke in tow. I knew all too well the rigors of travel that lie in wait and determined to use every available minute to relax and pamper myself.

What little sightseeing I did undertake was for the purpose of satisfying my curiosity about the fire. The bridge crossing the Allegheny from Pittsburgh had been fully engulfed by flames the night Dorrie and I had disembarked at Allegheny. We stood and watched the flames form a line as they reached halfway across the river. Now, I could see that the road bed had been repaired and so I asked my driver to take me across where I might spend some time enjoying the sunshine and fresh air while observing the resurrection of the new Pittsburgh. The sun was obliging, but when close to the burned-out regions, the fresh air oftentimes was not so fresh.

Upon completion of business in Pittsburgh, we boarded the ST. LOUIS SALLY, a steamer operated by one of Christopher's enterprises that would provide us passage downriver to the Falls of the Ohio at Louisville. Our accommodations were splendid, and Luke lost nothing in the way of fresh curiosities on this his second cross-country voyage via riverboat.

I said as much to Christopher while walking the deck after I noticed Luke talking to the riverboat pilot, who just happened to be an Indian.

"On our journey to Boston, Luke spent much of his time talking to the riverpilots of those vessels. Now, he is over there at it again. I find it quite coincidental that so far all our riverpilots have been Indians. He can't help but to feel the bonds that exist between them. I dare say, he is of yet, more Indian than they."

"Ho, ho. Not luck, my dear. Not at all. Nine out of ten riverboat pilots are Indians. They are the best pilots to be found."

"Is that so?"

"Beyond question. Who better to know the course of the rivers than the Indians who lived upon them for generations?"

"I see your point. As for my point, I was about to say that I understand Luke enjoys his Indian ties, and I hope he keeps them, but I do believe he will adapt well to his new life."

"I am sure of it. He is an intelligent lad, just like his mother."

"Just like his father."

"I would like to think as much, but we both know about my intelligence at times."

"For the record, it was you who said that."

I pulled Christopher in close.

* * *

We stopped briefly downriver at Beaver where I learned for certain it was Christopher's freight that had been transferred from all three rafts to a second riverboat while we stayed over in Allegheny. I now understood why all the attention paid to him. Both vessels were now heavily laden with goods bound for Christopher's interests out west. Needless to say, I carried a certain amount of curiosity about the freight in his care, wondering if one day I would count a thousand toys or confront the white head of a Lipizzaner sticking out a stable window.

Our first port of call was Cincinnati. The port was packed with boats. Commerce appeared good and I was not surprised to be told Christopher and Luke would be going ashore. I chose to remain on board because the boat would only be in port for about eight hours before embarking. In fact, it seemed we had but just landed and we were now only awaiting the arrival of Christopher and Luke back on board before raising the plank and shoving off. Our trip continued down the Ohio free of calamity or setback and we steamed directly for Louisville unhindered.

Christopher reserved the four largest cabins. One for himself, one for me, one for Luke, and one to be used as an office for his business affairs. It was here that he began in earnest to teach Luke the business of bookkeeping and accounts. The river was tranquil, time was plentiful, free of distraction, and so Luke gained experience and focused insight from Christopher that few men enjoyed. It was a father teaching his son. It was all the more sweet for Christopher because of Luke's Indian upbringing. Luke was accustomed to learning by listening to the knowledge being handed down by his elders. He paid close attention.

It was necessary to change riverboats and transfer freight at the falls. In fact, the Louisville-Portland Canal had long been in existence to bypass the rapids, but it was now too cumbersome for larger steamboats. To make matters worse, according to Christopher, it was particularly prone to filling up with mud and during low water times, many of the boats scraped or grounded on the canal bed. Even worse, it emptied back into the Ohio at a narrow stretch in the river with a dangerously fast current. Many of the riverboat captains disliked it. For all of these reasons, we spent the night in Louisville as our freight was being transferred to boats below the falls, a times-old tradition that put "portage" or "port" into the name Portland.

It was now expected that Christopher would take Luke with him whenever he went ashore or inland on matters of business.

I had planned to relax in the hotel, to read and watch passersby, but instead found myself hijacked by a group of women in the lobby who belonged to the Louisville Children's League. Clearly, this was Christopher's doing.

I was suddenly made the guest of honor at a luncheon where I was not only embarrassed to convey that I had not been involved in charity for many years, but also suffered to note I was the oldest of those in attendance. I managed to endure, even making myself polite and approachable. If I had any doubts about later voicing my dissatisfaction with Christopher, they dissolved the minute Luke came into the lobby where I was having my evening tea.

"Hi, Mama."

"Hello, Luke. Did you have a good day?"

"Very much so. We've been calling all over the city in order to address father's business. He has a shipyard here—."

"Luke, you will soon learn that if rain leaves a puddle with a bubble, your father will have a ship sailing around it."

"This one is smaller than the ones in Cincinnati and Pittsburgh, but well outfitted. Oh, and I wanted to tell you that I really enjoyed seeing Rebecca Claussen's coach. We were there when it was rolled across to the new steamer. I remember you speaking of it. It is nothing if not fantastic."

I just stared at my son.

"That would be *Lady* Rebecca Claussen's coach."

I added the respect I felt was due. Luke frowned at me.

"*Lady* Rebecca Claussen's coach if you prefer. I only wished to say it was a work of art, simply magnificent."

"I know well the coach you saw, and to be truthful, magnificent is most likely an understatement as you now know. Luke, I have no desire to cut you short, but would you leave me, sweetheart? I wish a moment alone to speak with your father."

"Yes, Mama."

Luke turned to take his leave. I looked past him so I might gauge the full measure of Christopher as he approached. He knew I was assessing him.

"I see I am in trouble, and I have yet to open my mouth. It usually happens the other way around."

"Not so in our relationship."

"Ouch. Forgive me. What have I done this time?"

"You have me waylaid by a gaggle of pretty young upstarts from the Louisville Children's League without bothering to first ask."

Christopher laughed heartily.

"If I had first asked you would have said no, and you know it."

"Then so be it. That is my decision, and you are to respect it."

"True enough, true enough. I understand. I do. Yet, I feel strongly, time has come for you to reacquaint yourself with your past. Ten years in the wild has made you many things, certainly a strong woman, but it hasn't stripped you of those former talents you still possess. I only wish to help you remember those admirable ideals for which you stood, those accomplishments that gave you so much enjoyment and reward. Can you fault me for wanting what I believe is best for you?"

"I would beg you to leave those decisions about what is best for me—*to me*."

"Never again, I swear...with crossed fingers—see. Anything else?"

"Yes, as a matter of fact."

276

"Ouch, again. I *am* in trouble. Have you been working at this all day?"

"Is it true, you are actually transporting Lady Rebecca's coach with us? Dorrie told me of the rumors along the canal, and now Luke...."

Christopher's expression went solemn. His head snapped about from one position to another as if he was spotting answers floating by in the air. He looked down at me.

"Yes. I am." He thought momentarily. "You may wonder why, but the reasons aren't so strange. First, I don't believe I will ever return this way again, Elizabeth. I expect to finish my days out around South Pass or at my place in Northpole. If I had any doubts about that, they were settled the moment you placed Luke in my life. He will soon be old enough to make the trips east on my behalf when I find the need. He is smart and strong and eager to learn. He already has more experience traveling than most men I know.

"Another reason, that coach is as much a part of my life as anything I find dear. In my heart, it represents the very best of times, the very worst of times. It reminds me of friends and family, you, Rebecca. It reminds me very much of my father, God rest his soul.

"If you must know, I only came to consider shipping it out west while traveling east to see you. Maybe the Ohio is too tranquil, Elizabeth. Maybe it affords one too much time to reflect.

"Remember, when I arrived, I expected to be attending your funeral, not falling foolishly onto your bed. I believed I had most likely lost the last person to whom I truly felt connected as family. My thoughts led me to remembrances of you as a child sitting beside me in the coach. And that brought me to think of Rebecca, and of course, my father, the coach being his gift to her.

Thoughts of my father brought me to memories of my mother and Sweden.

"As I passed through the years of my life I realized that Rebecca's coach was the one thing that remained unchanged and steadfast. Thoughts of it gave me a sense of foundation, an inner strength. When at last I went to the docks to see it after all these years, the sight of it filled me with peace; its scent of lavender gave me an overwhelming sense of contentment. If you open the door, the fragrance of Rebecca persists to this day." Christopher took a breath. "Anyhow, the next thing I knew, I was assessing the challenges and working out a plan to bring the coach home." Christopher studied me for a moment. He nodded his head. "What can I say? I'm happy about it."

"Well then, I am happy for you. If it pleases you, it pleases me. If it satisfies your heart's desire, then you have done what's best. I only wished to put the rumors and speculations to rest. And what about toys, Claus? Are you also transporting toys? Were Dorrie's rumors true about that as well?"

"Hmmph." Christopher looked surprised. "Yes—I dare say quite a few—more than I would have imagined. Did you find that unusual? I can say that it was not part of my original plan. It was only when I went to assess the condition of the coach, and see what would be required to ship it that I happened upon the toys.

"You must understand; I would never undertake a trip back east without making arrangements for a return shipment, especially when I am the one overseeing its care. How could I not procure something of all that is needed out west? It is simply that the toys came unexpected. Typically, it would have been kitchen utensils, pots and pans, tableware and the like. Tools...dry goods...fabrics.... A few toys for sure. Clothes...lots of clothes, they are light, and can be packed especially tight for easy transport. Oh! Now there's a thought. You asked about toys, but clothes always fetch a good price. In fact, if you knew how many red flannel garments I packed into Rebecca's coach, you might truly think me insane.

"Had we not busted a couple crates while moving them to reach the coach, I would have never seen the toys. However, be it as it may, I did see them. And in spite of the years, they appeared to be in good order. I made an effort to contact the charities, thinking them perfect for Christmas. I asked for their help to distribute them to the orphanages and churches around Boston, but there were just too many. It was after that, while buttoning up my affairs that I decided I might as well ship a few crates out west as well. And, why not?

"The more important question to be asked is how did the firm lose track of twenty some crates of toys, but that it did. I suspect Rebecca's passing clouded my accounting of those crates, like many other things. Or it may be I never knew of them from the start. As far as I can remember, all my imports went to the East End Warehouses without exception."

Christopher drifted off to search his memory, at which point I commented.

"I remember those crates...."

The look on Christopher's face was quizzical. I could see him working to understand how that could have been. It took a moment for him to respond.

"Now, that comes as a surprise. I guess your memory is the better. Please, do tell. How would you have known anything of those crates? They were down on the docks...no place you should have been."

"Yes, that's true, they were. I stumbled into them by accident one day. If I remember correctly, I was in charge of obtaining a large tent for a charity event—I can't remember what. And there was just such a tent recently made available that was laid out in a stall inside that building. I think it had just been repaired, but again I can't remember.

"Anyway, I was waiting for the proprietor to finish out some business and so meandered about the warehouse sticking my nose in places it probably shouldn't have been. In doing so, I happened upon a door to another stall. It spiked my curiosity and again, following my nose, I slipped inside. The room housed Lady Rebecca's coach, and seeing it came as quite a shock. It was a squeeze to get back to the coach, and it may have been then when pressed up against a crate that I observed the toys."

"I find that quite ironic," said Christopher. "At least you might understand how after all these years, I found the coach to be in near perfect condition. I believe the inability for anybody to pass beyond that perimeter of crates was what saved it from the devil's hands. What better way to shield Rebecca's coach.

"Shipping the toys proved to be a simple matter. I enlisted the talents of some crafty old wainwrights to brace the crates together, affix them to axles and wheels, and wrap them in canvas. Afterward, we rolled them out like wagons filled to the brim. They will end up in my goods store at Northpole."

I sat there looking at Christopher and realized that this man was yet the mystery he had always been. I wondered if now, being at his side, I would at last begin to unlock the many secrets of his life—the side of Christopher that haunted me since childhood.

"Tell me something, Claus, do you always do that, or should I ask if you still do that…ship toys and gifts for children? I mean as far back as I can remember you were always shipping toys, or on the docks handing out candies or toys or trinkets. I mean, I saw that firsthand on the docks as a child, but have you always done that? I mean, day in and day out?"

"Day in and day out? No, of course not. I have always shipped toys from our shops in Sweden. It keeps a lot of folks earning a wage on the estate. Remember, fields lie fallow in winter, but our lumber jacks are in full swing moving timber over frozen ground. After milling, we have much scrap wood, a wonderful resource for making toys. In fact, not only a wonderful source for scrap wood, but also for manpower that would otherwise sit idle while waiting out the winter months. Winter was the time of the toymakers, and Christmas time was always the busiest time of the year on the estate.

"As for the docks, well, aren't they always home to the beggars, those looking to work for a pittance, a meal—children rummaging through the garbage...the mudlarks of London? My heart goes out to them, to all of them.

"Listen...you tell me, Elizabeth, now that you have traveled far and wide. You know better than most that the joy of travel is the encounter with all things new and exciting, and it should be, considering the hardships one must endure. Unfortunately, one also encounters the downtrodden and the miserable should one choose to acknowledge as much.

"I, for one, choose to do so. I make an effort to recognize the unfortunates when I travel. I try to appreciate and fulfill their needs, even if only in a small way. It's one of the few things I truly enjoy. Always an embarrassingly small gesture considering my means, but one that brings me a moment of genuine happiness, as it does a wretched lot of paupers. Their pleasure and gratitude is pure. Even now, I am moved to think about it—such reward for so little effort."

"Claus, ferrying barge-loads of toys across thousands of miles of wilderness is not what most men view as little effort."

"True for most men, but then I have plenty of funds and no family, Elizabeth. Those urchins remain the only souls who would yet stand in a downpour, in a snowstorm, a blizzard, to wait my return. I enjoy their welcome. You may say they only wish to see me for my gifts, and I admit the truth of it, but is it less true of any other child? They wish something for themselves and I appreciate the honesty. I have known many men who lack the same honesty. They smile in my presence, run off with my fortunes, and curse me in my absence."

"Claus...." I let out a long wind of breath. "Between you, the toys, the children...I must tell you, at times, I thought I was going mad. Mary, bless her heart, truly thought I was losing my mind. She was just too polite to say as much. Every time you show up, I feel as though I am being mobbed, overrun, by children. First, they arrive and then you arrive, or maybe you arrive and they arrive. Who would know. The whole affair becomes unnerving to say the least. Then my imagination runs wild and I start conjuring up preposterous assumptions and reading way more into their arrival than I should."

Christopher was smiling at me. I could see that glint in his blue eyes.

"Oh, never mind. I probably am losing my mind, and you are laughing at me. I don't need to voice as much. At least I understand why half of creation's orphans fall out of the clouds whenever you're around.

"Just so I am prepared, are children going to be lined up out there as well; children waiting for you to bring toys?"

"Oh, I am sure of it. I always bring them something—always have. Soon as word gets out that I am off on a trip, they start coming around."

"Dare I ask? South Pass, Northpole, how many orphans?"

"Oh, lord. There have been days.... Let me think.... I mean, what can I say, plenty. At least that is what I am told at times. But then, you know that country. It's tough on men, tougher on families, toughest on children. There is an orphanage not too far from the cabin, but frankly, the west sorely needs your skills, Elizabeth. You could do much good out there."

"Alright, I see where this is going."

"Does this mean I am absolved?"

"No. No, not at all. It means I am wondering what you are getting me into."

EIGHTY-SEVEN

We departed Louisville the following morning, made superb time steaming down trip, and tied up in Cairo for a spell to take on passengers, freight, and wood for the boilers. Shortly thereafter, we rounded the great bend at the confluence, and upon entering the Mississippi, steamed upriver until arriving safely in St. Louis the following evening.

Christopher's interests maintained four plush rooms in permanent reservation at the Planters' Hotel. We immediately assumed three to wait out the duration of winter. Without our asking, the hotel management stationed two pageboys around the clock outside our doors.

Our time in St. Louis was splendid. In the company of Christopher, Luke and I were shown every courtesy by the fathers of the community. To be sure, those persons whom I previously met while dressed in the odorous leathers of an Indian upon my arrival at Rachel's were almost embarrassed to find themselves now seeking to be seen in my company. I sought to immediately dismiss this change in status, and in no time was bridging the gap between these fortunates and the homeless shelters of my dear friend, Rachel. Her pockets were now filling with the flood of monies.

"Elizabeth!"

I heard the scream carry across the lobby and at once broke into tears. The sound of that voice was as much a part of me as my own heartbeat. I spun around to see Gracie running toward me with outstretched arms.

"Oh, thank you, God. Thank you, thank you." I crushed her in my embrace and cried with joy. I pushed her away from me and wiped my eyes.

"Let me see you, child!"

"I just returned last night. I have been on the trail for the last four weeks with Taa—."

"Taa! Oh, my word. How is he?"

"He is fine. He is healthy and earns a respectable living. I wanted to say that I returned last night, and this morning I stopped in to see Rachel as is my custom. She told me at once you were in town and I came over straight away. She told me you are here with Luke and…dare I say it? Mr. Claussen?"

Gracie's brilliant green eyes worked to pry into my heart of secrets.

"Tell me, Elizabeth. Tell me it is true. Rachel told me things, but I want to hear the words from your mouth. Tell me, tell me, tell me!"

Gracie clasped her hands together as if praying for a long awaited gift. Her fingers touched her lips, holding back a certain explosion of joy.

"Yes."

My emotion showed.

"Yes, I am here with Mr. Claussen…Luke's father."

"I knew it! I always knew it! You wouldn't say it, but your eyes never lied, not once. You must tell me all! All, I say. Do you hear me? I want to know everything. I want to know the look on Mr. Claussen's face when you told him. I can't imagine! I want to know what happened when he saw Luke. I want to know what Luke thought. Do they get along?"

"Two peas in a pod. Claus goes nowhere without Luke at his side. He is so proud. He is an entirely new man—*a braggart.* Who would have guessed?"

"Ohhhh!"

Gracie was giddy with excitement.

"I am so happy for Luke. At last, he has his own father."

"Where are you staying?" I asked.

"Oh, at a boardinghouse on the north side of town. I usually stay nearby Taa. We work together most of the time now-a-days. Taa says that my being pretty, being a woman, signing, speaking Cheyenne, English, and a hint of French, I am making him rich. To be honest, he has offered me half of his business."

"That is amazing, Gracie. That is wonderful. I have so worried about your well-being. This is the best of glad intelligence. We have so much to discuss. You must stay with me. I insist. You must stay with me here at the hotel."

"Oh, Elizabeth. I can only do so for a few days. We have another party soon to depart. Taa will need me—."

"Gracie! I will soon be leaving to parts far west and I have no intention whatsoever of being robbed of my time with you because of some party looking to be led by the nose into that godforsaken country. You tell Taa, I don't care how much it costs; you will stay with me for the duration. I insist. I plan to pamper you, to spoil you, to hug and kiss you until you hate the very sight of me."

285

Gracie was laughing uncontrollably.

"Fine. I will tell Taa. No, actually, I will bring Taa to see you. He will like that very much, and you can tell him yourself. That way he won't blame me for abandoning him."

"I can live with that. Now come upstairs with me and enjoy a bath like nothing you have ever experienced. I have the best of scented soaps and lotions. I see you still wear those knives. Did you ever learn to wear a dress?"

"Are you serious?"

EIGHTY-EIGHT

Only one thing would have made my life more than perfect. Mary. If Mary had been here, I would have been as close to heaven as might any mortal. Dorrie came down for the winter with Mr. Dorset and stayed with us at the Planters.

Rachel and Caleb bowed to our insistence that they join us whenever possible. They were escorted by the staff to our rooms. Apparently, the hotel went to great lengths to stifle loose tongues for fear of raising Christopher's ire. Free slaves were not welcome at the Planters, but not a single derogatory remark was spoken in their presence. Still, it was sad, even deplorable that we should have to be on guard for their honor and safety. They were such fine people and these injustices were a disgrace, an embarrassment that not so much broke my heart as fueled my temper.

The Planters was plush, but the heart and warmth of love and life were best had at Rachel's place. Everyone was free in Rachel's home. Gracie did stay close at hand while we wintered over. Taa also spent whatever free time he had to be in our company. When the two of them started into telling stories during dinner or over tea and drinks, the dining room would explode into raucous laughter, embarrassed snickers, or silent disbelief. I was tickled to see how Gracie drew Taa out of his famously reserved character. She could fire him up faster than a good bottle of aged whiskey.

With the exception of my dearest Mary, between Rachel, Caleb, Dorrie, Benjamin, Taa, Gracie, Luke, and Christopher, I had all of God's blessings surrounding me, all the blessings of heaven here on earth. No better example of this than when we all came together to celebrate Luke's fourteenth birthday.

If I was unable to have it all for all time, then I was happy to have just one blessing for whatever time given me. And that blessing was Gracie. I was thrilled when during the party she asked if it was possible for her to stay with us just a while longer as we traveled west.

Taa understood Gracie. He urged her to go to us. Maybe because of his own past he was able to perceive her need to refill her heart with the love of family. Since childhood, her life had skirted the boundaries of separation. In spite of her indomitable spirit and independence, Gracie's soul knew the fear of loneliness, and until she chose her mate, only Luke and I could give her what her words would never be heard to ask.

When I brought her request to Christopher, he was not only agreeable to having her join us, but visibly pleased by her appeal. He may have believed his every prayer was answered the day I gave him Luke, but he had not yet recognized the emptiness that only the affections of a daughter could fill. A son could share his dreams, understand his drives, give him support and respect, but a daughter gave hugs and kisses, and love thrice returned.

Christopher was smitten. To say that he could not stop staring at Gracie only made him seem like all other men. But who could know better than I why his eyes followed her? I knew well that look from my childhood years, a world in which he watched my every move and so directed me to achieve my potential. He was searching, looking through her, studying her ways, her temperament, sounding her conscience, waiting for the opportunity to offer her the smallest or greatest part of his support. He would shoot her to the stars.

* * *

It was early April, and the preparations for the nation's westward thrust were running amok over all else. March was the month for obtaining supplies and equipment. April was the month for departure and catching up to friends and family already out upon the trail.

It was mostly about ice and mud. As soon as the ice softened and the mud hardened, and trails became passable, and rivers fordable, the wall of humanity piled up into itself like a giant wave cresting at the Mississippi then crashing onto the shores of western frontiers. To witness the flow of human cargo through St. Louis was more mind boggling with each visit. Everything in the city was geared to engage this massive flow of westward migration.

Most of the settlers traveled by wagon, but we stayed with the riverboats. Gracie was torn between the excitement of boarding a riverboat for the first time and the apprehension of being on water.

"Are you certain these are safe? I have learned how wicked can be these rivers. Don't anybody forget I cannot swim."

"Gracie, the water is the least of our fears. Worry about the boilers not the water."

"Now, you needn't be worrying her about boilers. The boilers are built to the highest standards." Christopher sounded a little defensive. "Gracie, you could probably wade across most of the Platte, but if not, then grab anything that floats. Hang on and enjoy yourself, the scenery is spectacular."

We were all laughing at Gracie's expense. She only felt better after Christopher began pointing out the advantages of the new boat designs that were now remarkably shallow, and their engines so powerful that they could navigate even the difficulties of this river. Most obvious to Luke and me, when compared to the riverboats of the Mississippi and Ohio, these were far smaller boats, and we fully burdened three vessels in order to manage our freight.

Every obstacle was taken in stride but one—that being a flash flood. As soon as those dark ominous clouds appeared on the horizon all hands were at heightened alert, ready at a moment's notice to secure the boats. There was often only seconds to prepare. Storm waters regularly roared downriver closer to ten miles an hour than not. It didn't have to be raining. In fact, oftentimes it was sunny where the riverboat steamed, but the rain having fallen far upstream was soon racing toward us as a foam-crested wave well beyond the blackened skies that gave it birth.

On three different occasions, a terrifying wall of water pent up behind a dam of floating trees, dead animals, and riverbank debris came rushing toward us, bent on staving in the hulls of our small vessels. Anybody not holding on for dear life would have been catapulted into the turbulence of the currents. The banks where we sought shelter simply vanished beneath the broad and boiling wave. We suffered considerable damage on two of the occurrences, lesser on the third.

Fortunately, we always escaped injury or worse.
Unfortunately, I was unable to escape the torment dealt by these three events. The only boat that failed to sustain any discernible damage was the one that ferried the coach. It seemed impossible when one witnessed the fury of the flood and the damage done

to the sister boats. The fact brought back childhood memories of unsettled sailors aboard the REBECCA. I was returned to recollections of the unrest over Lady Rebecca's coach coming through various disasters upon the open seas unscathed, not so much as a blemish on its glasslike vermillion finish.

As a child, I dismissed those things I did not understand. As an adult, I was annoyed by my inability to dismiss the very same realizations. In those days, I understood all things under the watchful eyes of Mr. Claussen were protected. I never thought to question the fact. Now I was an adult and provoked by the past to mention the oddity to Christopher.

"I agree, it is a coincidence. I see it as a matter of knowledgeable hands and luck…and very good luck at that."

"But, Claus, this boat has no damage whatsoever. This is the third time it has come through a major mishap without as much as a paint-scrape."

"Elizabeth, you are being overly dramatic. There is plenty of scraped paint on this hull. You are now exaggerating."

"Claus, please don't do that. Your comments are belittling and upset me. The hull may be scratched here and there or scraped if you insist, but it surely isn't battered into pulp and unable to carry on as is currently the condition of the other boats. The stores aren't torn loose from their bindings to be pitched and scattered about the decks or washed overboard."

Christopher now turned away from his business to give me full attention.

"Elizabeth, I am not sure what you want me to say. We secured all three boats to the shore, as we always do if time allows. When the flood passed by, the trees along the banks broke much of its force before us. The first boat took the brunt of the debris plowed forward by the water and has suffered the most damage. The second boat suffered less, it being protected by the first boat. And this boat saw little threat other than the swell of water. It has always been the last boat of three heading upriver and so stands least likely to suffer consequences, no snags, no sawyers, no sandbars. I find it as simple as that."

He studied me and waited for my response.

"Are you suggesting some other more mysterious explanation?"

I looked over to see Gracie studying me. She had overheard our conversation and now wore a most pensive expression. Her eyes were fixed upon me as if to be weighing my answer. I knew that Gracie had been raised to fully accept the ways of the spirits. I shrugged.

"I have nothing more. Your points are well taken. As always, they make perfect sense."

Perfectly sensible, I thought to myself. And yet, as I stood alongside Christopher while he inspected the coach and its fastenings, I stared at Lady Rebecca's name scrolled across the door in gold calligraphy and remained haunted.

Once repairs were made, we continued steaming upriver along the Platte until we reached the forks. Here was Eastpole or Forktown as is was also called, and it was here we felt ourselves to be nearing home. It was here that Christopher's western reach could be felt. We transferred our baggage, cargoes, and Lady Rebecca's coach onto his railcars. We then boarded the RMR for South Pass Junction.

Gracie started out with the same enthusiasm boarding the train as she did the riverboat. But, as the miles receded into the distance, she grew increasingly quiet and self-absorbed. By the time we were scaling the gentle slope that would rise to South Pass, Gracie was lost in another world.

"Sweetheart?"

"Yes?"

"Are you feeling agreeable?

"Yes. I believe so. Why do you ask?"

"I have been watching you for the last couple of days and have observed how you have been sinking deeper into your thoughts. It took awhile for me to figure out what was going on in that head of yours, but I am sure I know."

Gracie laughed.

"There is nothing going on in my head."

"You may say that, but I beg to differ. I'll wager you are struggling to remember something of your parents. You have been fixed on that mountain range for a long time. I too remember that range. I told you long ago, in time, you would cherish a soul who might have shared something of your past. Time has come. You were then a young girl. You were just full of it, Gracie. I fell in love with you the first day I set eyes upon you."

"You know me too well, Elizabeth. Yes, you do. I remember so much about this land, but barely anything of my parents or the woodlands in the upcountry that we trapped. But, I do remember that the first time you saw me, you were hardly in love. You were horrified, so I have been told a thousand times."

I laughed aloud.

"Yes, you are correct. That is true. I honestly thought I had gone to hell."

"Do you suppose my folk's graves are still to be found? I remember piling a great number of rocks and stones on their mounds."

"I would think yes, most likely. There aren't yet that many settlers poking around these parts, being desert and all. Miners and trappers would be about it, but in time, nature levels everything. I am certain you would find your mother and father at peace and undisturbed where you buried them."

The land where Gracie and I met years ago was slowly passing by. It seemed as though the memories preferred to cling to those vistas now behind us. Gracie became more herself once she realized that someone else could appreciate her sadness of sorts. It allowed her to open up, to leave her private thoughts for comforting conversation.

Christopher and Luke remained silent during our exchange. I knew for sure that Christopher was most interested in Gracie's life, but had the good sense to understand this was ground on which he had no right to tread uninvited. The day moved on, and as Gracie's spirits lifted, so did ours.

Gracie was all eyes when we pulled into South Pass. It was the place that her father instructed her to find before going to St. Louis. Her memories of her "dadduh" were again being resurrected by seeing firsthand the place of which her father spoke. This time her memories were heartening.

We spent three days in South Pass, for this was the center of Christopher's business activities pertinent to the Rocky Mountain Railroad. Once concluded, we departed the junction to ride the rails toward Northpole, the farthest point north on the RMR line. I had never before seen these rails, but the country they traversed was almost as familiar to me as Mary's backyard. We paralleled the mountains, and I stared eastward across the plains. I contemplated the number of seasons, the number of times Gracie, Luke, and I had migrated north and south along that horizon. My mind called out as my heart cried silently for Talk-a-Lot. How I wished to again see her face, to hear her voice.

EIGHTY-NINE

"So, how did you end up with a residence in Northpole?" asked Gracie. "Elizabeth always said that your cabin in South Pass was splendid. She said it had a great view down through a valley. She said it was surrounded by meadows."

"It was splendid," I concurred.

"I suppose it was. I could give many reasons for my moving to Northpole. All the years Elizabeth and you lived with the Tsistsistas, construction on the railroad continued north. I was intent on having it end in the vicinity of the Bighorn Mountains. I wanted to get in reach of Powder Creek basin.

"My very first journey into those northern latitudes left me in wonder. It may have been my getting away from the heat of South Pass, or more likely just getting away from the crowds that were pressing into the junction, that drove me to cherish what I discovered about the Bighorn.

"The ruggedness of the mountains, the unpredictable weather and the challenges of everyday life in those parts invigorated me. The sheer beauty of the land, the purity of the air, the abundance of wildlife, every untarnished feature thrilled me. The vistas brought me peace. They settled me. Life there was demanding, profound, too profound for mere mortals. It was a god's country in every way.

"I rarely leave there. On occasion, I travel down to South Pass on business, but even then, I do so only when my presence is imperative. Otherwise, all my dealings are conducted in full view of the last tie laid beneath the final foot of rail we staked down, where line's end butts up to the pole."

It was easy for me to hear his affection for the land and work whenever he spoke of it to Luke. In fact, aside from our long conversations during the nights of winter, when I first found

Christopher in South Pass, I don't believe I ever heard him converse with anybody as much as he did with Luke. I never joined the two on their ventures into the cities for business, so I never fully appreciated the closeness that had become. Sitting and observing them for these thousands of miles, I could see clearly that their hearts were now one.

Christopher looked out the windows of the coach and studied the passing country.

"It won't be long now...we're almost home. Thank the Lord; it couldn't come a moment too soon." He turned to me. "You will love it here, Elizabeth. Northpole isn't a boom town. It isn't a nightmare of confusion like Boston or even South Pass. Rather, it has been growing at a slow and steady even-handed pace. People in Northpole tend to stay put. They get to know each other and develop friendships that last. They watch your back.

"It isn't much of a place to settle when compared to South Pass, that being the gateway to California and all. Thankfully, the prospects for business and profit will never be as attractive. Northpole exists to do what it was meant. It accommodates the slowly growing stream of wayfarers moving up and down along the Rockies between the upper Missouri and South Pass. It does that well."

As we neared our destination, Christopher offered more to enlighten Luke and Gracie in regard to the development of the pass and pole towns.

"South Pass is now well established and ranks the largest of the five settlements, it being something of a gatekeeper for the pass through the mountains. Eastpole or Forktown as it is often called, is now the faster growing of the settlements due to its location on the forks of the Platte."

He explained how a major route of travel westward was now along that river, and how countless numbers of settlers passed through Eastpole as they ventured toward California and Oregon country. Of course, of most interest to the three of us was to hear about Northpole.

"Southpole and Westpole are little more than trading posts, but a fixed community of sorts has taken hold in and around Northpole. It remains the third largest of the settlements. It isn't a population to be readily seen, as in a town for example, for many of its citizens are hunters and trappers, and spend most of their time out in the wilderness plying their trade. When time comes to cash in their skins, they show up, and as a rule are recognized and welcomed by those who stay put in order to serve them. I'm one of those who stays put."

NINETY

The train came to a halt, but the noise remained in our ears, the smell in our noses, and the vibration still coursed through our backs. Our bodies were grateful for the cessation of movement. We seemed to hurt as much as from any other form of travel, but we made more miles for the same amount of hurt…many, many, more miles.

From the passenger cabin windows, we could look out from the station through the remaining clouds of drifting steam. We could see across the platform and down Main Street, a road flanked by many solid structures. The largest establishment by far was a boardinghouse with an attached trading post, or more accurately, general store located directly across the street.

"That is where I work. That's my office."

"It's impressive—looks to be busy in spite of your absence."

I observed the number of townsfolk milling about the place.

"Once I get you and the children settled in, I will bring you down. Now, I must oversee the freight. Luke, are you ready, son?"

"Yes, Father."

Christopher and Luke were first to step out of the coach. Gracie and I followed them to the edge of the platform. Christopher placed his hands on Luke's shoulders and turned him to face the end of the track.

"Do you see that pole there with the flags flying above?"

"Yes."

"Well, son, the town took its name from that pole, as did the other pole towns. That pole was near one-hundred and fifty feet tall. We drove it into the ground to mark the end of the tracks' northern reach alongside the Bighorn Mountains. The pole was made from the tallest pine that could be found, felled, and ferried to mark the site. It stands as a landmark; and for miles across the flats, and even farther from the upcountry, its flags can be seen flapping in the wind."

Gracie and I grabbed our bags and personals, and followed the men onto the platform. It felt good to straighten out my back on unmoving ground. I looked about. Freight wagons were already headed toward us and lining up alongside the tracks.

Gracie and I stepped down off the platform and strolled back along the road that paralleled the tracks. It appeared to be the only road in town. All the buildings faced the tracks from the west with the high hills behind in the background.

We stood by as our belongings were placed into the lead wagon. The cargo now emptying out of the rail cars was being placed into a revolving parade of uncovered wagons. After the lead wagon was loaded and pulled away, another wagon pulled up at the end of the line. Most of the wagons shuffled goods directly across the street to Christopher's general store and returned to load pelts and skins back into the cars.

We watched as railmen unhitched the locomotive and rehitched it to the opposite end of the train for the return trip to South Pass. We walked back along the tracks and then onto the road until reaching the cars where stood Christopher and Luke. I stopped out of harm's way as Lady Rebecca's coach was hand carried by a large troupe of muscled men and set down upon risers. The wheels were fitted and then the teams and harnesses were brought out into view.

"Oh, heavens! Look at that! Isn't that a maggoty sight," exclaimed Gracie.

"Yes, it is. Exactly as I remember them. Well…. I actually think they look bigger now than when I was a child. Isn't it supposed to be the other way around?"

"I can't imagine those horses ever looking bigger, child or no child," said Gracie.

Christopher signaled for his coach. It moved up alongside the wagons as he and Luke walked toward the road to join us. We climbed inside, and once seated, Gracie and Luke slid the glazed panels back and stuck their faces outside to avoid missing any activity at the tracks. Gracie was especially fixed on Lady Rebecca's coach.

"That coach is unbelievable….the nicest coach I have ever seen…. Oh, look! The horses are now being hitched. I can't believe it. Look at those horses. Aren't they spectacular? They are huge…magnificent…. I don't believe I have ever seen either a coach that splendid or horses of that size."

Gracie was gushing before Christopher and me, but we understood. Every word exclaimed was truth. Christopher beamed with pride and offered a few words for her benefit.

"The coach was always drawn by six or eight Lipizzaners that were also white. However, that was in the city where streets were mostly flat and paved...and hills tolerable. When I decided to bring the coach out west, I decided to exchange the team for Percherons because of their strength and hauling abilities. They are a larger animal than the Lipizzaner."

"I knew they looked larger," I chimed in, delighted that my imagination hadn't got the best of me.

"Oh, no. These animals are indeed larger. Those wheel horses are about twenty-five hundred pounds each, the swings about twenty-three hundred, and the pair of leaders are weighing in at about twenty-one hundred pounds. The steep grades in these hills should be no problem for them. I also believed they would handle the cold better. My concern now is that they adjust to difference in feed."

"How much do they eat a day?"

"Plenty."

"What's plenty?"

"I don't know, Gracie. A bale apiece plus a couple of buckets of grain, less if we don't work them."

"Humph." Gracie was taken by the teams. "I don't know that I've seen many white horses."

"You haven't. The problem I had replacing the Lipizzaners was color. I wanted white and Percherons can be found now and then, but interestingly enough, white is considered a bad trait. In fact, they are black when young. For that reason, I bought them for a good price. Unfortunately, it cost me ten times more to find them."

The coach and Percherons passed from view. We took the lead on the way home from the station. A good number of wagons followed us as we were carried along a lane that turned to rise steeply from the town until reaching Christopher's lodge built upon a broad ledge at the higher elevations. One could sense the crisper air of altitude. The views were sensational.

"It is beautiful, Claus."

"I said you would like it."

"I love it. The place is no shack. How many rooms inside?"

"A great room with a fine granite fireplace, a large kitchen and six bedrooms each with an indoor tub and toilet, and a number of storage rooms."

"The view is breathtaking."

"It never grows old. There is also a spring-fed creek that runs close by. You will soon see it. It floods in the spring and refuses to freeze until faced with the worst of winter. It provides a sufficient supply of water."

The structure was palatial by western standards. A number of large barns and stables were built on the grounds and it was in one of those barns that Lady Rebecca's coach was later returned to deep sleep. The horses were led to the stables for feeding and care. The remaining wagons disappeared into various structures to be emptied of their goods.

We enjoyed all the comforts that Christopher's wealth could provide. It became most obvious that neither place nor possession was out of reach for those in the heady league of Claussen. And yet for all the finery, for all the accommodation put in place for our comfort, we were never as happy as we were when in Christopher's company down below at the boardinghouse with its general store.

The boardinghouse was most prominent in the line of structures situated across the street from the train station and in plain view of the tracks. It boasted twenty-four rooms, six held for private use, the rest for let. It presented a great room with one wall of stone that transformed itself into a grand hearth and provided the heat for the building. Here the wild game stewed and roasted for hours, emitting aromas that filled the structure and spilled into the streets causing every appetite to salivate. The winds carried the taste afar and pulled in the hungry by nose and reputation. The kitchen served the best repast for a hundred miles and more.

Christopher had added a large wing that nearly doubled the size of the building. The wing contained a general store and trading post. It also housed his preferred office, in which to do business; for here he was in the midst of all activity and a mere shout from passengers arriving at the station.

More often than not, at day's end Christopher and I would dine immersed in the heat and glow of the great granite hearth and afterward retire in our private rooms at the inn. We would awake to the smell of hot coffee and breakfast already underway. A few steps removed from the breakfast table and we were at our work, he at his office and I now at my store. The lodge in all its grandeur was used more by Christopher's favored business associates who came out to hunt or came with families to vacation.

Unlike Christopher and me, Luke and Gracie tended to spend more time at the lodge. Much of Luke's time of late was spent in the company of Gracie. Luke was not one to shun his lessons with Christopher, but he was still very much an Indian at heart. Gracie was all about exploration and investigating potential work as a scout for hire. The prominence of mountainous terrain was new to both of them, and her determination to explore every crest and valley was more than Luke could handle. He refused to be left behind.

Christopher viewed knowledge gained from exploration as important as learning the books, and so encouraged both Luke and Gracie to use the lodge as their base camp. He outfitted them well to travel. They were given goods and advice.

"There is only one truly dangerous element in these parts...the weather. Don't ever take it for granted. Always keep one eye on the ground and one on the sky. To do less will leave you both dead of cold. It doesn't have to be snow. In the summer it can be rain that will sap the heat clean out of you. Do you understand the seriousness of what I say?"

"Yes."

"Always prepare for the worst. This isn't like the desert. You can't fall off the desert floor. Take an extra mule or two for supplies. Do you understand?"

"Yes."

In short time, not only did they not sleep at the boardinghouse, they also did not sleep at the lodge. As often as not, weather permitting, they slept out of doors miles distant. Because of their Indian upbringing, I understood how they approached and respected nature. This allowed me the freedom from worry, and the ability to go about my daily activities in peace.

Between the good food, clean beds, and well-stocked general store, the boardinghouse stood dominant as the social station for townsfolk to gather and jaw. A local tavern came in a distant second, it being a rowdy place for men only. In very short time, I came to know most of the folks in and about town.

Christopher wasted no time in getting back to his work. He managed the trip back from Boston with only minor chest complaint, but we had to accept the fact his health was permanently diminished. The days of attacking his passions relentlessly and taking his trophies by storm were behind him. His pace was slowed considerably. I didn't mind. It was the first time in my life I was able to keep up with him in his endeavors.

"You have been forced to slow down so you might remember to notice me."

"Oh, ho, ho! What gibberish, I dare say. Once, I would have said only a blind man would fail to notice such beauty, but I am now blind. So, I am left with only a deaf man would fail to notice you."

"You are sweet…. No, wait a minute. That was an insult! Are you saying I nag? Is that it?"

"No. No, ho, ho."

Christopher broke into a hearty laughter and then commenced to cough and clutch his chest.

"That will teach you. I hope it hurts."

"Ho, ho, ho. It does. It does. I've learned my lesson."

I leaned over his desk and kissed him on the cheek.

"I worry for you, Christopher."

"Pointless worry—drama. I am strong as an ox."

"Rightful concern, and pointed out—stubborn as a mule."

"Oh, ho, ho, ho," he continued to laugh as I left his office.

I settled into my new surroundings with ease, as did Luke and Gracie. Unlike the smoke and foul stench often encountered in the congestion of Boston or St. Louis, here was a world flush with fresh air and open space enough to flood us with vigor. I was again living in God's garden with the Tsistsistas. It was a place, a home that was second nature to Luke, Gracie, and me.

The following summer found all of us still together, in good health and spirits. Christopher spent most of his time in his office tending to business and socializing with faces new and old. I spent most of my time just outside his open door tending the general store.

Gracie divided her time between helping me with customers and suddenly dropping everything to leave with those same customers in order to investigate some heretofore unseen canyon, valley, or stretch of unspoiled river of which they glamorized. She was determined to become one of the most knowledgeable scouts in these parts.

When not out investigating with Gracie, Luke continued to spend most of his time being schooled by Christopher and learning how to manage the vast holdings of his father. There was no longer any doubt about his abilities, he was brilliant. I never doubted it. Since his days as a toddler, he was lost to his insatiable curiosity. He observed, he absorbed, he categorized, and he presented his case with impeccable logic.

The first notable change to our now routine lifestyle came shortly after Gracie began to pine for her lost boot. It was the childhood boot turned papoose, turned backpack, fashioned by her father. It was the only possession that connected her to her parents. It became an obsession. Ever more I watched her staring east across the plains lost in her thoughts. I could see it coming. I waited for the words. What I didn't expect was the announcement made by my son.

"I'm going with her."

"What!"

I was shaken very badly by his intention.

"I'm going with her, Mama. I already told her I was, and she said that was my decision, but it had to be cleared by you."

"I don't—"

"Elizabeth."

I turned to see Christopher, who had stepped out of his office, and was now watching me.

"Yes?"

"Let the boy go. He is sixteen and every bit a man. Gracie is twenty-seven and well seasoned to be sure, but even she is safer traveling in his company. He is a big boy—takes after his father." Christopher winked at me. "Besides, it would be good to keep his knowledge of the wilderness sharp. Too much time in the office studying the books will make him soft and insipid. Look at me."

I said nothing more. I was upset by the thought of the two of them roaming the wilds, but it was very much three against one. Luke and Gracie were adamant about their intentions and not to be dissuaded. The two were gone for most of the summer before returning to me safe and sound.

When next I laid eyes on them, in the fall of the year, they arrived brimming with energy and excitement. They had spent nearly two months with their old friends and renewed bonds. Ho'neheveho was overwhelmed to see them, fearing they had been lost to the captors. He asked about me and was overcome with emotion to know I had been fortunate enough to escape. He called the medicine man at once to prepare a ceremony thanking the spirits for my good fortune. The whole tribe feasted and danced before a great fire.

With a sad face, Gracie conveyed the news that neither Talk-a-Lot nor Hotoomee'e was ever seen again. I was broken hearted by the news, but I had learned to accept the pains of loss. Gracie and Luke had rekindled ties with the Tsistsistas and through them I began constructing an assistance program to aid the tribe in whatever small way I might be able. I had stores shipped out from St. Louis and set aside at the lodge until they migrated into the area. At which time, I was invited to again sit at the fire with Ho'neheveho and his braves as Chief Vehona'e, catching up on news and learning of their joys and heartbreaks.

Before I knew it, a second year had passed, and then another. Gracie was now thirty years old and in no way a child of innocence. She was as frontier hardened as she was beautiful. Gracie flew in and out as frequently as our store door opened and closed. She had reunited with Taa and assumed half the business as he had insisted. She brought far more to the business than her looks.

Gold had been found in the California territory and it fired up the imaginations of thousands. Madness and gold fever ran rampant. Even in remote settlements like Northpole, panners, miners, and fortune seekers were arriving with evermore frequency. They were looking to scour the country and competing for the best scouts for hire. Gracie was there to oblige.

Taa focused on getting the panners outfitted in St. Louis and safely across the plains, and Gracie focused on getting them resupplied at the stores in Northpole or South Pass and then escorted into the mountains and beyond. She kept an office alongside Christopher, but preferred galloping off on a horse to sitting behind a desk.

With the full measure of Christopher's support and logistics to back them, Gracie and Taa were not only successful, but famously reliable and that translated into highly profitable. Their fortunes grew rapidly. The panners, the hunters and trappers, the speculators, the rail crews and merchants, folks of every walk came and went or stayed and settled. The result was the same all over, whether St. Louis, Eastpole on the Platte, or South Pass, the towns grew larger as the migrations continued westward.

Gracie had yet to find a man, and so her free spirit lifted her to lead parties high into the misty realm of the Bighorn Mountains and beyond. Unknowingly, she was giving birth to countless stories about a blonde-haired, green-eyed angel that were certain to replace all the legends of the Blond Ghost of years past.

Luke was now eighteen years old and journeyed alone to the East Coast when he, not Christopher, determined the business required it. Luke was gently relieving Christopher of his duties at the helm of a boundless empire. It was now Luke's influence that was emerging from the Rockies to the harbors of the East Coast, from the ports of St. Louis to the bayous of Louisiana.

His father and I were both grateful to see Luke did so with humility and grace, for he was now a very powerful figure. His affinity for the Indians directed his heart to see to their welfare in any way he might. In this way, his interests paved a new road on the map of Christopher's charitable landscape. Christopher remained focused on managing his charities primarily in the east; I on the orphanages out west, and Luke along with Gracie and Taa worked to alleviate the misery of displaced Indians everywhere between.

Northpole only served to encourage more business and needs, and continued to keep Christopher busy from sunup to sunset. I worried constantly for him and his heart, but he would get downright belligerent if I should take it upon myself to fuss over him. He was big and stubborn, but I loved him. I loved him with all my heart. Marriage was never considered, nor did we ever again share a bed. Yet, I felt the full measure of his love and spent my days content in his company.

Though the trees did still the winds

They could not silence cries

Of wolves that crept beneath their limbs

With firelight in their eyes

Woe to thee, woe to thee

NINETY-ONE

Her adolescent body, driven far beyond mere exhaustion was grinding to a halt. It had run its course. Her lungs and legs burned fiercely. Her body had gone to the extreme in order to save itself from the horrible stalking death.

Frantic, she had driven those youthful energetic legs to the point of turning dense and heavy as lead. Their weight dragged her to a halt. Entirely spent, incapable of supporting her further, she fought to keep them from buckling. She was no longer in control and unable to manage one more step for the sake of her own life.

She was surrounded by the dark of night. Night filled with a haunting chilling chorus of howling wolves calling out to her creator, telling God to open the gates wide for her pitiful return. The blood-thirsty creatures boasted of her impending demise. Toward the heavens in a ragged harmony of whooping cries, they proclaimed the inevitable departure of her spirit and the delicious remains to be had. Their proclamations, as ghastly as the end about to befall her, echoed for miles between the steep wooded canyon walls.

Wolves as high at the jawline as her own small frame watched her through dark slits catching the cold light of the moon. Thin from starvation and salivating profusely at the sight of her, they began to seep out of the dusky twilight of evening. Seven...eight... nine...the pack emerged from behind the curtain of pine and scrub. They pawed at the ground, scraped it with their nails and sniffed the air. They were stretching their tight bellies, nipping at each other, teasing themselves, honing their talents for killing, all wanting the heat of her blood.

But her blood went cold as ice. She glimpsed fragments of their low fleeting images sprinting silently, indirectly toward her. The animals moved briskly across a deep carpet of needles fallen from the safety of the treetops to quiet the drama playing out upon the forest floor. She tried once more to run but it was hopeless. Resigning herself to this terrible end, she turned to face the predators.

The beasts were bounding at speed, moving in an effortless glide, flickering in the dappled moonlight as they criss-crossed the earth in tighter and tighter patterns. In that last moment, when fully confident of their strength and number, they turned in unison toward her and lunged. She threw up her frail defenseless arms to ward off mammoth jaws lowered from lips drawn back to clear the rows of flashing gnashing teeth. In her final second, she defied them with her only weapon, a primal instinct. She screamed for her mother.

* * *

309

Dakota sprang forward. Sitting up abruptly in her bed, she gasped for breath in an enormous convulsion. The howl of a wolf could yet be heard in the distance. Pain barreled through her head. Unbearable, impossible, pain throbbing so severely, each beat of her heart drove her into paralysis. She moaned in misery and again cried out to her mother.

She was gaining awareness, a realization she was no longer dreaming, yet, she was terrified. The experience had been so real; it was difficult to accept as only a dream. Dakota believed that she was awake, but her vision was dim, narrowed as if sleep walking, as if she were stuck in the darkness of a netherworld. She was confused about everything except the pain. The pain was real. Something was very wrong. She called out again half sobbing, but her mother remained deaf to her plea.

Dakota could not open her eyes because even the dim light of dawn drove pain through her head like skewers made of glistening morning-light icicles, each ray inflicting additional misery if that could be physically possible. She nudged her younger sister, Raven, with her elbow.

"Raven…. Raven."

She attempted to look at her sister, but her neck was so stiff and immovable, she could do little more than stare straight ahead. Her eyes shifted and she glanced at the top of the bunk ladder.

"Move, Raven", she spoke feebly. "Move Raven, I don't feel well. I'm gonna throw up".

Something needed to be done. She felt awful as if her insides were pushed up into her throat. She needed to get past Raven and off the bed, but Raven would not awaken. Dakota's stomach rolled with nausea. In agony, she climbed over her sister. She wrestled to free herself from the tangle of blankets. She grabbed hold of the ladder. She swung her leg out from under the bedding and over the bunk rail. She placed a foot upon the step and shifted her weight. Her world spun wildly. She hung on tight. She was confused. Her leg had no strength. She placed her other foot onto the ladder step and found herself quivering with weakness. A tingling sensation moved up her back and neck. It flowed in waves along the outside of her arms.

With concerted effort, Dakota clutched at the ladder styles to compensate for legs she could not trust. She lowered herself a step at a time and moaned at each surge of pain that shot up through her frame. It collected at the base of her neck and moved around to pound itself furiously into her temples. She grimaced, wishing it to pass. A bare foot reached the cold wooden plank of the cabin floor.

Followed by its mate, her feet moved her inward to lean across her mother. Dakota dropped to her knees, and laid her head upon her mother's back. She was dizzy. The room continued to spin. She closed her eyes. She tried to shake off her sleep. It seemed useless. It was so much easier to avoid all movement, to leave her eyes closed, to shut out the painful morning light and go back to sleep. But there was this extreme pain in her head, pain she didn't understand. She needed her mother's help to stop this, to make it go away. Why wouldn't she awake?

"Momma, wake up. My head hurts. I'm sick, Momma."

Dakota lay upon her mother for a moment, jostling her now and then. She was groggy and confused.

"Momma, wake up. Momma!"

She was irritated by her mother's refusal to respond. She was irritated by a creeping fog that hovered about the cabin floor. It was thick. It hurt her lungs. She wanted fresh air, something easier to breathe.

Fighting off the throbbing pain in her temples, she knelt up straight and twisted around to face the room. Cautiously, she cracked opened her eyelids into narrow defensive slits. Keeping out as much of the painful light as possible, she noticed dawn's light was mostly a gry-white cottony glow filling a room that appeared undefined and featureless. This was something she had seen before, but never like this. She sensed the smoke to be the problem.

Dakota turned back to wake her mother with renewed vigor. Braving the morning light, she opened her eyes wider. She leaned over and pulled back her mother's hair. Her mother was facing away, facing her father, but she noticed at once the odd grayish cast to her skin.

The look of her mother appearing more dead than alive smacked her senses hard. Thoroughly unsettled, thoroughly confused, she studied her mother's face. What was happening? What was this? Suddenly, the worst of all possibilities crept into her consciousness. It was as fearful a thought as the wolves in her dream, the ones that moved through trees in the shadows of her awareness.

Dakota blacked out. Her mind went totally blank. It might have been seconds or minutes before she returned from her mental oblivion. She was puzzled. What had she been doing? Did it matter? Why was she kneeling here staring at her mother? Her eyes were drawn to the curious blue mask that covered the face of everything good in her life. A second time, she was jolted by the sight of death before her, and her memory was jarred back into place.

She quickly reached across to her father, and in spite of her splitting headache, she pulled hard on his arm. She pulled again. It was to no avail, he refused to respond. She reached over with both hands, grabbed his wrist, and tipped him back against her mother's side. The exertion riddled Dakota's head with waves of agony. It forced her to step back, hands pressed on her temples, eyes pressed tightly shut. Behind closed eyes, she was further burdened to see an image of her father also cast in that same haunting shade of grayish-blue.

"Ohhhhhhhhhhh. Ohhhhhhhhhh. Mammmmaaaaaa."

Dakota stopped. She waited. The pain settled, but perplexed, Dakota stepped back from the bed and the scene before her. Her hands were still pressed hard against her temples as she raised her head to look up at her sister.

In was difficult to think clearly, but she pieced together the oddity of her parents' inaction, the deathlike sleep of her sister, and the thick smoke that wasn't natural. There must be a connection, she thought to herself, but for now all the misery convinced her it was time to vomit.

Dakota's feet scuffed the flooring, flopping beneath deadened limbs that she dragged over to the cabin door. She threw the latch and swung it open to the white wilderness beyond. She stumbled out onto the porch and dropped on all four, hanging her head off the edge to heave up her insides. It didn't happen. The brightness of the snow on the porch prevented her from opening her eyes more than a crack. But that limited view was enough to see the profound blue of her fingers and nails now spread out from hands placed to support her.

Her palms rested upon freshly fallen snow. The outside air slapped her silly with its icy mountain morning gusts. She shivered from the cold as the biting wind swept across her sweat smeared skin and sucked the heat out of her drenched nightgown. And yet, the frigid air seemed to wake her up, not just from her sleep, but also from her confusion. Her head still hung limp off her shoulders, but inside, the murderous hurt started to fade. She worked to bend the stiffness out of her neck. The pain was being blown away by the breeze. Maybe the wind was so cold it simply made her numb. It didn't matter; numb was a much better way to suffer.

The air was good. Her thoughts were no longer so disconnected. She raised her head, and eased back onto her haunches. Finally, she raised herself on legs that gave better confidence, legs that felt stronger and repaired. She rolled her head about with more ease, around and around until her neck loosened. Her thoughts were definitely more lucid and the pain was subsiding from intolerable to mostly miserable.

Dakota began to sense how grave was this situation before her, one not fully realized in her heretofore mystified mind. She shivered in her damp nightclothes but no longer had any urge to vomit. She turned to look back and study the shadows in the cabin. It was now easy to see the bluish smoke wafting out from the open door. It was the same color as her parents.

Shivering, Dakota stepped back into the cabin and went directly toward the bunks. She wished to stop her shaking. She wished to climb back into bed, to cuddle up next to Raven and surround herself with the warmth and security of their blankets. Yet, something in the mists of her mind warned her away; something instinctive surfaced to say danger was all about. She returned to her mother's side and then shook her as violently as she was able, but to no avail. There was no response, nothing, nothing at all.

The more her head cleared, the more aware, the more Dakota grew frantic. She stepped onto the bottom rung of the bunk ladder and looked at the back of her baby sister. Dakota was beside herself. She recalled those days of her eighth year, a time when her mother was pregnant with Raven, a time when she had another sister.

Her only playmate, Flora was five, two years older than Raven, when at winter's close, she came down with the fever. It felt as if she died overnight. Her death ripped the heart out of Dakota. Even now, the memory remained devastating, one she had no desire to experience again. She climbed another step, and another,

314

quicker this time in order to lean across the bed rail and grab a fistful of Raven's nightgown. Dakota pushed and pulled her sister viciously.

"Wake up, Raven! Wake up! Waaaakeuuuuuuup."

She struck her hard on the back. Raven murmured but little else.

It was enough. Dakota removed the cross rail and tossed it onto the floor. She dragged Raven across the bedding and pulled her sister tight to her chest. With much effort, she embraced Raven and drew her down off the upper bunk. Carefully, she balanced the weight, lowering her sister's small frame to the floor. Still holding the child in her arms, she carried her to the threshold of the front door and laid her upon the now snow-speckled floorboards. She worked to awaken Raven, but achieved little more reward than a faint groan.

By now Dakota's wits were fully about her. The pain continued to retreat and was mostly tolerable. Discomfort was now due to losing a battle against the cold. She was freezing, shaking uncontrollably. She understood the fresh air to be important, but also knew that neither she nor Raven could be left exposed to the winter air for more than a few moments.

She ran back to her bed, reached up, and with a forceful and determined yank stripped the bunk of its blankets. She dragged the bedding across the flooring to Raven and wrapped her up snugly. She considered the delicate blue mask buried within the last fold of the blankets. It was her mother's face; it was her father's face; it was a haunting face.

Dakota could no longer dismiss the temperatures that racked her with spasms. She could no longer uncurl her near frozen fingers, and so moved toward the woodstove. She knew well the bucket of hot water that rested permanently atop the stove. It was always there, always melting snow and warming water for morning wash or daily hot water needs.

She tickled its flat un-rippled surface with her fingers. She flicked small splashes of the heated water on her hands, and after a moment, ever so slowly, she lowered her numbed fingers into the pail. It was painful, but it was a good hurt, and in short time the heat was absorbed by her hands and wrists. Tethered to the bucket by frail arms, she was helpless to do anything but stare over at her parents. She refused to allow any unwanted thoughts to enter her safe place. Instead, she closed her eyes and focused on the warmed blood now moving up her arms and flowing back into her being.

As Dakota stood before the stove, she also took note of the fine wisps of smoke drifting outward from cracks and joints about the cast iron box. Believing the stove was the reason for the smoke and the disaster she cared not to consider, she opened its door. She peered into the guts of the blackened rusty monster.

The inrush of air ignited the embers afresh setting flames to roll about silently within, but before any heat might be enjoyed, Dakota grabbed the pail of hot water and threw it into the stove's belly. As if a demon writhing in the throes of death, the stove exploded, belching up its innards, clouds of suffocating ash and smoke. It hissed and coughed up a miasma of steamy filth before slowly fading away in a fit of diminishing creaks and pops. Dakota was forced to withdraw, forced back to the front door where she gulped more of the outside air. She ran away gladly, believing with satisfaction that she had killed the killer.

The temperature was brutal and it sucked the heat of the hot water from her in a heartbeat. She remained to shiver from the cold, or possibly the residual pain, or maybe it was the added burden of a fear she would not face. With good air in her lungs, she rushed for her clothes. She put on her heaviest slip and dress, her woolen leggings and boots. She put on two sweaters and her coat. She fetched her mother's shawls and wrapped them about her. She fitted her scarf and mittens. Lastly, she draped both her mother's and father's coats over her frame.

The poisoned air of the cabin was being bled off by the breezes that blew past the open door. The wind was sucking it out along with the last vestiges of warmth and family. It was now easy to breathe, the smoke barely visible. Whatever had happened, she sensed it now to be over. She slid down the back wall, and like a massive pile of dirty laundry sat huddled on the floor opposite the cabin door. She was unsure. She was lost. She pulled her knees up under her shawls. *Don't forget to pray*, she thought to herself as she called out to Santa Barbara, the patron saint who protected all from sudden death. She then waited patiently for a guiding thought to enter her head.

Dakota sat surrounded by the solitude of death, sudden death to be sure. Only the wind blowing past the door with its unrelenting howl, and the crack of icy branches giving way under the weight of snow broke the silence. Off in the far distance she heard the faintest cry of a crow. From within the shadowy atmosphere of the cabin, she stared into the featureless brilliance outside. She watched the streams of snow slip sideways past the opening, pushed onward by an impatient wind.

Dakota drifted back and forth, in and out of her thoughts while her eyes remained fixed upon Raven lying at the doorstep wrapped in blankets. Her baby sister was motionless, either fast asleep or dying before her upon the floor. The thought made her shudder. Snow had begun to collect atop her blankets. The floorboards about her were now dusted in white.

"Don't forget to pray," she said out loud. "Please, Santo Mauro, protect us from the cold. Please, Santa Barbara, protect us from sudden death."

317

Her momma raised her to believe there were saints whose job was to listen for prayers from the desperate and frightened. In those times of need the patron saints would come to guide and care for them.

'Pray when times take their toll,
for patron saints to save thy soul.'

Eventually, Dakota arose to her feet and walked over to where Raven lay yet motionless, yet knotted up in the bedding. She lifted the flap of material covering the wee face. She smiled. The blue mask was gone.

"Thank you, Lord. Thank you for leaving my sister."

Dakota gave thanks with a soft voice that soon shattered as it broke into sobs. She was grateful as she gripped the bulk of material and dragged her sister back inside to be near her. The air inside was still and fresh. With affection and concern, she embraced her baby sister now lying up against her. She rocked her, and the closeness warmed them both.

Dakota rocked and rocked in silence. Her outside belied the speed at which her young mind now raced in its struggle to work out a plan. She accepted at a distance that her mother and father were dead. She wouldn't let the realization come too close. She allowed herself to accept the possibility, but nothing more, preferring instead to know their spirits were powerful and protective.

Her utmost fear in the absence of her parents was the night. Death roamed the woods at night, and darkness would come sooner than later. The days were short in times of winter. Her mother taught her to pray to Santo Giles, to ease her fear of night.

Dakota had little time to consider the crushing loss awaiting its chance to ruin her life. For now, there were more pressing matters. It was all of five miles to Uncle Kib's cabin. Five long hard miles down a canyon buried deep in snow that stopped all motion. If she could get the mule hitched to the sleigh, she might be able to handle him, and bring Raven with her.

"No."

Her thoughts were expressed aloud.

"He's too big and mean. He will surely kill us both."

…And too hard to handle without help from her father or Uncle Kib. The mule was stubborn and disliked leaving its shed and food in winter. The animal could kick with a vengeance, and she was bound to get hurt messing with it. And that would be the end for Raven as well—better to leave the mule alone.

She could try and walk the five miles, but that would mean leaving her sister in the cabin alone with her mother and father. Raven would be scared to death if she awoke alone, unless she first froze to death. Dakota sighed, she thought hard in hopes of working out a way to protect Raven. It had to be done right for Raven's sake. It had to be done right for what she, herself, needed more than anything—*to keep this sister.*

Dakota determined the only possible plan would be to pull her sister along on their play sled for the five miles. She knew the way. She had gone down the trail many times both in summer and winter with her father. It was a long ways. She would have to take her time. Pack lots to eat. Bundle up.

"What if he isn't home?"

She spoke her concern aloud. She didn't want to think about the possibility. Yet, whenever Uncle Kib was going off trapping or to town for any length of time, he always told them so they wouldn't worry about his disappearance. She couldn't remember him making any mention of a trip. He should be there. He would be there. She was certain her uncle was home. If he wasn't, he wouldn't be far off.

Yes, she would use the sled. Her mind being made up, she uncovered Raven and dressed her for the bitter winter temperatures. It wasn't easy. Raven wouldn't stir. She wouldn't wake to help. Dakota refused to consider any injury to Raven. Instead, she stepped out to the side yard and retrieved the sled. Freeing it from the depths of a drift, she brushed it off and pulled it up to the front door.

Back inside the cabin, she packed up whatever food she could readily take and placed it into a backsack; biscuits, preserves, dried meat and smoked fish. She didn't need much because Uncle Kib would feed them as soon as they arrived. She reached for a cup, so she and Raven might drink from the stream if it flowed, and a knife to split biscuits and spread preserves, which in turn made her think of taking a bigger knife along for protection.

The chill of her blood-curdling nightmare returned as she spied her father's sheathed hunting knife draped across her parents' headboard. As if wishing not to awaken them from their sleep, she carefully took hold of the handle and withdrew it slowly from its leather sleeve. She studied the keen edge of its blade, touching it lightly with her fingers. She stepped away from the bed and suddenly split the air with a swipe. She swiped again, this time followed by a lunge and a thrust of the blade into an imaginary beast.

As if successfully killing the formidable creature, she lowered the knife that loomed larger than the skinny arm supporting it. Her attention was again drawn toward the bed and her parents. She wanted time to cry, to ask what would become of her, but her worry of what would become of her sister overshadowed all else. She understood her role in what would be the life or death of her mother's youngest child, her remaining playmate. She turned away from the bed and slipped the knife into her bag.

Deep in thought, assessing what was needed to survive, Dakota sifted through all she had placed inside the bag. Her gaze suddenly snapped toward Raven, whom had stirred. Raven was beginning to show signs of waking. This raised Dakota's spirits enormously, for if Raven could walk, everything would go much easier.

Raven was now wrapped up warmly in sweaters, a coat, bonnet, and two thick woolen scarves that left almost nothing of her baby face visible to the eye. Like a giant overstuffed rag doll, Dakota dragged Raven by her coat sleeve across the floor of the cabin to its door. From there, she struggled to carry her across the porch and settle her onto their sled. Once safely secured, Dakota walked back into the cabin, picked up her parents' coats from the floor, and carried them outside to spread over Raven for added protection.

Dakota walked back into the cabin one last time. She felt the truth of the circumstances pressing hard upon her young soul. She stood in that awareness gazing at her parents. There was no sign of movement. No sign of li...*never mind*. She wondered why this wasn't all a nightmare like the wolves that chased her. She wondered why she couldn't just wake up. In silence, Dakota stared at the lifeless forms.

Finally, concern for Raven being alone outside drew her back to things that must be done, and she pulled the covers up to her mother and father's chins so they might remember how she cared for them, tucking them in and keeping them warm. She leaned over and kissed her mother softly, she reached for her father's strong hand; the grief was coming to break her spirit so she backed away. She asked Jesus to watch over them.

Dakota turned about, picked up the backsack filled with food, and slung it over her shoulder. She closed the cabin door behind her. The wolves wouldn't get in. She crossed the porch and looked down at the bundle that encased Raven. She shook her shoulders to position the backpack and then stepped off the porch into the drifts. She picked up the sled's manila rope; looked at Raven once more for assurance, and then struck out against the driving snow.

Dakota pulled for little more than half a mile before beginning to wonder if she might have greatly erred in her ambition to make it safely to her Uncle Kib's. The snow was deep, still blowing hard, and it was much more difficult to tow the sled than she imagined. Its frame, along with Raven's legs and the coats, were plowing and dragging from the weight and bulk. The pace was dreadfully slow.

Her dream of the wolves haunted her. It kept her wary and hard pressed to make way. She continually spied deep into the surrounding woods. Her head had started to again pound with pain. The bright snow hurt her eyes and caused them to tear. She was tiring fast, and preferred not to consider the countless obstacles that confronted her every step, for she knew there was no going back.

After a mile, she was panting hard and her mouth felt dry and rough. Her lips were chapped from the constant passing of moist breath and eating snow. She removed her coat and scarf, tossing them onto the sled. She let the icy wind reach the sweat beneath her clothes to cool her.

At two miles, Dakota was utterly exhausted. Her head was swimming as thoughts of reaching Uncle Kib's faded into wishful dreams. She fell to her knees, this time, too weak to get up again. She toppled over face first into the snow and lay there, panting hard. It felt so good to lie down in the undisturbed fluff. She closed her eyes and allowed the pain in her head to subside. She felt the pounding of her heart.

Without opening her eyes, she swung her arm about to push more snow into her mouth. She savored its moisture. She would take a moment to rest. She was simply spent, exhausted, not an ounce of energy left to be had. She wanted only to rest a spell, to catch her breath. She was beat. She was sleepy and her head ached.

It took nearly an hour for Dakota's young body to call up whatever reserves of energy might be found. She was awakened by her cooled state. She was shivering badly after having fallen asleep without her coat and scarf. She remembered tossing them onto the sled. She opened her eyes to find herself partially buried. She raised her reddened cheeks off the ground and looked back at Raven who was still asleep and unaware that she too was now buried under a carpet of freshly fallen snow.

Dakota pushed up onto all four and then onto her knees. Much like a wary squirrel, she looked around for any sign of danger. She looked about the area carefully until satisfied, at which point she labored to stand back up on weak and shaky legs. Not only was it a struggle to wake up, but it was a struggle to call on muscles she had never known to be so full of complaint. There was to be no relief from the pains of her exertions. She stumbled back to the sled and shook off the snow covering her coat and scarf. She was shaking severely as she moved to put the garments back on. She stripped mittens off hands unwilling to open. She observed where the sled rope caused lines of blisters to form across her palms. Her fingers appeared nearly as blue as they had back at the cabin. She rubbed her hands back and forth briskly. She worked stiff fingers to fasten the buttons on her coat. She replaced the mittens.

Dakota was yet groggy and rocked back and forth in thoughtless rhythm as if ready to topple over and fall back asleep. Mindlessly, she looked ahead through the mist of her breath, past the flakes landing upon her nose, until she found herself focused on a small clearing far in the distance. Her spirits were suddenly lifted, for she recognized the place at once; it being where her father and Uncle Kib met to fell trees for firewood.

The clearing was supposed to have been midway between her house and Uncle Kib's cabin. And it was often said to be so, but in fact her father always protested that Uncle Kib cheated and insisted on it being closer to her father's home. Her uncle believed the closer the firewood, the less the burden on her father—a family man. The clearing was a place where her father and Uncle Kib met twice a week to talk, chop, saw, and split wood. They were the best of friends.

Dakota knew well this firewood found stacked in neat rows, high as her head. She used to play with the sawn wood, and make pretend cabins while her father and Uncle Kib worked. The clearing was a place of fun and good memories. A stream came in close to the woodpiles, and quenched her father's thirst when working the saw or swinging the axe. The memories made her thirsty. Maybe there would be some water yet trickling along.

Falling asleep had not been part of Dakota's plan. By the change in day's light and the dark, low-hung clouds, she knew she had lost precious time and twilight would soon be upon them. Suddenly uneasy, she searched the surrounding woods for the fearful eyes of wolves. She reminded Santo Vitus of her need for protection. The clearing beckoned her to hurry with its feelings of happiness and familiarity. It wasn't foreboding as were the woods that now frightened her.

Dakota felt anxious and yanked hard to free the settled sled. She leaned hard against the rope and blisters. She never looked up from her boots as she strained to keep the sled moving forward at speed. She only needed to reach the clearing and its woodpiles. Now stumbling badly from side to side and tripping over her own feet from fatigue, she arrived at the place she believed to be safest.

Dakota panted hard. She could barely stand up straight as she viewed the two rows of neatly stacked firewood that barely broke through the drifts which overran them. After taking a moment to catch her breath, she began kicking, stomping, and grunting as she pulled the sled across a snowdrift that filled the space between the rows. Pulling with persistence, a long succession of energy draining tugs, she fought her way through the neck deep snow stuffed between those rows of stacked wood until midway back along their lengths. At that point, she called it quits, let loose the rope, and dropped to her knees with an enormous sigh of relief.

Dakota was spent. Sleep was a poor word for what she had the past night, and she had yet to eat something this day for energy. She wasn't so much feeling sick or hungry as she was utterly drained of life. She felt unable to do anything more than fall back into the drift and stare up between the two rows of firewood, up at falling snow that was nearly invisible against that backdrop of grayish, low-hanging clouds. Nestled within the pillow-soft bed of snow, the faint touch of flakes upon her lashes forced her blinking eyes to finally close.

Dakota dozed, but this time her instincts kept her from the deep, restful sleep she so desired. The whispers of wind and wood would not be shut out by her dreams, and so they frightened her more by the minute. Behind closed eyes, her senses stirred and she understood that she would never make it to Uncle Kib's cabin before nightfall. It would have been hard if Raven was walking, but trying to pull her on the sled under such circumstances was impossible at best.

The thought of nightfall made her hair stand on end; she felt goose bumps move up her neck. Her eyes slowly opened to stare into the gray heavens as she listened for the call of the wolves. Except for the distant cry of those crows, the world remained deathly quiet. She grew to fear all she was unable to see, but for being between the rows of wood. Her only solace being, if she could not see out, nothing could see in. Better yet, nothing could move through the two walls. Wolves couldn't move through wood. That thought spurred her to think back on the pretend cabins she used to build. *She would build a cabin*—a cabin for real to shelter her and Raven from the wolves.

NINETY-TWO

Dakota pulled herself up the wall of stacked wood. She walked out from between the rows and studied the firewood that lay in orderly piles poking up out of the drifts about the clearing. These were piles of wood, sawn and sorted by lengths, none of which were cut small enough to fit in the stove or fireplace. There was also the splitting mound, a brush pile, and a kindling pile. She looked at the sky and the shadows now deepening across the woods. She tried to gauge how much time before nightfall. It wouldn't be enough to waste.

Dakota began to poke about the piles. Her father and Uncle Kib always halved their saw lengths right up to the final cut. The first pile was the longest, the second half that size, and so on until the lengths were stacked into the two long rows ready for splitting.

Dakota went to the pile that contained wood cut twice the length of those logs stacked in the rows ready to be split. She retrieved these longer logs and laid them between the two stacked rows, joining the two rows midway along their length to form four walls. She did her best to stack her wood as neatly as the rows stacked by her father and Uncle Kib. Her father's rows stood very solid. They were evenly spaced near four feet apart the whole of their length.

Dakota next went about toppling logs off the ends of the stacked rows. Those she used to backfill her walls and pack the space between the two original rows. Here, what she didn't gain in neatness, she gained in mass. Her freshly built walls were essentially two huge impenetrable piles of wood built up between the two rows of firewood stacked by her father and Uncle Kib.

With all four walls in place surrounding Raven, the sled, and their belongings, Dakota went out to another pile for the longer-trimmed limbs that would act as roof beams spanning the two walls she built. When she laid enough limbs across the walls to feel secure, she began to pack snow into the cracks and spaces until forming a very tight windproof enclosure. Lastly, she dropped a short log of larger diameter into the hut. It would be used as a step to help her and Raven climb out. Dakota stepped back to compare her latest structure to those earlier childhood attempts. She was pleased with the results. The end of her project was timed perfectly to the end of the day, short as it was.

As twilight settled, Dakota sat outside her shelter atop one of her father's stacked walls. Her feet dangled through the opening in the roof of her tiny abode. Methodically, she rocked her body back and forth in perfect measure as if keeping time with the clock of life.

Dakota was tired. It felt good to just sit and rock. As her mind wandered, she sucked on an icicle that had been clinging to a nearby log. She refused to follow her thoughts back to the cabin where slept her mother and father. Instead, she looked down through the opening to where lay Raven. Raven slept, and that was disturbing. Raven was rambunctious. Raven never slept.

Dakota steered clear of the mental roads to heartbreak, and instead focused on her need to reach Uncle Kib's cabin on the morrow. That would be all of three miles and there would be no woodpile to offer shelter should she fail to make it. She would have to start out early, as soon as the safety of daylight allowed.

It may have been an omen, or a reminder of the importance of her success, when her thoughts and the tranquility about her were dismissed by the first howl of a wolf. It was off in the distance, but the warning stole her breath. She was no longer in the protective walls of her father's home. Nervously, her eyes darted back and forth as she checked and double-checked her work. The walls were solid, immovable. Another howl, now closer, was enough to prompt Dakota to drop inside and seal the roof. From inside, she carefully slid the heavy limbs now balanced on one wall across the opening to the other wall. It was dark inside the sanctuary, but because she was unable to pack snow between the limbs slid in place overhead, a small amount of light was let in from above.

Dakota settled back to stare up at the roof limbs where slivers of dusky light faded to black. The howling of wolves now came from many directions, some off in the distance, some nearby. Oddly, the darkness inside the shelter brought quietude, a sense of invisibility, and a sense of security. The walls were built thick. The air inside was undisturbed, and the temperature began to warm.

Dakota felt a certain confidence. She paid rightful attention to disturbances outside, but now using only her sense of touch, she focused on quietly attending to Raven, checking her clothing and whatever else she required. Knowing that Raven was asleep and would remain quiet, Dakota felt it permissible to relax. She could do nothing now but wait. She spread out her parents' coats neatly across Raven and herself. She drew up her collar, positioned her scarf, lay down alongside Raven, and let out a long breath. Dakota closed her eyes and so gave herself away to a deep sound sleep.

NINETY-THREE

Hours passed while Dakota's young body worked to rid itself of the poisons, the fatigue, and return something of the energy she took for granted. At that point, she stirred. There yet remained a mild throbbing in her head. She sensed her stiffness, the hardness of her bed, the confinement of her clothes. She was confused about the unfamiliarity and closeness of her surroundings. She waited quietly for some familiar sound, her mother's stirring, her father's snore.

As she waited, her memories began falling into place and duly revealed the tragedy she chose to ignore. Tears began to seep from behind eyes yet unopened. She felt them trickle across the bridge of her nose and spill onto the scarf that separated her head from the cold hard ground.

Dakota felt the firm grip of grief begin to twist her guts. In the coffin-like darkness, the first sob broke past her lips to be heard by her ears alone, or so she thought. For her sob returned the sweetest sound ever—the sudden jabber of Raven. Her sister was awake. Dakota perked up at once. Her eyes opened wide striving to make sense of the shadows.

"Are you awake, Raven?" Dakota asked with emotion.

"Yuuuuuuhh-ehet-ehet."

"Ohhhh. What's the matter? Are you all right, honey?"

"Un-uh-ehet-ehet. My head hurts. Where's Mommy? I'm hungry. I want Mommy. I can't see."

"Shush, shush, you'll be fine. I'll get you something to eat. Shushhhh."

Dakota sat up and pawed about the shelter for her bag. She fumbled about its contents until she produced some biscuits.

"Here. Here's a biscuit. Eat this you'll feel better."

Dakota reached out into the darkness and nudged her sister. Raven grabbed Dakota's arm at once, following it to down to her hand and the biscuit therein. She took it. Dakota listened to the sound of her sister eating. It brought her much relief in the darkness where her joyful expression went unseen.

"I want some water."

"You're going to have to eat snow. We don't have any water."

"Can I have some snow?"

"You may."

Dakota started to feel about, but realized almost at once, there was no clean snow to be had inside the shelter. What hadn't been trampled down whilst building the hut was either full of dirt or had been turned into ice from the heat of their sleeping bodies. It wasn't snow she would stick in her mouth, and she wasn't about to give it to Raven.

"We don't have any snow right now."

"I have to go potty."

"Ohhhh, nooooo," Dakota uttered her despair.

"I have to go potty."

"I know. I heard you. I need a moment to think."

Dakota had no desire to open up the shelter. She had even less desire to wander about outside. She searched for options.

"Do you have to go pee?"

"Yup."

"Just pee?"

"Nope."

Raven's answer was reinforced by the sudden reek of poop permeating the tight space of the hut.

"Raven! Did you mess yourself?'

"Nope."

"Are you sure?"

"Yup."

"You still have to go?"

"Yup."

It was unfortunate, but Raven had to relieve herself. When Raven had to go, there was no waiting. Dakota had thoughts of a most disgusting smelly mess smeared across everything in the darkness of the hut. On top of this Raven wanted water. Dakota was facing little choice, but to go out into the cold and fearful night. At least, she would have the benefit of moonlight. Instinctively, she was already listening for suspicious sounds outside.

"I have to go potty."

"Shush! I know. I know, sweetheart."

Dakota strained to hear any sound beyond the walls of their hut. As she listened, she realized that Raven wasn't the only one who had to go potty.

"Alright, now you be quiet. I don't want any wolves hearing us. Do you understand?"

"Yup."

"Tell me what wolves do," asked Dakota with a stern voice.

"Wolves wait in the woods for little girls who wander."

Even at her tender age, Raven understood well the danger of wolves. Dakota knew she had just put the fear of death into wee

Raven. But Dakota wasn't kidding. On this night, if anyone could get them into trouble, it would be her sister.

Dakota stood up and slowly began to work the first limb back across the opening. Quietly, she worked back another, and another. A view of the night sky with all God's unblemished stars opened overhead. The frigid outside air poured down through the opening as if to emphasize how warm it had been inside. She shuddered and went on to work another limb back and then another when suddenly—.

"Oh!"

Dakota's hands shot out, but not fast enough. The limbs and been moved too far back across the wall and went out of balance. They slipped one and all downward off the snow covered wall, and disappeared from sight. Dakota felt the pangs of fear stab her insides. She fully realized that the opening to their shelter was now unprotected. She had no choice now, but to step outside if only to retrieve the limbs. Standing upon her log step, she slowly raised herself up through the opening. She was most cautious. She listened.

"I gotta go potty," Raven whispered.

"Shush."

Dakota listened to the sounds of the night but heard nothing. As least the skies had cleared away the suffocating snowstorm, and allowed the moon to shine bright for the time being. She was able to see a fair distance both up and down the canyon. There was no movement to be noticed. She could see into the trees and about the bank where a creek might or might not be frozen at this hour. In the daytime, the sun's rays often provided just enough warmth to flow water thinly about the frozen creek bed. At night it was usually too cold.

Dakota dropped back into the shelter, and the light of the moon followed her inside. She glanced at Raven who was looking up into the shaft of moonlight while making a full assortment of peculiar faces. She was blinking her eyes like an idiot.

"What on earth are you doing?"

Dakota couldn't help but to chuckle.

"I can't see."

Raven answered matter-of-factly, as often did a young child. Yet, Dakota thought her reply somewhat strange.

"Are you all right, honey? You got something in your eyes? You have to be careful when you look up or you'll get a face full of dirt."

"I can't see."

"I'm sure you can. It's not that dark. Looky here. Let me see your face."

Raven squinted her eyes and made more of those unnatural expressions.

"Raven? What are you doing? Now that's enough. Can you or can you not see me? Have you got something in your eyes?"

Dakota felt alarmed.

"You're blurry."

Raven raised her arm and touched Dakota, seemingly to reinforce her belief that Dakota was before her. Dakota thought Raven too young for such an ongoing charade, and so pulled off her mitten.

"How many fingers do you see?"

She held up three. Raven squinted and pulled Dakota's hand near to her face.

"Three."

Dakota succumbed to her anxiety long before she heard the answer. As soon as Raven reached out for her hand, Dakota knew the truth of it. Within the beam of moonlight pouring through the opening overhead, Raven should have been able to see three fingers from the other side of the canyon. Dakota sat stupefied while studying the murky image of her sister. It had to be the sickness. She couldn't begin to fathom what had happened at the cabin. Fortunately, during the brief moment she sat speechless, she gained enough foresight to keep her concern to herself. No good would come of further frightening Raven. She changed the subject.

"Oh! What was that noise? *You little stinker.*"

Raven laughed as Dakota stood up to see out the opening. Dakota refused to think on sad thoughts, whether they be of her mother, her father, or now, Raven. She shushed her giggling sister while warily scrutinizing the play of shadows along the woods' edge. She searched up and down the canyon until reasonably confident all was well for the moment.

"We can go outside, but you must be very quiet. I don't want to attract any wolves. Do you understand me?"

"Yup," Raven whispered an almost imperceptible response.

"Stand up."

Dakota took a firm hold under Raven's arms and pushed her up through the hole in their roof. She followed behind. Dakota helped Raven down off the treacherous pile of strewn wood backfill, and taking her hand, walked her between the stacked rows. In whispers, Dakota undressed her sister, and the two squatted side-by-side to relieve themselves. In one stomach turning whiff Dakota realized that Raven had a bad case of loose bowels. This too, was sure to have been from the sickness.

"Ohhh, honey. You are a mess. Ohhhh. Ohh, mercy. Now listen to me. You stay here and you be very, very, quiet. I am just going back to get something to wipe you clean. Do you understand me? Can you do that, Raven?"

"Yup. But hurry up, I'm cold."

"I know. Now stay here and be quiet. Don't move. Don't move an inch, or I'll never get you clean. I'll be right back."

Dakota raced back to the shelter and dropped back through the opening. In the moonlight she had no problem finding her father's knife. The steel stood out at it flashed in the darkness.

"Dakotaaaaaa?"

Raven cried out in a frightened whimper.

Dakota shot back up through the opening like a jack-in-the-box. She looked over at Raven and then her eyes swept the vicinity with sudden urgency. In a loud whisper, she scolded her sister.

"Raven, I told you to be quiet! Now you shut your mouth or I will paddle your butt. Quiet! Do you truly want wolves to eat you?"

Raven went silent. Dakota waited a second to be sure, at which point she dropped back into the hut, and taking her father's knife, sliced off the end of her scarf. She returned to Raven and began washing her bottom with snow.

"You are a mess little girl. Now, I'm a mess. Oh, that is nasty."

"That's cold, Dakota."

"I know. I know."

"I'm thirsty."

"I know, sweetheart. Here, eat some snow."

Dakota buttoned her sister back up. She washed her hands vigorously with snow until she could no longer stand the pain of cold. The two walked back between the rows and climbed up the wood strewn backfill. Once back atop the rows, Dakota halted briefly in the moonlight.

"Can you see me now?"

"Nope."

The answer cut like her father's knife. Dakota's eyes watered as she reached for Raven. She lowered her sister gently through the opening.

"Well, just sit on your sled and rest for now. In a moment, I'll slice you up some jerky, all right?"

"Yup."

Dakota looked out across the canyon. With care, she stepped part way down the strewn logs and retrieved the roof limbs. She hauled them back up into position atop the row, and then feeling all was again in order lowered herself down through the opening.

"My head hurts," said Raven.

"I know, honey. So does mine."

Dakota was overcome with a feeling of despair; it suppressed most of the appetite she might have enjoyed. The clouds hadn't completely left the valley, and they sporadically blackened the snow cover, snuffing out the brilliance with sharp-edged waves that swept over the shelter. Making best of the intermittent moonbeams that ventured into their sanctuary, Dakota opened up her sack of staples. She produced a slab of jerky, and using her father's knife, began slicing the dried meat and some hard biscuits into manageable pieces. She handed the morsels to Raven.

"I'm thirsty," Raven whined.

"I know, sweetheart."

Dakota knew Raven hadn't had a drink since before bedtime the day before. All the while Raven had slept, Dakota had poked around for icicles on which to chew. Dakota fished about for the tin cup. She was also thirsty and knew it would be near impossible to melt snow inside their hut. They could just keep eating the snow she brought in from outside or she could make a run for the stream. It coursed close by, only a short distance into the wood from the clearing. Dakota figured she could satisfy her own thirst at the stream so long as it flowed. She could bring back a cup of water for Raven, or at least a big chunk of ice to break up as needed.

After explaining her intentions, she stood up to leave, but was halted.

"I want Momma." Raven fussed.

"I know, honey. I do too. We won't worry about that right now. You rest now."

Dakota mimicked her mother's manner of comforting.

"I don't wanna stay here."

"It's just for a moment, while I fetch some water. You'll be fine."

"But I wanna go with you."

"You can't, honey. Remember? You have dirt in your eyes. You can't see…remember? You said you couldn't see."

"I can't see."

"I know, and I believe you. And I don't want you to trip and fall, or hurt yourself. The creek is dangerous. You could drown. That wouldn't be good. It's best you stay put. I'll be back along soon, I promise. I'll fetch some water at the creek, and be quick about it. Now shush."

Dakota had only been outside the hut for a few moments while cleaning Raven, but her teeth were already chattering.

337

Her clothes were still damp from the sweat of hauling the sled and building the shelter, and so she was quickly chilled. She reached for both her mother's and father's coats, and stuffed them out the opening in the roof. Once out herself, she donned the garments. She hardly moved with grace, but the warmth was worth the inconvenience. She climbed down the pile of strewn wood and walked off between the rows. Once away from the stacked wood, Dakota set off across the undisturbed snow of the clearing. Upon reaching the edge of the wood near where flowed the stream, she disappeared into the thick of the trees.

The day's storm had passed while the girls slept, and now there was only the stillness of night, the creaking of the forest, and the on-again-off-again light of the moon. Ever vigilant, Dakota crept warily through the woods as the oversized coats dragged smoothly across the snow until being snagged by the thorns and claws of summer's dead undergrowth. With much suspicion, her eyes scanned the slits between the trees for as far as she might see when the clouds allowed.

True to memory, she found herself immediately upon the stream. The rocky bank was steep, ice covered, and treacherous. She searched out any twigs or branches that were frozen securely in place. She gripped anything that might save her from somer-saulting off her feet.

Once safely down, Dakota stepped cautiously across the frozen current and studied its surface. There were no cuts in the snow cover to declare a flow of water, no glistening trickle to be seen. She squatted and began wiping the frozen floor with her hand. She cleared a swath across the creek from one bank to the other. There was no trace of wetness. Everything was iced up solid.

Dakota decided she would carry back a chunk or two of ice, and if she could fill the cup with smaller pieces, it would provide far more water than would packed snow. She next realized that she had lacked the foresight to grab the big knife. She set about scouring the bank for a suitable rock to break up the ice. To her dismay, every stone judged usable was held firmly in place by winter.

Dakota stopped short. She thought she heard something. She halted her business and stood dead still on the creek. She held her breath. She had allowed herself to be distracted. Did she hear Raven's voice? She turned slowly to look outward from within the creek banks. She studied the clearing as she listened to the creaks and groans of trees, sounds of night scattered about the woods.

In short time, she settled down. All seemed well, and Dakota's eyes dropped from the clearing back down to the creek bank. There, she spotted a shard of rock that likely protruded out sufficiently from the earth to be dislodged. She pushed and pulled, but it wouldn't budge. She wanted to kick it in the worst of ways, but it was too high up the bank. Yet, it looked so ready for the picking.

With no viable option, Dakota started hammering the rock with the bottom of her cup. It loosened, but the sounds of her strikes were amplified by the cup. It unnerved her to be making so much noise in the dead quiet of night, and yet, the rock was clearly loosened. So, with a few more strikes…. She clutched the shard, and after a moment of determined pushes and pulls the earth gave it up. With a sense of satisfaction, she took hold of her prize.

Dakota stood up and checked the clearing. She checked as much of the field about and beyond the clearing as she could see. She took close note of sounds and sights up and down the creek bed. Only after feeling safe did she drop to her knees to strike the creek ice with the shard. Chips of frozen water began flying in all directions. She picked up the first pieces and jammed them into her mouth. She started to suck on them, but impatience for the moisture drove her to crush them with her teeth. The cool wet ice brought relief as she hammered away. She hadn't realized how dry was her mouth. The pleasure would have been perfect had she not heard something beyond the crunching that now reverberated through her head.

Her jaws stopped at once. Her every muscle locked in place. Slowly, Dakota raised herself erect. The ice was suddenly too cold, and wanting no distractions, she pushed it out quietly with her tongue. She strained to hear. Turning her head, she listened, first out of one ear then the next. She again looked up and down the moonlit creek bed. She saw nothing other than black puddles moving silently along beneath the clouds, but her anxiety mounted. She rose quietly to her feet.

Dakota looked out over the top of the banks; again she scanned the clearing, again the flats of the canyon, and finally the woods that surrounded her. This time she wasn't comforted. This time she didn't immediately settle down. Her senses were peaked. Her thoughts were now only of Raven, and so her attention was fixed on the clearing. Her eyes hardly blinked as she stared and waited. All seemed quiet and in order, but there was this doubt. There was this inexplicable feeling. And as if to reward such doubt, there came the full measure of fright.

Dakota might have seen something, but if so, it was precisely when the world went black beneath an obscured heaven. Her chest collapsed. It went tight. She was working to get her breaths as she pleaded for a miracle.

"The light, where's the light?" she whispered to herself in a panic. "Santo Vitus, please, where is the light? Please, protect Raven. Please, please, please, protect Raven."

Outside the cluster of trees that lined the creek, the moon's beams drove down to split apart the clouds seemingly stalled above the clearing. Both rows of stacked wood instantly lit up bright in stark shades of ghostly white. There were no branches to bend over the clearing and dapple its ground with moving shadows. There was no reason to be fooled. She stood stock still and watched. She watched. She watched.

And then she saw it. Not a shape, but a blur of motion. It moved out from between the stacked rows of wood and slipped around behind the back row, out of sight. Fear ripped through Dakota like a gun shot. Wolves! She moved forward, but the earth went dark, and her body ceased to obey. It refused her will to move. She went senseless with dread. She feared making the slightest sound in this wilderness within which she could not see. Only her ears served to take account of movement in the distance. Was there only one? Were there more? Were they wary of the scent and so crept in quiet and cautious?

A sudden thought of Raven's blindness, of her inability to see, instantly racked Dakota with remorse and broke her body free of its bonds. She had to get back to Raven before the pack arrived. The valley went brilliant; Dakota leapt up the bank and straight away slipped on the ice-covered rocks. Falling hard onto her chest, she slid back across the creek. Her mind was flooded with worry for her younger sister. She rushed to get back on her feet before the light was lost and fell a second time. She rose and she fell a third time. She was acting out of emotion instead of good sense.

Dakota stopped to collect her thoughts. She quickly realized that stupidity and impulsiveness would spell doom. She would allow herself to be fearful, even frantic, but she determined to be level headed. She then scrambled on all four, and so crawled off the ice and up the bank only to reach the flat ground as the world was again lost to pitch black. This time Dakota moved forward blindly through the dark in spite of her terror. She arrived at the clearing just as the trailing edge of shadow passed over. In the glow of near daylight, she was filled with anguish. She was too late.

The fearsome creature stood proud and statuesque atop the stacked row of wood. With a black coat upon its back to reflect the night sky and white underbelly to reflect the snow, it boasted its oneness with the world in which it lived. The animal's command was obvious. The light that glorified the animal also exposed Dakota. She knew the wolf heard her approach long before it saw her. It stood unmoving, looking at her; at first curious, next calculating, and lastly emboldened.

Dakota felt every muscle tremble. She watched the wolf prance toward her and stop. The animal momentarily studied her. It then bolted in her direction, knocking snow off the stacked wood as it ran along the row until reaching its end, at which point the beast leaned forward and dropped its head. The creature lowered its stance and displayed the eruption of craggy hair now standing up across its shoulders and neck. It was easy to believe this demon could leap a country mile.

Eyes now narrowed, it glared in her direction. The beast pulled its lips back tight and nipped at the air. The sounds of its clashing teeth were easily heard. The wolf was lean and lanky, possessing a frame that enhanced its massive jaws now baring rows of large, glistening, saliva-covered teeth. It retreated back along the top of the woodpile. It turned to look back with an air of supreme defiance. Dakota felt the challenge. The animal then lowered its heartless eyes as if to dismiss Dakota so it might look down through the opened roof above blind Raven.

At this point Dakota was yet a distraction. The wolf kept her in his awareness, but was most interested in the closer smells of jerky and young Raven that emanated from within the dark chamber below. The wolf danced back and forth, back and forth, as it stared down through the opening from different perspectives. As it sniffed about the area, Dakota stepped gingerly forward. Her stealthy advance proved pointless as the wolf's head snapped upward to suck in her scent through flared nostrils. It met her eyes squarely, and growled its first blood-curdling warning to stay clear of its meal.

And then there came the worst premonition possible—*the pack*. Dakota strained to pick apart the tree lines for something distinct. There was only suspicion, a questioning of one's senses, of one's eyes. It was a matter of questioning one's superstitions as glimpses of ghosts and demons streaked through the light of the moon and the dark of night. These were images to be seen only in the peripheral vision. But Dakota knew beyond question; she could feel them in the chill of her blood. The pack was approaching with speed.

There was no time for thinking out this matter. Dakota was not ignorant of wolves. She spent countless nights listening to them pawing about the cabin. Countless mornings, she stepped out the cabin to see their tracks in the yard. She had on a few occasions frightened one or two away in the early morning light by opening the door to fetch firewood. The animals were a fact of life in the canyons, a lesson taught early to all. There was good reason to fear them. They were large, cunning, and vicious. Yet, when separated from the pack they were often wary. If un-cornered, they quickly vanished.

Most important, Dakota knew well enough that once the pack gathered it was over. Once the pack arrived, they would be here for the kill. Once the pack arrived, Raven would be shredded.

Dakota understood with perfect clarity that she would have to make her move now or forever be silenced. She knew with perfect clarity that she would forfeit her life this very moment in order to save Raven from a death too horrible to contemplate. The thought of her baby sister being mauled by the jaws now drooling above her was all that Dakota needed to replace fear with the euphoria of total resignation. She prayed to Santo Vitus and the saints for protection. Armed with her passion and a prayer, Dakota walked boldly forward to face the agitated beast.

The creature was made most unhappy by this unexpected affront. His teeth were splashed across clenched jaws that failed to contain the grizzly threats now rumbling toward her. The animal was infuriated. It dared her to approach. Every inch of its body backed up the challenge.

The black-backed wolf displayed its impatience, turning away from Dakota, to call on Raven. It drove its head through the opening with a growl yet trailing on its breath. Dakota panicked. She ran forward screaming, instantly earning the wolf's undivided attention. The animal pulled back from the entrance, but his head remained suspended over it. The large skull dropped low, its rage apparent as it sought to flaunt its power. The beast assaulted Dakota with fresh bone-chilling threats.

The snarling was too much for young Raven. She was lost in a world of obscurity. She saw nothing but shadows passing back and forth above her, shadows blocking whatever moonlight filtered down through the opening to wash across her face. This time it was she who let out a wail, a manifestation of loneliness, terror, and tears. Her fearful howl, erupting from the hole, was just sufficient to startle the wolf for a split second, time enough for Dakota to act.

Fate had provided Dakota with one chance only. She had spent the afternoon picking through woodpiles as she constructed the roof and sides of her shelter. She had managed to disperse a good deal of snow from atop the piles while digging away for her needs. In doing so, she uncovered all manner of useless scrap and kindling lying about the splitting mound.

Now, more by instinct than thought, Dakota dove for the kindling. Frantically, grasping anything that could be raised, she began slinging scraps in a crazed state of mind. Her supply was unlimited, and she dismissed any idea of sighting in the wolf. Her sole focus was on launching all manner of knots and debris, letting it rain down in an unending stream both about and upon the beast.

The wolf was thoroughly startled, and at first attempted a show of defiance, but after two or three good clobberings and a mess of confusion falling at his flanks and backside; it had sufficiently experienced Dakota's throwing arm. The wolf began to back away. There was little room to retreat atop the row of firewood, and the animal soon jumped clear. Dakota continued to let the missiles fly over the rows until she saw the animal retreat to a safe distance. It now began to bay, calling out its complaint, and calling in that barely perceptible motion moving ever faster through the shadows of passing clouds.

Dakota wasted no time. She ran for all she was worth. Raven was crying her heart out. Dakota sprinted between the stacked rows and scrambled up the pile of strewn wood. She eyed the entrance and jumped feet first into the hole without concern for the safety of either Raven or herself, but was fully stopped short in her descent. An involuntary scream escaped signifying the shock of surprise that riddled her through and through.

The extra coats, the extra clothing she had put on to keep warm had slid up her frame to gather as a massive clump of material at her armpits. She was wedged in, hung up, and to make matters worse; the coats had also snagged the ends of the balanced limbs that were to seal the opening. They toppled lengthways into the shelter.

Dakota kicked and squirmed like a tortured cat strung up by its tail. The steep slope of the roof limbs prevented her from gaining a solid footing on ground or her log step. The sense of impending horror suffocated her as she convulsed in fits. The mishap caused a mere second's delay, but time enough for her to see the returned wolf leap toward her from out of the darkness in a great arc of attack.

There was no time for her to consider the danger or her demise, for at once the bristling, snarling, monster of an animal, haloed by a swirl of drool and chomping teeth came crashing down onto the row of stacked firewood to stand before her. It roared out its fury and the hot mist of its breath swept past her face. She peed without control. She shrank from fear. Cowering, she instinctively threw up her arm as a shield. Without hesitation, the animal attacked, tearing into the frail appendage.

The enormous jaws snapped shut with the force of a steel trap. Once firmly within its grip, the creature shook Dakota senseless. It dug in and hauled upon her arm with such force that it pulled her halfway out the roof opening. Dakota had spread her legs and hooked her free arm under the remaining limbs. Her fingers were wedged tight between the logs of her father's stacked firewood yet frozen in place. She was momentarily keeping herself from being slung out and carried off.

The wolf would not relent. It snarled endlessly with such ferocity, and thrashed Dakota about with such force, it left young Raven to suffer the worst possible torment. She was out of her wits and so did the one thing that most likely saved Dakota's life. In an attempt to seek security, Raven clamped onto Dakota's leg. Her weight dragged Dakota back from certain doom.

"Momma! Momma! Momma!" she screamed.

"The knife! Poppa's knife! Raven! The knife!"

Dakota heard Raven's pleas of desperation floating somewhere far from reality. Hers was a second-by-second struggle between life and death, the balance heavily in favor of the beast. She hung on tenaciously, and this only encouraged the beast to pull the harder. It shook its massive head side-to-side, it pushed and pulled, but Dakota held on, as did her sister who now sensed the wolf's intent to separate them. Dakota's shoulder was badly strained, the ligaments torn and twisted. It burned with pain, but the thickness of the coats had prevented the creature's teeth from breaking her bones.

The roof limbs were now being lifted away as well by the animal's strength. The shelter was beginning to collapse amidst the battle.

"Raven! The knife! Give me Daddy's knife!"

It could only have been the intervention of Saint Vitus, the protector from wild animals, which saved the girls. Dakota was at wit's end when she felt the cold steel of her father's hunting knife brush the back of her free hand. Blind Raven was trying to locate her. Raven felt out Dakota's free arm and positioned the knife handle into her grip.

The second that Dakota unhooked her arm from under the roof limbs, she was ripped loose. Raven lost her grip and fell back as her sister was yanked up and out of the hole. The moon was bright, and so in spite of all the fear and confusion, she was able to site her mark. Her sacrificial arm was now bent at the elbow leaving the wolf's nose only inches from her own, its jaws locked tight with determination. The beast suffocated Dakota with hot breath that floated growls and snarls, but it was too close for its own good.

Dakota thrust the knife straight upward as she screamed with bold disregard. Every scrap of remaining strength was expended for the sake of Raven. With all her might, she drove the blade deep into the predator's neck with a twist at the base of the jaw. She was given no choice, no other place to strike. But fate knew best, the knife was sharp, and the blow delivered true. The animal, bent on killing his prey, hadn't seen the blade rise up from below, from beneath the arm within its jaws. It hadn't thought to release its grip.

Now, it was the ear-piercing yelp of the wolf to be heard. The beast jumped backward, which worsened the wound by forcing the knife's edge to angle away and slice open the throat. Dakota fought to keep hold of her weapon. The animal exhaled showers of blood as it choked for a breath. It attempted to retreat at once.

Bewildered and bleeding profusely about its mouth and neck, the wolf fell backward off the stacked row. The creature disappeared into the woods, its white bib soaked in blood, and dripping a dark spotty trail for the rest of the pack, now looking to find their next meal.

The forest broke into a frenzy of yips and cries before falling to an eerie silence. Sanity slowly returned to Dakota. She lay across the roof of her hut, her numb, lifeless arm hanging limp over the backside of the stacked row. At first, she was unsure of whether or not she was going to die from wounds she had yet to discover.

Raven's renewed whimpering broke the short-lived silence and distracted Dakota from her self-pity. Dakota was coherent enough to understand scant precious time was given her to repair the entrance, but for now, she wanted only to calm Raven. She eased herself back through the now broadened opening in the roof. She found her footing in spite of the numerous angled limbs underfoot.

Once inside the hut, Dakota lifted the limbs up out of the hole and balanced them on the stacked wall. The moon, yet dodging clouds, was presently shining bright, and prompted her to inspect her arm, which was now throbbing painfully. She removed her father's coat. Then she removed her mother's coat. She followed with her own and the two sweaters. She was shaking, but she felt nothing of winter. She was full of adrenaline. It could have been a hundred below zero and she would never have noticed. Having ripped off the garments, she moaned from the pain of raising her arm up before the light of the night sky.

She observed the black bruises that covered her forearm. It was decidedly numb, but at least she could move all of her fingers. She rubbed her right hand up and down the forearm and was relieved to find no sign of blood or puncture wounds. She then slid her hand up to rub her shoulder, which was ravaged to an almost immovable swell of badly bruised tendons and ligaments.

"Thank you, Jesus. Thank you, Santo Vitus, for hearing my prayers. Thank you to whoever else watched over us. Thank you for my life. Thank you for my arm. Thank you for keeping Raven safe. Thank-you, thank-you, thank-you, thank-you, thank-you."

Dakota continued to shake fiercely as adrenaline worked its way out of her system. The intensity of thunder in her chest eased as her heart returned to a more regular rhythm. She was grateful for whatever time given to gain back her wits, but the not too distant sound of wolves kept her pressed to consider repairs needed about the shelter. At least, the pack sounded to be stationary. She believed the animals were following the scent of fresh blood; otherwise by now they would have been back for more.

Being free of the binding coats, and feeling agile, Dakota jumped up out of the hole, and stood tall upon a stacked row to look down through the canyon. Slowly, she spun about, scanning the terrain. She believed the wolves had run off for a spell, for how long, she dared not venture. What she did know was that the animals would never forget where hid their next meal. The question was merely which would return first, the dawn or the wolves.

Impulsively, Dakota jumped off the stacked row and ran straight for the creek. She slid down the icy bank and reached for her cup laying on its side in plain view. She collected the spilled pieces of chipped ice and placed them back in the tin. A sizeable chunk she held in hand. She scaled the bank and ran back to the shelter with visions of teeth nipping at her heels. She had plenty of adrenaline left in her system to fuel her speed. Back in the safety of the shelter she handed Raven the ice to chew.

Next, Dakota climbed out to reset the walls and repair the roof. As she labored to replace limbs atop the stacked row of sawn wood, she relived the horror of staring into the eyes of the wolf trying to eat her. The memory was more than enough to convince her that would not happen again. She longed for some other weapon, something to keep a wolf at distance—*a spear.* She needed a spear. There were plenty of straight sturdy branches from which to choose in the scrap piles. She walked across the clearing, chose three straight and stout, and returned. She set the branches alongside the opening.

Her priorities now addressed, Dakota took a moment to raise her dress and wash the pee off her legs with snow. She dried herself with her scarf. Her stockings would have to remain soiled. She slipped back into her sweaters and coats.

She seated herself again on the stacked row of firewood; and with legs swinging in the opening, she consoled Raven with small talk as they chewed ice. During their chat, Dakota kept a watchful eye in all directions for hints of movement. She studied the canyon relentlessly as she began to stroke the ends of her sticks with her father's knife. One after another, she fashioned her wicked points.

The adrenaline, now emptied from Dakota's body, left nothing but extreme fatigue. She wished to face nothing more. She wanted no more worries. Raven had drifted off to sleep. The shelter was repaired and appeared in good order so she moved to seal up the entrance. She repositioned the limbs across both of her walls, taking great care to see they did not easily dislodge. There was nothing further she could do this night, but wait for the safety of dawn's light. Not unexpectedly, the calming effect of Raven's slumber, the rhythm of her breath, drew Dakota down, down, down, deep into a near coma where she remained. She did not dream.

* * *

Dakota awoke with a start after a spray of cold snow and dirt showered her face and neck. The wet gritty discomfort caused her eyes to open at once, but her awareness was intact. She had slept hard and nearly full cycle, and so might have soon awakened on her own. Considering her past morning of misery and sickness, she found herself incredibly refreshed and invigorated by comparison. In fact, she was so stable and collected; she was surprisingly unmoved by the realization of what loomed overhead.

Instead of panic, she lay perfectly still. Her hand slid silently along her side until she brushed up against the shaft of a sharpened spear. She remained admirably calm as she studied the movement of shadows across the spaces between roof limbs. She wondered how many wolves, how much danger, milled about above their heads. Listening carefully to the difference in yips and whines, she determined three, maybe four at most, were taking turns testing the limbs. They pawed lightly as they worked up courage to inch their way onto the roof and sniff out whatever was sheltered below.

One animal might have sensed the dangers of unstable footing, and so retreated to the row of stacked wood. It might have been a long howl of complaint that wrung every ounce of sleep from young Raven's groggy head. Dakota reached out at once to cover her sister's mouth and quiet her. She kissed her on the forehead for reassurance. The wolf's call to regroup was returned many-fold and the pack was soon at its side. The girls were now centered in a pack of wolves hungry for their trapped quarry.

The animals strolled restlessly atop the rows of stacked wood or sat shoulder to shoulder facing each other across the roof of the shelter. At their feet, they could smell Dakota and Raven and the scent both aggravated them and made them salivate with anticipation. They sniffed and scratched at the limbs that formed the roof. They did so with increasing curiosity and sense of reward.

Dakota whispered in Raven's ear to pray quietly, and ask Jesus and Santo Vitus to watch over and protect. She wanted Raven to

351

concentrate on something other than the peril overhead. Dakota drew Raven into her embrace. In their stillness, they listened to the whining and whimpering of their tormenters.

More frequently, the animals would test the roof and dislodge snow and dirt bent on blinding the girls should they look up. Moments now felt like hours as the determination of the wolves increased, and they began to become more aggressive. The wolves were now clearly obsessed with getting into the shelter. It didn't take long before most all the debris had been shaken through the piled branches. Limbs were spreading apart. Spaces were opening. Enough light was now visible above the roof to define the nightmarish silhouettes. The wolves were seated atop the four walls and looking down at them like perched vultures.

Dakota sensed there were many more wolves than before. She couldn't say for certain, but the commotion outside was more raucous. The animals were yelping and carrying on a great deal louder, more frenzied, more antagonistic. Members of the pack weren't lazily lying about after gorging themselves on a blood feast. At the approach of dawn they were yet grouped together and driven to hunt. It meant pickings for the pack this night had been slim.

The beasts were focused and scratching at the roof limbs with resolve. The difference in behavior was marked. They were impatient, growling and snapping at each other. They picked away at the limbs with determination. The moonlight outside suddenly flooded into the shelter as a limb was lifted high off the wall. Fortunately, it dropped back hard and into place. It was enough to notch up Dakota's anxiety measurably. She took hold of a spear and prayed for dawn's quick arrival. The wolves were getting desperate.

The roof was shifting, jumping about as if it had a life of its own. Limb by limb, the wolves nosed, pawed, pushed and pulled. One by one, she heard or saw the pieces of split wood fall from above into the snow beyond the walls. Suddenly, a snout pushed through, and sounds of sniffing filled the hut. The wolves were just about inside.

Dakota fingered her spears. She ran her thumb over the points she had fashioned. She took hold of one and slowly eased herself upright. She studied the roof, the shadows moving about, and waited in ready with the first spear now pointed straight up. She prayed for Raven. She called on all the saints that her momma promised would come to watch over them.

Another wolf stepped onto the limbs. It was easy to hear him sniffing down though the roof. He began to growl in low tones and sniffed more frantically. Just then its two front legs came crashing through the branches, scaring the devil out of both Raven and Dakota. Acting out of pure fear, Dakota instinctively thrust her spear upwards through the limbs as hard as her strength would permit.

There was wretched yelp. Dakota felt the spear slow and quiver as it passed into the mass of the wolf's body. The yelp turned frantic as she shook the spear back and forth, spreading ribs and plunging the point closer to the animal's heart. There was a great deal of thrashing. The injured animal, unable to use its suspended paws, attempted to drag itself back off the limbs. In the process, the animal dislodged much of the roof causing wide gaps to appear above the shower of debris. Its fur could be discerned in the darkness, and without question the warm liquid flowing freely down the spear and across Dakota's fingers was the blood of death.

She pulled back on the spear and sensed its slide out of the animal's underbelly. The animal had been released and nothing further needed be done, for the other wolves tore in to the injured mate, pulling it off the roof and tearing it to shreds. The sounds of the fight over its remains were horrendous. The first wolf hadn't even been devoured before a second and third animal leapt to the top of the wood stack and spread their shadows across the girl's faces. They went into frenzy, tearing into each other, fighting to lick the blood spilt across the limbs. The remaining beast wedged his head down through the blood-covered branches and growled with crazed fury at the girls. They cowered, sinking to the earth.

In the moonlight, Dakota watched her breath float up through the limbs and rise past the shadow of this enormous gnashing head. Whether or not bumped by another frenzied wolf Dakota didn't know, but just like the first, its paws slipped off the spinning limbs and it plunged down into the hut. This time the limbs were all that kept the head and paws from falling completely inside to devour them. As before, Dakota drove the stake up through the limbs, catching the beast in the ribs.

As before, the second wolf cried out in agony as it struggled to get to its paws, but each time the tree limbs rotated and the animal fell back to impale itself deeper on the stake which Dakota rocked vigorously. The yelps were the only invitation needed by the rest of the pack who were happy to feast on a second of their kind. They were starved and took him down without conscience, practically ripping him off the spear.

Two things happened in short time thereafter. One, the wolves had taken the edge off their hunger; and two, they became very suspect of the hut. A few of the animals leapt back upon the rows of stacked wood, but were now wary of advancing closer even in light of the blood smeared everywhere.

Instead, they remained content with what food was in their belly. Others stationed themselves along the stacked rows of firewood, and watched the hut with a mixture of curiosity and suspicion until the first pale pinkish rays of morning light touched the peaks high above the canyon walls.

A chorus of howls arose to announce morning's first light, and soon thereafter the wolves silently slipped away into the depths of the forest. The girls, overcome with weariness, and realizing they were alive another day to see dawn's light fell fast asleep wholly against their will.

NINETY-FOUR

Ernie Kibben started up the canyon to meet Joe Brooks at the woodpile. For fifteen years that had been his routine on Wednesday mornings during winters when the creek was frozen. It wasn't as if he needed more chopped wood or anything like that; it was about escaping "cabin fever" and getting a chance to "jawr'" with his life-long friend, Joe. It usually ended up with a dinner and a stay at Joe and Rosaria's cabin.

It was said misery loved company and maybe that was the truth of it. Joe and he had met some eighteen years back in St. Louis as young furriers. They shared a desire, a dream to see the continental frontier, to see firsthand the glorious legends of grandeur, to see a world beyond the great desert, a world of majestic mountains. And of course, fast-flowing streams overrun with beaver, and all the wealth that brought to bear.

They agreed to strike out together on an adventure into the wilds to trap beaver and pan gold, to make their fortunes. Unfortunately for them trapping proved a dismal disaster. Every bank of every river, in every canyon between every mountain they suffered to scale seemed plumb trapped out. They were too late. To make matters worse, beaver went out of fashion in Europe, and the price paid for pelts fell to a pittance. The two lads were broke and stranded out west. The only good that came of their wasted time setting traps about stream beds was in knowing if any gold was to be stumbled upon, their chances were better than most.

And that was the long and short of how Ernie and Joe happened to wade into a reluctant bed of pay dirt. Panning their newfound stake would not make them wealthy, but back then there was no place to spend money for a hundred miles or more, and the country provided all the sustenance they required.

Many evenings of a cold winter, the two shivered in each other's company while crowding a campfire and discussing notions of packing up and taking their load back east to St. Louis. But then they invariably touched on the traffic, the smoke and stink of cities, the crowds, neighbors, and the noise. Not to mention the fishing. Even when sitting half frozen at a fire, returning to the comforts of civilization was one prospect that always sounded terrible. It couldn't be denied; freedom was downright addicting. They loved being left alone to live by their own laws.

It wasn't a bad life, but it changed dramatically one day when Joe met a gal at a Snake River Rendezvous some fifteen or sixteen years back. It changed him overnight. Joe was smitten, crazy about her. He got her father's blessing and took her hand. Joe never let go of it. He and Joe brought her back to Partner's Canyon, and he sweated alongside Joe to build his best friend's bride a cabin.

The wife was a fine, hard-working woman, respectable, good for mothering, came from Spanish stock and could talk up a storm in some sort of Spanish-Mexican, French-Indian, English language of her own making. She went by Rosaria, and she could beat you to hell with a spoon or send you to heaven when she stirred up one of her stews. The woman could put on a spread. She was always insisting that Ernie stay over and eat. That always led to staying over for the night. That always led to sticking around for days. It was obvious that her heart was too big, and as long as he was about, she and Joe would never have a proper life as husband and wife.

Ernie decided it was time to move on. Truth was, he had no place to go, but in his heart, he knew it was for the betterment.

Joe was like a brother, like family to him, and because of it, Ernie felt obliged to respect the man's life. It took *a great deal* of pleading from both Joe and Rosaria before they talked him out of leaving— a great deal of pleading. But, an agreement was reached, whereby a second cabin was soon built for Ernie about five miles downstream. Ernie insisted it be far enough off so Rosaria wouldn't keep telling him to *"come on o-fer for dinner."*

Ten months after Ernie moved into a cabin too far away down valley to be convenient, Rosaria was pregnant with Dakota. Ernie was an uncle. He was too proud to contain his joy, and he stayed on at Joe's place two weeks until Rosaria got back on her feet. It was a good thing he and Joe spoiled her because by her account their cooking nearly poisoned both her and the baby.

He and Joe spent many a spring and summer day working the creek, swishing water round and round in their copper pans until their fingers were too cold to keep it up any longer. At that point, they would step off the banks for a spell and take to the trees. They might fell a tree or two, or saw logs, or split and stack firewood into rows for the winter months. The work was demanding, but it warmed up their blood quickly. It forced out the stiffness in their joints that bending over cold mountain streams induced. When feeling less ambitious, they simply strolled down to a favorite bend and let themselves be lulled by a warm sun while they fished away an afternoon *for Rosaria.* She loved big fish.

Wednesday morning was 'woodmans-day' morning during winter. That is to say, on Wednesdays, he and Joe worked the woodpile together, loading the sledges with split wood for hauling back to the cabins. Wednesday was the only day of the week that Ernie would see Joe. It was his only chance to talk a spell, because during winter the creek was frozen over and there was no reason to meet for the purpose of panning for gold.

And so this morning, like every *Woodmans-day* morning, Ernie was impatient and eager to have a day of conversation with his best friend. He delighted in hearing another week's stories about Rosaria and the girls. Joe could get him to splitting a rib with laughter. He hoped maybe Joe would bring them along to play. Well, play was no longer a term to be used, as Dakota was nearly a woman in her own right. She was a fine girl, bright, feisty but respectful, and easy on the eyes. She could talk Ernie out of anything her heart might desire. In fact, she and Raven both could. Just name it.

Ernie stood on the trailing edge of his sledge to keep the front climbing high over the snow. His sledge moved across the deep fluffy snow better than a sled because it didn't have the pronounced runners that sank under the weight of the wood. He thought about how much he hated starting a morning by having to clear snow off the woodpiles. It was entirely a waste of time because no sooner cleared, and it snowed again. Chopping wood was a great deal harder than clearing snow, but once chopped always chopped; firewood never went back to being a tree just to be split again and again.

Ernie coaxed his mule along the path that led up the canyon toward the clearing, and beyond, ending at Joe's cabin. He was still a ways off when he spotted the mess at the woodpile. The flawlessly white snow was splattered in every direction with the bright crimson color of fresh blood. In the freezing winter temperatures, blood could remain bright for many days before turning a dark brown. As he closed in on the woodpile he noted how the clearing was heavily trampled and disturbed. He had no doubt about what most likely took place. Wolves were a curse with which to be reckoned, as some hapless creature discovered the hard way, probably a deer. He drove the mule right up to the stacked rows and stepped off the sledge.

"Land sakes alive," He muttered aloud. "What a mess."

Ernie stood about for a moment sizing up the scene. He was mentally sorting out the blood and gore before him. Tufts of hair were strewn all about. Ernie was re-thinking his dead deer theory when unavoidably distracted by the obvious pile of wood wedged between the stacked rows. He was suddenly far more interested and puzzled by whatever Joe was doing. Joe must have come to the clearing unusually early, but it certainly wasn't like him to be so sloppy and just toss worked wood into a pile. What was he doing? Ernie rubbed the back of his neck out of habit when contemplating. Then, he spotted a wolf carcass.

"Whoa! Looks t' me, like a wolf got his ragged ass tagged by a cat. Sure looks that-a-way, yes-sireee," he chuckled. "Ya don' wanna be messin' with them cats. No-sireee. It's no wonder this place is tore up."

His assessment made sense, but the conclusion bled over into a more unpleasant consideration about whether or not it might have been Joe who got tagged by the cat. Ernie dismissed the idea at once, but it was obvious a lot of work was in progress here at the clearing and Joe was nowhere to be seen. Where was he? Where was his sledge?

The collection of limbs spread over the rows of stacked wood continued to puzzle him. He walked up to study the huge pile of firewood between the stacked rows and found himself utterly befuddled. The limbs were bathed in blood. The work was obviously done in the past few hours; nothing was covered by snow. The blood that drenched it was obviously spilled sooner, after the pile was built. Ernie was growing uncomfortable. Where the hell was Joe? He should have been around here somewhere. What the hell was going on?

Ernie's eyes first followed the trail up the canyon toward Joe's place. Seeing no sign of his approach, Ernie began to look around in earnest. Turning slowly about, he took a circular sweep of the canyon searching for any sign of his friend, or at least some clue as to what this was all about.

"WHAAAA!!! Damnation!"

The words exploded from Ernie's chest as his knees buckled. He had turned full circle, looking back to the piled up wood, and nearly collapsed when a blood-covered head suddenly appeared atop the mess. It might near have been called murder when the head opened its mouth to speak, and scared the absolute life out of him.

"Uncle Kib?"

"Ahhh! Ahhh! Dad burn it! Dad burn it, child!"

Ernie literally bent over. He needed a moment to work his heart. He looked back up to be sure of what he was seeing.

"Dakota? Dakota? Is that you girl?"

"Yes, Uncle Kib. I was sleeping. I thought I heard you talking."

She stood in place, her head poking up through a hole in what was left of the hut's roof, her body hidden entirely from view.

"Lan' sakes alive, girl! What in tarnation ya doin'? What ya doin', Dakota? Look at ya! What's all over yer face? Is that blood? You all right, child? What's goin' on here? Lord, ya gave me a fright. I was thinkin' a cat's out here a-killin' deer or wolves, then I sees yer head sittin' 'top that there pile an' I'm thinkin' we got Indians goin' crazy or somethin'. Ya 'bout scared every drop a piss right outta me. Where's yer daddy, child? I was thinkin' all hell broke loose out here. Where is everybody? What ya doin' out here all alone?" He spun around again, still searching the woods for Joe.

"Momma and poppa are in the cabin. Raven is down here." She looked down. "She's sleeping. She's sick, Uncle Kib."

"What ya talkin' 'bout child. Yer momma'd never let ya out alone. The two o' ya's nothin' more'n wolf bait. Where's yer daddy, Dakota?"

"Momma and Poppa are in the cabin. They won't get up. I think… I think…"

"Spit it out child, ya think what fer chrissake?"

Dakota looked down for a moment; then with courage she raised her head. It took every ounce of her fiber to hold back her emotions. "I think they died, Uncle Kib."

"What?"

It was a horribly absurd thing to say, and the words stiffened Earnie's frame as if the chill of winter slipped down his bare back.

"Gosh darn, child, don' ya be talkin' that way, never. Ya hear me? It ain't…it ain't…. Ya don' never say such things, ya hear?"

"They wouldn't get up, Uncle Kib. They wouldn't get out of bed."

She looked at him for an explanation.

Ernie didn't settle down, he just found himself thoroughly stumped by the comment and standing stock still while studying the bloodied and unsettling face of Dakota. He turned to witness the blood that appeared to cover everything in sight, but his eyes returned to take full measure of blood-covered Dakota. A sensation of dread began to creep over him. His speech came slow and low.

"What in tarnation…. What's goin' on here, Dakota? I'm gettin' a might bit spooked, sweet'ert. I love ya like my own, but I don' take t' this here talk. No sireee, ma'am, I don' much care t' be stumped. Ya best spit out somethin' child, somethin' that makes sense. Tell me what's been takin' place here. Ya best tell me right now, Dakota."

Ernie Kibben didn't wait for an answer. He waded out through the blood-stained snow and drifts to look around. He then walked back toward Dakota. Having made his way up between the two rows of stacked wood, he climbed up the hut Dakota had built and reached for her. She attempted to raise her arms, but the pain of her shoulder was now intense.

"I can't, Uncle Kib. My shoulder's in a bad way."

Ernie dropped to his knees and looked into the shelter. Raven was looking up at him with a blank expression. He looked at Dakota.

"Put yer arm 'roun' my neck."

Dakota did as she was told. Ernie couldn't help but think how Dakota was only eleven, and yet light as a feather. He lifted her out of the hole and onto the stacked row. He looked back inside the four walls and studied wee black-haired Raven, too small to climb out on her own, and waiting patiently for help she never questioned. She was staring upward into the light.

"Come here, Raven."

Ernie reached down to grab her. He noticed at once how she raised her arms but failed to meet his eyes or smile as was her way whenever she saw him. Ernie hauled her up and out of the hole. She promptly laid her head on his shoulder. He walked her off the woodpile and carried her to the sledge.

"Stay put, Raven."

Dakota followed in Ernie's footsteps as he walked back and forth retrieving the sled and bag filled with their belongings. The three of them sat for a moment on the sledge as Ernie tried to make some kind of sense out of Dakota's accounting, and Raven's condition. He listened intently as a morbid feeling of dread gripped his insides. This just couldn't be true, he thought to himself, but he knew the children would never be left alone under any circumstance. Whatever the reason, it would not be good.

"Hang on, we're goin' up t' the cabin."

Ernie prodded his mule to step off in the direction of the Joe's cabin. As they made their way, he demanded that Dakota retell her story, over and over from the beginning. He pried out every detail he was able. He listened as well, over and over, each time to every word.

Dakota recounted the how she awoke in great pain, how smoke filled the cabin, how she was unable to raise her momma or poppa from their sleep. She told her uncle about her journey to the clearing, pulling Raven on the sled because she wouldn't wake up. She told him about the hut she had built because of her bad dreams and how it protected them from the wolves that came for them. She told him how scared she was and how brave Raven had been.

Ernie only halted the mule one time to again check Raven's eyes. She might as well have been his own daughter, for he was sickened by his finding. He urged the mule onward as he slipped deeper into his own thoughts. He knew this was truth from a child's mouth, and he was anguished by Dakota's accounts. This was all about his closest friend and the only semblance of family he might ever have. He suppressed his gut instincts, preferring to see with his own eyes the truth of what he feared to face.

NINETY-FIVE

Ernie arrived at the cabin. He stood on the sledge, swallowed hard and stared. He studied the yard, the cabin, and finally the front door with much apprehension. There was no smoke wafting from the chimney. There was no sign of life, no sound to interrupt the chirping of birds or breezes buffeting his ears. Even the girls stood silent by his side. The silence bore down on him like an avalanche. He felt his gut twist tight. He fought for a breath.

"You girls stay put."

363

Ernie stepped off the sledge and walked over to the porch. He stepped across, removed his hat, and reached for the door. He looked down at his hand and realized he was trembling. His chest felt tight. He knew he had no choice but to walk into the most soul-crushing scene he might ever imagine. He unlatched the lock. Slowly, he pushed the door open. He hesitated. He looked back at the girls. Dakota's eyes were fixed on him. He looked away and stepped over the threshold.

Ernie stared along the shaft of light that penetrated the dark and cold of the cabin. It was a harsh light in comparison to the glow of a hearth that warmed him for winters beyond count. The hard cold light illuminated Joe and Rosaria, as they lie carefully tucked into their bed. He instantly broke apart.

Ernie's life emptied itself of meaning and friendship at that moment. He stood squarely in the center of the jamb so the girls couldn't slip around him and see the tears pouring down through his graying beard. He entered the cabin and walked up to their bed. It was as Dakota described. Rosaria lying peacefully, facing her husband. Joe was tipped back as if to be talking to her, his arm lying across her. Ernie knew a big part of him had just died. He fought to stifle his sobs. He struggled to keep any sound of his grief from reaching the girls, but he had to let it go. He covered his mouth, his face, to suppress his grief. Given a moment, Ernie collected himself and raised his head. He dried his eyes with the sleeves of his coat.

"Joe...Rosaria...I...I don' understand. Why...why must I live t' see such painful...." Ernie took a breath and settled down. "I promise t' keep the girls safe. I'll take 'em with me, an' if it takes my last dyin' breath, I'll see 'em grow happy. I promise, I...pro...," he sobbed.

Ernie had to wait. He stepped back to glance out the door at the girls. He couldn't step back outside or even into the light and face them in his current state. He cleared his throat.

"I'll be right there, girls. Stay put, ya hear?"

Ernie turned back to face the bed. He stood respectfully before them, arms crossed, hat in hand. It was his loyalty as a friend, and his love for Joe and Rosaria that steadied him. He understood they would expect nothing less than his inner strength to prevail. Their daughters' survival depended on it. He nodded to the couple, affirming his understanding of what must be done, affirming he had been called to task. He was the girls' uncle and their only hope.

"They're my only family now. They're all I have left, Joe. You go in peace. Go with Rosaria. You kiss her; you kiss her fer me, an' you hold her fer eternity. I promise t' love an' care fer the girls as if they were my own. I will see t' their happiness 'til that day when they's returned t' yer embrace. I swear it, Joe, so's ya might rest in peace."

He turned to join the girls. Ernie wasn't afforded the time or the consideration for personal grief. He held his head high, trying to be that pillar of strength the girls could count on. They were frightened, now in their time of need, but they never doubted 'Uncle Kib' could make some of it right.

Ernie found himself standing in the bitter cold before the Mistress of Winter, who whispered her taunts and mocked him. He had the bodies of his dearest friends on one hand and the responsibility of their daughters on the other. He had to determine what to do with the bodies and still trek five miles back to his place before twilight when the wolves roamed. He approached the sledge and looked at Dakota who was embracing Raven to keep warm.

"Dakota."

"Yes?"

"Honey, d'ya understand what's happened t' yer mother'n father?"

"I think so."

"What'dya think happened, child?"

Dakota hesitated. Her eyes were seeking out Ernie's. Ernie's eyes were beckoning her to accept the truth in her heart. The tears that appeared told him she had.

"They died."

"I'm thinkin' the stove pipe cooled down too much an' the outside air got t' goin' down it an' pushin' the smoke into the cabin. You an' Raven lived 'cause ya were sleepin' up high in that bunk, maybe near a draft. It's all I can figure, Dakota. D'ya understand, girl?"

"Yes."

"Yer ma an' pa are the two people closest in my life, Dakota. My heart is heavy an' breakin' inside. I loved 'em jus like I love you an' yer sister. I'm tellin' ya this here b'cause I can't jus leave yer folks layin' in that bed fer the wolves an' whatnot. I see ya tucked 'em in real snug, but honey, we gotta give 'em a proper send off t' meet their maker. D'ya understand?"

Dakota said nothing. She simply waited, knowing her uncle would do what was best.

"The ground is frozen harder'n the rock below it. I can't bury 'em, Dakota. We gotta take 'em with us. Listen, I'm goin' 'round back t' fetch yer mule. Ya think yer up t' helpin' me take care o' yer folks, girl?"

Dakota said nothing. She nodded. She went on to help Ernie bundle her parents in their blankets and bring them out to the sledge. Ernie closed the cabin door for what he knew would be the last time. He urged the mules to start back down the valley .

When Ernie and the girls reached the clearing midway, Ernie halted the mules. He walked over to the hut that Dakota had built.

366

He began straightening out the limbs she had used to build her roof. When he was satisfied, he returned to the sledge.

"D'ya remember all o' them cabins ya used t' build out here when yer daddy'n I cut wood?"

"Yes."

"So do I, honey. So do I. Yer folks'd be real proud o' what ya built here, Dakota. They'd be proud o' how ya saved young Raven's life. I think they'd like t' be a part o' that lil' cabin."

Ernie smiled at Dakota. He stepped back to lift Rosaria from the sledge and a sob burst from his chest unexpectedly. He coughed so as to make it sound like a grunt from the weight; he coughed to cover his emotions. He carried Rosaria over to the hut and laid her gently across the limbs. He went back and carried Joe over to Rosaria and laid him next to her. He was turned away from the girls and so let the tears pour. Ernie wanted to place Rosaria's hand into Joe's in the worst way, but their arms and hands were frozen and unyielding. He forced their hands to touch and accepted that act as final. He stood a moment to gather up his composure, and then turned to address Dakota.

"Come here, girl. Help me gather up the wood off the rows."

Together, Ernie and Dakota began dismantling the neatly stacked rows of firewood. From the ends of the rows, they brought the wood center to the hut and piled it. After half an hour of labor, they finished the task. Ernie said a prayer alongside Dakota and Raven, and then set all of the wood in the clearing on fire. Once it was well underway, Ernie removed Dakota so she wouldn't have to witness the consumption of the bodies. They started back down the trail with the roar of an inferno behind them.

The three reached Ernie's cabin safely before twilight. They made mention of the fact that not once had they heard the bay of a wolf. When darkness fully settled upon the land, Ernie and the girls stood on his porch looking up the canyon. They stood silent watching the enormous glow that lit up the surrounding countryside and the clouds overhead with a haunting orange cast. When the cold prevented them from watching further, they went inside, latched the door, and climbed into bed where they could each cry in the privacy of darkness.

* * *

The girls were most certainly secure and safe from any danger, but Ernie was at a complete loss as to what next he should do. The three of them spent a week doing little more than sit about his cabin staring at each other. Sadly, Raven never knew what she was staring at. Her blindness gutted Ernie.

When the next Wednesday rolled around, Ernie was beaten down by depression. Joe was gone. Rosaria was gone. His life was gone. Ernie no longer had any desire to remain in the canyon. He deemed it better all around if he collected the girls, his load, a few of his belongings, and left this pain behind. He would seek work closer to people, maybe something in South Pass…a scout or guide.

NINETY-SIX

Ernie lifted Dakota and Raven onto his mule. He checked the leather straps that held the travois fast to the animal. He next mounted Joe's mule , a temperamental beast that often needed a sound clubbing to settle him. It could be a mean cuss. He looked down across the animal's hind quarters and studied the belongings strapped to his travois. All looked secure. Ernie then took one last look at his cabin and the surrounding country that had been his home for nearly two decades.

"Let's go, girls."

Ernie started down Partner's Path Canyon.

"Where are we going, Uncle Kib?"

"Right now, we're goin' t' ride south out o' Wind River. Then we're goin' t' ride more easterly across the flats an' over t' a place goes by South Pass Junction. I reckon by that time you girls'll be more'n spent. I figer on buyin' us passage on the Rocky Mountain Railroad up t' a place goes by Northpole."

"What's in Northpole?" asked Dakota.

Reality was sinking in, and Ernie realized that he could love until he was blue in the face, but there was no possible way he could take on the responsibility of bringing up Dakota and Raven. Especially Raven, now that she couldn't see. He didn't know the first thing about child rearing, and they would prevent him from getting work, which in these parts always included some form of traveling. It required being out on the trail for days or even weeks on end.

"When yer daddy an' me were young, we used t' trap an' pan at a place called Powder Pan Canyon. We still got us land up that-a-way. We heard tell of a young gal called Mother Gail who kept kids. Heard tell it was the kindest place fer kids this side o' the Mississippi." Earnie stopped to think a moment. "But 'at 'as a long time back...long time back."

There was more silence until Dakota worked up her courage. Ernie wished he could be anywhere but here when the question came.

"So we won't be living with you, Uncle Kib?"

Ernie stopped the mules. His head dropped low; his chin resting hard against his chest. He turned to look at Dakota.

369

This time he made no effort to hide the tears that welled up in his eyes.

"Dakota, I love ya more'n life itself, but honey, I don' know a thing 'bout raisin' girls. If I'd be a-workin', I'd be out an' about fer weeks. Who'd be 'roun' t' look after ya? Who'd be carin' fer young Raven?"

"I'll be twelve this year , Uncle Kib. I could take care of myself."

"I'm believin' ya could, Dakota. I don' doubt but what ya say. But yer eleven and ain't gonna be twelve till near year's end, and what about young Raven. She can't see the way God intended. She needs someone special who can see t' her upbringin'. Ya'd have yer hands full jus' getting' by yerself, child.

"Most times, the likes a ya go t' kin. Yer daddy spoke o' havin' a brother back east Virginy way, but lordy, I never paid a mind t' getting' details. Yer mama always spoke o' bein' the only child o' four that lived. Ya got no kin t' speak o', girl.

"I always been there fer ya, Dakota. Always bin yer Uncle Kib. Proud to be such—."

"You took care of us before. You could do it again." Dakota's voice grew desperate.

"Baby, I only did lil' things. I watched t' see ya didn' get inta mischief, t' see ya dint get inta places ya dint b'long. That's differn't, Dakota. That ain' 'bout riasin' ya proper t' be a woman. Ya need t' be teached things like how t' cook fer a man, things like that. How t' mend clothes an' be a mother. I don' know nothin' 'bout any o' that. D'ya see what I'm gettin' at, girl? Ya needs a mother."

Dakota didn't answer. She only nodded that she understood. Now when they needed him the most, Ernie found he was powerless. He would do whatever he could, but it wouldn't amount to a hill of beans. He had to get them out of the canyon and into the home of someone who knew how to care for girls.

Ernie urged the mules forward. The weather was cold but held sunny and clear during their ride out of the mountains and onto the South Pass flats. Their journey was entering its second week as they neared South Pass. Ernie stretched it out for the sake of the girls.

Dakota and Raven had grown up with little or no chance of seeing another living soul back at the cabins, save for a trapper stumbling upon them when in need. The prospects of visiting a town made for better medicine than anything a doctor could prescribe. Dreams buried the troubling thoughts in their young and confused minds. A town would be a healthy diversion for them. 'Uncle Kib' would see to that.

Upon the South Pass flats they headed southeast until they spotted the RMR tracks cutting across the snow swept expanse. Once done, they turned east and followed the rails directly into South Pass Junction where Dakota got her first look at a town, not to mention a steam locomotive that pretty much scared the wits out of her.

Young Raven was no less overwhelmed. In spite of her blindness, she was awash in an unending stream of strange sounds. The extent of the wonder was apparent by the expressions on the girls' faces. The surprises weren't entirely their own. Ernie only got down to South Pass once or twice every couple of years. Each visit astounded him. The growth was unnerving. He rarely thought it a good thing.

Ernie was no fool. When he realized how many people were in town or milling about the station discussing gold and where best to find it, he took a gamble and rented out an entire rail car. He paid the livery to deliver a few bundles of hay and a wagon load of straw to be spread across the car bed. Finally, he led the mules inside to feed, closed the door and tied a bandana to the door handle.

Ernie led the girls to an eatery at the station. At the table, he barely spoke, telling the girls he had to pay attention to the conversations in the room. About midway through the meal, Ernie got up and walked over to a nearby table where sat four men. He introduced himself loud enough to be heard by all.

"Sorry, t' be interruptin' you gents. Name's Kib. I stepped over, but fer hearin' ya jawin' bout pannin' an' such, an' I was wonderin' if ya heard any further news 'bout the finds of late in Northpole?"

The four men went both silent and motionless. One spoke for all.

"Northpole?"

"Yes, sir. Ya know, 'bout a hun'erd fifty miles north a here, end o' the tracks."

"Mister, we knows about Northpole. Knows xactly wheres it is. But we ain't heard nothin' 'bout no gold in Northpole."

"Is that a fact? Gosh darn, I been hearin' creeks up that-a-way are pannin' out goodly. I been hearin' say from panners passin' by my place in Wind River that they's headed east o'er t' Bighorn 'fore everything good gets laid claim to. Said there's gold bein' found all o'er them hills.

"I finally heard enough an' packed up the kids. Figer'd I'd do some scoutin' 'bout the area myself. Can't hurt, if ya hear what I am sayin'. Gettin' down t' my point, I ain't of a mind t' ride that distance in this here weather, too damn cold t' be on a horse with kids, if ya git my meanin'. I took ta rentin' out a car on the RMR an' wanted t' say if there'd be others en route t' Northpole, I got extra room fer cheap passage. Comes with straw bed'n all.

There be a kerchief tied t' the handle o' the car. We'll be pullin' out later tonight."

Ernie went back to his table and sat down. He looked at Dakota, who overheard his conversation, as did most others in the room. She said nothing as she sat in silence looking back at him. Ernie winked as a smile broke across his face. He finished his meal, and made sure the girls were in want of nothing more. They were satiated, and it showed by the weight of their eyes. They had grown listless but for their full bellies and now only sought a warm place to lie and rest.

By the time Ernie returned the girls to the rail car, a sizeable crowd of panners and speculators were gathered at the kerchief-marked door. The number of fresh strangers appearing every few minutes only served to whip up fever as they competed for a place onboard the car. Their emotions were quickly proved out by the amount of money being offered for passage up to Northpole. The idea of applying the cost of lodging toward passage that came with a warm bed was too tempting to turn down. Ernie made a killing.

Nights were now long, and the trip on rails took a full 'dark to dawn' journey in order to reach Northpole town. The car was packed full of men pressed up against each other for heat. Blankets were shared and covered the entire lot. Any opening, regardless of size, was stuffed tight with straw to seal out the chill. The car warmed quickly and became comfortable. In time, cracks were reopened for fresh air.

The strangers took kindly to the girls, who spent most of their time making up for lost sleep. They lay curled up looking like a couple of sleeping angels in a hard land. The sight of them rekindled memories that softened leather-tough hearts. Stories passed from one stranger to the next, fond recollections of families and loves lost in their quest for gold.

Ernie had his story.

"I reckon it's goin' on six, maybe seven years in the high country since last comin' down. Was wonderin' if y'all have any word on the Union an' where it's getting' t'be."

"Most certn'ly do."

"I do remember Texas joinin' in…'bout forty-six or so—," said Ernie.

"Forty-five, t' be exact."

"Zat right?"

"Yes, sir."

"Shoulda 'member'd that, bein' with the war'n all."

"Yep. Then there'd be Iowa in forty-six, Wisconsin in forty-eight, and California in fifty, as last I heard."

"California in fifty?"

"Yes, sir."

"Now, I am surprised t' hear 'bout California. Now'n then there gets t'be a panner or two comin' through the canyon, up where I'm from, an' they always get t' talkin' 'bout California. It's always talked up t' be the place t' be pannin' an' such. But never nobody made mention of it bein' a state. Go figure."

"It's a fact. Been that way a few years now."

"Yut. Time's are a changin'…changin' fast. Yes-siree. Ain't seen Northpole in a good bit. Not since, we last come down. Been scratchin' my head tryin' t' get back some o' them memories. Hard t' make sense of it from a train. Not like sittin' on a horse an' gettin' back yer inner compass, if ya know what I'm sayin'."

The strangers understood, and agreed, all knowing full well the truth of what he spoke. Only a few of the men were yet awake, and taking part in conversations that were now softer and more personal. Ernie looked over at the girls and grew silent for a moment. His eyes moistened.

"Them girls' father was my best friend ever. Went by the name, Joe. Joe Brooks. Joe an' his wife, Rosaria went t' meet their maker a month or so back. That's why I'm headed up t' Northpole. Joe an' me spent our younger years scoutin' an' trappin' the upper Missouri River country. Spent years sloggin' up an' down the Yellowstone an' Powder. We crawled all over those Bighorn Mountains with traps an' pans. In them days, there's nothin' known as Northpole. There's nothin' more'n a campsite, maybe."

"Well, it's every bit a town now-a-days," said another. "The RMR saw to that. It's a nice place, though. Not nearly as crowded as South Pass and Eastpole. Man can still breathe in Northpole."

"Amen," chimed in two or three others.

"Yeah, we always liked the place, always did. Fer whatever reason, I don' know, Joe an' me settled a stream we panned west o' the Bighorn, that one bein' o'er Wind River way. I guess it panned out sufficient t' keep us in cash, but Joe an' me always said, if we were t' pick a civ'lized place t' kick off our boots, it'd look a lot like Northpole."

"Ya could do worse."

"I'd wager I could yet find some o' them ol' timers or at least kin. Ya gents ever hear o' ole Curry Jackson?"

"No, sir."

"Nope, can't say I have."

"Hell, Joe an' me traded more pelts'n I care t' count with that ol' buzzard. He's jus' one o' that batch from years back. Them ol' timers been at it 'roun' this place since the mid-thirties."

"They'd be all dead an' gone by now," said a stranger.

"Yeah. Same as Joe. Dead an' gone, rest his soul. I miss him sorely. I miss Rosaria. I miss em' all."

The conversation went silent, giving way to inner reflection until Ernie interrupted what thoughts remained.

"I guess it's a night fer me, gents. See ya in the mornin'."

Ernie slid down into the straw, and pulled his hat down over his face. He pulled his blanket up to his neck, and let the vibrations of the rolling car pass through him like a gentle back rub. He had never before been on a train. He might never have, had it not been for the girls. He could hardly fathom traveling one hundred and fifty miles from the south pass to the Bighorn Mountains in less than a week's time, let alone overnight. It was a modern miracle to be sure. Ernie drifted off to sleep.

NINETY-SEVEN

The train came to a halt at the Northpole station a little past daybreak. Those early morning hours were always the coldest. The pale whitish-blue cast of the sky both looked and felt like ice. Not one of the strangers sleeping in the rail car was anxious to leave the warmth of their bedrolls; Ernie was no exception. His plans were to stay in town until the following day and rest up. He saw nothing but advantage in taking a couple extra hours of sleep. For the girls' sake, he had determined to go it slow and easy every step of the way. Today was no time to start thinking differently.

Unfortunately, Ernie failed to find that sleep. Each hour's passing brought worsening thoughts of losing the last remnant of family he had always called his own. He opened his eyes a dozen time to gaze upon the girls while they slept. They were the essence of everything good in his life, everything that had been his life for fifteen years.

Ernie, at last opened his eyes for the day. He was still facing the girls.

"*In the beat of a heart,*" he whispered the last of a dream aloud.

Everything had changed. Everything had been replaced by anxiety and uncertainty—in the beat of a heart. It was a sad turn of events indeed. Fate was too often cruel, and he couldn't expect suffering to be something endured only others. He reached over to Dakota and gently shook her.

"Wake up, sweetheart. We're in Northpole."

Ernie would take whatever time necessary for the girls to get a hot bath and warm themselves. He intended to stay over the night before starting out on the trail up into Powder Pan. In the meantime, the girls would fill their bellies and enjoy themselves. He would have them pampered as children should while he saw to the mules and resupplied. He would leave the animals at the livery, and let out a couple of horses, which he believed would speed their journey up into Canyon.

Once off the train, the girls followed Ernie to the livery where he put the animals up for the night. Dakota asked if she might see something of the street with its buildings. South Pass was her first town ever seen; Northpole only her second. Unlike South Pass, here life moved at a slower pace, and so Ernie left their belongings temporarily at the livery. He then gave Dakota free rein to walk and investigate whatever she pleased.

Dakota was drawn to the details of the structures, how they were constructed side by side to work in unison, how they invited passersby. She was also for the first time able to wade into the commotion and interaction of community. It was exhilarating to say hello, and in return be asked, how was your day? Her face would beam the moment a person would take notice of her. Conversation was an alien experience for Dakota, and so she dragged Ernie and her sister around until poor blind Raven could no longer tolerate the biting winter air. Unselfish by nature, she voiced no complaint when Ernie suggested they return to the livery for their belongings and then head to the boardinghouse.

"Good day, ma'am. I'd like a word with the proprietor, if that would be possible."

"I can help you, sir," responded the woman.

"Very well…. Presently, I'm in need of a night's lodgin' fer me an' the girls. Also, I'd like t'enlist the services o' that person employed in the business o' preparin' baths suitable fer these here young ladies."

"I can see to both your needs. Please follow me."

The matron led them to their rooms. Satisfied with the lodging, Ernie turned to the matron.

"I have promised these angels a blissfully hot an' soapy bath, an' a good back scrub. They been two weeks out in the bitter cold, an' could use a good thaw. They're t'have their hair washed an' dried. I'd like 'em t'have fresh garments if ya got anythin' fer sale that'd fit 'em. If ya gotta bolt o' cloth that's good'n warm, an' a seamtress, I'd be agreeable t' the charges.

"Come the morrow, first thing after breakfastin', I'd appreciate a woman's hand t'get 'em brushed out with ribbons an' all, dressed, an' made up presentable fer introduction t'Mother Gail."

"Mother Gail?"

"Yes, ma'am."

The woman looked at Ernie quizzically.

"Are you referring to an orphanage up in Powder Pan Canyon?"

At once, the words cut wicked into Ernie's soul. His eyes flashed with emotion as he looked at the matron. She realized at once.

"Forgive me, sir. I am so very sorry," she whispered.

The girls heard every word. Dakota's eyes rose to meet Ernie. He looked away, and lowered his head in shame. He nodded his head.

"Yes, ma'am." Ernie cleared his throat and continued.

"I promised 'em afterward, I would seat 'em to a long overdue dinner o' hot food an' trimmin's."

"Of course! I promise you, I shall see to it they are treated like queens."

The matron wished to make up for her indelicacy. Ernie only wished that the girls' last memories of him be good. He was desperate to again see smiles that had long since disappeared with all the other joys at Joe's cabin far up Partner's Path. He raised his eyes to look at Dakota. Traces of emotion were yet there to be seen.

"You'd like that wou'n't ya, honey?"

Dakota understood. She was old enough to appreciate the brutal realities. More important, she never questioned her Uncle Kib's love. She could see it now in his eyes. She wished him no guilt. Slowly, a smile crept across her face.

"A hot bath with suds and a back rub? A dinner with all the trimmings? I don't know, Uncle Kib. I'm just not sure. What do you think, Raven? Yes, or no?"

"Yes! Yes, Dakota. Say yes!"

"Alright." Dakota looked back up at Ernie with a broad grin. "If Raven says yes, then it's yes."

"That a girl." Ernie looked back at innkeeper with an air of relief and the faintest of smiles. "Take 'em away."

* * *

Confident the girls were in good hands, Ernie was free to go about conducting business and getting better information on the whereabouts of Mother Gail. In answer to his questions at the livery, Ernie learned that Mother Gail's place was still going strong up in Powder Pan Canyon, about six hours' ride out of Northpole . For anyone having traveled the west, six hours was as good as being arrived. From Ernie's point of view, he was presently standing in Mother Gail's backyard. That news came as a relief.

Ernie also asked about a doctor. He was informed that a man of medicine lived in South Pass, and paid visit to Northpole once every two weeks unless summoned beforehand. He would be here on the morrow for regular rounds. Ernie determined to have the doctor call on Raven at the boardinghouse. It meant delaying their morning departure for Mother Gail's, but her place was only six hours by horse , and the delay would be small price for knowing the extent of Raven's affliction.

Ernie returned to the boardinghouse.

"The girls are both down for naps," said the matron. "They had a good hot soak. Hair washed and dried as you asked. I went with a seamstress. She suggested good lasting wool for warmth with cotton undergarments to keep them from itching. Poor creatures could hardly stand but for falling asleep. As soon as Madge got her measurements, the fittings came off and the girls were put to bed.

"Two weeks on the trail in the open weather. I dare say, Mr. Kibben, you ask a good deal of the two so young, especially that blind tot. It's no wonder they're sound asleep."

"I wish it'd been diff'er'nt, ma'am. I had t'get 'em in the care of a woman. I love them two more'n life itself, but I don' know the first thing 'bout raisin' girls. I pray ya b'lieve, I work only fer their best interests."

"I believe you, sir. It may please you to know that they have slept for almost two hours. Would you have me call them down for dinner?"

"I'd be most grateful, ma'am."

"Take up your place at the table, and I'll bring them to you."

Young Raven walked into the room, her hand held in that of the matron. Dakota followed behind. Dakota broke into a smile at first sight of Ernie. Both girls looked well refreshed and healthy. A feast with all the trimmings was ordered up. The girls ate until they were nearly sick.

"What ya need t'do now is walk a bit t'settle all that food. It'll make ya feel better. Why don't ya wander o'er t' the tradin' post? I promise ya'll find more t' see than yer eyes can take in. Know they got all sort o' toys an' stuff fer kids young an' old."

The girls were most agreeable to the suggestion. They would have their day, Ernie thought to himself. He would see to that.

The trading post had a vast collection of wonders to be viewed. Everything imaginable could be found prominently displayed on counter's tops, in bins, hooked on racks, or spread out on tables at the store. It adjoined Claussen's Boardinghouse, and patrons passed between both establishments by way of a large opening. From the trading post, the girls could look back directly into the great hall of the boardinghouse and see Ernie yet seated at the table.

Most of the items at the post were supplies for survival—cooking and homesteading, or hardware for the business of hunting and trapping, mining or logging. There was also a wonderful collection of cloth and some ready-made clothes. There were patterns for making dresses and one was hanging on display. There were piles and piles of red flannel pajamas, sheets, pillowcases, housecoats and jackets for tots and grown-ups as well. Raven squeezed a stack of the red cloth and rubbed her cheek with it. It was soft to the touch. Dakota found paper for practicing her letters. The whole place was stacked with wooden boxes full of colorful trinkets and beads mostly used for trading with the Indians.

Best of all, there was a collection of toys. Most all were made of wood or cloth, painted or sewn with bright colors or dressed in wonderful miniature clothes. Dakota spied the little wooden wagons, the carts, canoes, and boats. Her hands passed by the barns with cows, horses, and different little animals. She fondled the building blocks and inspected the wooden Indians for boys. Everything she touched, everything she saw, she put into words, describing all down to the last detail for Raven.

"Oh my word, Raven. They have dolls! Oh! They are beautiful. Come quick, come, come."

Dakota reached for Raven's hand and kept her in tow as she rounded the corner of an aisle to stand before a display of dolls. The sweetest, most precious baby faces the she had ever seen, cradled in thick heads of hair made of soft brown, blonde, or black yarn. Some were dressed in nighties, some in winter attire, and others in Indian dress.

"Well, what do we have here?"

Taken by surprise, the girls spun around from the doll counter to find themselves before an older woman. Dakota was visibly nervous, for Raven was yet holding a doll that didn't belong to her.

"I'm Elizabeth . Who might you be?"

"I'm Dakota and this is my sister, Raven." Dakota forwarded the information, but had no concept of offering a hand in greeting.

"Dakota and Raven, what perfect names for such pretty girls. Are you here to shop for a Christmas gift?"

"No, ma'am, we just stopped to rest."

"I took a bath," offered Raven in a weak voice.

"We both took baths and had our hair washed. We had dinner in that room." Dakota pointed into the adjoining boardinghouse. "My Uncle Kib said we could look about if we wished but not to touch. He said there would be a lot to see in this place."

"Yes, I'm certain for two young ladies such as you, it would be an eyeful. I see you found the dolls."

"Yes, ma'am. They are beautiful. My sister Raven can't see right now, and I was trying to show her how pretty were these dolls. That's why she is holding it. She has to feel it to know what I am saying, at least until she can see again." Dakota purred as she stroked a doll's thick brown hair.

"Don't you think she's beautiful, Raven?" asked Dakota.

"Yup."

Raven's lips puckered up to blow hair out of her own face. She then raised the doll to her cheek and smiled.

"I agree. She is one of my favorites as well. But, I like them all. Well, you just go ahead and look all you want, and if you have any questions, you be sure to come and ask."

The girls didn't respond. They simply returned to their fixation with the dolls of their dreams, minds far off in a world of make believe.

Eventually Ernie rose from the dinner table to make his way into the tradin' post. It was getting late, and he hoped to start the morrow off early. The trading post never truly closed, it being open to patrons of the boardinghouse that came and went at all hours of the day and night. There was nothing to tell the girls that is was time to call it a day except for fatigue or Ernie.

He suffered to ruin their fun, and so tried to be patient, but soon realized he was making no headway in the matter. Taking the low road, he moved to buy his way out of the treasure trove. It cost him two dolls, a large bag of flavored sugar drops, and finally a slew of promises for lavish gifts come Christmas. The girls were most pleased with their gifts, and so followed Ernie back into the boardinghouse without complaint. He saw them to their room. As he pulled shut their door, he last saw Dakota sitting alongside Raven on their bed playing make believe. Ernie retired to his room feeling a brief moment of peace. He held on to the image of the girls as he snuffed the lamp. The memory of their contentment was his ticket to sleep.

The next morning, Ernie jumped out of bed, and into his boots, as soon as he heard the RMR pull into town. He ran across the street, to the station, so he might present himself to the doctor. To his dismay, he was told by the train's conductor that the doctor had been dropped off some ten miles south of town to make a call, and wasn't expected to arrive in town for another three or four hours. The patient's family would bring him in by carriage.

Ernie left the station, and walked over to the livery where he squared away his dues. He then returned to the boardinghouse and had some breakfast. He made good on his debts so he would be ready to leave as soon as the doctor was finished checking on Raven. He let the girls sleep. He waited. He waited. Two hours passed, and then three. The girls came to the table of their own accord. They ate breakfast, and still no doctor to be seen. Ernie had the matron see to washing the girls, doing up their hair with ribbons, and donning their new garments.

Ernie was beside himself. It was fully mid-afternoon before the doctor came walking into the boardinghouse. The girls were having a snack when Ernie rose from the table to introduce himself. He explained Raven's condition to the man, who agreed at once to see her.

The doctor peered first into one eye, then the other, then he would repeat the process over and over. He ran his fingers across Raven's skull looking for signs of trauma. Finally, he dropped his hands and let out a long breath of exasperation. He looked up at Ernie.

"Only time will tell. She might get her sight back because she is young and strong, and yet growing; but I can't say, no one can. It's in God's hands, Mr. Kibben. If I was to venture a guess, I'd say it had to do with a lack of oxygen in the cabin. It must have somehow damaged her eyesight."

Ernie turned away from the girls at hearing the news. He wiped his eyes. Inside, he was suddenly full of anger, angry at God, angry at himself for being unable to do anything. How could the Lord allow such terrible misfortune to befall a child so sweet, so young…so innocent? She was blameless for the world's problems. He cleared his eyes and throat. He paid the man.

"Let's go, girls."

The girls weren't at all eager to saddle up. They knew all too well about bitter cold and isolation in the wilderness. Raven whined pitifully for the comfort and security she was forced to leave behind, but Ernie had gotten his directions to Mother Gail's, and it was now time to go. It might have only been a six -hour ride to the orphanage, but they had gotten off to a bad start, and it would be darned cold and late by the time they arrived. There wasn't a moment to spare. The sky was clear, but that could change with the snap of a finger. The days of winter were too short to be of use, and night was the domain of wolves. It was one thing for him to be caught alone in a blizzard or the darkness of night, but it was something else to be burdened with two young girls. They rode off in haste.

NINETY-EIGHT

By the time Ernie rode up to Mother Gail 's porch it was well into nightfall, most certainly brushing the midnight hour. Raven had gone past her ability to stay awake and ended up on his horse, cradled in his arms. Dakota was dead beat and drifting in and out of sleep, but managing to stay in the saddle.

Thankfully, the faintest hint of light came into view. As Ernie continued up along the trail, the distant pricks of flickering light turned into the glow of windows. He figured he had the right place because it was the *only* place. A couple of dogs met him with a ruckus that could have raised anything now dead in the canyon. The front door to the cabin opened, and a sturdy but attractive middle-aged woman wrapped in a large and heavily knitted shawl filled the space, haloed by the light of lamp escaping from behind her. She stood there unafraid with a passel of faces peering around from behind her.

"Who goes there, stranger?"

"Ernie Kibben, ma'am. I beg yer pardon, most certainly fer disturbin' ya at this late an' uncivilized hour."

Ernie brought the horses to a halt. He tipped his hat. She acknowledged his greeting.

"What brings you this way then?"

Not at all timid, the woman stepped off the porch and took note of the girls.

"I reckon yer Mother Gail?"

"There's those that call me that. These here girls are a might frail to be out this late in a bitter cold, sir."

The woman scolded Ernie mildly as she waded through the snow toward Dakota. She reached up for Dakota, who was tottering back and forth in the saddle with eyes closed, and mostly sleeping where she sat. Dakota toppled off the horse and melted into Mother Gail's arms. She laid her head up against the woman's breast and appeared to continue sleeping on her feet.

"I'm right pleased to see ya bein' more an' jus' rumor. Might I have a word with ya in private, ma'am?"

"You most certainly can…if you can find any privacy; if you can't, you can still have a word with me if you prefer it. But before you get to jawin' you best bring that child inside unless you plan on soon burying her. I'll warm up some soup and tea." She beckoned him to follow.

"Much obliged for the kindness."

Ernie dismounted, keeping blanket-wrapped Raven cradled in his arms.

"You kids get back inside and stay out from under my feet. Ya belong in bed, ya hear. Now git!"

She forewarned the young group of scattering gawkers, gathered to look over the new arrivals. Ernie stepped through the door and was taken aback by the suffocating lack of space inside. When shoved against each other, there was just enough room to fit the bunks and a table with four chairs. A stove in close proximity to everything had by some blessing of God failed to ignite the place.

"Cynthia, you and Mary sleep by me tonight. Let these two lie down and get some rest. They have been too long in the night and cold. The poor things are too tired to eat."

The lower bunk was cleared. Dakota fell into it and never moved. Ernie placed Raven, who never awoke, alongside her sister. Ernie went to remove the girls' boots so as not to mess the bedding.

"Leave them in their coats and scarves. It gets cold in here of a night."

Earnie glanced quickly around the room, wishing to size it up for his peace of mind.

"Ya surely have a way with space, yes ma'am, everythin' is well placed."

"Ha! You choose your words well. You are either too kind or too funny," she laughed. "Please, sit and have some tea to warm ya. Might as well take off them boots and get those feet next to the stove while ya sit. Go on, get comfortable. It's too cold to be wandering about outside, and I should hope you plan to bed here for the night, if not for yourself then, at least for the girls. Besides, it's been a while since I've had chance to converse with someone my own age. I'll even throw in dinner and fixin's an' if that don't get ya, you ain't worth talkin' to, anyhow." She smiled and poured him a cup of hot tea.

"Oh, ma'am, ya don' need t' be twistin' my arm. I'm more 'an happy t' take up yer offer o' hospitality. Yes-sireee, it's bitter cold out there jus' like ya said. I pray I'll not be too poor a talker."

Ernie blew across the cup of hot liquid and sipped the warmth nested between his hands.

"Ohh."

He needn't say a word. It was understood. He set the tea down onto the table.

"You can call me Gail."

"Yes, ma'am, Gail. Is there no man in this here house, then?"

"No, sir. Not for a few years, now."

"I don' believe I understand, an' if ya'll pardon me fer askin', there bein' no man how d'ya manage with all these children, them needin' t' be fed an' such?"

"Well , you might 'a noticed there's little fat to be found on any of us. Truth is, it's hard getting by, mighty hard, but we manage. There's the stream just there for fishing and the woods are full of game. We set traps, lots of traps. Then, we race the wolves to see who gets dinner first. Sometimes friends or maybe a hunter wanders in an' drops off what he can't eat. Quite often, I'll cook up what they fetch in trade for sharing the food. We see to it younguns eat first. To look at it from afar, I reckon I'd figure it impossible, but day to day we always seem to find a way. This time of year is the worst with the snow an' all. Anyhow, I ain't on your porch, sir. What brings you to these parts?"

"The girls," Ernie spat out.

Mother Gail dropped her head and then leaned back in her chair with a less than happy expression.

"You sayin' they're orphans?" she asked with disappointment.

Ernie nodded his head.

"Lost their folks a coupla weeks back. Their daddy was my life-long friend."

"My condolences."

"Much appreciated. I've known the girls since birth. Watched 'em learn to walk, to talk, watched 'em grow up. That Dakota is a clever one."

Ernie went on to tell how Dakota fought off the wolves. He went on to tell Mother Gail about how Joe and Rosaria died. He cried as he told her about how it cost Raven her eyesight, and the way it broke his heart every time he saw her and thought on it.

"Anyhow, I love 'em kids like they're my own, yes-sireee. I can't imagine 'em not bein' part o' my life as always been, but it's near impossible. I just gotta say it. Girls need mothers, an' I don' even know how t' be a father."

Ernie shook his head. He was genuine, truthful in heart. He looked away from Mother Gail's scrutiny. It was hard being a man and fearing a soul that would bleed openly from the mere utterance of a child's name. He adored the girls, and it was like ripping out his soul to leave them. It was the situation that left him with little choice.

"Don't you fret over it none, Mr. Kibben. It don't need no explaining. It's pretty much the same with most of these kids. Mamas who died delivering, fathers who went off trapping and panning in the hills and never come back. These things happen. That's God's way. Ain't no explaining it. But I'm fearing I gotta tell you truthful, I can't see how I can take on another mouth to feed, let alone two. You saw it for yourself, first thing." She shrugged.

Ernie sat dumbfounded watching the woman as the meaning of what she just said slowly sank in.

"God almighty, woman, are you sayin' ya can't take the girls?"

He was stunned. He hadn't prepared himself for the possibility of the girls not being able to remain at Mother Gail's. In the whole of the wild west, there was no other place. A moment went by and he was still lost for words. He was stumped pure and simple. What the hell was he supposed to do now?

"What are you thinking, Mr. Kibben?"

"I'm thinkin' yer sayin' ya can't take the girls an' I'm here t' leave 'em. Plain an' simple we gots t' do a lotta a' talkin' before sun-up. I'm pleadin' fer ya t' allow me the chance t' speak my piece."

"Take your best shot, sir, but it's going to have to be darn special words. I got seven mouths to feed as is, and you don't see no cake 'round here."

Ernie settled into his chair. Two people who had nothing in common the hour before, save for a desire to talk, faced off across a table and cups of hot berry tea. They listened to the words, they read the expressions, they exchanged warmth and an unconscious yearning between them as the cold of night filled the unheated spaces.

"It ain't like I planned on becoming a spinster, Lord no! It's just the way things work out. I never really had a choice in the matter. You see, my folks passed when I was young, and it made for a hard, hard life. Don't misunderstand me, it wasn't any worse for me than for any child in this room. A child only knows its own suffering, its own loneliness. In fact, I now know I was luckier than most here. You see, my brother Gabriel, who was seven years my senior, never give thought to leaving me or turning me out to fend for myself. He became my father. He watched over me as if I were his own.

"Anyhows, during my seventeenth year, let me see, Gabriel was twenty-four. That's right, he was twenty-four when he fell in love with the greatest gal ya ever want to meet. Her name was Betty Carson, and I always swore she could make a snake laugh. My Lord, she was funny. Ha! We never stopped laughing in this house. She was always saying she was the best 'Bet' Gabe had going for him. At that time, I was old enough to be married myself but Bet never made me out to be a burden to their union, she only made my days all the more worth living."

"I know just what yer sayin', Gail. It was that-a-way with Joe an' Rosaria."

"Same thing, I am sure. Well, day come to pass and Bet sez she's with child. We were so happy. Everybody was happy we talked and laughed, thinking about what it would be like to have a baby boy or gal and all them things you might figure on for such an announcement. She carried that child well all through her term, there being no problems of any sort to the best of my knowing.

"But all that changed the day she come to labor. She wasn't able to deliver and her labor went hard right on into the next day. Gabe and I were sick with worry. There was no one to contact for half a day's ride at the least and Gabriel didn't dare leave her side. I pleaded with him to let me go, but he forbade I do any such thing. So we sat side by side and prayed. God almighty did we pray. On the second night of her labor, the baby's head came through, but it ripped her open something horrible. It was a boy but the delivery had been too much for the poor thing and he entered the world still born.

"Bet had wrung every ounce of life from her body and passed out from pain or fatigue, I don't know which, probably both, but she never come back to us. She died about two hours later. Gabe was devastated. I was devastated. Gabe was never the same afterward. This house grew so quiet, so serious. It was no longer a home. It was simply empty without Bet's laughter.

"Life went on day after day, empty, until one afternoon when Gabe come riding up the trail with a young boy of about eight sittin' behind him on his horse. Good-lookin' kid he was. Went by the name of Carl. His family died of Cholera as so many of them settlers do. He came into South Pass with the wagon train and took up with a trapper for a couple of months. I guess he didn't care much for the man and he ran off. Showed up at Claussen's, and Gabriel happened to be in town when he arrived. He said there was never a second's hesitation from his first sight of the boy.

"Then came Nancy and Timothy. They were followed by Roberta, and so it went—maybe twenty in all. They come and they go. ...Seven with me now. The only difference is Gabriel passed on three years ago, and now I'm all they've got. It hasn't been easy without Gabriel. Actually, truth be known, it's been downright hard. Word gets out and each year sees more orphans than the one before.

"There's more people in these parts, and more things to go wrong, and more families to get busted up. Cholera or consumption or Mountain fever, you think of it and there's a kid standing alone at the end of the story. I hope you can understand now, why I can't just jump up and say I'll take the girls. It ain't that I wouldn't love to care for them, I just no longer have the means."

Ernie listened to her story with interest and understanding. He also mulled over ideas that might help both of them out. He decided to offer her his thoughts.

"Mother Gail. I'd be a askin' that ya give some thought t' what I'm a fixin' t' say. Like ya t' hear my figerin'. It'll take some gettin' used to, yes-sireee, but bite yer tongue an' give it some thought before ya might feel t' rush off an' say ya'll have no part in it. That's what I'm askin'. Will ya jus' hear me out?"

"Course. I'm not in such good way that I can afford not to hear ya speak your piece." She smiled.

"Very well, then. Dakota's daddy, Joe, an' I been all through these here hills an' I might add I'm most surprised I never once laid eyes on this place, 'specially if it's been here as long as you're a sayin'. T' me, was nothin' but rumor long ago. I reckon we jus' never got to walking this patch. Could be, I just plumb fergot the place. No matter, I guess. What I mean t' say is Joe an' I both got lands staked out in this here canyon an' others.

"I'd make the offer t' build ya a cabin t' care fer yer kids an' my Dakota, an' young Raven. It'd be downstream from here, nearby water, but a good deal closer t' town. I know it t' be scarce more 'an two hours' ride t' Northpole. I'd take my time an' build it good. All I'd ask in return is ya carin' fer the girls, an' allowin' me t' see em' when I can. Ya still have yer own place if the cabin doesn't suit ya."

Ernie looked to Mother Gail for a response. She leaned forward in her chair and looked him straight in the face.

"You're sayin' you'd build me and the rest of the children a cabin for looking after the girls and nothing more?

"Yes, ma'am. I'd a had t' do it fer a wife if'n I'd a had one. The way I sees it, if ya got my children, yer like my wife then. I'll build ya a cabin t' keep ya warm an' dry. In return, I trust ya'll give my girls a proper upbringin'."

"Hah! I can't believe my ears. It would be a fine thing to be but two hours' ride to town. Not that I got a horse, but I think townsfolk would be more apt to lend a hand if they knew about the kids; if we didn't live so far out."

"It's a deal then?" Ernie waited. Mother Gail thought for a moment then raised her eyebrows.

"It's a deal 'til I wake up with more sense. More tea?"

"Don' mind if I do. Thank-you."

Mother Gail took in the girls as agreed, and Ernie set out to build her a larger cabin as promised. It was about four hours' ride back down the canyon to the property he and Joe had staked out long ago. He raised a small shack to keep him out of the cold.

The structure would suffice, but Ernie relished any opportunity to return to the warmth and family atmosphere of Mother Gail's. He was more than happy to bring home fresh kill so that he might be invited to stay for dinner and spend the night having tea with the lady. Times of late were easier at Mother Gail's' because Ernie used some of his and Joe's load to buy supplies for the orphanage. His presence reduced the burdens of Mother Gail. He also could provide a fair but firm hand with the young ones when called for. Whenever he was visiting, he spent most of his time chopping wood, taking the boys out with him, teaching them to trap game, and seeing to everyone's needs in general. A grown up man was both a rare commodity and an oddity in the eyes of these souls, but either way he was worshiped. He was offered the affections of all, but most enjoyed the attentions of Mother Gail.

Ernie spent his time the following spring and summer, and going well into autumn, working on the new cabin. It would be large and divided into two living areas. It was to be built as two cabins facing each other with a suitable porch separating the two structures but at the same time joining them. The porch made for a covered breezeway and idyllic gathering place for the children during foul weather or in the evening hours of a summer.

As one approached the porch steps, the cabin to flank the right side of the porch would be a kitchen with a stove, a fireplace, two nice cup boards, a counter's top, and room for a large table and a batch of chairs. There would be a small loft overhead that allowed for storage and two small beds for Mother Gail and a guest should she choose not to sleep with the children.

The cabin now being built to the left of the porch, would be the sleeping quarters. It would be larger than Mother Gail's kitchen cabin, large enough to house twelve bunks or more and still have sufficient room left over to be fitted out with a table and chairs for playing, actually for keeping the children out from under Mother Gail's feet while she worked in her kitchen.

Ernie spent the spring living in his shack, while he cleared the trees and formed the beams. It was much more difficult an undertaking than he had supposed. Joe had always been his left hand, his face always to be seen at the other end of a beam to be carried. Now beams were dragged and hefted alone. As soon as the first cabin had a suitable roof in place, he moved inside with a sigh of relief and made himself a much more comfortable life.

The children were always clamoring to see Uncle Kib and their new cabin. The pestering was so persistent that Ernie and Gail had to agree to a day every week or so, whereby he prepared for their arrival by starting up the fire pit for Mother Gail to roast game and bake corn and sweetbread over the coals.

It was a welcome visit, one he looked to enjoy, not only because of the company but also because the older boys eagerly offered a hand with work that required those extra hands. Every child wished to say that he or she had helped in the construction of their new home.

Each week the orphans arrived to marvel over Ernie's progress and await their instructions. Ernie finished the left cabin first, it being simple sleeping quarters and the easiest to construct. It was an open rectangular room, and so the walls went up fast. As soon as the older boys helped him finish the roof, the pattern of the visits changed. Now, oftentimes, the Mother Gail and the children stayed over for a second day or even a third. Extra bedding began to find a permanent place in the new sleeping quarters. The speed of construction improved markedly at that point.

It wasn't uncommon for Ernie to travel the four -hour round trip down to Northpole and back for purpose of procuring sweets from Claussens' to hand out to his crew of orphaned visitors. The youngsters had long since forgotten the pleasures of candy. In fact, it had become such a routine purchase that he had begun to raise the Claussens' interest. They had taken an interest in his activities and were most pleased to learn more about the orphanage and it being moved closer to town. They expressed a sincere desire to see his progress when deemed convenient. The Claussens soon insisted on donating the candy and other stores for the orphanage. The candy and gifts made visiting day cherished by all. A great cloud of disappointment and silence snuffed the children's exuberance when time came to leave. The end of day marked long faces and resignation, maybe more so for Ernie and Gail.

It had been a wonderful and fulfilling year for Ernie, rich with new relationships. He couldn't remember ever having so much contact with people. There were many times when he felt compelled to escape all the commotion and head for the woods. Fortunately, there was never any shortage of wilderness to find solitude and his lost wits. In truth, he had become quite attached to the children. They would wait on him hand and foot, and compete with each other to be his favorite. They had come to accept him, not only as their savior and hero, but for the youngest, he was in every way a father.

Ernie grew depressed whenever he considered leaving Gail and the children. It was hard to keep up spirits knowing the cabin was finished. He reached for every extra moment he could find to fix this, or make that a little better, but now everything appeared perfect and it was obvious he had no further reason to stay.

He longed to stay in the worst of ways, but could find no reason to propose such a thing to Gail. Their relationship had developed into more of a 'dear friend' alliance. It was wholly understandable, for the children never allowed them the privacy needed to sort out their feelings. Ernie understood why Gail was not married. What man stood a chance against the demands placed upon her time and heart? Ernie had few doubts about where his heart sought comfort, but to say it, was the most difficult and embarrassing task he had ever been put to, and as autumn approached, he still wasn't up to it.

The dinner arrangements changed once fall arrived and everyone was settled into the new cabin. Ernie tried to make himself useful by hunting and trapping, but finally faced the fact that it was time to seek work in South Pass or possibly finish out his days back at his old cabin in Wind River where he could go back to trapping and panning gold. Thoughts of the old cabin were just thoughts. He knew he could never go back because the memories caused his insides to feel like lead, they suffocated him with depression. He would most likely depart the orphanage and drift.

The farewells were filled with tears and most memorable was Gail's approach and kiss. It was awkward and they weren't able to meet each other's eyes, but Ernie took the kiss straight to heart all the same. The kiss was so thrilling a sensation that it stayed with him, long, long, after he rode out.

NINETY-NINE

Ernie spent some time in South Pass, but it was a bleak existence. The pass was a magnet for stragglers and the downtrodden. These were mostly men who chased dreams of fortunes out in California and Oregon, but ran out of funds and food by the time they reached the mountains. Without the means to cross the barren desert beyond the Rockies, they ended up stranded at the pass. For that reason, workers could be hired for meals only, and there was no hope of him making enough money to get ahead. These facts, coupled with countless nights packed into unheated sleeping quarters, horse stalls and the like, and too many missed meals for the lack of game to hunt, and Ernie decided to go back to his cabin in Partner's Path Canyon.

If Ernie thought that his earliest days of adventure in the company of Joe had been a disaster, he now realized that it paled in comparison to trying to live in a place crammed full with memories of his best dead friends. Coming up Partner's Path proved to be bearable, more so than he thought, even inviting to some extent, possibly due to the familiarity and the peace it had always provided. It was also to Ernie's benefit that his cabin had been built down valley from Joe and Rosaria's, thereby making it the first and only place he need happen upon. But that was about as good as it got.

After a week of rest in his cabin, Ernie ventured up to the clearing. His stomach was in his throat. There was little left of the woodpile, most all of it had been burned to ash.

"Lord, I beg ya hear my prayer. I thank ya this day fer savin' me the sight o' Joe an' Rosaria. I thank ya fer takin' every sign o' their existence from this earth, dust t' dust, ash t' ash."

Ernie waded back into the creek. In time, he was again bent over in much the same manner as done for years prior, swirling the icy water around the worn copper and separating out the fines. The only difference being, now he had only his pan and his memories. The memories were killing him.

In spite of any wish, any determination different, Ernie was no longer in his element. He and Joe had lived five miles apart, and that was like standing on each other's toes. Now with Joe and Rosaria gone and no longer sharing the canyon, the countryside was as desolate and bleak as the desert. If there was one thing in life more empty of heart, it had to be his existence.

Ernie's loss haunted him terrible. He finally took it upon himself to ride up to Joe's cabin. He was searching desperately for relief, longing for companionship. The one trip turned into many. He now regularly rode up to Joe's place to go inside and sit...nothing more, just sit.

Ernie would talk aloud. He would talk to his ghosts. He would talk and laugh about the old times. His memories went all the way back to the core of their existence. He looked at the cabin wall and remembered busting an axe handle notching out the seventh log up. He remembered losing his grip on the door while hanging it, and dropping it on the very ends of Joe's toes as he tried to set the hinges. Poor Joe bounced and bounced all about the front yard. He laughed but he felt terrible to cause Joe so much pain.

Then there was the pain when Joe stepped back into one of his traps. His leg was gashed horrible and bloody. Joe cried out as he pried the trap open. He remembered carrying Joe back on his shoulder to Rosaria who was nearly hysterical.

When light of day diminished and darkness weighed heavy, Ernie could smell rabbit stewing over the fire for dinner. Rosaria was so happy to make a meal in her new home. And a home it was. He thought of the evenings they had sat together making a crib for Dakota, who's birth was close at hand. Joe worked the crib frame, he whittled the dowels, and Rosaria made the bedclothes. Those were good times, times to sit on the porch and smoke a pipe and laugh. When Rosaria laughed, everybody laughed.

He and Joe had always been two of a kind, chopping the same tree, panning the same bank, living the same life. When Joe died, they both died, one physically, one spiritually. The tears streaked down Ernie's face and he cried hard in the darkness, in the silence of the cabin, in the silence of his world.

The day finally arrived when Ernie asked Joe and Rosaria to understand he had to leave. He believed he was going insane with loneliness. He was supposed to go to Gail's for Christmas and spend time with her and the kids, but the undeniable truth was he didn't want to come back to be haunted by all he missed.

Ernie tried to explain how the canyon no longer had the feel of home. He was always looking back over his shoulder. He was always spooked by things he never saw. He felt as much an orphan now as the children with whom he wished to be. Especially to be with Dakota and Raven, who represented his only concept of family, a fact made more apparent each passing day as his heart searched the empty countryside for their laughter. It was addicting, if he had never known it, he could have gone on, but he was as tied to them as a kite to string. He could fly, but only if he was rooted in their lives. Ernie sobbed. He would take Joe and Rosaria with him in his heart. He would never forget them, but he had to leave. He was miserable.

The days dragged, the weeks seemed eternal. The inability to talk to anybody was unbearable. He wished his time away. He hunted, he fished; he panned from sun-up to sun-set. Ernie rationalized every excuse imaginable in his search for a sound reason to stay with Gail and the children once he arrived for Christmas.

The trouble was he understood the only reason to stay, which rang true from the heart, was the feeling that he belonged with them. It wasn't only for love he wished to be with them; it was also a basic human desire to be needed. And they needed him, but no more in fact than he needed them. On a day-to-day basis, they gave him a reason to exist. The kids needed him for the silliest reasons, but that silliness brought fulfillment to his heart. If only he knew how Gail felt.

Gail did very well managing her affairs, requiring little or no help other than donations of food. She was now closer to town and much of her struggle had been alleviated. Ernie could see plenty of reasons why she could use him, but he was never a polished man, never been learned or mannerly. Maybe he was too high a price to pay for what good he could do in return. Women were different and he didn't understand them. They made him uncomfortable. Women did everything by instinct and feeling. You could stand the tallest, run the fastest, be the strongest and all of it meant nothing if you didn't know how to properly ask for something, how to say *please*. You couldn't just strike a deal and shake on it, as you might do with a man. If a man reneged on a deal, you could shoot him. If a woman did, you just had to bite your lip and cuss the wind.

The occasional wind now came to take a hard bite out of a summer turned autumn that somehow managed to stave off the brutality of an overdue winter. The water in the creek was at its lowest save for the downpours that came with the change of seasons. The water had lost all the warmth of the summer and pained the fingers and hands without conscience. The banks were now broad and exposed, ready to be filled again with ice.

Ernie was bent over his pan when that cold wind sliced up beneath the backside of his coat. It stood him straight and prompted a serious thought to heading out for Northpole and Mother Gail's before the onslaught of winter storms made snow deep and travel murderous. The idea of being right close to Gail and the orphanage as Christmas neared warmed him.

"I oughta jus' get the tarnation outta here."

Without thought he bent back over and scraped up some bank with the pan. He was thinking hard on Gail and that kiss he carried in his heart when suddenly a clunk in his pan distracted him.

He was stunned. Ernie stood up slowly. For the first and possibly only time after returning to the canyon, his mind was blank. There was simply no thought, no memory that could overtake or sidetrack what sat nestled amidst the sand in his pan. He reached in with cold fingers and plucked out a nugget of gold the size of a grape. He twirled it in his fingers as he held it up to the light of a cloudy gray autumn sky.

"Joe?"

Ernie couldn't help but to call out to his friend.

"Look at this."

He rolled the nugget around in the palm of his hand.

"Who'd a figered this miserly ol' creek could cough up a nugget like that?"

Ernie knew better than to dare think there could be any chance of finding a second such nugget. He stared down as the depression in the bank where he scooped out the sand. He then looked back at his pan. He didn't even need to swirl the sand. There were a number of sizeable nuggets in plain view. Ernie settled himself, and began to wash the sand and pick out the gold. He then scooped out another pan full of sand and immediately spotted the glitter.

Most men would have only seen the potential for spectacular wealth in hand, but not Ernie. He saw only his reason to go back to Gail. He now had something more to offer her than just another mouth to feed. If given a little miner's luck, he would bring Gail security. Ernie was almost in tears at the thought of his possible good fortune.

"I can't believe it, Joe. Look at this. How many years did we sit aroun' scrapin' this here bank wishin' an' hopin'. Mebbe, it was yer doin'? Was that it, Joe? All my cryin' 'bout bein' lonely an' needin' t' leave. Are ya givin' me my way out? Are ya sendin' me back t' Dakota an' Raven?"

Ernie bowed his head and wept—*for joy*. The vision of that grape-sized nugget could return the spirit to a dead man.

"Hooooooooooo-weeeeeeeee! Haal-laaay-luuujaaaaaaaahh!"

With a purpose not felt since he and Joe were lads in St. Louis, Ernie shoveled his way through that bank. He kept hard at it until the easy pickings passed and snow was pressing upon his back.

Ernie stood up at last from the ice skimmed creek, tossed his pan aside, and called it a season. When he closed up his cabin, he did so with a smile, great satisfaction, and the highest of hopes. The weight of his gold was directly proportional to the lightness of his heart.

ONE HUNDRED

Maybe for the sake of polite conversation, the Mistress of Winter waited until the bitter end to make her appearance. Maybe she desired an "entrance" or maybe she just felt cruel. Either way, she was absent and allowed a warm and balmy Indian summer to have its innocent way, stretching late into the year. Unseasonably warm days were still making a show in the latter part of November and early weeks of December.

When her connivance was found out, it was too late. A trap of death had been set. She rushed in, winds screaming and temperatures killing. She sliced through the unseasonable warmth like butter halved by a butcher knife, splitting a clean line between the hot and the cold. She hit hard and unexpectedly with little more than a day's notice.

Eighty-seven stragglers, diseased, half-starved, frost bitten or frozen solid, entered South Pass Junction in a state of hysteria and twenty-two busted up wagons. These tattered souls had been the late starters, the ignorant, the fools, the left behinds from earlier trains that could not make the strenuous pace. The misery painted across their faces was all the explanation needed to understand why only twenty-two of the forty-three wagons leaving in a train from Independence, Missouri, managed to arrive at South Pass. They had paid the price of venturing into the unforgiving wilderness with dreams instead of diligence.

It wasn't difficult to fall behind. It was said: *"every torturous mile of Platte River trail is marked by a gravestone."* The life-giving waters that drew settlers to its banks dealt out death in unforeseen currents of Cholera. In some places, the rows of grave markers were so numerous, from a distance they appeared as picketed country fences. There was most certainly enough wood lying about from broken down or abandoned wagons to build the fence.

Ernie rode through the deepening snow and grumbled about the long overdue blizzards. He retreated as far as possible into the warmth of his coat. It was more of a thought than an action for there was no escape from the screaming squalls that swirled relentlessly across the flats stretching out about him. It had been cold in Partner's Path Canyon; it was colder on the open plains.

He concentrated on the warmth of a woodstove and the welcoming embrace of a passel of kids and a strong willed woman. Buried deep beneath his hat and blanket, behind an upturned collar and closed eyes, was also his insecurity.

The Mistress of Winter wailed. She whirled about his frame, drawing off his heat, all the while wearing Ernie down with whisperings in his ear. He could hear Mother Gail asking if he was delirious. ...Asking why would she have need of him? Asking what future of worth might he ever offer? He feared looking the fool, and it seemed his situation was bent on ensuring just that. What was his worth? What would be his retreat?

During every passing hour of his journey toward Mother Gail's, Ernie's mind rehashed the same hopes, the same worries. He found himself becoming more fatigued from all the hard thinking than the winter ride against the storm. South Pass Junction was more or less the half way point to Northpole and Mother Gail's when measured in miles. But when measured in time, the ride out of Wind River mountain country took near ten days, whereas it only took a day, two at most to reach Northpole from South Pass Junction by train. He would be facing Mother Gail and all his fears soon enough. Knowing it made his stomach twist into a knot. He pulled up his wraps tight about him to force out winter with all its worries. He closed his eyes and focused on the heat of Mother Gail's stove and hot berry tea. He buried winter's misery beneath his determination to recount every spoken word and sensation of their first conversation.

Ernie followed the RMR tracks eastward to South Pass Junction. The raised bed of rails was about the only feature in his flat, colorless world. The man-made scar kept him on course. It was in the twilight of late afternoon that he rode into town. Ernie raised his head just enough to lift the snow-covered brim of his hat off the upturned coat collar that supported it. He peered over his woolen scarf, through the mist of his breath, and beyond the blinding snow that filled the air between him and the emerging sight of a stationary wagon train.

It was too late in the season for a train to be underway. The sight wasn't one to be welcomed. Ernie feared it would prove to be a scene of disaster. For the first time in days he was distracted by something profound enough to overshadow his trepidation about Gail and the kids. He rode slowly past the wagons, one after the next, and listened to the crying and confusion of families inside. He imagined them to be huddled together in darkness beneath blankets and spare clothes to keep from freezing to death. The wagon hoops strained beneath the ice and snow piled atop the canvas.

Ernie rode up to the livery and dismounted. His knees felt frozen into a permanent crook. Looking around as he straightened out his back, he assumed it was the arrival of the wagon train that made the livery and blacksmith shop an exceptionally busy place this night.

Working the stiffness out of his legs, he entered the establishment, if for no other reason than to get out of the hard blow. Inside, it was wonderfully warm. He stepped lightly across a floor crowded with slumbering wayfarers wrapped in bedrolls with feet pointed toward the furnace. Ernie removed his ice-caked leather gloves, placed them atop a large worn anvil, and held his hands out over the glowing coals of the furnace to steal away some of its heat.

The manager barely took notice of him. He was addressing a myriad of problems. Most stemming from animals removed to him from the wagon train. Horses and wagon teams where pressed in tight wall to wall. The tortured creatures looked like a herd of walking ribs. A long row of broken wagon wheels was leaning against his bench. A riotous chorus of snoring and snorting, by all manner of men, women, children, and animal reverberated throughout the place.

"Howdy, stranger." The blacksmith approached him.

"How do."

"Can't say I know your face. Come in with the train?"

"No-sireee. Travelin' alone."

"Lucky man. In view of the goings on with that miserable lot, you can count yourself fortunate. What might I do for ya?"

"Jus' lookin' fer some feed fer the night, an' hopin' t' get my horse outta the cold fer a spell."

"Mmm. Let me see. Put your horse over there by that mare. That's about all the space I got left."

"What news o' the wagon train? Terrible late in the year fer traveling with kin, ain't it?"

"You might say that," the man snorted. "I never seen such a herd of greenhorns. Ignorant fools, if ya ask me. Maybe not so ignorant anymore. Lot of 'em died...two younguns just last night from the cold."

"Ahh. That would explain all the cryin' in the street, yes-sireee."

"They're a pathetic lot. Cholera took out half of 'em. Now they're stranded here in South Pass and they don't know what to do. Supposed to be headin' into Oregon territory, but that ain't about to happen. Even if this snow clears, they won't make a mile before the next storm hits and freezes 'em all to death. Hay or oats?"

"Oats. I'll be by fer 'em jus' before the train heads out fer Northpole."

"Hey, if ya need a place to bed down, still some room on the floor for a roll; got a good fire a-goin'. Fifty cents for the night and that'll get ya a coffee at daybreak."

"Much obliged, but I been too many nights on the ground. I'm hoping fer a right hot bath. Yes-sireee. Got ten frozen toes wantin' out o' these boots an' into a good hot soak."

"Alright, then. In the morning."

"In the mornin'. Much obliged."

Ernie slipped on the warmed gloves and pulled his collar back up to the brim of his hat. He stepped back out into the cold. He walked up the street toward a string of oil lamps that brightened the entrance to a respectable-looking boardinghouse. Inside, he was greeted by a woman, the proprietor's wife, and was soon given a room and a towel.

His bath was prepared. Ernie got himself a good hot soak to return life to his frozen appendages. His clothes had been removed to the kitchen for drying and warming beside the hearth. Ernie paid for pot after pot of boiling hot water to be brought in until he was fully saturated to the core with heat. Feeling truly warm for the first time in ages, he climbed out of the hot water, wasted no time toweling off in the cold room, and climbed back into warm dry clothes. He felt invigorated.

"It's time to eat, Ernie."

At the table, Ernie was gorging himself on bread and roasted buffalo when a woman, visibly distressed, escorted a slew of children into the building and approached the proprietor's wife. There was nothing to prevent overhearing the conversation.

"May I be of assistance?"

"I pray you can. I am party to those unfortunates traveling with the train. I wish to know if you might open your heart and offer these children a warm floor upon which to retire. They are recently orphaned with no next of kin. I have watched over them best I can, but there is no room in the wagons, they are overfilled with survivors.

"We have many orphans amongst us, but for the most part the others have gone with family and taken up what little space is left. My wagon is large but already occupied by older children better able to stand the cold. Whereas they once slept under it or the open sky, the sudden show of winter has further prevented such arrangements. So, I moved them off the ground and inside the wagon, and I hope to find a warmer place for these youngest of the lot. I don't believe any of us has enjoyed the benefit of sleep for the better part of a week. There are only seven, ma'am, and they mind well, and God would surely look upon you with favor for your compassion. Please, I beg you take them in."

The lady in service looked at the woman, speechless, but with eyes that revealed a genuine mother's concern. She stood there in an obvious state of distress and indecision. She looked around searching for some answer. She turned back to the woman and children.

"Madam, I would do whatever I might, but I am not sure what that would be. The rooms are all let and the kitchen offers possibly room for one or two, but…. Please forgive me. I…I…"

The proprietor's wife shook her head in dismay.

"Maybe, I could ask around. There may be someone…"

The stranger held out her hand and stopped the lady in service.

"No. Please, I can see you mean well, but I shan't be the bother…"

"No, it's no both—."

"It's no bother, ma'am."

Ernie interrupted the conversation. He arose from his table and stepped into their midst. The women turned to face him somewhat startled by a man's approach.

"Ernie Kibben, ma'am. I have a room an' I would be honored if ya'd take it fer the night, yes-sireee. As fer the younguns, if ya'll follow me over t' the livery, I know fer a fact there's space enough fer the lot t' put down a roll before a warm fire."

The woman appeared nervous to accept Ernie's offer. Sensing this, he continued.

"No need t' be a fearin' me, ma'am. My offer's honorable."

"It's a fact, madam. He has two young girls here at the inn," said the matron.

The woman, having scant alternative, thanked him and gathered her children without a word. Obediently, she followed Ernie back out into the cold. At the livery, Ernie conferred with the blacksmith, settled on a price, and within a few minutes had the children bedded down in a soft carpet of hay. The strangers who shared the room were happy to move back from the fire so the orphans might enjoy the warmth.

"I'm ov a mind t' offer ya my room at the boardin'house. I hope ya'll take it an' get yerself that night's sleep ya been longin'."

"Oh, no thank you. You are too kind, Mr. Kibben, but I can't leave the children. What if they should awake or get underfoot—."

"Ma'am, I didn't get yer name...."

"Please call me Emma."

"Miss Emma, there ain't a snowball's chance in...in...tarnation that them kids are gonna wake anytime soon. I'll put down next to 'em an' be sure they remain settled. I'm askin' ya t' take my room an' get yerself that sleep. Ya can't keep up with this lot unless ya keep yer strength. Please...take the room."

"I don't know—."

"Take the room, Miss Emma."

Her eyes locked onto his as she searched for the comfort of trust in Earnie's face.

"Very well, Mr. Kibben. If you insist."

"Fine. I'll just walk ya back to the—."

"No. I will be fine. My walk back will be easier knowing you are with the children when I depart."

"Very well, Miss Emma. Sleep as long as ya like. I will await yer return come mornin'."

Ernie took up a place on the floor alongside the orphans. He sat with his back up against a post and studied the faces turned his way. He tried to understand what possible gain God might fathom by doling out such hardship and ill fortune to the innocent and helpless.

"Go and sleep, Emma."

"God bless, you, sir."

"Sleep tight."

Earnie watched the woman walk away, slipping out through the door that held the freezing weather at bay. He let out a sigh. In the minutes that followed, all but one of the children had fallen fast to sleep. He could see they were hungry and exhausted. A young boy of about ten was close to him and he could hear him sobbing quietly into his blanket. Ernie slid his foot over to the boy and nudged him. The boy turned to face him and the firelight danced off the moisture on his face.

"What's yer name, boy?" Ernie spoke in a low hushed voice, so as not to disturb the other sleepers.

"Jeremy."

"Jeremy what?"

"Jeremy Larson." The boy wiped his face with his shirt.

"What happened t' yer folks, Jeremy?"

"They died of the Cholera."

"What about the rest o' 'em?"

Jeremy looked over his shoulder away from Ernie. He turned back.

"Same. Those two boys are William and Clifford. Their folks are dead. The three girls are Cynthia, Louise and...I think...it's Melanie. Their dad was one of the first to die. I don't think he died of Cholera, because it was way back, just a short while after we left Independence. Their mom was pregnant with twins. Cynthia and Louise are twins. I think Melanie was a twin, but her sister died in delivery. At least that's what was said. Their mom tried to continue on with the train, for fear of turnin' back and runnin' into Indians, but after two months she was deliverin' and she died with her babies. It was said, she was too tired from driving the teams and cookin' the meals and washing the clothes and raising the girls. I remember because everybody was real sad that day. The other kid is Jeremy too, and the other girl, over there with the red hair, is Bess. They don't talk much and I don't know anything about them."

"What about the lady who brought ya in?

"Mrs. Gardner. I don't know. She's real kind. She didn't have any kids and said she was going to Oregon Territory. I think her man died, but I don't know anything about that. She never speaks of him. I think she was rich because she had a large team and a large wagon. It had a lot of stuff in it but when everybody got scared and starting throwing away all their things to lighten the load and move faster, she got rid of everything. She said she had a lot of wonderful things, but they didn't mean squat to a dead person.

"I know her husband was dead for a long time because once everybody started dying, the wagon master, Mr. Stanley, asked if she would take some kids. She took the seven of us too sleep inside her wagon because we had nobody. She watched over another six or seven who slept outside. All the rest of the kids went to friends or kin. It was no problem riding or walking, but there wasn't any place to sleep ceptin' for outside."

"Lay yer head down boy, an' get some sleep. It won't be of'en ya get t' feel the warmth of a fire, 'specially when being dry at the same time."

The boy turned his head away once again, and this time fell asleep without crying. Ernie sat and dozed on and off for at least an hour thinking about the children and their lot in life. He ended his night in a deep sleep, the first night in many when he didn't suffer the worry of facing Mother Gail and her rejection. He had been too involved with the tragedy at hand.

ONE-HUNDRED-ONE

Ernie opened his eyes at the first stirring of the blacksmith stoking up his furnace. It was a good many hours before daylight, being that dawn came late during winter months, and clouds heavily laden with snow often kept the lid of darkness tight upon the land. He overheard a couple of the men near him discussing the slumbering children.

"Excuse me, gents."

"Are these children in with your lot?"

"Yes, sir. ...What remains of it."

"I promised t' keep an eye on 'em fer Miss Gardner, but I'm of a mind to walk over an' breakfast at the boardin'house where she's taken her rest. Would one o' ya's be willin' t' take my place fer a spell?"

The men were more than happy to oblige Ernie. And so, he stepped carefully over the children, leaving them to their sleep, and walked back over to the boardinghouse. He ordered a cup of coffee and some breakfast sweetbread with cinnamon and sugar sprinkled on top. He asked the proprietor's wife to escort Miss Gardner to his table when she made her appearance. This, the woman did.

"Good morning, Mr. Kibben."

"Good morning, Mrs. Gardner. I trust ya slept fer the better last night."

Ernie rose to his feet.

"I did indeed. I remember nothing; my eyes closed, my eyes opened. I don't know how I might repay you for your kindness. I feel guilty being one of the few to sleep inside. May I ask about the children?"

"T' the point, Miss Gardner. Rest assured ya may be at ease. They are bein' watched o'er by the menfolk of yer party. I only departed a short while ago after bein' given assurances to their care. In fact, two o' their wives made an appearance as I removed myself here to the boardin'house. Would ya care t'join me in some coffee?"

"That is very kind of you, sir, but—."

"Miss Gardner. I insist. Have ya never been a mother?"

Miss Gardner stopped short with a puzzled look.

"Why do you ask?"

"No disrespect, ma'am, but I'm guessin' not. Otherwise, ya'd know full an' well the only time ya might take in a cup o' coffee in peace is when the younguns are asleep. Now, I insist, join me fer breakfast. It'll do ya some good."

"As you wish."

Ernie forced Miss Gardner to cut loose her stress. He watched her take a deep breath and resign herself to his insistence. He stepped around the table and offered her a chair.

"I lay in bed last night before falling asleep and chastised myself for being so mistrusting of your good intention. I hope you'll forgive me my disgrace. I am very sorry." She smiled at Ernie.

"Oh, ma'am. Ya did right. I can see yer a carin' soul. Ya had nothin' short o' the best in mind fer the kids. Are ya then a mother, yerself, or is it as I supposed?"

"No, your assumptions were correct. I...."

She shrugged her shoulders. She held her head high, unashamed to display a certain disappointment.

"Well, I must say ya do seem t' have a way with the young uns. I conversed at length with one o' the boys an' he spoke very highly of yer kindness. I believe he spoke truth."

"I do like children, I can't deny it."

"What 'comes ov 'em now?"

She looked at Ernie. She shook her head in dismay, lost for an answer, saying nothing at first.

"I really have no idea. I suppose some have family back east, but who, and where, and how does one find them? I can only address the now. And now, they are living out of my wagon on handouts. The worst part of it is how they look to me for shelter from the storm fate has presented. They simply accept me as the guardian, the shield that stands between them and all they fear... never questioning my abilities...never seeing my inabilities. I must confess, Mr. Kibben, at present I am fearfully insecure. I don't believe I have ever suffered such responsibility...or such incompetence."

"A day at a time, Miss Gardner. Surely, incompetence wouldn't o' won yer daily battles up t' this point. ...Day at a time, day at a time. What'r yer aims, then? Have ya any thoughts 'bout next week an' the followin'?"

"Aims?" Miss Gardner blurted. "I have no aims. I am every bit as lost as they. If only I had a guardian...." She laughed to herself. "My plans were to move to Oregon. I was fortunate to have made a few good friends while on our journey west. I was unfortunate to have picked friends that all died. I am alone. I have no commitments or schedule. I reckon I'll just sit tight in South Pass until spring breaks."

"Mrs. Gardner, I know I'm outta line a-askin' this, but I gotta know. How is it yer travelin' these parts alone without a man? I see ya can fend fer yerself, but it ain't a common thing."

"I don't mind." Ernie watched the woman sip her coffee as her history unfolded privately behind her eyes. "I had a man for seven years. He was a handsome man, a hard working businessman who did very well for himself. I know because I kept his books. His father was in the business of warehousing hides and made a fortune doing so until demand slowed in the forties. Ben, my husband, assumed his father's affairs and did an admirable job of leasing out his buildings for all sorts of commercial enterprises.

"Unlike many ventures, leasing warehouses does not require one to remain on the premises watching over employees or grinding one's fingers to the bone. It is more about having coffee in various coffee houses with other successful businessmen and concluding arrangements beneficial to all. This lifestyle leads one to an unlimited stream of social activities and the freedom to pursue other activities.

"For Ben, those other activities proved to be very young women. It reached a point where he actually began boasting publicly of his conquests. It was incredibly humiliating. However…while he was bent mindlessly over those young bodies, I was bent mindfully over his books. I discovered precisely how to forgive him for his indiscretions.

"Of course, you must understand, his ego would never allow him to reveal my successes. He would have suffered my same humiliation. He would have appeared the fool he was. I am satisfied to know he suffered sufficiently enough to kill me should he scrape up enough funds to find me. For this reason, I have elected to move to the unknown reaches of California or Oregon."

By the time Miss Gardner finished her story, Ernie was red-faced and enjoying a good laugh. It was his first in a long while.

"So's I reckon ya could have paid fer yer own room after all."

"That is for certain, Mr. Kibben, but you mustn't forget, there were no rooms. Either way, you were kind and nothing can detract from that. You are a gentleman."

"Heh, heh, heh, now that's somethin', yes-sireee. In the whole o' my life, one thing I ain't never been called is a gentleman. I lived my life in the woods, a trappin' an' pannin', fergot my pleases an' thank-yas. Gosh darn, I ain't no gentleman, Mrs. Gardner, no-sireee. I ain't never been one."

"You sell yourself short, Mr. Kibben. I was married to a man who appeared to possess all the social grace imaginable, and yet he was little more than a horse's ass. A gentleman is known for his actions and not his words. Your actions have spoke for you, sir. Now please call me Emma."

"Emma, I assure ya, you'll be havin' no problems figurin' out how t' get you an' them kids through this hardship, no ma'am. I am certain o' that much."

Ernie accompanied Emma to the livery where she collected the children, and returned them to the boardinghouse for a meal. Meanwhile, Ernie pulled back the flap to Emma's wagon and climbed in. He looked around. It was pretty much as the boy said. She had tossed all her belongings to make space for the children. He nodded his head. Emma was a good woman, a woman with heart. She was another Mother Gail. He lit an oil stove to put a small amount of heat into the wagon.

Ernie decided to postpone his passage to Northpole for another day or two . He hovered around the wagon to help Emma and to talk. She was far above him in the social graces, but was she was every bit as kind as Jeremy had said. She made Ernie feel comfortable in her presence. Ernie wished to learn more about women and he watched her with interest.

In the evening, Emma paid for the children's stay at the livery stable and had a plentiful stew brought to them from the boardinghouse. She and Ernie sat next to each other and ate in the warmth of the blacksmith's furnace. The fast pace of their growing friendship prompted Ernie to offer up a suggestion that he knew Emma would accept as sincere and well thought out.

"Emma, from all ya said, I see nothin' here fer ya but hardship... hardship fer four or five months till sping. I want ya t' know that I'm a-fixin' t' head up t' Northpole; t' that place I spoke of; the one I called Powder Pan Canyon. It's 'bout two hours west o' Northpole, up in the Big Horn Mountains. It's real nice country up that-a-way an' I know ya'd like it, o' that I'm certain, yes-sireee. Thing is, I'd like fer you an' the kids t' consider goin' up that-a-way with me t' Mother Gail's. Stay fer the winter an' then come back down here t' South Pass an' go on to Oregon if yer still of a mind.

"The place is small, but I built it, an' it's warm an' dry as a bone on the inside. I'm sure Mother Gail'll let the kids stay an' I don't doubt she'll keep 'em once she knows 'em an' you'll be free t' move on west when ya see fit. Or, I can take the kids with me if ya prefer t' remain here an' wish t' be relieved o' the carin'. I guess that's up t' you."

"That's a decision I am unable to make over one coffee after eating at the blacksmith's, Ernie."

"Of course. I understand. I do. Let me fetch the pot, an' I'll pour ya another."

Emma laughed.

"I wish it were that easy to quiet one's conscience. I would be lying if I were to say I am of a mind to become a mother of seven. I don't see that in my future. However, I am not prepared to abandon the children either. It's only two weeks before Christmas and isn't it bad enough, they have lost their folks and homes, let alone having me walk out on them during the holy days. I...I—."

"Emma, ya always talk sense. I'll give ya a week, but no longer. Come hell or high water, I aim t' be at Mother Gail's spendin' Christmas with my girls. They're expectin' me, an' I am not of a mind t' let 'em down. I've waited near a year t' see them kids. I just plain miss 'em."

Emma used up a week considering her options, none of which were attractive. She spoke with the children, trying to explain the situation and helping them to understand what might have to be done to ensure their well-being. She spoke with others in the wagon train and many of the townspeople as well. The picture painted for the future, or even the present, for the children was bleak. There were some possibilities being discussed for the older orphans, earning their keep in the shops or boardinghouses, but nothing for seven small helpless souls, standing only one step ahead of an early grave by exposure or starvation. Ernie had offered them the only opportunity for a safe haven, even if Mother Gail proved to be only half as good as he made her out to be. Emma decided to accept.

The blacksmith, who Ernie had come to know as Jerome, swung the stable doors wide open. Outside in the falling snow was a team of eight oxen hitched to a large, low, heavily built wagon. Cradled securely in its bed was a massive black tank-like apparatus. The oxen hauled it inside and were unhitched and removed to the outdoors. Ernie closed the livery doors for Jerome. No one wished to waste heat. Jerome was yet outside talking to the men who drove the team to the livery. Ernie looked over the tank and imagined it to look a great deal like a locomotive's boiler. Jerome entered the building and walked up to him.

"Sumpin' ain't it?"

"Yes-sireee. Looks a lot like a locomotive boiler t' me."

"I guess you ain't nearly as dumb as you appear," Jerome chided him.

"Yer sayin' that's what it'd be?"

"Yep. The ole' RMR plumb froze up. They fired up her boiler, but her inner workings were split." Jerome was looking inside the end of the boiler, but Ernie was looking at Jerome.

"What are ya sayin' t' me, Jerome? The train ain't a-runnin'?"

"Not lessin' you got one of these in your pocket."

"Oh! No, no. Tell me it ain't so. I ain't likin' the sound o' this one bit, Jerome. No-sireee. How long ya figurin' it'll be 'fore she's back on the tracks?"

Jerome studied Ernie's face. He took on a more serious manner.

420

"I'd figure two or three weeks. No, wait. We got the holy days ahead. Three weeks for sure."

"Dad burnit, man! I gotta get my hide t' Northpole 'fore Christmas!"

"Well, I wouldn't wish to be the one riding, but you could make Northpole in five days give or take, depending on the weather being with you or against."

"No-sireee. It ain't like that, Jerome. I gotta party a-goin' with me. Miss Gardner an' them kids are goin' up with me."

"Sheeeesh." Jerome exhaled through his teeth. You're talkin' a wagon. That'll be a full week's pace, long as the snow holds back. Ain't been as deep this season as most. Could be done, Ernie. Like I say, I wouldn't care for it, but it could be done."

"Jerome, I gotta go find that woman or I'm gonna be in a heap a' trouble."

ONE-HUNDRED-TWO

It was Monday the twenty-third of December, year of our Lord eighteen hundred and fifty-three. Two days before Christmas, and Mother Gail's kids were as excited as any child in any fortunate family. It was clearly understood from the start, Mother Gail had nothing in the way of money or presents to give, but the children never let that stop them from indulging in the heady anticipation of Christmas. They dreamed of all the gifts they wished to receive. They beamed with generosity as they promised with all sincerity to fill the wishes of others. They accepted the fact that their gifts were not for eyes but for hearts.

Today was special. Today they were to go into town and look at the toys for children in the Claussen store, weather permitting. Again they understood they wouldn't return with even the smallest of treasure. Still, it was considered by all a worthwhile price to pay for the privilege of seeing all the wonderful things. It had been *thee* topic of discussion, *thee* center of conversation for the last couple of weeks.

Taking into account the younger children, the trip would take about three hours going downhill on foot and everyone was eager to embark at first light. It wasn't a difficult matter during summer or decent weather, for one merely followed the old Indian trail down toward the plain. The trail was probably as old as the mountains, having served the needs of deer or wolves, sometimes a black bear or a mountain cat, all manner of creatures on the move long before man.

The trail might twist this way or that as it descended, but it never split off to go in a wrong direction. The forest floor was generally open and there was scant underbrush to be seen trampled or parted by travelers. For this reason, oftentimes there would be little more than a tree marked here or there to keep one following the route.

Confusion only occurred when crossing clearings during foul weather, a time when visibility was poor. It was in the clearings that the trail would be first covered with snow, and one had to look ahead at the opposite stand of trees for the tell-tale arch that marked where the trail continued onward.

The morning proved bright and clear and spirits were high. The younger children were quicker to tire and necessitated a stop at the stream for a drink of cold mountain water and a chance to lie down and refresh themselves. At about ten o'clock they arrived at the front porch of Claussen's trading post. It was everything they had hoped, and the miles were replaced with smiles and wide eyes, all the proof townsfolk would need to understand simple joys.

The children filed in through the front door, and putting forth all possible restraint, mobbed the counters of wonderment. An elderly woman approached them.

"I remember you two."

Dakota and Raven looked up at her.

"It's been a long, long, time. Did you came back to see the dolls?"

"Yes, ma'am," Dakota answered.

"I remember they were soft," Raven stated.

"I saw scrap paper in some of your bins. May we take some for wrapping?"

"Of course, you may. Any scrap paper, or string, or ribbon you find in a trash bin is yours for the taking."

"Oh, thank you, thank you very much. Say thank you, Raven."

"Thank you, ma'am."

"You are both more than welcome. Well, I am happy to see you. You certainly have grown since our last meeting when you arrived. Go ahead and enjoy yourselves and remember Santa knows all his little girls. He never forgets."

The woman smiled down at them and then walked off. The girls stood there thinking about Santa.

"I don't think Santa knows we're here, do you Dakota?"

"I don't know, Raven. If he goes to our home, he'll see we're not there."

"Do you think Momma and Poppa will tell him?"

"If they see him, I am certain they will. You know if I saw Santa, I would tell him how much I wish we could give something to Uncle Kib."

"Me too."

"We need to find something nice for Uncle Kib. It just isn't fair. Everything in this store is nice, but we can't buy anything."

"What are we going to give Uncle Kib?"

"I don't know." Dakota shrugged her shoulders. "Maybe if we looked around, we might find some more of that wrapping paper. We could bring that back with us and make a gift out of it. Do you want to help me?"

"Yup."

The girls left the group and began to scout for anything that might catch the eye, any discarded item that would spruce up a gift, something special. They wandered to the back wall of the store that separated it from the inn. They looked about the tables and into the corners and Dakota kept a sharp eye open for both her and Raven as they worked their way toward an office. It was there she spotted a wastebasket brimming with a fabulously adorned assortment of discarded gift wrappings. It appeared as though the gifts were gathered upon the desk. On an engraved plate upon the desk, amidst the collection of displayed gifts, was the inscription MR.CLAUSSEN. They stood there quietly as Dakota studied the treasure stuffed into the trash bin. She looked up at the man sitting behind the desk.

"What is it you are up to, child?"

She stepped forward as Christopher looked up from his desk. Dakota stopped short, unsure of this man. She was about to explain she wished to have the paper but was interrupted when Mother Gail stormed up from behind.

"Dakota Brooks, you come at once; you too, young lady."

Mother Gail grabbed Raven and spun her around, patted her on the rump, and sent her back into store. She turned to Mr. Claussen.

"My apologies, sir. I hope they didn't have time to make a nuisance of themselves."

"No matter." Christopher looked back down and continued working at the books.

"How many times must I say, we remain together as a group or I simply will not allow you to come to town. Do you understand?"

"Yes, Mother Gail."

The girls sported frowns. Raven had no idea what Dakota was looking at, but she understood it was what they needed.

ONE-HUNDRED-THREE

Mother Gail and the kids wrapped up their midday in town and prepared for the walk back to the cabin. It was about a two-hour trek on horseback, three going downhill, but it was certain to be four or more heading back up into the hills on foot with the little ones.

Fortunately, if one overlooked the distance to be traveled, and instead enjoyed a good conversation, one could cut the time in half, or at least so it seemed until reaching the front door of the cabin. By that time, it was near dark, and everybody was exhausted, too tired to wait even for a supper. Instead, many curled up in the bunks and were fast to sleep with dreams of Santa and the toys in Claussen's Trading Post.

Nobody awoke the following morning until hearing Mother Gail's call to the breakfast table. As soon as the meal was finished, and chores completed, the children eagerly set about preparing handmade gifts for Christmas. That is all children save for Dakota and Raven, who moved about with a dark, disillusioned, cloud over their heads. Their spirits were beaten down over the issue of Uncle Kib.

The problem was everybody loved Uncle Kib because he had done so much for all of them. Everyone worked together to form and bake special cookies for him. Everyone drew pictures and decorated things for him. Everyone practiced songs to sing for him.

It wasn't fair. Dakota and Raven believed Uncle Kib was their uncle and not an uncle to everybody else. There should have been something special for him, something just from the two of them. Not something *shared,* but something special *only* from the Brooks girls. It was Christmas Eve and Dakota and Raven removed themselves from the others and sat at the table in the bunkhouse. Dakota sat dispirited and glum for hours as she looked out across the stream through the lightly falling snow.

"It isn't right, Raven."

"Nope."

"I have thought about this for a long time today and I know what I am going to do. It's gotta be a secret. Do you wanna know the secret?"

"Yup."

"Well, if I tell you, then you have to be part of the plan. Just you an' me. Are you sure you wanna know the secret?"

"Yup. I can keep a secret."

Raven shook her head as she looked at the wash of bright light from the window.

"All right, now listen carefully. I aim to go back to town, back to Claussen's Trading Post, and get some of that fancy paper. There were mountains of it in that man's room. Just being thrown away. Real nice paper. We can wrap Uncle Kib's gift with it.

We could make him a Christmas hat with it. The main thing is the gifts would be just from us. Do you wanna go with me?"

"Will we get in trouble?"

"We will be in so much trouble you can't imagine, but Uncle Kib's worth it, don't you think?"

"Yup."

"Well, let's go then, come on, hurry up and get dressed. Mother Gail is so busy in the kitchen getting her fixin's ready in hopes of seeing Uncle Kib, she won't even know we're gone. We'll be back before she ever finds out. Let's go."

The girls were quick to dress up in an attempt to slip out. They were questioned about going outside by one of the other children, but Dakota lied saying they were only going outside to play in the snow. She said it with enough sincerity to clear their way of suspicion. Once outside they ran as far and as fast as Raven's little legs would carry her. Due to the difficulty of leading blind Raven down the trail, the trip was taking far longer than Dakota would have imagined. It was mid-afternoon but it seemed much later for unlike the day before the skies were heavy with the dark clouds of snow.

"We don't have enough time to stay. We get in, grab our paper, and get out. Do you understand?"

"Yup."

ONE-HUNDRED-FOUR

Our trading post was busy, swamped. It was Christmas Eve, and the place was packed with patrons. Needless to say, far more children were running about than usual. The youngsters were exuberant and in constant motion as they crowded the toy crates to assess handfuls of miniature treasures. Ever since Christopher brought out the crates of toys, the trading post grew to be the focal point of children's fantasies.

I paid scant mind to their number. After all, it was the season to be merry and nothing made the season merry quite like a mob of children. Every year since our arrival, the Christmas crowds grew larger in number. This year was no exception, and even I was suddenly caught up by surprise. We had children packing the place from wall to wall.

It was their exuberance that triggered my feeling of something being amiss. I realized there were very few parents, or at least adults to keep those unruly characters in line. A second look to assess this matter entirely changed my outlook. I became focused. There was more to this than met the eye. It was the look of them. They were urchins—street scamps. I could spot one a mile away and I had a whole store full of them. Their eyes were glued to me. What I had here was a large gathering of clever little thieves doing their own Christmas shopping. They were all about watching me turn my back so they could clean me out. I was watching them as closely as they were watching me. I found myself growing uncomfortable but for their number.

To their advantage, my attention was diverted by the arrival of the Brooks girls. I was quite surprised to see them, for this was their second visit to the store in two days. I knew it to be a fair distance between the orphanage and town, and couldn't imagine how a woman caring for a dozen children, many quite young, might manage such a feat twice in so few hours.

It certainly raised my suspicions about Mother Gail in spite of everything positive I had heard. On the other hand, maybe the girls were brought to town by somebody else. But on that point, where then was the *'somebody else'*? The two girls had entered the store alone or so it seemed.

428

I watched Dakota head directly for the doll display with Raven in tow. I did the opposite. I headed straight for the front door to step out onto the porch and have a look up and down the street. In spite of foreboding weather, the street was crowded with people, but I saw nothing of Mother Gail. I did see a good number of children walking in my direction, and they might have been Mother Gail's, but their attention seemed fixed on me and more likely party to the band of brats having a go at it in the store. It was the last thing I cared to see.

"Hey! Take that out of your pocket. I'll have no thieves in my store. Do you understand?"

The rascal flipped the toy back into a bin and sprinted down the aisle out of reach. As my eyes lost him in the crowd, I glanced around in search of the girls. I spotted them behind a crowd of those unruly urchins pressed tight against the toy counter. That lot of saucer-sized eyes, bulging out of heads filled with pleading desire, resolutely refused to give way to anybody. They were hypnotized by the assortments of porcelain headed dolls for girls and colorful wheeled toys for boys.

The girls had small chance of getting anywhere near their beloved dolls. I decided that as long as they were standing there in wait, I would say hello, and possibly inquire as to the where-abouts of Mother Gail. I approached them from behind.

"Well, this is a surprise! Twice in the same week. Two days in a row! You must really like those dolls."

In perfect repetition of our first encounter, Dakota spun around startled by my greeting. She faced me wide-eyed and outwardly nervous. I couldn't help but to smile. They were two wonderfully attractive children who possessed an air of innocence that simply stole my heart. I wanted to grab them and hug them half to death. How could I be blamed after comparing them to the little devils and rascals now flooding my store?

I suppose in some inexplicable way, Dakota reminded me of Gracie. Of course, Gracie carried knives from the first day I met her. Yet, in my eyes, even into her older years, she possessed an air of innocence. A good many men paid a steep price by taking advantage of perceived innocence that proved nothing short of an illusion. Still there was something about that Dakota. I felt this inexplicable connection.

A twinge of discomfort moved through me as I looked across the room. The isles were packed with urchins that might have seemed more interested in me and the girls than the toys about the store. I met their stares as they stepped back to give me room.

"I beg your pardon, move along now. Hear me now, you rascals, move aside."

A narrow space opened at the counter and I encouraged Dakota to move forward and fill it. She pressed her hands together prayer-like, and brought them up to her lips.

"Oh. They are so beautiful." She turned to me. "May Raven hold one so she can again feel it?"

"Of course, what good is a doll that can't be snuggled?"

I reached for the one that I remembered Dakota liked the best, and handed it to Raven. As she pressed it to her face, I felt the crowd press in on me, which was unpleasant. I looked up and around. I noticed the countless dirty faces glancing back and how ragged and hard was this collection of children. They were equally young, equally adorable in their own right, equally orphaned, but definitely of a different breed.

"Where is Mother Gail?" I asked.

With a mild sense of urgency, I looked about the store for their mistress. I thought there something secretive about these two. My instincts alerted me to their suspicious nature, and I recognized the subtle expressions of guilt. Dakota was obviously nervous, fidgeting and looking in every direction but mine. She looked over to the store entrance and commented.

"It's getting dark outside."

She turned back to me.

"We were wondering if we might be able to fetch that paper we asked for yesterday? Do you remember, you said we could have it?"

"Yes, I remember clearly, and of course you may, but where is your...where is Mother Gail?"

"Oh, she doesn't know we snuck over here. That's why we're in a hurry. We're going to use part of the paper for her Christmas gift, but if she finds out, the surprise will be ruined. You said we could have some paper, so we came back. It is still all right for us to have the paper, isn't it?"

"Ahh...yes...yes of course. All right, go on. Go find yourself some paper, and then come back, and maybe I'll have something extra for you to give her as well."

"Oh, thank you, ma'am." Dakota gushed. "Isn't that nice of her, Raven?"

"Yup."

"Say, thank you."

"Thank you, ma'am."

"You're welcome, Raven. You're both welcome, now go on hurry up before you ruin your surprise."

The girls wasted no time removing themselves from my presence as they waded through the currents of children. I didn't believe that Dakota had it in her to lie, but I did feel as though she were twisting the truth to her advantage. One thing for sure, the girls appeared most relieved to get away, and that made me all the more uneasy and suspicious. I found myself squeezing through the throngs of bedazzled urchins as I walked over to the front door and again stepped out onto the porch to have a look up and down Main for any sign of Mother Gail or other orphans.

I saw nothing of the woman, but I did see a staggering number of children, orphans or otherwise, milling about the street. That concerned me, for above their heads I observed how threatening appeared the oncoming weather. It was getting dark. Not because of the hour, but because of an especially ominous collection of blackened clouds that were moving in overhead and choking out what little light we had been given on this dismally overcast evening. I certainly didn't think of this afternoon as a good time for Mother Gail and her orphans to be out and about. They were at least some two hours or more from their place up in the canyon. I wondered if I might arrange a wagon for their safety.

The entire affair seemed risky to me, too risky, and it made me again question the character of this woman. She had spoken to me yesterday for the first time during her brief visit to the store. I found her to be a very amiable person, but private, almost secretive. I had inquired about the children, but she side-stepped the issue. She never once said the children were orphaned. In fact, she never called them orphans. She did say that she had moved closer to Northpole, and it was now easier to get into town, hence her appearance with the children. Her new place, now being in walking distance on a good day, permitted the children to accompany her.

I felt guilty or at least uncomfortable about my questionable thoughts. And to be truthful, our conversation stirred up something inside, an emotion from my past that had long since been buried under the dust of daily activity. I felt certain regret; I found myself somewhat saddened by my disassociation from a former life working with orphans. Christopher had hoped I might again take up the cause, but he respected my right to make my own choices and so refrained from forcing my hand. Until this moment, I never overcame the belief that my life's dedication to orphans was meant to remain behind me in another time, another place.

I turned my attention toward Christopher's office and watched Dakota dodge the patrons and the street brats, all the while looking back at me as if to seek safe distance. She knew I was looking her way, watching her. She led Raven by the hand along a balustrade that edged the landing which led to the offices. As they climbed the steps to the landing and approached Christopher's office, I realized that she had seen her coveted wrappings in his trash. Observant soul, I thought to myself, for Christopher was deluged with fine gifts from his business acquaintances. Most arrived encased in fine wood boxes and wrapped in expensive coverings, all now set aside or discarded. I watched Dakota walk up to his door and stop short.

I could see Christopher working at his desk, buried in his books. I could see him sitting there deep in thought, and I knew he wouldn't especially want to be bothered. The season was now at a close, but he had endured all of it with the added burden of his complaining heart. The pain left him annoyed and on occasion ill-tempered. He seldom spoke of it, but the discomfort affected his mood adversely. Ask anyone about the boardinghouse, and you would know he was evermore irritable and short tempered.

Christopher's mood was indicative of his pain, and I knew today he was suffering more than usual. Earlier in the morning, I had insisted that he retire to the lodge and relax, but he wouldn't stand for talk of that nature. He was as stubborn as an ox. Knowing these things, I decided to move closer to his office in case I needed to rescue the girls or Christopher, whomever needed rescuing first.

I moved slowly through the crowd, working my way toward the landing. Even from across the room, I could see that Dakota was nervous. As I continued toward the landing, I could see she was hesitant; I watched her biting her nails as she peered inside Christopher's office. She didn't know whether to enter or not. I saw her draw Raven up close to her side for support. She stepped up to the office door and stood there silent, fearful to go farther. She waited to be recognized.

For a moment, I thought she might lack the courage to interrupt Christopher as would most. I decided it might be best for me to go to her aid, or at least stay close and keep an eye on the three of them. Maybe Dakota decided that she had come too far to be scared off. For as I reached the balustrade, and peered through the balusters, I heard her tap on his door and speak out.

"Excuse me, sir."

Christopher kept on working.

"Sir?"

Christopher sat there trying hard not to pay the girls mind. I felt a tinge of annoyance, but I understood when he was mired in figures, he disliked being bothered. I also noticed he was rubbing his chest. That wasn't a good sign. He would be irritable, but I didn't want to intervene just yet. I would rather give Christopher a chance to redeem himself and display a little Christmas spirit.

"Ahem-hem-hem."

Dakota cleared her throat. The gesture made me smile, but I could see that their breaking into Christopher's concentration only served to increased his annoyance, as he did mine.

"Be gone, child!"

"But, sir…"

"I said be gone, you've already caused me an error in my work, and I needn't any further annoyance, now be gone."

I raised my hands and clutched a baluster in each. It was as if I were behind the bars of a jail, ready to reach out and strangle a certain old fool. I felt the furrows fold deep into my forehead as I dipped my head and looked up at Christopher. It was a good thing he couldn't see past the girls to where rose the balusters that now framed my eyes and ire within. There was simply no call for such rudeness, especially toward a child.

As if to slow my escalating irritation, one of the girls party to the hardened lot of urchins, the girl standing closest to me, suddenly started crying as did another. At first, I assumed there was a disagreement between the two over a toy or some other item. Then a third young girl erupted into tears, and then another, and another. I glanced across their lot to see not only these disheartened souls, but most of the others looking at me as if I held the answer to some mystery.

The incident was a profound and unsettling distraction that caught me off guard and confused me. The strangeness of the occurrence would have been impossible to dismiss had it not been for my immediate concerns regarding Christopher and the Brooks girls. I was pressured to look away from the distraught children, and thereby ignore a profound inner foreboding. Against the demands of the crowd, I wished only to aid the girls.

"We just wanted to…"

Dakota's final attempt to make known her request was cut short. Christopher in his state of irritability acted in haste. It was an action no sooner taken, than woefully regretted.

ONE-HUNDRED-FIVE

Christopher and Raven shared a singular disadvantage. They both suffered from poor eyesight. By every measure, Raven appeared to be blind. Christopher not quite, but he endured other suffering that she escaped but for youth. One notable and most apparent difference between the two was Raven's gentle demeanor—that in direct opposition to Christopher's advanced state of surliness.

His irritability was provoked by the increasingly painful discomfort in his chest, the increased workload of the season, and the general pandemonium of Christmas shoppers. I hardly need mention the added burden brought on by the horde of urchins now running about the store stealing him blind. In Christopher's attempt to gain some immediate relief from the noise of the crowd, and two nosey kids in particular, I watched him rise to lean over his desk and to my utter mortification...*fling the door shut.*

"Claus! Noooo!"

Bad luck was not something to which Christopher was accustomed, and so when it arrived, he took the full brunt of it. Two of the worst possible happenings occurred at precisely the same time. First, the door met Raven before it met the jamb. She was too blind to see it coming, and unlike Dakota, who instinctively jumped backward, Raven remained to have her nose driven straight into her face.

The force of the solid wood slab swinging recklessly closed upon its hinges crushed her tiny upswept appendage, it being the only thing blocking the door's arcing path to the latch. She barely kept hold of consciousness as her head careened backward from the blow in a spray of blood. The bloodbath was immediate and relentless. The floor where they had stood only seconds before to spy the splendid wrappings was now a slippery mess of red soup.

436

I watched Raven shudder in a spasm of shock. My stomach turned as I observed the torrent of blood burst forth from her nose to stream across her lips, teeth, and chin as it rained upon the floor. I could have easily wretched from the sound of her choking on the blood rushing down her throat. Regaining her senses, and with them the full pain of her injury, at first breath, Raven let loose a screaming crimson mist of pure agony. The wail brought a crippling sensation of dread that stood on end the hair of every mother within earshot.

The second happening, and certainly the one to be most damaging for Christopher, came from the other scream, not one of agony, but one of blood curdling despair from me. My motherly instincts had forced me to keep an eye out for the little blind girl's safety, and so I was made to suffer as witness to the entire heart-rending mishap. Screaming from below the landing, with all rudeness, I yelled for patrons and youngsters to move out of my way so I might pass through the crowded isle and go to the child's aid.

The store was packed with buyers, sellers, goods, and people spinning around in circles, sorting out their confusion between a child screaming hysterically on one side of the store, me screaming for clear passage elsewhere, and the wail of street children crying aloud from places invisible and for reasons unknown. It would have been no less traumatic if one had been shot to death in their midst leaving them to stumble about in a fog of gunsmoke and fear. I was desperate to reach Raven, but it was to no avail. Curiosity pitched the crowd forward into landing and held me fast.

Meanwhile, Dakota was traumatized, scared clean out of her wits by the rivers of blood, by Raven's screams, by my screams, by the screams and cries of compassion that ripped through the crowd of adults and urchins alike. The chorus of agony swept over her from every direction.

437

I thought Dakota a timid child, not one accustomed to strangers, let alone crowds shuffling about, bumping, and pressing up against one another. Now, the eyes of an entire mob of unknown faces bore down upon her, carving up what remnant of confidence remained before their bold and curious stares. Visibly terrified, I saw her step backward against the closed and bloody office door. There, her anxiety and fear spiraled out of control. She stood frozen in place staring down at her younger sister, who was now fully overtaken by uncontrollable sobs and convulsions.

Pressed against Christopher's door, pent up in a place she didn't belong, her eyes rose from Raven to stare out at us wide-eyed numb. She was lost. I saw the insufferable fear scrawled upon her face. I struggled to make my way to the girls.

"Please! Step aside. Please! Allow me to pass. Step aside. Children, please…."

Dakota looked every bit the cornered animal, trapped, near mindless, as the patrons rushed toward her en masse with eyes starved to see more of the bloody spectacle before them. Their jaws hung slack, some covered by hands to suppress involuntary gasps. Their arms flailed, reaching out to the left, to the right, but always reaching closer to the frightened girl. They were closing in on her, about to entangle her, about to crucify her for a sin she never saw coming. Her ears must have rang numb, but for the uproar, the questions, the demands, and worst of all, young Raven's ongoing screams of agony.

* * *

Inside his office, I imagined Christopher standing mortified by the pain he feared to have inflicted. I imagined him standing behind that door immobilized by dread, unable to approach the

438

portal, afraid to see what misery his tantrum brought forth on the other side. I imagined him to be staring at the latch, listening to scream after scream, the pangs of guilt ripping away at him. He would see nothing, but the young girl's wailing left no one, especially Christopher, to doubt the scene upon the landing.

In spite of my disbelief and horror, I knew Christopher was kind to the core, and his error in judgment was brought on by his torments. I knew he wished the office door would never have to open. I was confident Christopher did some serious soul-searching by the time he worked up the courage to face his incorrigible act and lift that latch.

* * *

Dakota heard the latch release behind her. It being her only protected side, she lost the last of her sensibility. She bolted across the landing like a wild animal under attack. Her bloodied hands clamped down on Raven's wrist and yanked her frail arm hard, snapping the child through the air like a blur of red ribbon. Dakota dragged her bloody bawling sister behind her as if a beloved rag doll. Hell bent, she flew alongside the balustrade that held the crowd at bay, leaving hand prints, red and perfectly spaced upon the rail. She leapt off the landing and sailed past the wall of groping fingers and flailing arms, past me, past the collection of wailing urchins, past the nightmare until disappearing through the front door at a dead run. The girls left me standing amidst the dumbfounded crowd of patrons yet howling in her shadow. The orphans vanished into the snowy twilight far beyond the footprints outlined in a trail of tears and blood.

Desperate to reach the door, I managed to free myself from the tangle of children and so ran outside in pursuit. The blood was everywhere. It drew me south across the porch and down

439

onto the street. It was the stain of remorse, of guilt by association, the color held fresh, frozen in snow and memory. I was physically sick by the sight of it. In haste, I followed the disheartening trail toward the edge of town until the painful bite of numbing cold forced me to retreat.

I turned back into the wind, retracing my steps, unable to look up from the abstract pattern of red dots that sickened me. They reminded me of a mortally wounded animal fleeing for refuge in the forest. Only after a snaking curl of blowing snow swept them from view did I raise my eyes above the road, past the random street urchin, and toward the glowing lamps of the trading post porch.

I was hysterical. My emotions ignited the long forgotten and now unknown temper of my youth, a temper that blinded me from reason, and could drop the mightiest goliath when certain conditions were met. Those conditions were all met the moment I saw Christopher lumber out into the light of those porch lamps. Weak heart or not, he should have run.

Christopher stood there looking deeply embarrassed and very sheepish before his patrons. He watched me approach and appeared ready to accept his punishment. Anybody who knew Christopher knew he would never have harmed the girl intentionally. It was an act of idiocy, they knew as much, but the fact didn't make him any less guilty, especially not in my eyes.

If the good Lord had plucked out both his eyes, he still would have seen the anger swirling about me. My clenched fists, the snap in my step, the throw of my shoulders and my dead ahead stare amounted to what might have been the worst wave of explosive fury to ever come his way.

I was hardly about to wait until I reached him. The concussion of my rage, the lash of my fiery tongue split the air and cracked worse than lightning as it slammed forcefully into his soul from ten paces out. My voice was shrill and shredded by anger. For starters, I never called Christopher, *Christopher.*

"Christopher Nicholas Claussen!"

I screamed out his name as I stormed toward him.

"Christopher Nicholas Claussen! I have never, never in my life seen as shameful an act as done by your hand. It was by your hand, Christopher, your hand! I cannot imagine anything on earth or heaven above that could possess you to commit such an odorous and despicable deed as to bloody the face of that helpless wretched soul of a little girl."

Even in my state of rage, the thought of the little girl's agony broke me down to tears, tears that fueled my wrath.

"That…darling…little girl was blind! Do you hear me! Blind!" I bellowed through my sobs. "She was hardly a day over five, if that! You brute! You're a beast Christopher, a beast! I declare there is a river of blood that flows from your door to the edge of town, a river of blood on your hands. I say it for fact because I followed it." The tears streamed down my face. "They were orphans, Christopher, asking only for some scraps of paper in your trash bin. Scraps! Do you understand! It was I, Christopher, I who encouraged them to fetch what they wished wherever they might chance upon it.

"As God is my witness, Mr. Claussen, I swear, Hell will freeze over before I forgive you unless substantial amends are put into place, unless I know you haven't truly sold your soul to the devil. It can't be done any too soon! Do you hear me! It can't be done any too soon!"

I wiped my eyes across my sleeve and then drove Christopher to the side with a deliberately brutal strike to his chest. It was an act of frustration that must have diminished all but the pain in his heart. I turned back to him.

"You best get someone out to find those girls this very moment before they freeze to death or you will live with that tragedy on your conscience as well."

Christopher bolted forward. He reached out to follow me into the store, but I forcibly slammed the door in his face. I wanted to provide him with a less than subtle reminder of his misdeed. I hoped it brushed his nose.

I only wandered a short distance into the store. It was as if I expended all my energies without knowing. I coasted to a stop. I was embarrassed to return the stares of the urchins still inside as I struggled to regain my composure. I heard the door open behind me. The children were watching as I wiped the emotion off of my face and turned around.

Christopher stepped through the door and even though there were still plenty of patrons and others in the store, we stood in a private world of two. He raised his head high and closed his eyes as if directing the activity of life to halt. He then looked at me with an expression of resignation. He had done wrong. He had little choice but to accept what was rightfully due him unless he wished to serve out the rest of his life in the misery of my judgment.

"Thank you for sparing my nose. In light of my actions, it was generous of you."

I listened, but I did not reply. I was fighting back a fresh wave of tears, and thinking how amazed I was to have given him that much.

"I am angry with myself, Elizabeth...."

I saw Christopher flinch. Apparently the old pain returned to overshadow my blow to his chest. He clutched his shirt with his fist and rubbed his breastbone hard. His rotated his bad arm. It wasn't that I didn't worry for his health, but this pain was an ongoing occurrence, an unending affliction that I wasn't about to let diminish my anger this day. His pain was nothing in comparison.

"How was I to know she was a blind orphan—? No! No! I didn't mean to say that. That was unforgivable. Of course…it makes no difference if she was blind or not. Slamming the door in the face of anyone, blind, not blind, adult or child is inexcusable. I wouldn't do that to an animal."

I watched him wrestle with his conscience. I continued to listen as I nodded my head in agreement—*not even to an animal.*

"Elizabeth, I have no desire to go to my grave with an epitaph that reads, here lies an ornery old man, a brute—here lies Elizabeth Dennison's shame. It was a silly, stupid, thoughtless act, purely impulsive, but one that ferried appalling consequences. I cannot undo what I have done, Elizabeth, but I can and will do everything in my power to make amends."

I remained silent.

"I am sorry, Elizabeth. I know you believe me. I just don't know when you will find it in your heart to forgive me."

Christopher moved past me and slipped quietly through the store trying to avoid eye contact with the patrons and the remaining children who chose to observe our every move. The gossip would run amok. He headed back toward his office, and as if drawn by the wake of his passage, I also moved in that direction. The children stirred in toward me. Christopher stopped short of his door. He could not enter without walking through the bloody mess that painted the floor with an invisible arrow pointing directly at him. He shook his head as he attempted to step across the disgrace.

"Excuse me."

The children parted so I might fetch a pail of water and some rags. I returned to clean up, and Christopher had little choice but to sit at his desk and watch me while I knelt and wiped up the mess. The crimson soak spread quickly across the damp ivory-colored cotton. I am certain I was twisting the knife of guilt as deep as it might go. I certainly hoped so for my tears were mingled with that water.

As I finished mopping up, I waited impatiently for whatever action I expected him to take in haste. I watched him stare blindly into his accounting books. His mind was racing behind his furrowed brow. He kept glancing up at me, each time with more courage, but yet insufficient to speak unless able to precisely address my concerns. He knew his words had better be good. Finally, he called out to me, understanding I was yet primed to ignite, my fuse still smoldering.

"Elizabeth, please…come in a moment and sit. I will not hide behind some feeble excuse for my intolerable action. I can see how very angry you are with me, and justifiably so. I am the first to admit. I can only ask you believe me when I confess, my eyes are not what they used to be. I failed to see the young girl was standing directly in the path of the door. My spectacles distort distances before me. I was annoyed with the noise and the crowds, and all of commotion. I admit to that. I admit I acted in haste without thought of the consequences. But I stress I didn't realize the child—."

"There is—."

"There is no excuse." Christopher stopped me from speaking. "I was wrong. I confess forthright, I confess here and now, there is no excuse for slamming a door in anybody's face, for any reason. Elizabeth, please, I beg…forgive me my stupidity. I am terribly ashamed. This is not who I am. You must know that after all these years. Now, let us see if any good can come of it. Please, sit with me a moment."

I arose from my knees and entered the room to take a seat at his desk, but not without again stressing my concerns.

"You send someone at once to fetch those girls, Claus. It is black as night out there. The sky is most disagreeable, stormy, and I fear they may die out there in the weather."

"I understand. And I aim to do better than that with your help."

I was not yet ready to offer up the warmth of forgiveness. Not yet.

"I must step out for a moment, Elizabeth, but I will return quickly to address your concerns and see to the care and safe transport of the girls. Wait for me."

True to his word, Christopher returned after about fifteen minutes and signaled me to meet him back in his office. By then, I had settled down considerably. I pulled the door for privacy.

"I have sent for Rebecca's coach."

"What?"

His comment seemed to fall out of the sky. It was an utterly meaningless statement to me. I was expecting his first words to announce an immediate plan of action, and not some waffle about Lady Rebecca's coach. To my credit, I knew to hold my tongue and leave Christopher time to expand. He was not, nor had he ever been a fool. He never spoke a meaningless word.

"I have given instructions for my lads to fit the skis, and to hitch up the Percherons. I have told them to dress the teams in their holiday blankets, bells and all, and then to bring the coach around here to the store."

"Lady Rebecca's coach?"

"And if you would be so kind, Elizabeth, my dear, I would ask you to go through our stores with a generous heart and hand, and remove whatever brings you pleasure, place it in the coach, pile it in the coach. Pile in as much as you wish, anything, everything; pack it to the roof. Empty the store. It is a very large coach,

Elizabeth, as you well know, and I will see it gets to the orphans tonight. I will drive it myself. You said they were orphans...I assume from Mother Gail's up in Powder Pan Canyon, is that correct?"

Christopher was waiting for my answer, but I was still trying to fathom what was going on. Why Lady Rebecca's coach? What was he doing? Again I bowed to his judgment and simply answered his question.

"Mother Gail has never said as much, but everyone claims they are."

"Of course they are! I have listened to people speak of Mother Gail for years. What truly matters is two little girls and a wrong I have to right. What truly matters is a woman who has given up a life to care for the homeless. What truly matters is our countless conversations about looking into her orphanage. Let us presume it is an orphanage. I shall give them a Christmas they shan't soon forget. Help me see this through, Elizabeth. Help me now.

"Let us pack sugar and dried fruit. Tell the boys to give you a hand. Pick out some blankets and rugs for Mother Gail, some new cups and plates, and some silverware. A lantern or two would be nice for those treks into town—don't forget lucifers. Grab a couple of good sharp axes and hatchets, and I want them to have plenty of warm clothes, clothes without holes, clothes that don't need darning. We have more flannel in house than I care to count. Load the coach up full; flannel stockings, shirts, pants, coats, whatever you can find, whatever you can fit inside. Pack it full, Elizabeth. The Holy Days are over tomorrow so let's empty the shelves tonight. We have a whole year to restock."

Christopher stopped for a moment lost in thought.

"Dolls?" I suggested.

"Oh heavens, yes, dolls! Be sure to include dolls for the girls. Lord knows, we mustn't forget the dolls. Little girls need dolls to love."

Whereas, Christopher's mind was racing, mine was stuck at a dead stop. What on earth had gotten into him? I sat there speechless, simply stunned.

"Grab whatever else takes your fancy, Elizabeth. I was just thinking, maybe a box of tea for Mother Gail. …Maybe a box of English tea or coffee. Make it a crate of tea. Cakes! Biscuits! …Pastries…what would tea be without pastries? That should encourage guests to stop by on occasion and give the poor woman a hand. Whatever you think best, Elizabeth—but be generous. The more the better, I have a lot of wrong to right. I want tonight to be remembered as Christmas Eve and not Christopher's calamity. And one last thing..."

He paused and looked at me with an expression of unspoken love.

"Yes."

"Say you forgive me. Say it now, Elizabeth. Say you forgive me."

My eyes were locked to his. Our emotions were evident.

"I forgive you, Claus." My eyes moistened. I shook my head, yet spinning, but for all his carrying on. With a shaky voice, I continued. "I love you with all my heart. And I apologize for those things I said in anger. I wanted to hurt you. I don't know what came over me. I guess it's the mother in me, but then I don't know what came over you, Claus. It…. It…was so unlike you. Honestly, what could you have been thinking? Are you so unwell? Is that it? Is it your heart, Claus?"

"No, no, I am fine, thank you. Don't fret about that. It was sheer stupidity, plain and simple, mostly going a little daft and a lot blind in my old age. And you needn't apologize to me for being a mother, and for doing what mothers do. I believe I had a hand in your affliction so I should have known."

Christopher never dwelled on his discomfort, and instead chose to reassure me. And I did laugh at his comment.

"Mmmm, yes...maybe more than just a hand."

Christopher rose from his desk. I stood up from my chair and was immediately embraced by him. He kissed me tenderly on the side of my face.

"I am repentant," he whispered.

I moved him back from me.

"I know you are. I also know that I wish I could believe you are fine, but your brow is beaded with perspiration. It's that heart of your, Claus. It worries me, and don't tell me different. I know."

"What would you have me say? This heart will be the end of me. I know that. We all know that. But we've been saying that since our days in Boston, and I am yet here getting into trouble."

"True enough, but scant comfort. I trust you will take care... and now, we must hurry for the sake of the girls. I'll go through the stores as you asked, but only if you promise to rest yourself. I must have rocks in my head, the way I worry for you. Money and gifts are too easy an out for you, Claus. I pray your conscience suffers you to no end, but I do forgive you. You brute."

I opened the door to exit Christopher's office, and was surprised to find only a few patrons remaining in the store. All of the children, but one young girl, had disappeared. The girl was sitting on the floor up against the wall near the woodstove.

"Hello."

"Hello," she answered.

"Are you cold?"

The child nodded her head quickly.

"I'm freezing."

"Are you hungry?"

"Yes."

"C'mon."

ONE-HUNDRED-SIX

Raven finally stopped screaming. Dakota finally stopped running. She halted so her sister might catch a breath. Raven was winded and struggling to breathe. Her nose was blocked off with packed blood that forced the remaining flow back down her throat. The hard run from the trading post did nothing to stem the hemorrhaging and left her teeth and chin bathed in red saliva. Her pleas to stop running were understandable.

Dakota knelt down to size up her sister's condition. Even in the last remnants of light, it was not a pretty sight. Her face was badly swollen, the bridge of her nose was turning dark and the discoloration was filling in the space below her eyes. Shadows made darker by shadows. Given the light, Dakota inspected the wound as best she could. As best she could tell, the nose yet appeared to be centered and in its proper place. She struggled to forget the memory of Raven staggering backward from the blow. The vision turned over and over in her mind, turning her stomach with every remembrance.

Dakota lamented over her failing to protect, her failing to pull Raven out of harm's way. Knowing she was Raven's eyes, knowing how Raven placed all faith into her hands, she suffered with remorse. But it happened so fast. Dakota's body saved itself. It simply moved without being willed. She hadn't the time to think. She had plenty of time to think now, and her thoughts were full of regret and pity. She embraced her younger sister. She consoled her and smothered her with kisses.

On the other hand, Dakota knew her own suffering was yet to come. A person could only imagine the amount of trouble in store once back at Mother Gail's and everyone got an eyeful of that face. If it wasn't enough that Raven was badly injured and looked utterly horrid, and it wasn't enough that sneaking out was her idea, and it wasn't enough that a storm was upon them; she could consider the approaching dark, the wolves, the fact they were yet miles from the cabin , and finally…visions of Mother Gail worried sick and wandering the forest while frantically calling out to them with lantern in hand. Dakota wondered if there could ever be enough forgiveness to save her, or a fitting enough punishment, or any hope of escaping her stupidity and guilt.

When the two set out for town, the sky was clear and the sun streamed down through the branches of trees leaving lace-like patterns of shadow lying across the trail. While enjoying the warmth of an overhead sun, and busy hop-scotching across the patterns of shadows, the girls would have been hard pressed to appreciate the wall of dark clouds piling up behind them, about to break over the crest of mountains to the northwest.

These ominous clouds tripped over jagged peaks to fall down the faces of those high-rising formations. They descended like liquid into the upper valleys, flowing over vanishing treetops. They swamped the forests and spread outward across the glens and snow-covered meadows. They rolled onward to smother the lower canyon, moving eastward to change the air, forcing out the warmth and the last light of day. The clouds spread darkness that nipped at the girls' heels all the while they sang and skipped their way to town. Had they not entered the store, they would have been soon overrun.

The trip back to Mother Gail's was now mired in the murkiness of that ominously dark and hazy world. Light, dark, thick or thin, a haze was irrelevant to Raven, but for Dakota the markedly diminished visibility meant the difference between courage and cowardice.

A showy fall of large white snowflakes could yet be seen and therefore caught by thirsty tongues. Raven enjoyed the distraction enough to offer up some giggles without too much renewed bleeding. Her giggling was funny in itself, the result of her head being plugged with coagulated blood. Raven held out her tongue, and Dakota guided her head into position catching one flake and then the next. For those few moments, fear was put aside, and they danced toward the flakes making zig-zag trails up the canyon in the fluff of fallen snow.

Short-lived stiff cold gusts began to race down through the haze prompting unseen trees to roar in fits, to moan and creak. The closer trees could be seen twisting and swaying in complaint. They thrashed about whipping each other senseless with limbs until cracked and snapped, until made useless and flung to the ground. The harsher gusts would relent in short time to be followed by less forceful but respectable blows that in turn settled down to become a stillness lying in wait for the next agitating turbulence.

Meanwhile, the Mistress of Winter descended quietly from above their awareness. By the time Dakota realized the worsening weather was upon them, it was too late. The weather in a canyon was unlike all other. It presented little rhyme or reason. It could ferry in the biting cold, and moments later send in a heat wave, a warm rain, a blizzard, or a drenching downpour of liquid ice and sleet. The skies above the mountain peaks were never settled and all things living beneath suffered their erratic fallout.

The girls had been warm, almost sweaty as they climbed upward along the trail. Dakota seldom released her hold on Raven, but now she found herself wishing to keep both hands steeped in the warmth of her pockets. Her hands were balled into fists within their damp and tattered mittens. Her head was now fully wrapped and dipped low to deflect the snow of a blizzard that was blowing hard out of the northwest. It howled as it barreled down between the unseen cliffs, driving flakes directly into what little was visible of Dakota's face, forcing her lashes to flutter and eyes to close.

"I'm cold, Dakota."

Dakota turned to look back at Raven.

"The snow keeps blowing up my sleeve. It's cold."

She realized that Raven was holding her hand and arm outstretched to be guided, instead of keeping it in close for warmth. The front of Raven's coat was completely covered in snow.

"You look like walking snowman. Hmm, we both do."

Dakota brushed the sticky snow off Raven's scarf and shoulders. She worked Raven's collar up tight to her neck. She adjusted her sister's scarf about her head to better protect her ears, cheeks, and of course her injured nose.

"There. Now you look like a winter turtle."

"My toes are cold."

"I know. Mine are too. Maybe we should try and run for a while."

Dakota took a firm hold of Raven's hand. They broke into gentle trot that was short-lived. The first time Dakota looked down at Raven, and saw fresh blood seeping through the scarf, the running stopped.

"Well, that won't do."

"How much farther, Dakota?"

"I don't know. It's snowing so hard, I can't see a thing to get my bearings. We'll just keep to the trail and watch for the trees that are marked. And Raven, don't talk so loud anymore."

Dakota didn't have to explain. Wolves were understood. As much as the near white-out conditions presented discomfort, and prevented her from seeing her way, it also prevented wolves from seeing them. The howling winds kept them from being heard and also dispersed their scent. It was the only possible blessing for one freezing to death.

They managed some success moving up through the canyon. The way was discernible, marked by the trees that bounded it like guide posts, and they were able to keep marching along in a proper fashion. And so it went until the trees abruptly fell away, and the world turned into an all-moving, milk-white, featureless wall. Dakota remembered the clearing. She knew it was large. She was forced to stop, to assess her next move going into a place with no boundaries. Dakota strained to see something of the trail ahead. Up to now, in spite of the storm's strength, the forest shredded snowflakes into a fine mist, a fog of sorts that afforded them better visibility, allowing them to pick out the path.

"Wait."

"What's the matter?"

"We need to go back."

Dakota firmed up her grip on Raven's hand and quickly backtracked a short distance until the trees came back into view.

"What's the matter?"

"It's the.... There's no path. We're at one of the clearings."

"Why are we stopping?"

"Because I can't see anything out there, it's just white."

"You can't see anything? You can't see anything at all?"

"Nothing. No trees, no shadows, no outlines, nothing but a blur of white. It's blowing hard, Raven. It's blowing right at us. It's like looking into a pitcher of stirred milk in the dark."

"Everything looks that way to me."

"I know, but you're used to it. I'm not."

The air was thick with snow. What fell to the ground was kicked back up by gusts of wind and blown about to wash over them, melting against their faces like a shower of water and freezing solid into the fabric of their scarves. Dakota was growing anxious.

"I think it would be a good time for us to say a little prayer, Raven. Remember how the saints watched over us at Uncle Kib's woodpile when the wolves came around? It was just like Momma said, remember?"

"Yup."

"We should say a little prayer. Bow your head."

Raven complied.

"Dear Lord, Momma and Poppa, and all the saints in heaven. Raven and I know you can hear us, and we know you will watch over us. It is snowing hard, and it's fiercely cold; and we need to get to Mother Gail's. Oh, and I am sorry I left without telling her. She is probably very angry. Amen."

"Amen."

The girls made the sign of the cross.

"You stay right at my side, Raven. Do you hear me? If I lose sight of you, I will never find you in this storm. Here put your hand into my pocket."

"What are you going to do?"

"Walk straight across. There's woods on the other side. We just have to walk until we find them. Are you ready?"

"Yes."

"You keep your hand in my pocket, all right?"

"I will."

"Let's go."

Dakota stepped out into the white. It wasn't but two minutes before she was gripped with full blown fear. She was walled in. It was if the only way she could keep her balance was to look down at her feet or Raven and make sense of the ground. There was nothing else. After looking down at her feet for the second time in as many minutes, she looked up and realized she had no idea of her direction.

She fought hard to keep her composure. She didn't wish to frighten Raven, and so she kept on walking ahead...into what, she had no idea. She tried to recall the look of the clearing. All her thoughts were now being crowded out by the fear wandering aimlessly until found out by the wolves. She was simply walking and waiting for trees to appear, but then what. How would that help? Without the trail, trees would mean nothing. She was in a terrible state by the time Raven interrupted her thoughts.

"Dakota...."

"Dakota?"

"What?"

"Why are we not going to Mother Gail's?"

"What?"

"Where are we going?"

"We're going to Mother Gail's."

"Mother Gail is that way."

To Dakota's utter disbelief, Raven pointed off somewhat to their right without the slightest hesitation. In her fear, she was scrambling for anything that would help.

"How do you know that she's over there?"

"The wind."

"What do you mean?"

"You turned away from the wind."

"The wind? Oh, for heaven's sake. Oh…. Thank you, Raven. That was a big help."

Dakota wanted to break down and cry where she stood. In her thoughts, she thanked Raven, she thanked Jesus, she thanked her patron saints and then she corrected her course. The wind was such an obvious thing, but she was so filled with fear that she had stopped thinking coherently. They would walk into the wind. It blew from up valley.

The confidence she now enjoyed was soon offset by the deepening snow. The winds were pushing it across the ground and forming waves that were now reaching waist high in places. A couple of times, she had to pick Raven up and carry her through the drifts. She was being pressed to think of another plan.

"Raven?"

"Yes."

"I've been thinking. If we were to keep the wind to our left side and we walked in that fashion, we would not only find an edge to the clearing, but we would also find the stream that leads up to the cabin. Can you walk with me that far?"

"I think so, but I am really cold, Dakota."

"I know, honey. If we can find the steam, I can get us home. C'mon."

Dakota felt entirely responsible for her younger sister's well-being in this world, and so tried to carry an air of strength and security. She concealed her concerns and the unending prayers to her mother and father for guidance as she worked her way through the white pulsating walls of motion that made her eyes go crazy. It was a tremendous relief when at last trees began to appear, and soon thereafter the edge of the clearing.

"We're back in the woods, Raven."

"It's harder to feel the wind."

"I know, but I am certain if we continue in this direction we will come upon the stream. C'mon. Be quiet now."

Dakota was nervous. She couldn't shake her fear of the wolves. Fortunately, in short distance she spotted a change in the lay of the land and rightfully assumed it to be the creekbed.

"There it is. There's the creek," she whispered.

"Do you know how much farther it is?"

"No."

"I'm cold, Dakota. My toes really hurt."

Dakota was having thoughts. She was studying the heights of the trees overhead.

"C'mon."

Dakota towed Raven back toward the clearing where the trees thinned out and the spaces between them made for easier observations. She continued to study the pines until she found one in particular. The wind was again blowing cold and forceful at the edge of the clearing, but the tree stood alone with nothing close enough to block views up-valley.

"I wanna go home, Dakota. I'm so cold."

"I know, Raven. I am too. I can hardly move my fingers. Listen, I want you to wait right here and do not move. And I mean don't move. If you walk away, I will never find you in this blizzard. Do you understand me? I will never find you."

"Yes. I understand."

"You wait here. I am going to climb this tree. If I can get up high enough, I can probably see up the canyon. I am sure Mother Gail is probably looking for us and I am certain she has put out lanterns on the porch so we can find our way home. I might be able to see it if I can get above the blowing snow. If they are out looking for us and carrying lanterns, I might be able to see them. I might even be able to see the trail at the other side of the clearing if I can just get above the blowing snow. This tree looks to be our best bet. You wait right here and don't move!"

"What if the wolves come?"

"If I see any wolves, then I will climb back down and bring you up, all right?"

"Don't stay up there a long time looking around."

"Don't be making any noise down here."

"I won't."

Dakota looked back up along the height of the tree. She studied the positioning of the limbs and once confident, turned back to Raven. Raven was shivering. She adjusted her sister's scarf and then kissed her.

"I'll be right back. Now stay put, Raven."

Dakota had to leap to reach the first sturdy branch. She hung momentarily by one hand. She grabbed it with her second and clamped her legs around the trunk. Slowly, she began to work her way upward slowly, picking her handholds carefully. She stopped to blow warm breath into her mittens and look down at Raven who had turned her back to the wind and now stared into the woods.

"You stay right there, Raven."

"Hurry up, I'm scared."

Dakota wedged her knee into the crotch of a limb and reached up for a branch. She knew her sister was frightened. It broke her heart to know how helpless Raven felt standing alone down below worried about wolves and cats or bears, or sounds made by harmless things that would always be worrisome.

Dakota was also afraid. She reached up for another branch. Each time, the snow was disturbed and toppled off the branch to fall into the coat sleeves of her upheld arms. Each time she ratcheted herself up, the disturbed snow doused her. The branches were small and numerous, always in her face, but easy to reach. Branch to branch, she climbed quickly.

Dakota looked back down at Raven and the height unsettled her. She looked out and the distance of her view was gradually increasing. Most important, the blowing snow was thinning out at this higher elevation. Still, she had to climb higher to see farther. She had to climb higher or else, or else she didn't know. She reached for another branch and a second and a third, each time easing herself up another foot or more.

She had climbed a good forty feet or more by any lumberjack's reckoning, and reached the threshold of both her nerve and endurance. She could climb no farther. She was weak and her arms and legs trembled from the exertion of her efforts. Sensing her loss of strength, alarms sounded in her head. She panicked. She shut her eyes and locked onto the trunk of the tree. She feared losing her grip. She feared losing control. She feared the height.

Dakota tried to relax. She opened her eyes and looked down. The forest floor dropped right out from under her. It fell miles away. Suddenly, one of those forceful gusts came ripping through the trees. This time being the one tree standing alone from the others was not to her advantage. It swayed mightily.

Dakota gripped the tree with such fear, that she chose to endure the pain of her arms and hands cramping rather than consider any other option. She was taxing her muscles to their limit. She knew her hold was the only thing that kept her alive. Her limbs were seized up. She was frozen in place now fully sensing each sway of the tree as it gave way to the buffeting wind.

Something told her to let go. What if she just let go? …So simple a thing to die; so quick—death so close to life. She scolded herself for such thoughts. Her chest felt thick. She struggled for her breath. She began to hyperventilate. She was becoming dizzy, which brought on more panic, more loss of control, more stress to her muscles.

"Hurry up, Dakota."

Raven's voice interrupted the escalation of her fear. It offered her a brief moment to focus her attention on something else. Raven needed her. Raven needed her. Her eyes remained closed but concentrating on her sister's helplessness helped relax her. Trying to steer herself far away from thoughts of height, she hollered out.

"I think I see lights up ahead. Yes, I believe I do. I'm coming down now."

It wasn't true. She saw nothing but blowing snow, but the yelling relieved much of her tension and her lie gave Raven hope. The wind was forcing its way beneath her coat. Her hands were numb both from the cold and from holding on so fearfully. The sleeves of her coat felt packed with snow.

She was numb. She knew she would be frozen for real if she didn't get herself back down off the tree, but first she had to release her grip. She struggled to move a hand. Only an inch, she thought to herself, only an inch. She tried hard to relax, but she couldn't. She was breathing hard and fast. She willed herself to move, to release her grip. It was an action to be taken against all her instincts.

"Hurry up, Dakota."

The sound of Raven's plea again snapped Dakota barely out of fear's grip, but enough for her to attempt sliding a hand down along the trunk of the tree. She felt the various branches searching for one that gave her faith. She found the courage to look down and select a branch for her foot. Hearing nothing now but the sound of her breath, she closed her eyes and felt for another limb. She began to work her way down. Her legs and arms were burning with fatigue.

Dakota's foot next settled upon a branch that was too small a diameter. It didn't snap away as might something dead. Instead, it held fast until the instant she lifted her opposite foot to descend. At that moment it folded over, allowing Dakota's foot to slip across the snow-covered limb as if it had been greased. Her opposite foot had not yet found its place, and so she dropped at once forcefully with only the grip of numb, stiff, fingers in mittens to stop her fall. They did not.

She screamed without conscious effort, without any awareness of doing so. Her scream followed her down through the bending branches that eventually flung her out away from the trunk. Her body plummeted toward earth, tumbling through a cloud of disrupted snow and snapping branches when she was fortunate, and ricocheting between the unyielding limbs when she wasn't.

461

There was no sense of direction in those last seconds of being flung and flipped. A large limb caught her across the chest and knocked the wind out of her, but mercifully, she was relieved of any further pain or fear as her head met a last stout limb that delivered her to the ground unconscious. She sensed nothing of the frozen field that brought a final unforgiving brake to her fall.

Little Raven sensed it all. She let loose a scream driven by the sheer horror of everything she imagined, but could not see. She covered her head, and crouched in fear at the sickening sounds of her sister crashing down through the tree above her head, and slamming into the ground but an arm's length away. It was over in seconds. Suddenly, there was nothing but the sound of blowing snow, the moan of trees rubbing in the distance.

Raven slowly straightened up. She turned about, still cowering under the shield of her arms. She lowered them, and peered past her mittens at the dark shadow in the white haze before her. She stood focused on the motionless form, awaiting some sign of reassurance.

"Dakota?"

"Dakota?"

Dakota remained stilled and silent. Raven lost her mind. Now truly filled with fear, she crept toward her older sister and eased down to her knees. Her outstretched hands brought sense to the shape before her. She ran her hands tenderly over Dakota's body. The leg was wrong. It was underneath her back. Raven understood that was unnatural and not good. She brought her face close before her sister's and now crying hard, she tried to arouse her.

"Dakota?"

"Dakota? Please…. Please, wake up. Please…."

Raven toppled over sideways into the snow and placed her head onto her sister's lifeless form. Afraid to make noise, she muffled her sobs. There was snow in her sleeves, her mittens, and her boots. Her fingers and toes were so cold they burned. She didn't know the way home, or how to get warm, or how to help her sister. She was lost, alone, and terrified. She thought of her patron saints and began saying her prayers. She prayed to her momma and poppa for help and for sight.

She tried desperately to overcome her blindness, to see clearly through her tears. The snow was quickly covering her sister, shrinking the shadow before her eyes. She reached up with her mitten to brush the snow away from Dakota's face. Uncertain of what should be done, she held her cheek up against her sister's and waited. She felt the heat of life in her sister and noticed that Dakota was breathing. Raven couldn't really accept death because it was still beyond her reasoning, but she did understand that Dakota needed help. She thought of Mother Gail and how Dakota had said she saw lights. Maybe they would hear if she called out.

Raven didn't know how impossible were the odds of anybody answering her pleas for help in the middle of a deafening blizzard far into the backwood. She simply followed her instinct. She stood up and cried at the top of her lungs for her mother. Tears and blood streamed down her face as her nose gave way to the pressure of her emotion.

She paid no mind. She screamed from her soul to her poppa who had always been there for her when she needed him. She just had to cry loud enough for them to hear. Wherever they had been on earth, wherever they might be in heaven, she believed if she screamed loud enough, they would hear her. She screamed and screamed and screamed.

* * *

463

ONE-HUNDRED-SEVEN

Christopher stepped out into the night, out onto the raised porch of his frontier store. I didn't believe he was prepared for the torrent of emotion that appeared to sweep over him as he stood outside facing the gleaming work of art from his distant past. The high polish of Rebecca's vermilion coach reflected the warm glow of flaming wicks that spilled forth from the four massive brass coach lanterns and those smaller lamps suspended beneath the overhang of the porch.

I saw Christopher's expression tighten. It was true he had kept the coach as well cared for as possible, but over a lifetime, the wedding gift had become a shadowy image, a dim memory pushed far to the back of his mind. It had become a vision of old discolored tarps dirtied by dust and webs, tarps tossed over the coach to conceal and protect him from the sight of Rebecca's name and the painful recollections of his past. No longer, now it seemed to float in all its resplendent magnificence. Not a scratch, not a blemish of any kind, it presented as perfect as the day it was given to Rebecca.

He stared into the depths of the rich vermilion finish. We both saw his reflection, the curly white haired and bearded bull of an old man he had become. How many years, how many lifetimes of memories had passed since this glorious coach was seen in public? In the mirrored reflections, I imagined he saw the faces of those he loved and missed, his mother, his father, his wife Rebecca. I wondered if he saw the brilliant white billowing sails of her namesake, the ship REBECCA, within the random patterns of snowflakes that swirled in waves across the glassy finish. I felt as if he saw more than he was prepared to witness and the visions filled him with aching melancholy and sadness.

An astonished crowd gathered to surround us, all whispering disbelief in murmurs and hushed tones. There had always been rumor, but until now, nothing like this had ever been seen on the street. It was inconceivable that anything of this value might exist on this side of the Mississippi, let alone in a small frontier town called Northpole. The townsfolk were yelling and whistling, calling out to their families and friends at the boardinghouse and up and down the street to come and feast their eyes. Only Christopher's eyes remained fixed upon the delicate tracery of hand-painted gold filigrene that worked up to kiss the name REBECCA CLAUSSEN.

"Rebecca Claussen," he whispered with a sad smile.

In spite of the years, Christopher's heart still tripped at the thought of Lady Rebecca. In spite of the years, I knew his longing for her remained constant. He closed his eyes and most certainly allowed memories of her to wash over him. I watched him rub his eyes. He wished no one to see the tears that welled up.

Lady Rebecca was taken when they were young and wonder-fully alive. She was taken from him in a most tragic manner, and for these reasons, his heart would never be released. Christopher's love never matured, and so she remained forever a perfection of passion, a mystical experience, a legend that would never be surpassed, forgotten, or overcome. I saw him swallow hard.

"Claus, why are you standing out here in the cold?"

I wasn't sure if he would appreciate me stepping up from behind to take his arm and ask what he had in his mind to do. I drew him back from his past.

"You are so very special to me, Elizabeth."

"I already said I forgive you."

I was taken somewhat aback by the unexpected comment and so brushed it off with a tease.

"No, no. I was thinking back on all the years, and sometimes I forget how much of my life is about you. Sometimes I fail to appreciate how rich it has been made by your presence. You have given me a son and all the love and joy a man could desire."

"Claus, whatever has made you so sentimental. I am going to start worrying again. It's the coach, isn't it? Are you thinking of Lady Rebecca?"

"I suppose I am. The coach brought it on, I reckon. I try not to pay it mind for just that reason. But here it is before me. I can't walk away from my past. I miss Rebecca, I will always miss Rebecca..." He turned to look at me. "...but I love you no less, Elizabeth."

I turned away from his gaze to look at the coach. It stole my breath away as a child, and even now as an old lady, I still found it breathtaking.

"The most beautiful coach I've ever seen Claus, but nothing less would have been fitting for the lady that she was."

"Thank you for your kindness."

"I have never desired to take her place, Claus. To stand by your side, yes; to be loved by you, yes; but never to stand in her place. Never. I love you from where I stand."

Christopher's eyed flooded with emotion. He nodded his understanding. We stood in silence until Christopher spoke up.

"Anyway...I have amends to make. Have you packed the coach full as I asked?"

"To the roof—packed, just as you wished."

"Good. I aim to find two girls, and bring Christmas to the orphans, for I repent. Do you hear? I repent!"

I looked around for Christopher's hired hands.

"I trust you will have some of the men accompany you while you are out in the weather doing all this repenting."

"I think not, I prefer this to remain my private matter."

"No, no, no. Now, don't be foolish Claus. A bad storm is upon us. The hour is late and your heart isn't about to put up with such nonsense."

I was stern. Christopher stepped off the porch and walked up to the coach. He inspected the collection of goods and wares heaped high inside.

"Claus. Don't be foolish. You can wait a moment while I call up some of the help."

He stepped forward to the driver's bench and then stopped. He turned around to face me with a distant look in his eyes.

"Elizabeth, my love, this is something I choose to do alone. Please understand."

He reached over and slid his hand across the golden scroll of REBECCA CLAUSSEN, and then turned away from me to step up to the bench. He pulled his large frame up to the driver's seat; and once situated, he took up the reins. The crowd was mesmerized by the sight of him atop such a spectacular coach, a coach that was as much a part of Christopher and my life as the air we breathed.

As my eyes took in the amazement that crossed their faces, I suddenly realized that hundreds of children had gathered, children who looked past Christopher and the coach to stare at me. I was overcome with a dreadful premonition. They had come to warn me, to tell me with their eyes that it would be this night. …That it would be this night. I panicked.

"Claus! No! I forbid you to do this, Claus. No! It is foolish and fit only for the foolhardy." I moved to step off the porch. "I implore you let the men accompany you for your own safety. Please. Claus! What if it rains and you get soaked. It'll be the death of you. Take Luke with you, Christopher. Please! There is no point in being so pigheaded."

I reached up for him.

"Not this time, Elizabeth. Pigheaded or not, I have long since forgotten how to be foolhardy and foolish, and it's a pitiful shame. What worse than to go to the grave on spindly legs too weak to raise one's ass from a cushioned chair before the hearth. Now... go inside and wait for my return. I shan't be too terribly long. I give you my word."

"No. Claus, please. Please, I beg. Why do you persist on this foolishness? You are too prideful a man, Claus, an unfavorable virtue to say the least. Why am I not surprised you would prefer I remain here to worry myself sick until your return. Do you enjoy being heartless the whole of this day?"

"I am not yet in my grave, woman. Do you enjoy rushing me?"

"Why must I beg before deaf ears? Have it your way, Claus. It's too cold to stand out here and argue with a pig-headed fool. See to it your coat stays buttoned up, and pray take care."

"I have never felt better, Elizabeth. Now, I beg before good ears, go inside and see to it you stay warm."

I looked into his eyes, eyes that had enraptured me since the youngest years of my life—eyes that had given me the warmth of security, the heat of passion, and the cruelty of rejection. Eyes that blended a lifetime of memories and emotions, warming me as I looked into them, but eyes inexplicably fixed on some distant place, someplace from where came these children to stand amongst the crowd and watch my suffering. Christopher was leaving me. I could see it in his eyes. They were caressing me, but receding, growing cool and clear like the blue ice of a frozen mountain stream that was at once flowing away and permanently stilled.

I looked up into those eyes, blue as a clear winter sky, framed by his unruly crop of thick white hair, rising and falling on the wind, swirling about, blending and becoming one with the clouds.

His beard cascaded in beautiful curls with the snowflakes below it all. I saw at once an illusion, an incarnation of Old Man Winter himself. His face and the face of winter were one and the same. I was overcome with emotion, the most unsettling sensation, a chill to the bone and disorientation. I shivered.

Christopher's eyes kissed me and turned away. He looked ahead into the falling snow and then back at me one last time.

"We must save the children, Elizabeth. I trust you remember… we must save the children."

He winked at me with those twinkling blues, and then urged the team forward. By the time Christopher departed for the orphanage, a sizeable crowd had gathered. As soon as he cracked the whip, they applauded him with heartfelt admiration, cheering him on for the good he was doing. They high-stepped with merriment and rejoiced at the sight of him driving his team through town, captain of an arc filled with gifts. It was as though Christopher were the physical hand of God. The children lined both sides of the street and he made his way between them. They rushed to follow.

A thousand bells jostled to the ground-pounding stomp of six majestic white horses. The bells rang aloud, resonating between the buildings and bringing to the townsfolk the long forgotten sound of Christmas. Folks of every age were visibly inspired by the red spectacle as it glided forward through the snow. The music of Christmas wafted through the air. People were suddenly singing.

* * *

As Christopher drove the team beyond the limits of town, he came upon Luke on horseback about to pass by on his way to the boardinghouse. Christopher halted the horses. Covered head to foot in snow, Luke looked like a white specter. His head was tilted to keep his hat square to the gale. The men hollered over the roar of the wind.

"Father! My word! What is this? What are you up to? Why do you have Lady Rebecca's coach out on a night like this? Wait-wait-wait…why do you have Lady Rebecca's coach out at all? What have you got inside there? Does Mother know you are out here?"

Luke was baffled, filled with more questions than time in the cold would allow.

"The coach is out because I needed it. It's big. It's full of toys and gifts. Yes, your mother knows I am out here. No, she isn't happy about it. When you see her, tell her I made it safely to the end of the street. Ho, ho. You are a good boy, Luke. You make me proud. Now, I must be on my way."

"No, no. Wait, Father, hold up a moment. That does much for my heart, Father, but little for my comfort, or the weather. Why do you need to drive the coach? Where are you going? I presume farther than the end of the street? I trust you realize the storm is hammering everything out here. This is dying weather, Father. Forgive my asking, but what could be so important it's worth risking your life? At least allow me to accompany you."

"No, son, I appreciate your concern. I would expect nothing less, but you must stay. It is my wish to correct a wrongdoing. I am making amends and lives lay in the balance. Now, I must go."

"Amends? On a night like this? My word, Father, did you kill somebody? What amends?"

"I apologize, my son, but the concern is mine, and mine alone. Now, again, I must be on my way."

"But Father, I beg of you, consider the storm. It is not safe to be out in such dangerous conditions. Can it not wait until tomorrow? Think of your heart, Father."

"I'm afraid I am of a different opinion, but have no fear, son. The team is plenty strong, I am well dressed for weather, and I am in no hurry. I suggest you look in on your mother, she is dear to me and prone to exaggerate things for the worse."

"I don't know, Father—."

"Luke! I beg you honor my wishes."

"But Father—."

"Luke!"

"Yes, Father, I understand…your wishes, your honor. I apologize."

"And son…."

"Yes, Father."

"When you are back at the post, open the doors to whoever is still in town. Open the boardinghouse and make coffee and food available to all. It is Christmas time, Luke. I don't believe Christmas has ever made it to Northpole, but it most certainly will tonight. Tell the folks to write down what they would like to bring home to their kids. You and Elizabeth see that their wishes are met. I want gifts flowing from Northpole to all the needy that ask. See to it, son. See to it that it is a merry Christmas for all and for all a memorable night! Can you do that for me, Luke?"

"Yes, Father. If that is what you wish."

"It's Christmas Eve, Luke. Don't look so downtrodden. Go now, go with God to your mother's side and do my bidding."

With that, Christopher cracked the whip, leaving them to their separate commitments. Luke looked back over his shoulder as the bright red coach disappeared into the storm. Luke returned to the post in haste, hoping to find his mother and get answers to his questions. Christopher headed up into the mountains, up into

471

Powder Pan Canyon, where he pulled his collar up tight and drove the team headlong into the merciless gale.

The gusts drove flakes of snow deep into Christopher's white beard where they were secured in place with frozen wafts of vapor from his breath. The storm coated his shoulders and packed itself against his chest. Christopher would not be dissuaded. He continued hauling the gifts up the slopes against weather, gravity, and the pain of a faulty heart.

Deep inside his snow-covered chest he was in the highest of spirits. He sang aloud in the wind. He sang to his mystical horses. They were powerful, plowing through the drifts with ease. He sang songs of his past. He sang his favorite love song learned from his old friend and salt of the sea, Darin O'Kurk.

"Tell me now me maties, tell me then again!

'av yer eyes laid rest upon the lovely lady o' the Thames...

Er name, it 'as been ferried across the seven seas

In the 'eart o' every sailor man that's been by West Indies

Oh, Rebecca, Rebecca, Rebecca darlin' dear

Think on me forever, an' forever I'll be near..."

Oh, Rebecca, Rebecca, Rebecca darlin' dear

Save yer 'eart, an' I'll be back, me promise be sincere

Hya! Get along there now, my lovelies. Hya! Hya!"

ONE-HUNDRED-EIGHT

Christopher had been on the trail for almost an hour. He had lived in these parts plenty long enough to know the truth of Luke's claims; this was indeed a killing storm. He was now deeply concerned for the girls' lives. They had been in the weather too long. The seriousness of their predicament was upon him in no diminished way. It would have been impossible for them to survive in such weather unless they had found the orphanage or a miracle. He thought of Elizabeth's warning about additional blood on his hands. He shielded his face from the blow, and urged the horses onward into the whiteness.

Christopher had seen neither hide nor hair of a dwelling so far. He wasn't about to admit he was too blind to spot one, and so preferred the certainty he hadn't passed by anything. Elizabeth had said Mother Gail claimed to be living some three hours up the canyon trail by foot, and that the course was plainly marked by the trees for the most part. Surely, he had gained on the girls by this time.

Until now, he hadn't questioned his course, for the trail was as Mother Gail and Elizabeth said, plainly marked, right up until he entered into the large clearing. Now, it was precisely the opposite as he moved apprehensively into a flurry of snow so thick he could barely see his leads. He snapped reins that disappeared into oblivion.

He was unable to take a bearing, and so unable to make sense of his position. He was compelled to wait at woods' edge but for common sense, for the storm was particularly ferocious in this place. In the woods, the snow fell dusty and the winds were held to bay near the forest floor. It was nothing like the roar in the treetops, or the wind of this clearing where the full force of the blizzard was to be reckoned.

The snow fell with such intensity that it would bury him soon if he should remain. It should have raised an ear-deafening roar, as it pelted the ground and piled up before his eyes. His fear for the girls mounted. He snapped the rains and the leads set their forward pace, steadily, and seemingly unbothered. It was the thought of a snow-covered bog lying centered in the clearing that gave finally gave Christopher reason for pause. No ice or bog would support the weight of his team.

He wished only an opportunity to see clear of the field, to locate the trail on the other side, for many a man had walked to his death while in a blizzard looking for his barn. But, wish as he might, there was no letting up, and hopes to see across the clearing were without merit. He halted the horses for fear of the terrain, and a lingering hope for a break in the white-out.

Wishing to see beyond his team, Christopher climbed down off the coach with a lantern in hand and waded through the waste deep snow past his wheel horses, his swings, and finally up to his leaders. He continued to head into the clearing by foot until the coach lanterns grew dangerously dim, mere flickers to be seen and then not.

Ahead in the darkness was nothing. No hint of trail or treeline, no distinction of any kind, only his being centered in the soft glow of a lantern, its light nearly suffocated by the dense snowfall. Christopher turned his back to the wind and sought out the faint glimmer of the coach lanterns. He followed the beacons until arriving back where stood his leaders. He lowered the lantern and inspected the wrappings on their legs. Satisfied they were secure and protecting the horses, he stood up and looked off to his right, sideways into the blow, but saw nothing beyond forty or fifty feet. He cupped his hand to his mouth.

"Hellooooooooo!"

He listened with intent.

"Hellooooooooo! Can you hear me!"

Again, he listened. Again, he heard nothing. He feared his ears could well be the death of the young girls, ears that barely served his own needs. He moved back along the team toward the coach, checking the harness at each of his horses and their leggings in the lamp light the best he could. He climbed back up onto the bench and replaced the lantern. He turned up the wicks of the four coach lanterns to project as much light as possible. Maybe their eyes would be better than his ears.

Christopher sat stalled in the clearing. He wasn't one to be lost for a plan, but he knew driving a team with leaders fifty feet down his reins across unknown ground when blind was nearly as dim-witted as coming out in this weather alone. Fortunately, Elizabeth knew nothing about driving teams. If she had, at this moment he would likely have been shot.

It was there, just then when thinking about being shot, that a notion popped into his head. He grabbed the reins for the ready. He pulled out his revolver, held it up high, and fired off a round. He listened.

He fired off a second. He listened.

He fired off a third. He listened.

He snapped his head bringing his best ear to the wind. Did he...? He listened. Had the wind carried an unnatural sound past his ear? His senses sprang to life. He moved his head slowly about, directing his good ear, striving to hear above the frigid rush of wind through the trees. He worked his eyes with effort to see anything, anything at all, but the cloud cover was thick, the snowfall heavy, and the night black. He glanced at the lanterns. They were hot, but not hot enough to keep the snow from creeping up across the glass. He wiped them down with his fingers. They brightened.

He raised the revolver and fired a fourth round.

He listened. Was it the wail of the wind and nothing more? He wondered. A specter hidden amidst the swirling patterns of snow before the light of his lantern, he thought to himself. The thought was just folly, but it served to translate the sound into a sensation akin to fingernails moving up and down his back. He shivered and unconsciously sucked his large frame farther into his coat. Admittedly, he was feeling altogether alone and somewhat unprotected. He looked down at the driver's bench. Its corners were filling with drifts of snow as he waited at a standstill.

There! There! Did he hear it? Again! Yes! He heard the cry... broken by the turbulence of the wind, but clearly not of the wind. It was more the sound of a cat. A stupid cat...too stupid to find shelter from the storm—stupid as was he. Animals usually hunkered down in a bad blow unless they happened upon an easy meal. No sooner had that thought emerged than a vision of a cat finding the girls exploded inside his head and nearly stopped his aching heart. The girls!

"Hello!"

"Hello! Can ya hear me!"

Christopher stood atop the bench seat with hands cupped to his mouth.

"Hello! ...Can ya hear me!"

As if an echo, the scream came back at him from the dark. A scream far more frantic and forceful. Christopher nearly collapsed from exhilaration.

"You scream, child! You scream and I will find you!"

Christopher climbed down off the coach and grabbed the lantern. He plowed his way through the snow. He plowed his way into the darkness.

"Hello!"

The screams returned, but the wind in his old ears kept the source hidden. He worked his old eyes, shifting his gaze back and forth, back and forth.

"Scream, child!"

He continued forward through the waist deep snow. The scream was returned to draw him in. How could he hear so clearly and see nothing? Then at last, he saw the figure of a young child breaking in and out of the blowing snow. She was nearly buried neck deep in snow, and backed up against the black trunk of a tree for protection against the wind. Christopher was amazed, for the child was in every way virtually impossible to see.

"I'm here. You'll be fine, child. I've come to take you home."

The child continued to howl—crying in desperation. Claus knew the child heard him, but never looked his way. He understood. This was the little blind girl—the little blind girl who he so badly injured. His heart poured out its guilt.

"Shushhhh. Shushhhh, child. You're safe now. Shush. There's no need to cry my child. Everything is fine. I've come to take care of you. Shushhhh."

In the light of his lantern he could plainly see the deplorable injury he inflicted upon her, for she was a mess of frozen blood from head to toe. Her eyes were blackened. Her face and scarf were caked in a scab of frozen blood-ice. Christopher's stomach was in his throat. He cursed himself to an eternal whipping for what he had done. He hooked the lantern on a limb and raised Raven up from the snow. He embraced her tightly against his chest. He dropped his head upon her shoulder and his eyes flooded with tears. Her blood was indeed on his hands and it coursed through his conscience.

Raven barely realized he was present. She had worked herself into a stupor, screaming hysterically until she blocked out her ability to discern any outward activity or attempts by Christopher to respond to her cries. When he finally calmed her down enough, to stop convulsing and catch her breath, she merely looked at him with a mindless gaze. He knew she was exhausted and in a state of shock. He surmised the energy she expended bellowing was all that kept her from freezing to death. That and standing in a chest deep hole of snow that served to reduce her exposure to the wind. Slowly she returned to the world of reality.

"Oh, child. What have I done to you? You're fine girl. You'll be fine. Shushhhh. Tell Claus your name. What would I call a girl who cries so hard?"

"Ray-Ray-Ray-hay-ven," she blurted.

"Raven, is it? That is a wonderful name. Tell me Raven are you alone?"

"N-N-N-No-ho."

Christopher looked around.

"Can you tell me where your friend is? Do you know?"

"Y-Y-Yup." She nodded.

"Where is she then? Tell me so we can find her."

Raven began to stir mentally, turned her head, and looked about the freshly fallen snow.

"There." She pointed.

Christopher scanned the ground the best he could through the storm, but to no avail, he could see nothing.

"Where, Raven? You must take me to her."

He set her down. She first returned to the tree, to the hole in the snow, and then stepped away struggling to walk through the drifts. She only moved a short distance from the tree. She stopped abruptly and pointed down.

"There."

Christopher was stunned. He had been scanning the woods, looking out across the snow that buried the fallen body. He felt the weight of death placed squarely upon his shoulders. He stepped over to Raven and dropped to his knees. He began sweeping away snow, going deeper, brushing away armfuls until there came to view the other child.

Christopher was mortified. He moved to raise her, when suddenly she whimpered. She was unconscious, but she was yet alive. Being buried in the snow probably kept her warm enough to survive, but she would surely die from the cold unless he acted to save her at once. He turned to look at Raven who was standing silent at his side.

"Raven, do you know what happened here?"

"Yup."

"What happened, sweetheart?"

"She fell out of the tree."

Claus began brushing away the snow about the girl's legs and discovered soon enough that one leg was missing. He stood up and returned to the tree for his lantern. He returned and spread the warm glow across the girl's legs. He unbuttoned her coat and raised it. He lifted her dress high enough to see a leg lying at an impossible angle. The child's legging was soaked in blood. With great care, he lowered the legging to see the bone partially visible through a break in the skin.

"It doesn't look good. She's broken her leg."

"Yup."

Christopher glanced at Raven who nodded her affirmation. This was not good. Time was against him; the weather was against him. He was under pressure to resolve the situation, but that pressure was extreme and his heart suffered the consequence. A stab of pain shot through him. It was severe enough to immobilize him. He felt the sweat break out upon his forehead. He looked up to the heavens.

"Please, dear God, if you must take me, do so after I give aid to these children. I beg."

Christopher struggled to get back on his feet.

"Raven, I want you to lie down next to...."

"My sister?"

"Yes, your sister. Lie next to her and keep her warm. I am going back to the coach. I will be right back."

Christopher left Raven with her sister and trudged his way back to the coach through snow that taxed him physically. Upon reaching the coach, he stopped, head hanging low and breathing hard. He tried to regain his breath, but struggled with the increasing tightness in his chest. He understood he had pushed himself too hard. He needed to relax, but the life of the girl surely depended on every second. Again, he looked up to the heavens.

"Oh, God. Give me some time. The child needs us both."

Christopher had to figure a means to protect her from the weather and he had to do it fast. But how was that to be done without moving her? There would be no moving the child until the leg was braced. To do otherwise might kill her well before the weather. What to do, he thought, what to do? Maybe something in the coach, blankets, oilcloths, whatever else that might protect and warm her; yes, he would bury her and Raven in the clothes. The coach was filled to the roof with clothes. That should do it until help arrived.

He stood leaning against the vermillion glaze, eyes closed, still fighting for air as he finalized his plan. He was a long ways removed from the strong and virile man of his youth. He was hot, to the point of overheating. He wanted to remove his coat, but the wind would kick up in fierce gusts and it made his sweat freeze to his skin. Yet, he was warm. His hands felt warm, he removed his gloves, and as he looked at them, a drop of water splashed upon them, then another. He was puzzled at first, thinking it to be sweat off his brow, but only for a moment before he looked up to the sky, and was promptly pelted in the face with more drops. It began to rain. He spun around. He scanned the canyon. He hadn't even noticed the snow had stopped. The treeline across the clearing was yet impossible to see but not because of snow. It was blocked by the fog of warm air crossing over the cold snow cover. The warm air would have been welcome had it been free of rain, but rain meant death.

"Oh, Lord. Please, not the rain."

This was the worst of all possible situations. In the mountains, one could face the coldest of temperatures providing he was well dressed and dry. But to be wetted could bring one to his death from exposure even during the middle months of summer. These fast, unexpected temperature changes were not uncommon in the mountains with their towering heights and enclosed valleys, which trapped cold pockets of air and disrupted the normal currents. The weather was always in turmoil and this rain could wreak havoc with the ice that usually accompanied it.

There was no time to waste, and at once he lunged for the bright brass door handle and gave it a twist. Pulling the door open, he leaned in, and pushing and pulling, he sifted through the enormous pile of presents searching desperately in the light of the lantern for anything to aid his cause.

The beams of light snapped back off the cutting edge of an axe. He moved it out of the way. He began to pull out a blanket, but

481

knew it to be useless without an oilcloth. His search for an oilcloth moved him back past the axe, and this time he grabbed it. It was razor sharp and preferring not to get hurt, he moved to place it outside. The rain was now falling across his back as he pulled away from the coach. He closed the door to keep the gifts dry.

The cutting edge of the blade held his attention as it reflected the light of the lanterns. He ran his finger cautiously across the sharpened edge. It was sharp, wickedly sharp. Something about the axe was forcing him to recognize something. It was there in his mind, he could feel it just below the surface of his conscious-ness...think...think. Maybe he could cut some tree limbs, maybe form a shelter of sorts. No, he thought, his heart would never hold up, and besides the rain would simply stream through to soak the children beneath. He needed to think...an oilcloth, a cover, a roof....

ONE-HUNDRED-NINE

Christopher looked at the coach. He stared at it. His head was suddenly filled with an intuition, a near premonition. It was a vision that was too inconceivable to be considered, and yet he moved to unhook the lanterns from their hooks and set them upon the chassis as he thought it through. He stepped back.

Christopher stared at the coach. He broke into chest-heaving sobs, sobs that filled his lungs with air. He filled his heart with one last look at his wedding gift to Rebecca. Then, with the precision of experience gained in the forest as a youth, he drew up the axe and sent it slicing through the air. He brought the razor edge of its steel to bear upon the flawless vermilion finish.

CRACK!

The deluge of rain and ice failed to muffle the sound of the blow, which sent the woodwork splintering across the field.

CRACK!

Only a man of great character could withstand the wretched sound of such a sacrilegious act. With each powerful swing came a fresh memory of his past.

CRACK!

...The rides of summer, the romance of love, the look upon Rebecca's face; the look upon his father's face.

CRACK!

...The remembrances of Rebecca seated at his side, remembrances of her standing atop the bench thanking the crowds in London, the days of Elizabeth's youth, the coach passing through the cemetery.

The axe split open the coach as it split open the vault of his life story. He swung, he cried, he swung.

CRACK....

Through tears and billowing clouds of hot breath, he watched as the top slowly parted from the body at the base of each window post. What he lacked in strength from his age, he more than made up by the efficiency of accurately placed strikes. It was a finely built coach and the strikes never loosened an untouched joint, but he forced the top to relinquish its integrity and it collapsed cleanly upon the mound of gifts packed inside.

He collapsed as well from fatigue, for each blow he delivered to the coach struck another to his heart. He hung over its side, struggling to breathe. Christopher prayed for relief from his pain. He prayed to find the strength he desperately needed.

"Oh God! Where is the air I so badly crave? Have you already sucked all the life out of my bones? Hear my prayer, dear God, it isn't for my doing that I ask your help, it is for my undoing. It is for my misdeeds. Have mercy I implore, and help me to prevail."

Christopher went on to struggle with his age, as well as the gnarled and splintered edges of the severed top that insisted on snagging in the tangle of gifts, blankets, and clothes that bloated its innards. He pushed and he pulled, he worked it from side to side, attempting to dislodge it from its resting point. He wrestled with it until his arms were numb. Eventually the roof gave in to his persuasion and fell free, flipping over upside down onto the snow. Once done, it was then possible to drag it across to the girls like a sled, but not without an additional cost. The strain was destroying all that remained of his already overworked and failing heart.

The fallen girl never stirred all the while he worked his way toward her. Raven huddled close to her older sister and remained as still as a stone. She paid little mind to Christopher, for whom the scale had been tipped. Now the conflict with his heart was the more pronounced battle. The struggle with the coach roof forced him to stop and rest far too many times. He wondered which rest would be his last.

He focused on the girls. He pushed himself. He was soaked with sweat. He was soaked with freezing rain. He was feeling chilled. His system was out of accord, out of balance. His chill was from a summons he wished to ignore. He swore at himself for being so old, for being so slow. After much determination, and what seemed an eternity, he reached the girls. They were both soaked by the time he dragged the roof to them.

One look at Raven shivering uncontrollably drove Christopher to renew his efforts. He upended the coach top and carefully flipped it, bringing it down over the girls where they lay. He knelt down and crawled inside through what had once been the cabin door. He began pulling snow out from beneath the roof. He pulled it out from the center and packed it up against the now paneless window openings. In time, he formed a comfortable little chamber.

He moved back outside and piled snow up to the window openings and sides to block out the cold air. The falling stream of freezing rain quickly coated the vermilion roof with a cake-like topping of clear ice. Christopher was thoroughly soaked by the time he finished. The shivering caused his muscles to constrict and this added to the pain in his already tightened chest.

Christopher gasped for breath as he plowed back through the snow now acting like a sponge to soak up the downpour of sleet. At the coach, he reached beneath the upper gifts now heavily coated in the wet slop. He picked through the buried gifts yet dry, grabbing up an armful of the blankets and red flannels Elizabeth had packed away. His arms supported the burgeoning stack hooked in place by his white bearded chin. He brought the garments over to the shelter and stuffed them inside.

He made a second trip to retrieve food items. He believed little Raven was most likely half starved, probably not having eaten the whole of the day. Food would go a long way to warming her. He reached for another lantern atop the bench. He located the second axe and brought both back to the shelter.

Christopher dropped to his knees a final time and pushed his armload of goods inside. He took off his coat and tied the sleeves to the brass rails atop the roof. He next lay down upon his back and attempted to slide his large frame through the opening. It was no small feat, but once inside, he reached outside atop the roof and pulled his coat down over the door opening to seal it. Inside, his girth helped to warm the small confine, but not quickly or sufficiently enough to save blue faced Raven, who was soaked and succumbing to her exposure.

"Raven, we must get you out of those wet clothes and into something dry. Come to me, child. Let's us undo you."

In the warm glow of the lantern, Christopher helped Raven remove her coat and wet clothes. She undressed before him without shame as a child does for a parent. He was disheartened to see how fragile she appeared. She was but a wisp of life, a creature so delicate that only a world of care could see her though. He clothed her trembling frame with layers of flannel, one upon the next. He rubbed her feet briskly, trying to warm them. He cupped them in his hands and blew breath across them. He held them to his cheek. He tickled them. She broke into laughter. It did him good to see her dressed in the bright red of flannel instead of the dark red of dried blood.

Christopher wrapped Raven in blankets and laid her down. He handed her a box of biscuits that she delved into, paying scant mind to choking. While she occupied herself, he began sorting through the pile of flannels. His hopes were realized. Somebody in the store simply lifted an entire stack of garments and stuffed them into the coach. Had it been Elizabeth, she would have seen the assortment was specific to children. This person was simply following orders to stuff the coach. There was more than enough to satisfy his needs.

Christopher took hold of the large bundle and waited for a break in the weather. As soon as it occurred, he dragged the garments outside with him. He stood up and quickly stripped down. He began to shake violently from exposure. His chest murdered him at once and again the pain of his injured heart tore apart his insides. He struggled to get into the dry clothes. First, dry flannel pants that fit fairly well, a couple of shirts, a nightcap, dry sox, a robe and coat. He looked at himself in the light of the lantern and in spite of the pain began laughing aloud.

"Ho, ho. My word, Elizabeth, I look like a grand tomato."

Christopher spread his old garments like a carpet across the snow covered floor of the shelter. He then crawled back inside. Raven was now warmer and much calmed down. Her eyes were closed, but she continued to feed and fill her belly with biscuits, albeit much slower.

The lantern offered a gentle and cozy glow to the inside of the shelter. It also provided a respectable amount of heat. The shelter offered a haven from the harsh sounds of falling ice, winter winds, and splintering wood. As the sleet accumulated upon the roof, it insulated those inside from the sounds of winter's havoc. The peacefulness was made more profound by the soft breathing of the girls.

Christopher laid still and willed his heart to ease its infliction of pain. He contemplated what next must be done about the broken leg. The girl's leg would have to be addressed before she could be moved. As he sought a plan, his attention drifted back to Raven's bruised face. Her coal black hair parted across her forehead at the bridge of her nose, and was lost before eyes blackened by his hand. Again he was moved to tears of shame. If only he could take it all back. He noticed she was yet nibbling.

"Raven?"

"Yup."

"Do you know who I am?"

"Yup."

"Who am I, sweetheart?"

"You hurt my nose."

Christopher winced. In the light of the lantern, he noticed how she never looked his way. She only laid back and stared at emptiness off to the side. It made him feel terrible. He understood Elizabeth's fury. The child never saw the door fly toward her.

She simply stood at the mercy of others as he kicked it into her face. He was riddled with guilt, crushing guilt. Elizabeth was correct to ask what kind of beast would do a thing so despicable.

"I am very, very, sorry, Raven. You must believe me. I was wrong. I didn't mean to hurt you, but I did, and for that I was wrong. God is not happy with me. Do you understand?"

"Yup."

"I brought you a gift. I hope you will accept it. I want to be your friend, Raven. Will you forgive me for hurting you, for the pain I caused?"

"Yup."

"Here, this is for you. Please take it."

Christopher produced one of the dolls that Elizabeth said the girls so wished to have in the store. Raven reached up into the void before her and waited for something to touch her hands. He offered the doll and she took it up in her arms and rubbed her face in its hair. She recognized its feel at once and smiled. For Christopher it was a windfall profit for a trinket of a toy.

"Do you like the doll?"

"Yup."

"I have brought another for your sister as well. Would you tell me her name?"

"Yup."

"What is it, sweetheart?"

"Dakota."

"Dakota. That's a pretty name."

"She's my sister."

"Yes, I remember you saying as much."

Christopher nodded, and sensed a deepening of the tragedy. He uncovered a box of chocolate.

"Are you warm, Raven?"

"Yup."

"Do you like chocolate?"

She didn't answer.

"Have you ever had chocolate?"

The girl said nothing but shrugged her shoulders.

"Here taste this. Tell me what you think."

Christopher handed a piece to Raven. She ate it quietly, and when finished, she rolled her head toward him focusing her blind gaze in his direction.

"I like chocolate."

"I thought you might. Most people do."

"What's your name?" she asked.

"Christopher Nicholas Claussen. But that's a mouth full, so my good friends call me Claus. You may call me Claus, if you prefer. I think you would make a great friend. That's why I have come to see to it that you're out of harm's way, to see that you're warm and that you have something to eat. You may go to sleep if you wish. I promise I'll stay here and watch over you. I promise."

Raven laid there, eyes shifting, blinking, following movements of thoughts moving through her mind.

"My momma said saints watch over us."

"Oh, that is true indeed. Your momma it right. We would be in a lot of trouble if there were no saints to watch over us."

"Dakota said a lot of prayers. Is that why you came?"

"Well...I suppose it might be. I guess it could be, why not. Your sister prayed to God for help and He made sure I found you. God must have wanted it that way. He must have told my heart *'Claus, go find that little girl.'*"

"Really? Are you a saint? Are you Santa Claus?"

"Wha...oh.... Oh, ho, ho, ho! Oh, ho, ho, ho!

In spite of the terrible pain within his chest, Christopher was forced to laugh. He laughed without reservation. He laughed long and heartily. His large frame shook, nearly with convulsion as he roared.

"Oh, ho, ho, ho! Ho, ho, ho....

It was a merry laugh that brought both tears and a sparkle to his eyes. Raven enjoyed hearing him laugh. It made her feel good.

"Oh, ho, ho.... Santa Claus! Santa Claus! My word, child." He shook his head in disbelief. "If only one could measure innocence. Dear, one, Santa Claus didn't go about giving little blind girls black eyes."

"But Momma said saints come to watch us when we are afraid. I was afraid and you came. Doesn't that make you Santa Claus?"

"Well, maybe just for tonight," he laughed. "I reckon it is Christmas Eve and there will be no harm in that. Now, if you want more gifts tomorrow, then hold your doll tight, close your eyes and go to sleep. I have much work to do before the night is over."

Christopher laid back a moment to collect his thoughts. He did still have much to do, and it wasn't pleasant. He rested only a moment more, listening to the falling ice, which had started up again. He waited for Raven to drift off to sleep with the doll cradled in her arms. He waited until his heart settled and then he went back to work.

He fumbled badly with his almost useless fingers; they were warm, but remained numb. Reaching for his knife, he cut through Dakota's wet clothes. He collected her garments and along with Raven's, and laid them out as carpet to protect them from the cold of the snow packed floor. Christopher's stomach tightened as he looked at Dakota's deformed body in the light of his lantern. He cut away at her leggings and uncovered the bone of her leg protruding through her skin just above the knee. Raven stirred.

"Go to sleep, Raven."

Christopher began to ramble mindlessly to sooth Raven while he studied Dakota's leg. He didn't want her to awake to Dakota's screams if it should come to that. Raven would never understand that he was only trying to help.

"Think of my bright red coach…." Christopher stopped to think a moment. "Forgive me, Father, but I reckon it's a sleigh at this point." He then continued to talk to Raven. "Think of the gifts I've brought this night. I've brought them for you and all the other children at the orphanage. Think of the sugarplums and the sweetbreads and the dried fruits. And what about that chocolate; wasn't it delicious? Think of the warm flannels and the toys. … All the toys. The dolls I have brought you, my child. Tomorrow will be a wonderful day, but tonight you must sleep. Go to sleep, Raven, and dream. Go to sleep, my angel, and dream of wonderful things."

Raven drifted off with a faint smile upon her face. Her plugged nose made her snore. The sound stopped Christopher. He looked over at her and blew her a kiss. He then looked back at Dakota. Christopher raised Dakota's frame carefully as he pulled the dangling leg out from underneath her. Struggling to position himself to advantage in the cramped quarters served only to further aggravate his discomfort, but the sight of Dakota brought stamina to his being.

491

He thanked the Lord profusely for blessing Dakota with unconsciousness. Christopher looked over to Raven, who was now fully asleep, snoring through her mouth. He then grabbed Dakota's fawn-like leg and pulled it firmly until it took a set. The bone was now retracted back from the open wound and so it was allowed to close. Dakota cried out from someplace far away and then went silent as before. He held the lantern over the broken leg and watched with intent to assure himself that the bleeding was abating. He mopped up the blood with a clean cloth.

Christopher again looked over to Raven, who slept soundly and dreamed on unaware of Dakota's condition. He reached for his knife and slit a couple of the cotton towels into strips. He reached for the two axes and wrapped each in the strips of cloth until soft and cushioned. He then laid the two handles side by side, one on each side of Dakota's leg. He applied a fresh cotton swab to the tear in her skin and then began wrapping towels tightly around the leg and the handles.

Christopher stopped to rest. He grabbed a pieced of scrap cloth and mopped his forehead. With the last of the strips, he tied bands around the towels to keep them from unraveling. He inspected his work and was satisfied that her bone would remain immobile and have a chance to mend. He dropped back off his aching arms. He closed his eyes.

Christopher was concerned about injuries to Dakota's back. He needed to raise her up off the ground in order to get her into dry clothes. If he failed to do so, she would freeze to death. Her skin was bluish and cold as ice. Unlike Raven, who could remove most of her own clothes, he had to slice through Dakota's with his knife. He did so and then worked to dress her in the flannels. He placed the final articles of clothing and blankets across her frame. These things he managed to do gently, in spite of suffering the burning discomfort in his shoulders, that being the strain of so long supporting his large frame on elbows.

Finished with his work, he mopped his forehead and face. He gazed upon both girls and was filled with an appreciation of their pristine beauty...perfect creatures. Injured, yes, but otherwise flawless in every respect. What was it Rebecca used to always say?

"...And so God doth keep...sacred, children of the street."

How rewarding it must have been to know such devotion. Rebecca was an orphan who lived for her own kind. She understood all the joy and horror behind the meaning of the title "orphan." Regrettably, in contrast, Christopher only looked into the window of that world. He felt his life was badly spent pursuing evermore empty successes that prevented him from having the empathy and understanding of these lost miracles.

Christopher wished only to rest, to have a reprieve from the pain in his chest. There was no manner in which he might lie or position himself that brought relief. In fact, even while lying still, the pain only seemed to increase. He picked up a scrap of packing paper and retrieved a piece of graphite from the pile of his emptied pockets. In case his condition continued on its present course, he determined by the light of lantern to write two letters for whoever might find the girls. One addressed to Elizabeth, the other on caring for Dakota.

To whom it may concern...

Take care to move Dakota gently. She suffers a serious injury to the leg, a break above the knee and possibly the back. She suffers an open wound at her thigh. Set the coach roof aside, and lift her by means of a board. You can transport her best by making use of the brass baggage rails as handles. I have used two axe handles to splint the leg. I am afraid I have done this thing only once before, that being a favorite dog. I am unable to advise you on her back. She has not regained her wits since falling from a tree. Pray, take care! May God be with you and the child.

C.N.C.

By the time Christopher finished this letter, and his second to Elizabeth, he had slipped into a state of morbid agony. Rivers of sweat crossed his face and chest. He was burdened with unbearable pain and concluded that, in fact, his time was at hand. All things considered, Christopher was determined not to die within the confines of the shelter.

Christopher placed Elizabeth's letter on Dakota's flannel nightgown, near her breast. He leaned over awkwardly and kissed both girls with heartfelt affection. He then began backing his way out from underneath the coach top. It was done with great difficulty for his left arm was near useless. The numbness in his hands and legs may have spared him the burning kiss of winter's mistress.

He pulled himself up the coach top and from there raised himself to his feet. Staggering slowly, he made his way over to what was only shortly before Rebecca's wedding gift—the most magnificent vermilion coach ever seen west of the Mississippi. It now rested in place, roofless, filled with slush and ruined forever more. It looked to be a poor excuse for a carriage—and when fitted with skis—it looked most to be a sleigh. He stared at her name upon its door, the sweeping gold calligraphy. The hand-painted scrollwork that wrapped itself around the wooden remains like fancy ribbon.

"It is the most beautiful sleigh I have ever laid eyes upon, my darling. I am sure you would love it."

He spoke aloud into the night air. Christopher was becoming disoriented. He struggled to lift his boots over the snow, and he summoned what little strength he had left to make a final climb up onto the driver's bench. It was the most difficult climb of his life. One step then another, he hung on to the sides seemingly forever before finally falling across the leather snow-covered bench. The effort consumed all that was left of his mortal energy.

"Christmas Eve, Rebecca. The night you were taken from me. Now, I go to you."

He gasped for breath and sat upright just in time to endure one last decisive shudder, whereby his heart succumbed to the fact of its age. It resigned itself once and for all, to everlasting peace. It beat no more to the rhythm of life with all its memories and emotion.

In his dying throes, Christopher sat up tall and clutched his chest. In his last vision, the sky was clear with only a hint of snow falling delicately into the clearing, now a place of overwhelming tranquility surrounded by a thousand crystallized trees. Standing there before him with outstretched hands, in all her radiance, was his beloved Rebecca. She was calling him, calling his name. She had come back for him. She had waited, as had he.

He lifted his arm upward offering her his heart. He reached for her, as once again he was filled with the passion of youth and swept away by the rapture of Rebecca's love. She beckoned him to her bosom and he went gladly, wholeheartedly. He stepped out across the threshold of death and left behind forever the memories and constraints of his mortal life. His spirit moved into her glistening realm, into the radiance of her presence, into the light of her, so bright it bleached the earth white. He was with her now for eternity. She was his Mistress of Winter.

ONE-HUNDRED-TEN

The Good Lord set upon my shoulders a capable noggin, and I am fortunate to have never been taken for a fool. Not in my early years at the Claussen estate as I stood on shaky legs to serve Christopher and Rebecca, not when I traveled with them across the ocean, not in my adolescence at school or my work in Boston. My adventures in the west served only to give me more of the grit needed to face my new life in Wyoming. I had earned and been given the respect of a woman who had paid her dues. No one ever accused me of being slow of wit. Fortunately, I passed on some of that wit to my son Luke.

When Luke entered the store, he was calling out to me before the door had closed behind him.

"Mother!"

"Mother!"

"I'm here in your father's office!"

Luke came rushing in. I could see the anxiety about him.

"Mother, what is going on? I just passed Father. He's driving the vermillion coach and headed out of town in a blizzard that will be the death of him. Do you know this? Mother…did you let him go?"

"Let him go? Let him go? Luke, I did everything in my power to stop him, but he was adamant. He sent me back here to worry myself sick. I only dare go so far against his wishes. I was just about to have a few of the hands saddle up and chase him down— at least watch him from a distance. He's headed up Powder Pan."

"Powder Pan? Powder Pan Canyon in the middle of the night, in a blizzard? What is this about, Mother? Amends? He said amends. What amends?"

I went on to explain what had taken place in the store and how Christopher had determined to right his wrongs, by finding the girls and taking them up to Mother Gail's with a coach filled with toys and needs.

"No, no, no, Mother. He'll never make it. I have been out in the weather for the last four hours, and I know he will never make it up the canyon in this blizzard. I must ride out after him at once."

"Absolutely not! I'll not stand to watch the same mistake made twice, Luke. Go summon the help if you must. We'll ride up in company. A party should have been sent up after girls in the first place. I already sent word for McKenzie and some of the hands."

"Very well. I'll ride out to meet McKenzie, and round up some more help. I will return shortly. In the meantime, don't you be running off."

"I'm not going anywhere, Luke. Now go get McKenzie, and be quick about it."

Luke rode off at once to rouse Sheriff McKenzie and give him an account of the night's happenings. Luke and the sheriff went about on my behalf, collecting volunteers from around town to form a search party for Christopher and the girls.

Volunteers soon arrived on horseback or by wagon. Many were still in town talking about the beauty of the coach that they had seen for the first time only hours ago. They were quick to sit down and discuss plans that wouldn't cause others to end up in peril. As they waited for Luke and others to arrive, the snow had drifted to depths of nearly six feet and was pushing upwards of two feet on the flats.

To everyone's relief, while formulating plans, the wind suddenly dropped off and the snowfall abated. The spirits of all were substantially raised, but only for a brief moment. A very warm breeze blew through town. The old-timers turned to look at the door. Suddenly, two or three stood up and stepped out onto the porch. I followed them out and observed them step down into the street and look skyward into the blackness of night. As I moved to approach one of the old men, I noted there was now on the street a good many volunteers seated on horses or gathered in groups ready to set out.

"What's happening, Anthony? Why the look of concern?"

"Warm wind...'at's not a good thing."

"How can that be worse than freezing to death?"

"Rain."

No sooner uttered when a torrential downpour of freezing rain and ice soundly doused the town. The old-timers and I, along with those close by, jumped back under the porch roof. The crowd in the street was caught unaware, and ran every which-way desperate to find shelter. Anthony turned to me.

"Now we 'ave a problem. A good soakin' can kill ya in a heart beat."

As if to reinforce his comment, the street crowd disappeared. Only the children, the street urchins, remained to be seen. They had no place to go. They stood around watching us on the porch. Or maybe, they were watching me.

"Everybody's leaving," I remarked soulfully.

"They'll be back. They got a good soakin' in the street. Heh-heh-heh. Don't ya worry yerself, they'll be back soon enough. It's the horses, we'll be losin'"

"What do you mean?"

"Look at those folks, walkin' about. They're in fear o' breakin' their necks. It's the ice. It's buildin' up thick. 'At's bad news for animals. It lays atop the snow like broken glass, an' it'll slice them horses' forelegs open clean to the bone. Good as any knife. Nasty business. Can make a horse lame in five minutes."

"What about leggings?"

"Most certainly. Them's that got 'em on hand'l might use 'em. More likely they'll leave the animals in the livery and go it on snowshoes. That rain an' sleet'l pack the snow down, makin' it harder, an' easier to walk."

Just as Anthony said, many were now returning with snow shoes in hand. A couple of teams had been fitted with leggings because we would be in need of wagons. The rest were retired to the livery in light of probable injury. The wagons to be pulled were abandoned. It seemed as though one setback followed another.

Sheriff McKenzie, who had more or less been expected to take the leading role, assumed the final voice of the search party. He brought what remained of the volunteers to order inside the trading post. I was standing just inside the front door with Luke at my side, and listening intently to the men both inside and out presently discussing the odds of the girls being able to survive. I was praying for the sleet to let up, when someone in the street hollered.

"Thar's a wagin' a comin'!"

"A wagon or coach?"

"Someone's coming."

"It's big, big team. Six horses."

"It's a big team, six horses!"

"Six horses, it's gotta be them!"

The news raced along the street to be repeated by those standing outside on the porch. The strangers were yet too far off to identify, and so talk was mostly rumor and speculation.

But emotions were running high, and once overheard by the volunteers inside the store, a rush for the front door was underway. They pushed their way onto the porch, and in turn drove those standing under the overhang onto the street. Caught up in the excitement, a dozen or so volunteers dismissed the freezing rain to rush into the street and greet the approaching vehicle. They ran off into the distance, their oil cloths flapping in their wake.

My heart raced. I prayed it was Claus and the girls being returned to me safe and sound.

"Sure 'nough. It's a big team, but it ain't the coach," said an observer. "She's round topped with canvas. Coach is square topped with driver up high. Coach had four large lanterns."

"Ain't got no lanterns lit," said another.

Those in the know agreed. The onlookers went quiet. My hopes plummeted as the men moved back off the street. They glanced my way, some with expressions of sympathy as they again sought shelter under the overhang. Everyone was presently distracted from the business of rescue and departure by this unexpected arrival. They wished to know what fool or circumstance of desperation would bring about traveling at night in this drenching misery.

ONE-HUNDRED-ELEVEN

When the clouds opened up on Ernie, he was taken no less by surprise than were the folks in Northpole. He should have climbed back into the wagon and drove the team from under the protection of the canvas, but he was already under his oilcloth, and the town laid spread out before him only a stone's throw away. He was soaked and mostly too cold to move off his seat for what little road remained. One could get mighty miserable in a short distance.

Ernie watched through the downpour of ice and rain as the crowd of volunteers came running into view. It wasn't odd they should be collected under the shelter of the covered porch, even a dog had that much sense, he thought. Question was, why were folks pouring into the street. Why were so many running in his direction? He would have been a might bit surprised to know something was in the road behind him...in this mess? Hardly... not in the middle of the night. Truthfully, he didn't much care, for he was mostly grateful just to reach Northpole, a welcome sight for frost-burned cheeks, frozen hands and a soaked butt. He was barely hanging on, in all honesty driven as much by dreams of a hot bath, as the children's salvation. The dream dissipated.

"Emma, looks t' be somethin's goin' on."

Ernie spoke over his shoulder and into the wagon where Emma was sitting with the children. She pulled back the curtain and peeked outside. The cold air slipped in, but she and the children were huddled close for warmth and unbothered beneath blankets that covered them. Unlike Ernie, they had escaped the drenching sleet, but for the protection of newer canvas drawn secure over the wagon hoops. It had leaked little, but more important stood the test of buffeting winds that tried to shred it.

"My word, Ernie, you are a mess. You are soaked. You'll catch your death of cold sitting out there."

"It's only fer a few minutes more, Emma."

Emma looked past the team and now observed all that Ernie was witnessing.

"What's going on? Is it safe?"

"Oh, they ain't goin' t' be a welcomin' party in this weather, no-sireee. But Northpole is a right civ'lized place. Good people. I don' 'xpect no trouble."

501

Ernie drove the team into the midst of the crowd. He halted the team alongside the porch. The children were climbing over Emma, pulling the curtain farther back for a look outside. Their faces were full of curiosity and their chattering mingled with the talk of the crowd. He raised his head to meet the stares of amazement lined up beneath the overhang.

"Eve'nun, gents."

"Eve'nun stranger." Sheriff McKenzie stepped forward. "You must be dern hard pressed t' be git'n ahead. No un else'd be travelin' this hour in this slop. Lordy, an' with a parcel of kids to boot. Don't get me wrong, sir. It's always good t' see a new fam'ly 'riving, but ya sure pick fine weather. Anything, we can do t'help ya by?"

"Much obliged, Sheriff. But I'm jus' passin' thru, takin' the lady an' kids up t' Mother Gail's fer a place t' winter. I gotta say it feels a might good t' be in town. Ain't at all pleasant on the road. No-sireee, nasty bit out there."

A murmur raced through the crowd upon the porch. It raced outward from the wagon through those standing in the street. The reaction caught Ernie off guard. He looked about with some surprise. The crowd went silent, all awaiting his next word. Sheriff McKenzie spoke again.

"What's yer name, stranger?"

Ernie was now unsettled. He studied the faces that seemed to be sizing him up. He wondered if Mother Gail had given up a life with orphans for life with outlaws.

"Uhhh…well…I'd be Ernie Kibbin, an' this'n here'd be Emma Gardner. Like I said, the kids are all orphans off'n a train out from Indy-pendence. Pulled in t' South Pass Junction a couple o' weeks back, but too late in th' year. Got snowbound an' a lotta of 'em died...most of 'em t' be precise. I was lookin' t' reach Mother Gail's in hopes o' findin' 'em some care."

Ernie noticed how the crowd swelled with whispers and side talk every time he mentioned Mother Gail's place. He thought of Dakota's and Raven's well-being and was growing anxious. He sensed the change in his heart. It was beating with concern. He waited on the sheriff.

"Pleased t' meet ya ma'am, you too, Ernie. Name's Carny McKenzie. Reason for my being interested in your business, is we got us a situation. Man named Claussen, old fella, well known in these parts, bout owns half the town if ya must know the truth of it. Anyhows, he's a good sort an' all, but went bounding off t' deliver a load of gifts t' Mother Gail's orphanage an' keep an eye out for a couple a young uns wanderin' up the trail in the weather. They were headin' up to Mother Gail's." The sheriff then confided in a lowered voice. "We're fearin' they may be lost in the storm, even feared dead.

"Trouble is, Mother Gail's gotta a new place built for herself an' no one knows exactly where it is, ceptin' it's up in Powder Pan Canyon. I'm assumin' ya can see the 'portance of knowin' anything bout Mother Gail's whereabouts. If you'd be knowin' something, it'd sure mean a lot t' us folks if you could take a party in tow an' lead us up the canyon, that is if yer up to it. That is if ya know it yourself."

"Hell, I know it fer certain, Sheriff. Yes-sireee, I do, I built it... built it with my own hands."

The crowd let out a chorus of hoops and hollers and Sheriff McKenzie barked out his order.

"Boaz! Some o' ya git with Sammy an' fetch a fresh team for this man. Git them legs wrapped up good an' we'll head out at once! Luke! Can ya fetch some hot coffee for the man an' his lot?"

"Yes, sir!"

The crowd exploded into action. They splashed through the slush-filled street and unhitched Emma's team. Others came around with a fresh team from the livery and wrapped the leggins on the horses up high, for the crust of ice was higher on the leg in the deep snow of the canyon.

ONE-HUNDRED-TWELVE

I was very interested in the conversation between the driver of the wagon and Sheriff McKenzie. I wanted to be sure everything possible was being undertaken to bring Claus and the girls safely back home. But I was also impatient to learn everything possible about Mother Gail, the girls, and the orphans in her care.

I made a quick run into the boarding house and pulled a stew pot off the hearth. I placed it into a basket, and then raced into the kitchen for spoons and bowls. Lastly, in all haste, I reached for my shawl and headed out the door. I stepped up to the wagon, and addressed the driver.

"Good evening, sir."

"Ma'am."

"I'm Elizabeth Claussen, and it's my man that we're about to go searching for up in Powder Pan. He went looking for a couple of younguns on their way up to Mother Gail's, but he suffers terrible from a failing heart. I worry for him and…. Oh, I beg your pardon. This is none of your concern. Forgive me; I'm certain you must be weary enough having traveled all night in such miserable weather.

"Here, please take this basket. It holds a pot of hot stew. Be careful, the pot's fresh off the hearth and it will burn you something fierce. I brought it out so you might warm yourselves. I would think you all to be freezing. I heard the children from the porch, and I see now by the look in their eyes, they are indeed hungry. Is it true what you said, they are all orphans?"

"Yes, ma'am. This'n here is Emma an' she's been watchin' o'er 'em fer some time. We're fixin' t' take 'em up t' Mother Gail's, give 'em a place t' call home."

"It's true then, you know the whereabouts of Mother Gail's place?"

"Yes, ma'am, I do. Lived there most o' last year."

Ernie turned around to pass the stew and bowls through the canvas opening to an overwhelmed Emma. The children were climbing over her like a litter of pups fighting over a teet. I chuckled at their impatience. I sized up the situation in the wagon and decided to make a proposal.

"Ernie, it is Ernie, is it not?"

"Yes, ma'am."

"Ernie, would you be willing to bring on one more? I would be grateful if I might join in your party. In return, I can offer you fresh baked bread and cheese for the children, extra blankets, or whatever else you might be needing. I am concerned for Mr. Claussen's well-being and am of a mind to join the search party. However, your wagon is certainly more accommodating than riding a horse or walking in the weather. I have also invested a good many years of my youth working with orphanages, and I am most interested to learn more about this Mother Gail. I have heard much good about her, and I believe I can further her cause."

"That there would be a wonderful thing, Miss Elizabeth. She surely could use a helpin' hand. I'll tell ya right now, ma'am, I'd be speakin' honestly t'say Mother Gail is a fine woman in ev'ry way. An' I have no objection t' takin' ya ceptin' it's Emma here's wagon. Ya'd be havin' t' ask her, not me."

"Oh, for the love of God, you needn't be asking anything," said Emma. "Just the thought of conversing with a woman who knows her way around orphans…. I mean to say, here you have arrived with a hot dinner before we even know your name. Please, climb in, I insist, no…I beg; I beg you join us. We have plenty of room under these blankets."

Emma laughed from behind the dripping, ice covered canvas. She waved her hands with impatient encouragement, beckoning me to climb aboard.

"Thank you, Emma. I am truly grateful."

"Go on then, git yer stuff. We'll wait," Ernie prompted.

"I thank you indeed, I'll be right back."

I turned about and hurried into the store to grab my winter wear. I climbed into my boots, and on my way out, I swiped a basket of bread, a block of cheese, and a jar of jam. I stepped into the store and reached for a dry overcoat to give Ernie. I returned to the wagon. Ernie stepped down to offer me a hand. My only thought was how uncomfortable it must have been for him to move when he was cold and soaked to the bone.

"Here."

I handed him the dry coat and then pulled back. I could see him shivering as he stood waiting under the oilcloth.

"No, no. This will never do. Come with me now—quickly. Quickly! I will fit you out in dry clothes at once and we will be on our way. They have yet to hitch up the team."

"Mother, what are you up to? Where are you going?"

506

"Never you mind, Luke. This man has been all day traveling and is half frozen. He readily offers us his service, and we can't return the courtesy with a dry pair of trousers? It won't take but a moment to fit him out. I don't wish to have him die of cold on me as well. You can wait. The team has yet to be hitched. You tell Carny McKenzie he can wait too."

"Yes, Mother." Luke spun his horse around. "Hold up, Sheriff."

"Oh, ma'am. You are an angel fer certain. Yes-sireee."

"Emma, if any of them children are needing to relieve themselves, the outhouses are back behind the store. There's paper in each."

I led Ernie across the porch, and encouraged him to follow me into the store.

"Find your size in that bin of clothes. Go on, hurry up. You can change over there in Christopher's office."

"Yes, ma'am. Ya might be wantin' t' take an armful o' blankets with ya. It's lookin' t' be mighty damp this night."

"Of course."

In a matter of minutes, I had him in dry clothes head to foot. I threw a fresh oilcloth over his shoulders and we were back outside at the wagon with extra blankets. Emma and the children were waiting inside. They wasted no time freezing in the outhouses, and returned in haste to the warmth of the wagon and blankets. Ernie helped me ascend the slippery step and climb inside. Once I was safely seated, he situated himself back on the bench. As I snuggled up beneath the blankets next to Emma and the kids, Ernie released the brake.

"Are ya ready, Sheriff?"

"Ready as ever, Mr. Kibben."

"Let's git 'em up. H'ya! Git up there! H'ya. Move outta the way, kids, watch it, watch it. H'ya. H'ya."

Ernie snapped the reins, turned the team about, and drove us all south back through town and toward the trail that headed westward up into Powder Pan. There simply was no trail that I could see, but for Ernie it was as obvious as need be. He knew the canyon like the back of his hand and kept us on course. The party following behind the wagon was most relieved to hear that Mother Gail's new place was much closer to town. They were being sorely tested by the drifted snow below and sleet above.

Emma was a woman of means, and so elected to pay for the extra security of a six-horse team. It was larger than necessary for her sized wagon even when fully loaded. Her team of six was replaced at the trading post, the number of horses never being questioned. I looked around and felt ashamed at discovering this fresh six-horse team was drawing a nearly empty wagon. It was a morbidly bleak vision. Emma noticed my eyes wandering about the interior of her wagon, and correctly assumed my misgivings.

"It's not as bad as it looks. Ernie talked me into storing my belongings in South Pass. He said the added burden on the horses in such foul weather and deep snow was too much of a risk to take with children in my care. I can't say we wouldn't have made it, but I can say that we did—all safe and sound."

The foresight was a blessing. Not only did Ernie transport Emma up to Northpole as promised, but the now fresh team was easily able to hold its own as it dragged the lot of us up the canyon trail through axle deep snow. If the six-horse team hadn't trampled down the drifts, the wagon would have been light enough to float across the snow all the way up the canyon.

Ernie kept the lead, with Sheriff McKenzie, Luke, and a few others on horseback riding directly behind, taking advantage of the trampled snow. After Luke and the sheriff, there was a second wagon following our tracks. It had been hitched up at the livery the moment snowfall had eased. It was presently filled with stores of food and drink, and a rambunctious lot of kids who should have long ago been in bed, but whose folks were part of the search party.

The wagon's unspoken purpose was to return the dead—a grim thought. Hopefully, it would only be used to haul the same children back to town while slumbering. A few of the search party were on horseback, but the majority of folks in our party were on foot. In time, it became evident that most of the conversation and carrying on was amongst children and not adults. One of the older boys looked up at Emma.

"Can we go outside with the rest of the kids?"

"Yeah, can we?" said a second lad about the same age.

"I should say not," said Emma.

"Why not?"

A chorus of complaints rose from the group. The first boy scampered out from under the blankets. He untied the back curtain and poked his head out the back of the wagon.

"George! Close that flap. We're trying to keep what little heat we have. What's the matter with your head?"

"Miss Gardner, there's kids everywhere. I never seen so many. Why can't we go outside?"

"Because I said so. Soon enough we will be at Mother Gail's, and then you can horse around outside all you wish, but not until then."

George's observation did not escape me. I left Emma's side to send George back, but before tying off the flap, I also took a look outside. The field, the woods, the trail of our wagons, were dotted with children. In a glance, I guessed seventy or eighty at least. I retreated back from the curtain and tied it off securely.

Chills moved up and down my frame, but not from the cold I was shutting out. My throat felt dry, but for the first time, I was not afraid. I was filled with a sense of sad understanding—feelings that possibly this growing procession of children were here to see I was spiritually prepared.

A fresh blow broke over the high peaks, and barreled down through the canyon. The temperature dropped like a blacksmith's hammer. The brutal cold dampened the high spirits, the conversations, and the excitement that had been heard floating in the air. That space was now filled only with frozen clouds of breath and numbing pain. It caused the inside of one's nose to stick closed when pinched.

Complaints of cold hands and feet echoed in all directions. Warnings were given to only breathe from behind scarves or risk freezing a lung. Everything heretofore wet was now frozen solid as rock. Everything underfoot was now brittle, and cracked in complaint. Ernie was worried about the ice, and complained about being unable to see the leggings on his leaders. I was worried about a hundred children walking alongside us many without the benefit of blankets to warm them. Maybe that was intentional on their part, for I soon heard a boy call out.

"Sir! Sir!"

"Yeah," replied Ernie.

"The cold is gettin' the best o' these few. Would ya give thought t' lettin' 'em have a spell in the wagon to warm their hands an' feet?"

Ernie didn't have time to answer the child.

"Ernie, can the team take on the extra passengers?"

"Miss Gardner, we can prob'ly board as many as ya like."

"Wonderful. Let them come in and warm themselves."

We stopped the wagon long enough to take on seven children of about seven or eight years in age. It was difficult to assess the ages of the undernourished. They were small and thin by nature. The unfortunates were soaked and shivering badly from the unnatural cold. The children stood on the bench seat next to Ernie, and removed their coats to shake them out and kick the snow off their boots, trousers, or leggings. They were then hustled inside and pulled under the blankets where they remained packed together hidden from view and shivering away their chills. Their coats were turned into mats or blankets.

The canvas held tight across the hoops overhead. It was also drawn up tight to the wagon sides. Even so, we stuffed the smallest gaps with cloth, and every attempt was made to keep heat from escaping. There was an element of comfort to be had for all but poor Ernie seated on the bench. Inside, the canvas glowed from the lanterns that also produced a small measure of heat. The canvas glowed from the warmth and chatter of children whose movements were amplified by distorted silhouettes parading across its curved surface.

Ernie halted the wagon three more times. He went forward to inspect the leggings, and also to take on board an additional eight children that he deemed to be the youngest and most suffering. At that point we were twenty-two children and three adults. Ernie preferred not to tax the horses further, but knew the distance to Mother Gail's was within reason for the added burden. The older children who had clamored to go outside were set free to ease the load. The additional passengers did much to increase the warmth inside the wagon.

In the meantime, the stew pot had been essentially licked clean, so I uncovered the basket of bread and began slicing it along with the block of cheese for our newcomers. Emma coated each slice sparingly with huckleberry jam. We goaded Ernie into taking another blanket and eating as much as he could stomach to keep him warm. The children who had previously eaten stew followed our example and gave up their treats for the benefit of those new passengers who looked to be starved and worse for wear.

I passed out the smaller portions to our new guests, making every attempt to distribute the food evenly and fairly. Each child that held out a wanton hand stared at me with eyes that spoke to me of more than hunger. In spite of their distressed state, I was convinced they were more concerned about my well-being than the reverse. I felt the goose flesh begin to creep across the back of my neck. I turned to Emma in order to break the spell.

Emma was a wonderful conversationalist, and I questioned her at once on a variety of personal matters to distract me from my illusions. As she spoke, I glanced repeatedly across the blankets. The entire troupe of newcomers was sitting quietly, peacefully, watching me with faint contented smiles. Was I losing my mind? Of course not, why shouldn't they smile? I had just fed them and they were warm. Nonetheless, I elected to keep my focus on Emma.

"So tell me about your trip along the Platte, Emma. I remember that country from years back, when Claus first brought me out to the Rocky Mountains. We called them the Stony Mountains or Shining Mountains in those days."

My intent was to continue a good conversation, but it was poorly thought out. In my attempt to avoid the attention of the children, I completely forgot about the tragic events Emma endured on the trail. Fortunately, she was not put off by my blunder, accepted my apology, and gave good account of the trip... misfortunes included. I listened as she described in whispers the scenes of horror when Cholera swept through their party.

She described the fights that erupted because of fears; how starvation was setting in, how bewildered were the orphaned children, and about how they were dealt the final blow by an icy blast of winter weather. It played a part in killing two children on the day before arriving at South Pass Junction. The latter part of the conversation was made cryptic for the sake of those children in our company for whom she had cared, all related to the dead. I applauded Emma for her bravery and compassion.

ONE HUNDRED-THIRTEEN

The farther up the canyon we traveled, the quieter we became. Conversations dropped to a minimum, for everyone now feared the worst. The focus of the search party was one of listening. After every fifteen or so minutes of progress up the trail, we would stop and wait while someone fired off a round or two. The entire troupe would remain dead still, not so much as a whisper to break the silence. We listened to the report echo back and forth, back and forth, up between the walls of the canyon. Everyone prayed to hear a plea for help, or better, an acknowledging echo back down through the stillness of night.

Snow seldom worked its way through to the skin, and so cold and dry was always preferable to warm and wet. The hard blow that had driven showers of snow, ice, and rain to torment us earlier in the evening had thankfully blown itself down through the canyon and out onto the plains. The wailing of wind was lost in the distance, the storm having left us far behind.

Now, it was the cracking of ice underfoot, the repetitious squeaks of wagon wheels, and the endless chatter of children that drifted through the stilled air. The countryside seemed to be asleep, exhausted after having put up with the Mistress of Winter and her tantrums.

"May I ask for what reason your man would choose to risk his life in this wickedly wild and haunting place?"

I began to give my account of the past day's events.

"Yesterday was the first time I recall ever seeing orphans from Mother Gail's visit the store. They came as a group, and I suspected they were all orphans; they had that look about them. I had spent so many years working in Boston with orphans that I never questioned my instinct. I just knew. Well, as it happened, early this afternoon, two of the girls returned to ask if they could have some fancy paper to make Christmas gifts. I was delighted to help the poor creatures out, and I told them to go about and find what they may.

"I must ask you to understand two things before I proceed further with my story. One, during those last weeks before the holy days, the store is a rat race of activity, mayhem. And two, Claus is the finest man I have ever known, but as of late, he suffers intolerably from a disagreeable heart. It worries me sick. But it makes him irritable, easily agitated, and at times wholly out of character. You must accept what I say, as I have known him the whole of my life.

"That being said, I watched as the girls made their way to his office. At the time, I had no idea what business they pursued with Christopher, but I could see at once that he felt pestered by their presence. They distracted him from his bookwork. I quickly realized, they were drawn to the decorative wrappings and bows from his trash bin. Unfortunately, Christopher did not, and not wishing to be further bothered, he reached for the office door in order to fling it shut."

What took place only hours earlier remained fresh in my mind, and the vision still served to make me ill. I dropped my head into my hand and nodded it in ongoing disbelief.

"I must tell you, Emma, continuing from this point is unpleasant and most difficult for me. I can only assume you will be compelled to think the worst of this wonderful man. Let me say straight out, the door swung to shut, but did not. To Christopher's misfortune, the younger of the two girls didn't see the door coming her way, only to have it catch her in the face. It was a horrible mess, a horrible bloody mess.

"I was beside myself. I agonized, having seen the mishap first hand. I was so upset; I lost any sense of composure and gave Claus a very unkind piece of my mind. The girls ran out of the store in a panic. I had hoped to chase them down, bring them back so I might tend to the injury, but as you can imagine they were terrified and fled at a run. By the time I worked though the crowd, they were long gone. They wanted me to believe they were in party with others, but I am now certain they were not. They headed back up into the canyon alone. Clearly, they were too frightened to seek help.

"Christopher was appalled by his action, truly repentant. He swore before me that he would make up for his misdeed, by offering them his apologies and gifts galore. I believed him for I know this is his way. When he said he would see to it personally that they and the other children, all of whom we assumed to be orphans, would have a Christmas they would never forget, I never doubted his word. He instructed me to pack his private coach full to the roof with gifts and supplies, and off he went. Our son Luke and I both firmly objected to his going out alone in the storm, but he insisted on going by himself. He felt it was he, and he alone, who should go to make amends for it was he, and he alone, who caused the injury.

"I must beg you understand that there is no excuse for his action, this by his own confession. Yet, it might never have come to pass had the younger child not been blind—."

"Blind?"

515

Ernie's questioning voice came rumbling through the canvas drape. He stopped the horses and swept back the curtain. He eyes bore clean through me.

"Blind? Did...did ja say the child was blind? ...From Mother Gail's? My God, woman! Was she a wee thing o' four or five? Did she have black hair an' eyes? Oh, pray don't be sayin' it's my Raven. Please, Miss Elizabeth, say it ain't my Raven that's lost out here."

I was absolutely mortified. Could he know this girl? Was she kin? Oh my word, what must he think of Claus and myself? He would never understand. I looked at his face. It was filled with despair. I was struck dumb. I was made numb by the sound of his pleas.

"Please, tell me ma'am. Was the young girl's name, Raven? Aw hell, it's her an' 'er sister that are missin' out here ain't it. Gosh darn, I've got t' find 'em kids. I can't let 'em down. I promised 'em. I promised 'em things 'ud work out."

He dropped his head into his hands, and by this time the search party, now gathered around the wagon could hear all he was saying as he bemoaned the unwelcome news.

"Dear Lord, I'd be on my knees if I 'ad the time. Fergive me, but I need yer help, Lord. I ain't worth a hill a beans as a person, but them girls been raised proper by their mama t' know right an' wrong an' t' be God fearin'. Thems two are pure in heart an' 'ave suffered more'n any young uns rightfully deserve. Take everything I got Lord, take it all, but don' take my girls. I'm beggin' Lord, I'm beggin' please show me the way t' my girls."

He shook his head and unclasped hands of prayer to wipe his eyes. I lost the courage to say anything. I sat silent, feeling the weight of the world upon me in the confines of the wagon. No one spoke. Emma placed her hand on my shoulder. I looked her way fully guilt ridden. I hoped she understood we were better people than it appeared. She raised her fingers to her lips to quiet me. She gave me a nod of reassurance and whispered.

"Things will work themselves out for the better. It'll be fine, you'll see."

ONE HUNDRED-FOURTEEN

Gail placed her fingers against the frosty pane of glazing that Ernie had mounted into the cabin wall. It was a wonderful piece. The light it allowed into the cabin was uplifting, cheery, during the short and often overcast days of winter. The light always made her think of him.

Ernie had promised to return to them at Christmas, and that had made the past year one of Gail's longest and loneliest. All summer she had collected fruits and berries, a portion that she dried and set aside for his return. She had spent the last week baking breads and pastries. This morning she awoke early to feed the children, but also to fill the cabin with the smell of freshly baked pies. She had wanted his arrival to be warm and welcoming. Waiting for a sign of Ernie was unbearable for the children, but no more so than for Gail.

Up until this afternoon, Gail would have gladly dropped to her knees and kissed his snow-covered boots had he come walking through the door. Up until this afternoon, she had spent a year savoring memories of their many walks and talks, the picnics they shared with the children while the cabin took shape. She dared to think the unthinkable…the possibility that someone might hope to care for her. Up until this afternoon, she had a song in her heart, a dance in her step.

Gail had everything in the world for which to look forward up until this afternoon. It was then that she discovered Dakota and Raven's absence. It was then that hours passed, each longer and more fearful than the previous, until she resigned herself to the horror of possibilities and the crush of her failing. It was then that she suffered to think of Ernie's despair, his devastation, should harm have come to his beloved girls. The children were gone as were her dreams, gone in an instant. What could she possibly say, what excuse could there be? How could he know it was but a moment's neglect in a year full of heartfelt care?

It was but an innocent distraction; the tug of a longing heart, feelings she could never be forward enough to admit, feelings she never learned how to convey. Feelings mattered little now. That was an embarrassment she no longer feared to face. It could be dismissed. If Ernie walked through that door before the girls were found, her world would be emptied. It would have been so much easier had she never met him. But she had, and she made but one promise, one promise in trade for everything good...one obligation to keep safe and dear his two girls. Up until this afternoon she had done all of that and more.

The hour was near midnight. Ernie's failure to arrive was as much a blessing as a curse. She was tortured, as would be Ernie. He most certainly would blame her. The guilt was overwhelming, but it had to be put aside. This was no longer about her, but about the girls. The welfare of the girls was now all that mattered.

"Oh, God, Ernie. The girls are gone. I am so sorry. You were supposed to be here. Where are you? I need you, Ernie. Where are you?"

Gail whispered at a semblance of her reflection. She scratched at the glass, running her fingernail quickly back and forth across the pane as she had done numerous times before during the evening. The cold white dust flaked away and fell to the floor. She leaned in close to the window, squinting hard, resigning herself to the

518

futility. In spite of the brilliant light of the moon, the window was caked with ice on the outside, making it impossible to discern anything other than wavy images of light or dark.

Four times she had placed the younger children under the care of the older while she went out to search the countryside. Four times she had returned with nothing more than despair. There was no sign of the girls to be found within a mile radius of the cabin or along the trail. Each time out the storm proved more dangerous, and so she ended her efforts. She feared for her safety, losing her way back in the white out.

Each time Gail returned from the forest, the orphans stood shoulder to shoulder at the door. They understood the dangers of storms, and were relieved to see her return. They loved her dearly. They had warm tea waiting, and offered their assistance and words of encouragement. They could plainly see how she had been reduced to a bundle of nerves, unraveled, unable to eat, unable to sit still. They watched as she paced with worry. They watched with concern each time she warmed her hands over the stove and readied herself to go out again into the weather. She was desperate, and that desperation flowed through the hearts and souls of all the children in the cabin. They milled about quietly and out of character.

Gail's thoughts churned while she was out scouring the nearby forest. She sorted her recollections of morning and the activities undertaken. She attempted to put times and order to every instance of her noting the girls' whereabouts. She now could see flashes, images of the girls' somber disposition. Mother Gail couldn't recall anything having occurred that might explain their poor attitude, but concluded it most likely had something to do with their expecting Uncle Kib.

She questioned if Dakota would attempt a trip to Northpole. The problem was in knowing Dakota. It was hard to accept the girl might act so foolishly as to risk an hours' long trip to town, especially with Raven in tow. Gail believed that Dakota was not so irresponsible as to take on the dangers of returning after dark in a blizzard. Gail felt this especially true, considering the many times she listened to Dakota tell the fearful tale of wolves at her Uncle Kib's woodpile. It was the favorite story of the older orphans.

Gail's only ray of hope was in believing that Dakota had indeed set out for Northpole and after being confronted by the storm elected to seek shelter in town. It was a hope that Gail clung onto with every breath of her prayers. The alternative was to find them frozen to death somewhere along the canyon trail. There was no way to know one way or the other without searching the canyon at length from cabin to town. That had been impossible during the blizzard, but now the world was quiet and the sky clear. It was cold, but as she knew, cold was always better than wet, and in both cases time was of the essence.

Gail would need the help of the older children. Not only for the additional eyes, but they would be safer in the woods as a large group. Unfortunately, she would need the help of the older children, and they couldn't join her without leaving the young ones behind to fend for themselves. That wasn't about to happen. One tragedy this day was plenty. Gail would need to take them all. She could only hope a kind heart in Northpole might offer them a place to rest should they make it that far. Maybe she could find a place for the children to bed down in the livery or at the blacksmith where it was warm. Maybe the woman in the trading post would offer her assistance.

Gail left the heat of the woodstove to step outside into the glow of the lanterns hanging on the porch. For the hundredth time she yelled for Dakota. In fact, it was more an act to relieve her stress, for there was no more voice to be used for hollering. She had been hollering since after noon and was long since hoarse. She adjusted the lantern wicks for brightness, and was about to step back in from the cold when unexpectedly there came the report of a gun.

The echo bounced off the cliffs to be returned to her again and again. The gunshot was soon followed by a second and a third. She stood in silence on the porch waiting for whatever else might follow, but there was nothing.

It was a very strange occurrence indeed. She wondered if there could be a connection to the girls. In a land of trappers and panners, gunfire was rare, especially in the dark, especially in the middle of the night. ...Unless there were wolves stalking about. That thought stiffened her. It twisted her insides with anxiety until there seemed no alternative, but to leave at once and search the length of the trail

Gail raised her eyes to view the heavens. She was encouraged to see clear skies overhead and the hard blue light of a winter moon as it lit up the path down through the canyon. Here was the change of weather she desperately needed. Even though somewhat rested, warmed, and in a change of dry clothes, Gail was being driven back inside. The temperature had dropped significantly since late evening when clouds kept the earth warm. Gail didn't object. It meant the sleet had frozen and little feet would stay dry. The sky showed no sign of rain, and so Gail was determined to head out. As a group, they would search the trail. They might even meet Ernie if he kept his promise to return by Christmas.

"Gather around children. Come, come. I have things to say."

The children pressed in close around her. They remained remarkably quiet.

"I don't have to explain to you my worry for Dakota and Raven. You know I have been out most of the day searching, and I am distressed to have returned each time empty handed. It is possible the girls went to Northpole and the storm kept them in town, but I fear they would have made every effort to return and see their Uncle Kib, even risking the gale. I am most concerned they chose to return home, and for whatever reason didn't make it back to us.

"I want everybody to get dressed to go to town—."

"Now?" asked one.

"You want us to go to town now?" asked another.

"Will we make it, Mother Gail?" asked a young girl.

"Yes, we must leave now. And yes, we can make it, but you will need to dress very warm. Jeremiah, as soon as you are dressed, I want you to hitch the mule up to the cart. Gather up the oilcloths in case the sleet returns."

"Yes, Mother."

"What if Uncle Kib comes and we're not here?"

"Uncle Kib can only come by way of the trail, and we shall be on it. He can't pass us by without notice. That would be impossible. But you must give thought to how Mister Kibben will feel should he arrive to find Dakota and Raven are nowhere to be found."

A murmur of concern moved through the children. Gail dreaded to consider the outcome of such a meeting. She kept searching for the right words to soften the bad news. She suffered to think how he would react. She found herself praying they were safe and sound at the boardinghouse, maybe even in Ernie's company. It was late. Maybe he determined it prudent to remain in Northpole for the night and wait out the blizzard with the girls.

Gail and her wards poured out the door and flattened the drifts that had rolled up onto the porch. In places, the snow stood higher on the porch than half the kids that chose to wade through it. Gail was filled with trepidation, torn between leaving the younger children alone in the cabin or keeping them close by her side while out in the cold searching the woods. At least the children were in high spirits believing they had a mission to accomplish. They were excited and anxious to get on with it.

The youngest of the lot were placed on the cart and wrapped in blankets. The remainder battled drifts and tugged playfully at Gail, pulling her along behind them much as the mule was pulling her youngest. The children called out to Dakota and Raven. There was no lack of energy as they all competed to yell the loudest. It was a good thing. Their energy kept them warm.

ONE HUNDRED-FIFTEEN

Ernie raised his head. He looked out across the canyon. I watched as all the vigor and determination of the man drained. He was being emptied before my eyes. Having heard the words spoken between Ernie and myself, having heard his prayer, his plea of desperation, Sheriff McKenzie, Luke, and a few other associates stood back respectfully unvoiced. It was an unbearable silence for me. Thankfully, he spoke up, and the words eased the rash of guilt that felt baked onto my face.

"All I can do is hope. That Dakota…. She is a smart one, yes-sireee. Fought off the wolves, single handed, she did. An' she saved both herself an' that little Raven t' boot. Bloodiest mess I ever did see, yes-sireee, but there she stood in the middle of it, alive an' well as a girl could be…." Ernie's chest heaved. "…Talkin' like nothin' ever 'appened." Tellin' me her momma an' poppa were dead…."

Ernie bit his lip hard. He took a deep breath to settle himself. He raised his hands to snap the reins, and head up the team when Willie Parker yelled out with irritation for some talkers nearby to shut-up.

"Quiet! Quiet! I heard bells. I'm certain of it. I know I heard bells."

523

"Bells! Aw, now what the hell's he talkin' about?" someone scoffed.

"Yeah, it's probably more like bats! Bats in the belfry!" another whispered back. "Ha ha! That Parker is as—."

"No, it's true. We heard them as well," said others standing ahead of us.

"Bells? I perked up at once. I looked at Emma. I was too afraid to hope.

"The horses are dressed in their holy day blankets! They are covered with bells, Emma, thousands of bells!"

Emma sighed aloud at the revelation just as a third voice outside was cut off abruptly by another rush of the light tinkling sensations, delicate traces of near indiscernible resonance moving unseen through the trees.

"Hush! Shush! Quiet!"

All at once a number of folks exclaimed in unison.

"Bells!"

"Bells!"

"It came from up ahead!"

"Yeah, we heard them. They're up that a-way!"

"Them's were the bells we heard on the team hitched to the coach," someone added.

Sheriff McKenzie spoke up with his gruff voice.

"Kay, boaz! Listen up! Could be stray animals got loose. Don't get hoopin and hollerin' too loud jus' yet. It's cold, an' sound travels a long way in a canyon, can fool ya, could be a mile or more off. Stick by the trail an' keep yer eyes an' ears open. Let's go."

Some of the search party moved forward with Sheriff McKenzie and Luke as they rode past in a renewed state of excitement, like hounds on the scent. They passed our wagon, and we watched them ride their struggling horses through the undisturbed snow. Occasionally, the bells could be heard, but they were very faint.

The moon was bright, but we were unable to see anything from within the wood. Nobody cared to believe the bells belonged to stray animals. Besides, this wasn't the clang of cowbells, but the rush of many bells, a sound heard by some for the first time only hours before when Claus passed through the streets of Northpole. I feared that daring to hope or even thinking of the girls and Claus would mean losing them forever. Yet, I knew at once without question folks were hearing the holy day bells that adorned the horse blankets.

The storm's passing had given way to a brilliant pock-faced moon playing hide-and-seek about the last dawdling clouds to pass us by. Intermittently, the nightlight illuminated the forests that flanked us. It splashed its brilliance around, badgering intense black shadows that poked along slowly across the snow-covered distances. It ushered them out of the canyon with vivid definition in the clear, crisp atmosphere of night.

The murky shadows haunting us along the wooded path parted ways as we broke out of the treeline that bordered an enormous undulating expanse. Above the expanse, clouds vanished, leaving boundaries that separated heaven from earth blurred and undefined. The universe collapsed upon us. It descended at once to touch the mountain tops, to touch us with breathtaking displays of constellations, and nebulae. The speckled light of Milky Way galaxies seemed to rush headlong through the canyon to stream past our crawling lot.

Ernie called the children at once from the warmth of their blankets to look outside. He directed their attention to an intensely iridescent rainbow of ice that ringed the moon. It might well have been cast downward to be seen, to be soaked up, collected in a billion prisms of ice that frosted the snow-covered fields. The fields were on fire, the clearings shimmering with reflections that sparkled and shifted hue with each step of our passing.

Just above our reach, trees strained to support branches hanging low, burdened with the weight of thick, clear coatings of ice. It was as if they had waited our arrival, holding steadfast a moment longer, not daring to move lest they shatter the fleeting moment of glittering splendor. Millions of diamond-like flashes raced along their lengths arcing from tree to tree through the forest that bordered the expanse.

Between the cold bluish light of the moon and the warm orange glow of torches and lanterns, the entire spectrum of color was to be seen within the innumerable sparks, glints and glitters that flittered about us like fairy dust. We were engulfed by the glow of a mosaic of mirrored light.

Conversation would have been sacrilegious as we entered into this realm of spellbinding scenery. In this place of magical illusions and fantasy, millions upon millions upon millions of pin point bursts worked on this night to construct the most mystical crystal universe one might ever imagine seen by mortals.

The miraculous paradise swirling about wooed us away from our mission. For those enraptured, it stole away reality. For those lost to the inspirational euphoria, our mission grew suddenly less relevant. So overwhelming was this distraction that misery seemed an impossibility amidst such magnificence. One wished only to remain in place forever as if compelled to do so—*maybe we were.*

My hypnotic trance was lifted only by happenstance. I had been drawn to a visual disturbance far off at the opposite end of the canyon. The distinct flickers of lamplight could be seen moving through woods that descended from the upcountry toward the clearing. A party of some size was approaching us from ahead.

The distraction prompted all in our troupe to resume our march forward, but it was done in silence, heads turned, ears cupped in hopes of capturing the slightest hint of voices in need. Our number, now free of the confines of the path, was spreading out, coming abreast of our wagons. In that flanked fashion, we uniformly scaled a gentle swell of land, and upon breaking over its crest, we came to overlook a most strange and haunting sight.

A heartless drop in temperature was exemplified by a ground cover of creeping, snaking mist that flowed out across the clearing from deep within the woods. It was the result of frigid air settling upon earth kept warm by the presence of an unseen spring. The mist as a whole possessed a glowing quality as the moonlight passed through it from above, only to be reflected back through it from below by the snow. The field was awash in this unnatural illumination.

The milky air slipped along in a slow, circular pattern, pooling within a broad and near negligible depression. In particular, from the center of these rotating mists emanated an eerie glow of light. All eyes were fixed warily upon this ghostly unnatural radiance as we moved forward with apprehension.

In short time, as our distance closed, the silhouette of a mound amidst the glow of lanterns could be seen breaking out above the mists. Each step taken added definition to the apparition until it was possible to discern the backs of horses.

"It's a team of horses, a team of horses," someone hollered out excitedly.

"Yes, a team of six horses to be exact."

"It's a large team to be sure, but...."

…But the team looked to be hitched to a wagon with lanterns, and not Lady Rebecca's coach. The lanterns may have explained the source of eerie light that unsettled so many of us, but what remained was nothing if not entirely baffling.

"That is not Lady Rebecca's coach," I uttered dumbfounded. "Where's the coach?"

We continued forward filled with impatience, but no plausible answers. It was a mystery of no small proportion that left us with only questions, and all of those mouthed in whispers. The folks at the end of the line came forward to join in muted conversation, for there was much curiosity about not only what was before us, but also about the strangers closing in from afar. They had reached the clearing and appeared to share our sense of awe. Quietly, they approached to join in our ranks and investigate this haunting spectacle. It was only as we concluded our approach, covering those last few feet that the brutal truth before us became evident.

I first observed how the moonlight danced off the sharp edges and profiles; how beams snapped across the numerous angles and planes, all shapes and outlines that made up a massive mound of gifts all backlit by the surrounding snow-covered slopes. By the light of open skies, I clearly recognized the assortment of shapes and silhouettes as the same collection that I placed into the coach only hours before. I was stymied for an explanation. But what I next realized stole my very breath.

"Oh my, god! It is Lady Rebecca's coach! Oh my, god…oh my, god…. What on earth…. *What happened here?*"

I was stunned. I shuddered with disbelief. It was as if the entire roof had been blown away. Instinctively, I questioned what explosive article might have been placed inside. Where was Christopher? My eyes were riveted to every detail of the vehicle as we came around to its side. What we all thought to be a wagon, and later a sleigh burdened with unknown wares, proved to be

Lady Rebecca's coach split and splintered, its roof nowhere to be seen. There was no escaping the name REBECCA CLAUSSEN scrolled in shimmering gold across the door. There was no mistaking the impeccable team of Percherons standing tall and draped in bell-studded holy blankets.

My immediate thought was of Claus's well-being. And so, that which I next observed would be burned forever into my memory, and most likely the memories of all in our company. The manifestation before us appeared so surreal, I found myself shivering with goose flesh, too overwhelmed to speak. I could only observe what seemed to be a vision from another dimension, an afterworld, a spiritual place that opened our souls to awareness and immersion into the wonder of the beyond.

As though answering the call to heaven from atop a brilliant red sleigh heaped high with gifts was Claus seated upon the coachman's bench, his huge frame fitted in bright red flannel. He sat there in the stillness of death, wearing his flannel cap and coat, his high black boots, laces undone. He was frozen solid.

From head to toe, he was clad in icy armour that looked to be moving liquid. His left hand yet grasping the reins rested upon his heart, now partially covered by a white storm-sculpted beard. His blue eyes and reddened face were fixed, staring upward across the valley and onward to the heavens. His right arm was outstretched, resting across the bench backboard.

His hand was ungloved, uncurled, opened and fallen away as if pointing off to our side. So much so, I noted how many like myself, were compelled to oblige by looking off in that direction. As if spiritually connected to the forest trees, the flashes of light danced along that ice-encrusted arm to leap from his frozen fingertips and join the thousands of glittering branches that cradled us.

Everything about us was dreamlike, near incomprehensible. Even the extensive damage delivered to Lady Rebecca's coach was for me overwhelming. I felt my heart rupture as I observed the tragic wreck of her wedding gift. The entire crown to this work of art was missing, delicious lines lost, as if to show me in the physical world, what was being lost spiritually. Only I would appreciate the emotions, the memories embedded within the once cherished workmanship. Only I would be witness to the evaporation of history once relevant, but eventually to be forgotten.

What might have warranted such disaster? I began to scrutinize the massive mound of articles. The gifts now appeared as though they had been drowned in a pour of clear sugar icing. To my amazement, the coach showed equally magnificent as an open sleigh. What richness of vermilion yet remained welled up through the ice as if the finish were a foot thick. Lady Rebecca's name stood intact, undisturbed to iridesce in the glow of the surrounding light. As happened time and time again through my life, I felt her presence whenever I found myself lost in the curves of gold calligraphy.

"Are you all right, Elizabeth?" Emma interrupted my thoughts.

"What? Oh...yes, thank you. I am fine. I was just thinking; how can it be possible that a coach so demolished can yet appear so majestic? It must be I am only able to see it through my heart."

I was suddenly overcome by emotion. Emma placed her arm around me. The world about me held steady, stilled...silent. Save for the movements of six snow white Percherons standing in a cloud of their own mist. The wisps curled about their hides as the heat of their bodies dried out the passing sleet. It mingled with frozen breath that erupted from large nostrils to circulate about their space.

These ectoplasmic mists twisted and turned to rise and fall from the dense fog that carpeted the ground. The creamy opaque currents concealed the horses' hooves and skis beneath the sleigh. They made the sleigh appear to float, or about to fly above the clouds and carry Christopher to the heavens. Each time the Percherons stomped, maybe out of their impatience to be off across the skies, a chorus of bells would ring out above the clearing and strike deep into the waiting wood.

"Is that Santa Claus?" asked one young lad aghast.

He spoke aloud what everyone else asked in private. It was enough to raise the hair on every living creature in that field. If ever there was sacred ground, it would feel no less spiritual. If ever I felt that the Lord and all his angels of heaven had descended to be amongst us, it was now. My temples, the back of my neck and arms, all tingled. I shook to relieve myself of the sensation. No one moved a step; no one uttered a sound. All my instincts to rush to Claus, to take him into my arms, to cry for him, seemed to have been tempered by an awareness of something that transcended sorrow or grief.

We simply waited in silence, dumbfounded, transfixed in that circle for what seemed an eternity, lest we desecrate the memory, the passing of Christopher Nicholas Claussen. We waited without consideration, without contemplation; we waited for reasons unknown.

We waited until the spell was broken by a silence that heralded the only acceptable sound, a sound as sweet as a baby's first cry. It was the plea of a young child. It came to us like a message faint as the rush of bells first heard floating across the field to summon us. It would have gone by unheard had we not been held hostage to what may have been a miracle. Had we not been compelled to remain mesmerized at length to ponder the sight of Christopher frozen in death before us, had we not been driven to that state of silence, the plea might well have gone unanswered.

Instead, heads turned in unison. The cry came from the same direction that Claus seemed to be pointing. At first, only heads turned, for everyone was wary and unsure. All souls now questioned the smallest things. Then, as if to jolt us back to our senses, the woman I saw descend from the wooded upcountry, and approach us from opposite the clearing, came catapulting across the drifts of snow making a mad rush in the direction of the child's cry. It was if her seemingly rash movement had awakened us from a deep sleep.

Ernie jumped from his seat, landing on the ground to leap in giant bounds across the field. He thrashed his way through the snow, screaming out Raven's name until he met up with the woman. Together they dropped into the snow digging frantically until they exposed the vermilion roof of Lady Rebecca's coach. The brass rails were now clearly visible as they gleamed in the lamplight of those arriving to assist. Any hint of the roof had been buried completely by drifted snow coated with a thick spread of ice and so perfectly sealed from the weather.

"Oh, God. Oh, God. Please let 'em be safe."

Ernie and Gail shoveled snow away in shared desperation. They reached a pile of clothes and ripped them away from the wooden shelter. An entranceway opened to them. As the fresh air moved into the sunken chamber, a blast of very warm air escaped to surround them. It had the sweet smell of life.

Ernie dropped onto all four and crawled part way inside. Gail could hear his muffled cries of joy. He gently pulled Raven out from the warmth of her den. She sputtered and sobbed. She was drowsy and confused. She wanted her mother. Ernie passed the child over to Mother Gail, who embraced her wholeheartedly. She was crying tears of joy, tears of relief.

"Mother."

I turned to see Luke looking at me. He came to my side with a tortured heart. He didn't have to explain. He had become as close to his father as any son might. Luke adored Christopher and whereas my pain was tempered by history and understanding, Luke's was only the pain of loss.

"I know, Luke. It's difficult. I'll be fine. What about you?"

Luke nodded and then bowed his head. There was a lot of Tsistsista in his make-up, and Tsistsistas only knew bravery. Luke didn't know how to accept this loss. His emotions had been altered by a western culture that was more acclimated to grieving and viewing death as something tragic in life.

"Go walk, Luke. Walk away and wish your father well on his journey. Let him know how much he has taught you. Let him know how his lessons will serve to guide you through life. Tell him how his examples will show you the way to humility and generosity, the ways of a chief. That is the way of your Indian upbringing. Go walk. I am sure he waits for you. Go, I'll be fine. I'll wait as long as need be. I'll ask Ernie to wait until your return."

Luke left my side and wandered off, a lone shadow on the moonlit field. I watched him until I knew he was speaking with his father. I then returned to the crisis at hand. I walked to join those searchers collected about the coach roof. Ernie dropped back down onto his knees and again slid back into the chamber. This time he backed out in haste. He was distraught and demanding.

"I need light! It's Dakota! Light! Light! I need light! I think she's...." His voice was breaking. "I think she's.... She isn't responding!"

Ernie's emotions surfaced briefly before he stormed into action. He hollered across the bystanders who bolted forward to assist.

"Lift the roof! Help me raise this roof off Dakota."

Sheriff McKenzie amongst others stepped forward at once to free the roof from the clutches of winter. All manner of lanterns were produced and held high and low about the floor of the shelter now removed. Ernie held one of the lamps close above Dakota, first passing it over her, and then bringing it near to her face. I saw him retrieve two letters tucked within the wraps covering her breast. The first, he opened to read aloud Christopher's assessment of Dakota's injury and his suggestion how best to move her. The second letter, he pocketed for safekeeping.

They followed Christopher's instructions to the word. The coach top was cleared of snow and Dakota was carefully laid upon it. She was being prepared to be carried to Mother Gail's cabin by hand if at all possible. Those present feared further injury should the broken bone be separated by the jostling of a wagon. The men lined up six to a side and took hold of the brass baggage rails. There were many more waiting in line, eager to take a turn at ferrying her as gently as sympathetic souls could manage. Although she didn't regain consciousness, she would have appreciated the heartfelt consideration given during her move.

Now, that all appeared under control, and my attention was no longer riveted to the issue of Dakota's injuries, I began to assist Emma in getting her orphans back into the wagon. As I counted them by number, I noticed at once that we were back down to the original seven. My eyes made a sweep of the surrounding area and I was astonished to note that there were very few children to be seen anywhere. It seemed incredulous. I looked to Emma.

"Where are all the children?"

"I was about to ask you the same. We took on fifteen and they're nowhere to be found."

"Emma, look across the field. Where are all the children?"

Emma straightened up and scanned the clearing. She studied the woods that surrounded us. She looked back at me and shrugged.

"I presume they have all begun their journey back to town. The excitement is over and it must be uncomfortably cold for their lot."

"Well.... I suppose...."

I knew it was possible, but I also believed it was highly improbable. Of course, believing anything other than Emma's suggestion meant I was back to losing my mind. As I pondered the more realistic possibility of my being delusional, I noted that Ernie and Mother Gail were walking toward us with five children in tow. Ernie held sleeping Raven securely in his embrace.

"Emma, I think it may be a good thing we're back down to seven."

"Emma...Miss Elizabeth...I'd like t' introduce ya t' Mother Gail."

"It's a pleasure to make your acquaintance."

She offered her hand.

"Likewise. I'm Emma."

"Hello, Gail. It's nice to see you again."

I welcomed her.

"Gail, would you join Elizabeth and me in my wagon? We would be delighted to speak with you, and at the same time ferry you and your children back to your cabin. It get's quite comfortable inside."

"Oh, bless you. Thank you for your consideration."

"Okay, where's my seven?" Emma suddenly demanded.

The seven wards stepped forward.

"Go on get up there."

The children did as they were told, struggling to climb back into the wagon.

"All right, who belongs to Mother Gail?"

The five remaining stood awaiting their instructions.

"Go on, get in. I'll take ya back in the wagon. Wrap up in the blankets. There are plenty of 'em t' be used thanks t' Mrs. Claussen."

"Please, climb in, Mother Gail."

Gail passed Raven back to Ernie so she could climb up into the wagon. In doing so, Raven awoke and was at once fussy. We were more concerned with Gail's safety while scaling the ice-covered steps, and so no one paid close mind to Raven.

Finally, the danger passed, Mother Gail reached out to take the child, but Ernie hesitated.

"Raven, why're ya cryin' so, child? Are ya tired an' needin' sleep, zat it?"

"I want my doll."

"Yer doll?"

"I want my doll"

"What doll, honey?"

"I want my doll, Uncle Kib."

"I don' know where yer doll is, sweet'ert."

"It's in the house."

"The house?"

We three understood and looked in the direction where once lay the coach top.

"Oh, Raven…."

Gail sighed, not wishing to climb back down the wagon.

"I'll take her back," said Ernie.

"No! I mean forgive me; that was rude. I was about to say, Mother Gail and Emma should get their children settled. You should look over the team and I am yet free to take Raven back and find her doll."

"Wou' ja like t' go with Miss Elizabeth, honey?"

"Yup."

"All right, then."

Ernie handed Raven over to me.

"Alright then, indeed, let's go have a look."

I walked back to the depression in the field, and sifted about the snow with my boot, but could find no sign of a doll.

"I don't see a doll, Raven."

Raven rubbed her eyes. She was tired and fussy.

"I want my doll. I know it's here."

"Raven, are you certain you had a doll?"

"Yup."

"Honey, I'm sorry but I don't see a doll, maybe someone picked it up."

"I want my doll," she fussed.

"I know, Raven. It should be around here somewhere. We just need to find it. Oh! Looky there."

I bent over to pull the doll out of the snow and shake it clean. It was Dakota's favorite, identical to the one I gave her in the store.

"So, Raven, do you remember who gave you this doll."

"Yup."

"Really? Who was it?" I teased her.

"Santa Claus."

"San—. Ohhhh…."

A chill crackled down through me. I felt as though the Mistress of Winter had reached out from the dark of the wood and took hold of my soul. I looked back only once.

"Come on, Raven."

I took off running for the wagon and the company of others.

* * *

While Ernie, Gail, Sheriff McKenzie, and some of the town's folk rescued the girls, there were others who removed Claus from the bench of Lady Rebecca's coach. He was being carried over to the other wagon—the grim wagon. I removed myself from Emma, Gail, and the orphans to be escorted by Sheriff McKenzie over to where lay Christopher. The mystical experience was now waning, and I felt the looming onset of my crushing reality.

As I was about to climb into the wagon, Ernie approached the sheriff and me.

"Mrs. Claussen…."

Earnie held out his hand. It clasped a piece of paper.

"I found this'n here letter on Dakota's breast. I was told that your name was lettered across it."

I took the paper. I was perplexed.

"Thank you, Ernie."

"That's all right. Ahh...Elizabeth, ahh...I..ahh..."

He couldn't meet my eyes.

"What is it, Ernie?"

"Ahh...this is hard fer me t'say proper. I'm not a man o' words, an' I'm a fearin' it might come out all wrong."

"You have no reason to fear anything from me, Ernie."

"I thank ya, ma'am, yes-sireee. But, I jus' wanted t' say that I'm truly ashamed o' the way I was actin', yellin' an' all. I'm sorry it 'ad t' be you who lost someone in the end. I know, I was carryin' on an' mostly out o' control, but bless me, ma'am, I was so scared fer 'em girls, I can't begin t' tell ya. Joe and Rosaria...I don' know...I jus' don' know what ta say, ma'am. Jus' I'm sorry. I'm sorry."

He shrugged his shoulders and looked up to me for forgiveness.

"It's alright, Ernie. It's fine. Christopher led a full and rich life. I don't know if anything in God's heaven would please him as much as knowing in the end he saved those lives."

My eyes swelled with tears and I dropped my gaze to the letter in my hand.

"Thank you, Elizabeth. I'll leave ya be with yer man."

Ernie walked back to Emma, Gail, and the children.

I began to cry hard as I sat alone with Claus under the canvas of the wagon, and hidden from view. The enormity of my loss was beginning to surround me as the memories of our lives together began to fill my head. This man was the only constant in my life for nearly as far back as I was able to remember. He molded my life and gave me every opportunity to live it to its fullest. Under his care, the whole world was there for me, at my feet. He alone had made my life not only special, but fulfilling. He had given me Luke. I turned up the flame of the lamp.

My dearest, Elizabeth,

I write to you as the wife I never married, the child I never had. I fear this night is my last. My chest has not relented in its complaints. I sweat dreadfully, and feel it freeze upon my brow. My arm pains me severely, and we know these signs well. They bode ill fare. In these past few hours a conscience long buried in complacency and indifference has been awakened. I felt the warmth of love and the moisture of tears shed with emotion.

I am determined not to die in the company of these children. The horror of it would be more than anyone could be expected to bear within the confines of this shelter. I write to you now as they sleep. Should Dakota die this night, remember to Raven, she died for her, and will surely walk with the angels.

I am now of sound mind and ask you to amend the dispersal of my estate as follows. Administer one half of all I own to support Rebecca's foundation. We must save the children. You have been named executor of my estate and should encounter no difficulty. Remove one half of the remainder for your care into old age, and to be passed on to my son Luke. It is more than you could spend in a lifetime of lifetimes, but now it seems a small gift in my eyes for one who stood behind me all these years through good times and foul. I felt your love always, and so regret that never did I show the depth of my need for you.

Finally, reserve the remainder of my worth for these two ladies, Raven and Dakota. They have opened my eyes, and hopefully led me away from the hazards of darkness, to the light of our Lord. They have renewed my belief in compassion. I have cried for them as I cried for Rebecca, as I cried for you.

I must go. I feel Rebecca is now here. I beg you remember us for our failures as well as our accomplishments. I beg you remember our unfaltering love. We give you that and all our worldly possessions. We give you responsibility, but also opportunity. We must save the children. Now, go with God, Elizabeth. Do his will, for out of an infinite collection of souls, God placed you in our hearts. It was you, and only you. You were His chosen one.

Christopher Nicholas Claussen

ONE HUNDRED-SIXTEEN

Elizabeth folded the letter back up and slipped it into a card that she kept bundled with the original fifty orphan slips. She retied the same worn red ribbon that kept them stacked together for almost fifty years. The letter kept her close to Christopher. Whenever she read it, it moved her. The letter filled her with both peace and longing. She raised her eyes.

Brig looked at Elizabeth with that hard calculating stare, and Elizabeth understood well how it was that Brig was able to keep a rowdy crew in line on an old sailing ship. She felt small.

"Child! Let me get this straight. What you are saying is Christopher Claussen is Santa Claus!"

"I didn't say that."

"Trust me, darling, you did indeed! You said it every which way possible, except with words."

"I didn't say anything about anybody being Santa Claus."

Elizabeth regretted even insinuating a connection, for it singled her out as being totally out of touch with reality.

"Pray tell, child. Do you hear yourself? You understand, of course, you are telling me that I shared a bed with the King of Christmas for five years of my life, and have been pining over the loss of some folkloric hero for the rest of it."

"Enough! Enough, I am sorry for having such a big mouth! I deserve to be mocked, have your way with me. Obviously, it's a notion derived from a demented mind, the mind of a fool. Folklore couldn't possibly have had roots based in truth. I see that clearly now, thank you."

Elizabeth made her point, but Brig got most of what she wanted, and she sat back somewhat bemused.

"Aye! Pay me no mind an' I'll be kind, for t'is spooky. I'll give ya that. …Could give a person goose flesh. I'll say this, Elizabeth. When one has traveled the world, as have I, one tends to see more than a fair share of absurdities. Aye, I have seen strangeness beyond measure. This would however, be by far the most bizarre account I might know, something I would be forced to think hard upon…maybe during a winter gale." She grinned.

Ernie arrived at the cabin with Brig's companion, Richard. The ladies had conversed to the very last minute, and now, not a moment was to be wasted escorting Brig back to the train station. The bags were in place, the ladies helped aboard, and Earnie started the carriage down the lane. As they were jostled about, Elizabeth looked across to Brig.

"Should that winter gale come to pass, I beg you write me your thoughts. I have been hopelessly lost in these musings every Christmas season since Christopher's passing. However, I am not alone pondering these things, nor will you be, for there are many in these parts who are now changed."

Brig glanced back at Elizabeth and smiled. She wished to lighten the mood.

"I never thought of him as acting like St. Nick, that's for certain. Well…maybe that's not true. He did come bearing a mighty fine gift. As I recall, he could perform saintly. Maybe the trouble with me is I always thought Santa was for wee ones."

Both women started laughing. Elizabeth shook her head, wishing to steer clear of comments regarding Brig's sexual delights.

"All I would ask is this. If you happen to lay awake some December night, and things Christmas happen to dance through your head. Ask yourself this. If myth was based in truth, what truths would have to be realized to make a man the mythical Santa Claus? Now, before you start rolling your eyes—convinced

I have grown into an old senile woman too long living in the clouds about the Rockies—keep a thing or two in mind.

"Begin by considering Christopher's wealth. He was fabulously wealthy. I think far wealthier than those families on the Hudson Riverbanks. I am the executor of his estate, and I still have not been able to obtain a reasonable accounting of his worth.

"Consider his attachment to snow country, just as we were always told when sitting around our Christmas trees. It's a little thing, but why couldn't he have been born and settled in Mexico, or Italy, or New York, for heaven's sake? For the duration of Swedish winters, he fills his mansion with workers manufacturing toys that he delivers around the world.

"Know that in his heart, he was generous and kind-hearted to a fault. He finances the largest organization in the world for the welfare of children. I believe fate intentionally brought Lady Rebecca into his life to do his will. She stood in the limelight for him, an orphan herself. He loved her with all his heart. He worked though her, channeling his enormous power through her gentle hands. She raised awareness and social conscience; she was his voice, his call for good will among men.

"And after his death...well, they might as well have chiseled Santa Claus into his tombstone. Raven never stopped calling him that, for her mother always said a saint would watch over her. The entire town embraced her story straight away, and now they claim unabashedly that Northpole is the home of Santa Claus. I admit most do it because the notion is romantic. But no one will deny it brought law and order to that place almost overnight.

"Christopher's death changed a lot of people up there. The following month was spent completely refurbishing the church. The whole community was involved. Now, it has to be enlarged to hold the congregation. Five years ago they used it to store whiskey barrels for the tavern. It's strange, Brig. All of it is strange, not just for me, but also for those many folks standing in the field that night. They left changed. They left with something in their hearts that you won't hear them discuss directly, but you will see it in their eyes.

"Oh, Brig. There is so much more if you just take the time to see it. There are the letters. You should read the letters. There must be thousands of them that are filled with wishes, prayers of thanks and dreams for the future. I remember when it was only from the fifty orphans who had been encouraged to write letters because they had no books to study and they were so afraid to leave each other's company, only fifty slips with addresses.

"They sent their cards and letters to Lady Rebecca at her ship REBECCA, and then it was delivered to the Claussens' residence at the Barrington. Then it was Mary's place, God bless her soul. I know this better than anyone; because in the beginning, it was I who answered the mail. Christopher took over where Lady Rebecca left off. Now, children from all over write him every Christmas.

"Who could foresee the postings would end up being forwarded to 'Mr. Claus' at Northpole. It was nothing more than a distant north-country stop-over, a logical name for the place where a timber stripped of bark, a singular pole, would be driven into the ground to mark the end of a rail bed. There was nothing more to it.

"All of this good will that moves across the country was started because Christopher paid for the postage to make it possible. It is true he never lifted a pen to answer a letter, it was the rest of us who wore out our bony little fingers, but you would be surprised to know how many of those letters he read. You wouldn't believe how many he answered in actions, responding to their misery, to their cries of desperation, fulfilling their wishes through gifts and help by utilizing his innumerable connections.

"I never had any idea how much of his wealth he gave away until after his death when I assumed control of the ledgers.

Claus is the lifeline to orphanages beyond count. He has delivered relief to thousands of children around the globe. In those books, I discovered how he used his ships to deliver gifts and aid all over the world, and the more I reviewed his diaries and logs, the more I realized to what extent he used them for just such purpose. The holds were never empty. If there was open space, it was filled with donations. I often wondered if the business cargo was on board solely for the purpose of covering the cost of transporting his good will. How fitting he should die delivering his gifts in person.

"I know what I say next sounds terrible, but the fact is, Lady Rebecca, Christopher's greatest love, died in a Christmas Eve fire *saving the children*, as he would say. I mean what terrible irony. I can accept irony. I can accept coincidence. I have a much harder time accepting years of it without end.

"And don't forget about your precious engraving. You said it meant the world to you, and you were very special to him. Now, against all possible odds, it is back in your possession. It was you who insisted that was impossible, not I. Yet, I was witness to much impossibility. I remember the Brenner family; three stillbirths and three sons, three boys who should have been scooped up instantly by other women all hopeful to adopt. Yet, Mrs. Brenner came to the REBECCA and left with three sons against all the odds. It was more than impossible.

"Look at me, Brig. Against all odds, I crossed an entire continent to fill an emptiness that I could not explain. I fought forces that I could not see, I could not hear, I could not feel, I could only succumb. ...And for what reason? I certainly had no idea. I do know it felt as if fate selected me from the beginning to remain untouched, to suffer the life of a spinster, a virgin, until time to bear his child. I had never even been kissed before that union.

"I mean when I should have died in the Missouri River rapids, I lived. Impossible! Why? How could that have happened? The man I thought pulled me out was not Dusty Peddler. My first thought was Christopher, but I ended up in Dusty Peddler's wagon after having followed his postings all the way across the country. Why was I attracted to those bits of scrap in every ticket office? Do you think anybody else was hunting up those silly little pieces of paper? I saw that wagon roll down the road as clear as day. The innkeeper said it hadn't moved in four months.

"In his final letter, he said *'we must save the children.'* I understand anybody involved with orphanages would say something of that sort daily. But that is what Dusty Peddler or Claus, or somebody, said to me at a riverbank a world away from humanity when I was essentially in my grave. Maybe I imagined it. Maybe I imagined most of this. Maybe I just want all this to be true because it gives me hope, but I believe I am of a clear mind, and yet I remain taunted by questions and haunted by coincidences. I am not crazy, Miss Rings, I have been witness to all this and more."

Brig was fondling her treasured gift, spinning it slowly around as she listened politely to frustrations Elizabeth struggled to explain.

"I don't wish to have fun at your expense, Elizabeth. But, aye then, it is a tantalizing affair. And I must add with some embarrassment that my conscience and sense of good will is wider-awake than it has been in years. It may be that my pondering these matters is Christopher's way of keeping me in line, keeping me to wonder until I go to the grave...giving me just enough worry so I might make a more concerted effort to be compassionate. I could see him doing that. It would be like him. I give you that.

"Elizabeth...I won't laugh at you. I promise. But I can't just say Christopher was Santa Claus. For me that is just...preposterous. It just sounds...well...it just sounds like something that would get us locked up. Maybe, at this time in your town, in Northpole, you can imply these things, but try it in New York or aboard the CHROSUS and you might as well paint a circle on your ass and say 'kick me.'" Brig frowned.

"I understand. Truly, I do…and I hope I haven't made you uncomfortable. I am driven to sort out these things for my own peace of mind. You see, nobody really knows where Christopher was for most of his life. Only in his later years, after he discovered Luke, was anybody actually with him on a regular basis. It was almost as though by then he completed his work, and now it was time to pass it on to someone other, maybe a son—someone to continue on with this mission.

"Those earlier years were when you knew him best. Yet, meeting you was more than just asking about Claus. I did wish to meet you again as an adult. All my years, you loomed bigger than life…when you jumped overboard into a shark-filled ocean, when you captained your own ships. Christopher was very proud of you. I, on the other hand, was very jealous of you. So, you see, you are as well very much a part of my lifelong memories.

"Christopher was my father, my mentor, my friend. He was my heart and soul. He was my security; he was the answer to my questions. He loved me. He made love to me. I think, much like me, he was confused. I mean, he was a man for certain. It was that part of him that you knew better than anyone aside from Lady Rebecca. I don't know; I was confused. I am confused. I guess, I have nothing else to say…."

Earnie halted the horses at the station. Brig and Elizabeth sat silent at last, folding back into their thoughts as they looked out from under the canopy to view the waiting train. The locomotive's formerly dusty black carcass was now washed, turned about, and pointed toward Eastpole. It was hissing incessantly as blasts and trails of steam escaping from indiscernable places, remained visible even in the heat of day. From a grand funnel, a soiled cloud of smoke rose nearly straight up through the unmoved air.

Elizabeth and Brig crossed the platform. A conductor checked his watch as they embraced and offered their final good bye, most of it lost to the blast of the train whistle. Brig turned to accept the conducter's hand, as Richard followed with their baggage.

The conductor closed the door. A final blast of the whistle sounded out across a land that offered no echo. The locomotive might have shuddered as waves of steam billowed out from its underbelly. It lurched forward as if bucking, the giant steel driving wheels struggling to grip hold of sand sprinkled rails. Brig leaned out the window, her hand waving, her rings flashing as they scattered the blinding rays of sun. She asked a final question.

"Brace me through hell, child! Do you think he knew?!"

Elizabeth heard the question. She didn't answer. It was a question she had asked herself many times over the last few years. A question, exactly like all the others, a question she could not answer yes or no. She hardly dared risk the questions let alone expect the answers. She simply stood her ground, shielding her eyes with one hand while waving a final goodbye with the other.

Elizabeth watched the train carrying Brig Rings disappear into the shimmering veil of hot desert air. Only after good measure did her eyes leave the receding black dot in the distance, to pan across the hard edge of the horizon until she was nearly turned about and facing Ernie.

"It's going to be another one of those hot, merciless, Colorado days. We better get on with our lives, Ernie. There isn't enough left to squander."

"Yes, ma'am, ain't that the truth of it."

She took his arm, and allowed him to lead her back to the carriage.

Hush my love, be still. Lay back upon my bed.
I'll be quilt and cover to caress your sorrowed head
I'll be sleep that calms you and let no fear awake
I'll be breath of kisses for every tear you make.

Hush my love, be still. My pillow remains where
I'll no longer live to lie beneath your locks of hair.
I'll ask your eyes to open when you're sound asleep
I'll wipe away reflections your soul so longs to keep

Hush my love, be still. My bedroom beckons you
I'll be door and window to dreams you must go through
I'll not announce when I arrive but know when I depart
I'll take away forever memories from your heart

Hush my love, be still. My nights they are with number
Given me to set you free whilst I watch you slumber
You heart will find another, but think of me you will
If just to say with your smile…. Hush my love, be still.

Friday December 11, 1857

Dear Brig;

I have already thanked the Lord for your well-being and trust this letter will arrive to find you in the best of spirit and good health.

It did my heart a world of good to hear from you, for I feared you might choose to forget about me—good riddance. Rachel and Caleb wrote to say you had paid them a visit on your return, and I see you impressed them every bit as much as you did me. From all I read, it appears you impressed the entire city. They wrote to say you were most entertaining and enjoyable.

They also sent me a copy of the St Louis Times article— which I happen to have before me—noting amongst a good many interesting facts, how you were hauled out of the river. I'm still laughing. When first reading it, I laughed as hard as I did over lemonade on the porch in South Pass. Dakota rushed into my office to see what all the fuss was about. I read the article to her and further cried from laughter. She was unable to grasp the moment. I explained if she met you, she would better appreciate the humor.

Much has happened since your visit, some good, some sorrowful. Let me say, it never fails that winter brings to me my most memorable emotions. I must say, I have seen firsthand, the misery of desert heat and summer drought, but nothing compares to the snow when it flies. The desert can kill a soul in a day or two, but in snow country a gal loses her life in minutes. In the worst of situations, she watches her body freeze before her eyes, long before she dies. In the best of situations death still comes, but for reasons of damp, hunger, or sickness.

I suspect the Mistress of Winter will forever pay visit, and before she takes her leave, she will seduce many of those we love. Should I damn her for taking precious life from us, or thank her for bringing an end to the suffering? I don't know. I was faced with these thoughts amongst others after I received a letter last winter from Allen Sawyer, informing me that my oldest and dearest friend, Mary, had passed on. She went to our Lord in peace, expressing not only concerns for the well-being of her children and devoted husband, but obliging him to write me, so he might convey, her last thoughts were also of me.

I was in her heart to the very end. I always believed that to love is to share. We had shared much of our lives together. We built our dreams in the berths of the REBECCA and on the picnic blankets of Boston. We shared those dreams, and finally those memories. I had never questioned her love for me, and my life was markedly better for it. It was difficult for me, having to accept her death, for I had no desire to relinquish my half of those shared facets. I reread his letter, time and time again. At least, my heart was mollified in knowing her life was lived to the fullest, knowing she died in the company of those who loved her most.

12/12 Saturday

I am forever looking into the fresh and youthful eyes of my Luke and Dakota. She recovered from her fall and goes with a slight limp that disappears a little more each year. If you hadn't known about her fall, you would never imagine such suffering by the look of her. But, then it is impossible to note such small imperfection when all is overshadowed by the blessings of a wonderfully handsome face, so bright with ambition and spirit.

Dakota fared much better coping with her injury, than accepting the death of her last remaining sister. Young Raven was lost to consumption. The wound to Dakota's heart will take a long time to heal. Gail stood by Ernie through his suffering. I wept openly a good many days, for I adored the child, having come to love her dearly. I care not to question the ways of the Lord, but it was a dark and depressing time for us all. To this day, like Dakota, Ernie, Gail, and the rest, I miss Raven's chatter in the air. We yet talk of her as though she is still with us. She was laid to rest next to Christopher, at Rising Rocks Cemetery, close by the orphanage in Powder Pan Canyon. I am sure he enjoys her company.

I admit to occasionally spending a day of my winter solitude quietly grieving the deaths of my mother, and Mary, Christopher, and Raven. After a life nearly spent, I yet pine for Lady Rebecca. My feelings for all of them are dear, made more so over time. I fear most losing the memories of these people I so cherish to the fog of old age.

I find it interesting the way more and more of my emotional relationships reach into the afterlife, as though to ensure my place in their hearts when I am called to join them. I am not at all depressed, for my life, even now, is far from being empty or meaningless. Instead, for me the future and the past are both sources of solace and comfort, of promise and satisfaction, of accomplishment and lessons learned.

12/13 Sunday

I still travel a bit, making appearances for the Rebecca Foundation fundraisers, but have kept the lodge in Northpole as my home. After all, who should answer the boxes of Christmas mail, if I am to leave? The land is rugged, and altogether impossible to cope with at times, no place for a lady, I reckon. Still it has its merits, and you for one would probably thrive on its rigors. It is never boring, especially with the gold rushes and the hordes of sorrowful souls left destitute after failing to find their treasure.

The continental railroad will soon be connecting to the Rocky Mountain Railroad track, and at that point we will be overrun by those people who have dreams to fulfill. We will also be overrun by those who have fallen to the wayside, the ones forgotten in one fashion or another, the ones that could stand for a little of our compassion.

This area often reminds me of my childhood and the forests in Norway and Sweden near the old Claussen estate. It seems strange that I exist on the other side of the world from my place of birth and family, and yet, I find so many people traveling through Wyoming that are from Sweden. I have met a few who personally knew of my family. I see many more womenfolk in these parts now, and that will mean families. Families bring order out of necessity. I am certain Luke and Dakota will see this country tamed.

12/14 Monday

The Rebecca Foundation is forming a strong organizational body that is now being directed as much by others as myself. Not only is Mother Gail's orphanage no longer destitute, but it represents the head office for the foundation's western branch. Gail is just the right kind of woman to bring order to mayhem.

She and Ernie tied the knot, and I laugh because one has to look pretty darned hard to find the knot. I challenge anybody to see the bond of marriage between these two, so long steadfast in their ways. It is there, and unlike the fleeting flames of passion that are quick to die down, the radiant glow of embers beneath that thick black covering of ash is impossible to extinguish. The stable heat of love keeps them warm.

As for ol' Ernie, he is working his hide off, trying keeping up with the pace and the crowd of people. He keeps running off into the mountains for a day or two to 'gather his wits' and find 'unused air to breathe,' as he puts it.

We can't fault him for deserting us, for during the Christmas season the place is a mad house. There is so much activity.

The orphanage houses nearly fifty children. It also recruits boys and girls from all over to become members of Santa Claus's workshop. They are the biggest help in answering all the postings. As with the original fifty, it is the still the best way to learn how to read and write. The children study a great deal, and are offered opportunities to travel. They travel to orphanages all across the country during the holiday season, putting on plays and delivering gifts in one very special red sleigh.

It is still considered Rebecca's wedding gift, and bears her name in the original gold cursive. I had it repaired by a man who was a true craftsman, a tribute to his trade. He went at it with loving care, converting it into a proper sleigh. The job went so well, that the man joked about the sleigh practically repairing itself. I said nothing, as you may well understand. It is once again a sight to behold.

We send it off to South Pass Junction and the 'Poles' in its own rail car whenever possible. It arrives all polished up, the vermilion and brass gleaming bright, heaped full of gifts, and ready to be drawn by six white horses through crowds of screaming children all up and down the tracks.

As for Christopher, to say he influenced my time is positively inadequate. Whereas Mary, Lady Rebecca, and the rest gave me love, Christopher gave me life. I crossed oceans and coursed countries and continents in his wake. The wealth of my experiences is immeasurable. I don't know if you gave our conversation any further thought, but I am convinced that he set out on purpose to mold my character from the day we first met. This I believe.

I probably shouldn't tell you this because you already think I am daft, but there has been a time or two, in the fury of a winter night's storm that I have peered into a white out and sworn to seeing Claus sitting atop that sleigh. It gives me the worst case of goose flesh, setting me to shivering terrible, but always feeling the better for it. I always sleep well on those nights. Of course, I've always had a run-away mind; my days in the desert proved that out.

I am afraid I must put away the pen for my eyes are beginning to strain in the dimming light of day. I will close by saying let us see how plays out the final mystery left unresolved in my life, that which surrounds the future of my son, Luke. He tries hard to hide it, but I know he has feelings for Dakota Brooks. She won't give him the time of day and it breaks his heart, but he's no fool. I give him credit for that. Ernie always swore Dakota was special, and I believe Luke is keen to sense it.

Whenever he is about her, he changes. He becomes serious, manly; his eyes follow her every move. He studies her as carefully as a cat watches a mouse. The atmosphere crackles when they are about, and it is all the talk at dinner, for there is something magic about these two that fills the air. They don't know it yet, but we can all feel it when they are together in a room. I wouldn't doubt if there came some fatherly assistance from an unseen hand, to guide Luke, showing him how to handle a very wealthy, headstrong young lady full of teeth, nails, and spit. And in the end, I'll wager, the divided Claussen estate may very well come together again.

12/15 Tuesday

Today, I must tell you that I decided to become a grandmother. I thank my daughter, Gracie, for that honor. She will always be a daughter to me. After Christopher's passing, she returned to us and stayed by my side for three months in spite of the hardships place upon her business. Of course, Taa supported her by insisting she do no less. In fact, he escorted her to the lodge and stayed a couple of weeks to help in whatever way he was able.

I am unsure if Gracie's stay rekindled longings for family, but she has one now. By her accounts, after her stay here at the lodge, she set out on a lengthy excursion that took her into the timber lands of the Northwest Territories. As she tells it, she was out in the middle of nowhere, when she happened upon a scout working for a lumber firm out of northern California that belonged to his father.

I never laughed so hard, as when Gracie told me that after only one look at the man, she hid her knives around behind her back. That alone is beyond my comprehension. Almost as improbable, was my seeing the lady in a dress of her own accord. But there she was in a white gown standing at the altar. They were married here in Northpole at our newly refurbished church.

Gracie Castleman is now Gracie Martinez. Her man goes by the name, Travis. I know exactly why Gracie hid her knives. I can't imagine how many broken hearts lay in his wake. He is indeed a handsome man, but I can't imagine his heart stood a chance after one look into Gracie's eyes.

His family is well established in the lumber business along the upper Pacific Coast, especially in the Oregon territories. You cannot fathom how interested was I to hear of this. I had a monumental hole in Christopher's timber operations after his passing. I suppose it was my being selfish that prompted me to offer Mr. Martinez compensation far beyond reason in return for his services with our firm. I knew he could not refuse, his family would have thought him insane to dismiss such income. Needless to say, he did not.

Travis is no fool. He well understands my desire to keep Gracie close. She and Travis presently live here at the lodge, where they often work together out of the offices. I do feel openly guilty about buying my way into their lives, and so I make every attempt to respect their privacy and not meddle. I ask only to enjoy my grandson, Easton. He is a healthy, rambunctious lad, and I can only wonder what his eyes will come to see as he passes through life.

12/16 Wednesday

I have answered too many letters this Christmas. By contrast, I have taken my sweet time in responding to yours. It has been a pleasure to think of you at length. Having so much news to convey, it seemed I might never manage to have it posted. There is now this final matter, my last, saved for the only soul who might savor the implication.

It is the sixteenth of December. It is my birthday. I am sixty years old this day. I have lived as full a life as could be asked. For me, the past, the present, the future, lack nothing. I am content. It is important to me that you know this, for there is now much talk about town of children.

As of late, many have passed through Northpole to settle here at the lodge. I write, and I gaze out the window through an old brass spy glass from Gracie's tatterted bootsack. I believe there to be a hundred or more graceless souls dotting the snow-covered meadows. From my window, I see four or five yet walking up the road. There is no end to the arrivals. The usual questions are aired. The usual concerns are expressed by all for their welfare. The usual accommodations are made for their betterment. After all, here is the Mistress of Winter and she is unmercifully cold and unforgiving.

I have come to grow fond of these curious faces. I often go out in the worst of weather to walk amongst them and converse. They bring to me gentle smiles and countless memories. They are a cheerful lot of rascals, but as always, they come to ask only one question. It has always been the same question...how do I fare? I can hardly help but to wonder if they aren't the eyes and ears of Lady Rebecca yet fretting about my well-being. Fear not, my friend, it is then that I think of you, and remind myself to be rational. I ignore the obvious and hold to the truths....

Claus is but a man,
and these but the faces of urchins and mudlarks, orphans at best.

May God always be with you.
Elizabeth Dennison Claussen

Days Long Gone

How could one know in days long gone, those days of youthful bliss
those days of summer, days of song, those days our fathers miss

How could one know whilst so young what soul mates were in place
as innocence waned and kisses reigned upon one's blushing face

How could one know of strings attached that kept us so entwined
and formed the knots that bound us all together in our time

How rich those pages of our lives but for the wealth of friends
who wrote the diaries of our days that seemed to have no ends

By no account has it been said what starts will never stop
We may wish for all we're worth but cannot keep what's not

So songs of youth are set aside or quieted when it's feared
knots have come to be undone as friends have disappeared

For with them went a part of us in stories that they knew
embellished to perfection from other points of view

And with them went the heart of us, the only ones who care
about the diary of our days and what was written there

All that God hath joined together, He hath put asunder
leaving those of us behind amused and here to wonder

How could one know those days long gone, days our fathers missed
would in turn, revisit us, and again be reminisced

C. John Coombes

www.ingramcontent.com/pod-product-compliance
Lightning Source LLC
Chambersburg PA
CBHW030236030726
47493CB00022B/45